DREAMS of DROWNING

Patricia Averbach

Dreams of DROWNING

Bink Books
Bedazzled Ink Publishing Company • Fairfield, California

978-1-960373-17-5 paperback

Cover Design
by

Bink Books
a division of
Bedazzled Ink Publishing, LLC
Fairfield, California
http://www.bedazzledink.com

With love to my husband
Mark Averbach

Acknowledgements

First, many thanks to Claudia Wilde, Elizabeth Gibson and C.A. Casey of Bedazzled Ink for their belief in *Dreams of Drowning* and for all their work bringing this book into the world.

Next, I recognize with appreciation:

My Second Life writer's group: Adele Ward, Colin Bell and Chris Mooney Singh, real friends I met in a virtual world.

The Chautauqua Writers Center

The Tucson Festival of Books

Literary friends: Haviva Ner David, Monika Becker Amy Brown, Kate Borduas, Maureen Fielding, Carolyn Gold, Maris Soule, Lu Anne Stewart, and Judy Rousseau

My alpha reader, Karla Bell

And last, but not least, special thanks to my wonderful family: Mark, Ann, Elana, and Les for their boundless love, encouragement, and support

"Time expands, then contracts, all in tune with the stirrings of the heart." — Haruki Murakami, *Kafka on the Shore*

"People like us who believe in physics know that the distinction between past, present and future is only a stubbornly persistent illusion." — Albert Einstein, from 1955 letter of condolence to the family of Michele Besso

"Help!" Joanie's shouts are barely audible above the wind and the roar of the outboard motor as she struggles to keep her head above the waves. I put my hands over my ears and close my eyes, but she's still there, still struggling to stay above the water, the panic in her eyes a mirror of my own, her pale, freckled skin, her green eyes fraught with horror, identical to mine. I watch helpless, my heart pounding, until she disappears, as she always does, beneath the roiling waters of Lake Ontario.

Part One

Amy
April 1973

"AMY, WAKE UP." Mrs. Klein was shaking my shoulder. "You can't sleep here. If you need to sleep, go home."

How had I fallen asleep with the clatter and bang of the old linotype reverberating through the shop? I picked my head up from the drafting table and struggled to bring Mrs. Klein into focus. She was as solid and gray as the presses she ran. I felt a chill as her steely eyes took in my tousled hair and bloodshot eyes then moved to the floor where a chaotic mess of colored markers, X-Acto knives, and technical pens lay scattered.

"I'm sorry. I didn't sleep again last night, but I'm okay now. I'll get back to work." I was already on my knees gathering up the fallen art supplies as quickly as I could.

"When was the last time you had a proper night's sleep?"

I took a moment to consider. "Nineteen seventy-one."

Esther Klein was my mother's best friend, more like my aunt than my employer, but she wasn't amused. My literally falling asleep on the job had pushed her too far.

"That's not funny. You need to see a doctor."

"Now that *is* funny. How am I supposed to do that?" Legal Ontario residents had magic OHIP cards that entitled them to almost unlimited medical care, but she knew I'd slipped into the country illegally and had no papers.

"You can pay him in cash, the same way we pay you, so there's no record. I'll explain the situation to my doctor."

"Sorry, can't risk it. I've got to stay under the radar, but thanks anyway."

Mrs. Klein's face darkened, and a deep crease appeared between her eyes. "Go home, drink some tea, take a hot bath, and think about whether you want a future here or not."

My heart skipped a beat. Was she threatening to fire me? She knew I'd be on the street or worse without this job. I could hear a slight quaver in my voice as I responded. "What about this poster?" I pointed to the design job I'd been working on. "They need it by tomorrow."

She examined the work on my design table and nodded her approval. I'd hand drawn shadows beneath stenciled letters making the company name, Revolution

Records, appear to float over a background of brightly colored discs. "You can finish in the morning. Now go home and get some sleep."

What was the point of going home? It was easier to sleep in a noisy print shop than back in my apartment where Joanie's ghost followed me from room to room. It had happened two years ago, yet her desperate calls for help still woke me from panicked dreams of drowning. I gathered up my coat and purse, wondering if I'd just ruined my last chance for a new life.

I was half-way out the door when Mrs. Klein called me back. "And don't forget the party tonight. We're expecting you at seven."

I thought of rushing out the door, pretending I hadn't heard, but Mrs. Klein was only a few feet away. I paused and took a breath. "Thank you, I really appreciate the invitation, but like I said, I don't do parties."

She stepped between me and the door, blocking my only means of escape. "This has gone on long enough. You're not the one who died."

Mr. Klein and Eddie, our pressman, were watching from the back room. I didn't want to make a scene, but . . . a party? "I'm sorry, I know you want to help, but I'm just not ready." Me, the good-time girl of Fairport High, turning down another party. Joanie wouldn't have believed it.

Mrs. Klein took an umbrella off the coat rack and handed it to me. "You'll need this, and you're coming to the party. There will be people your age from the sailing club."

Was she kidding? Sailors were the last people I'd want to meet. The very thought gave me the willies. I started to say no again, but she wouldn't listen.

"Consider it a condition of your employment, and I mean it. Oh, and bring a box of baklava from that Greek bakery near your apartment. No excuses."

Then she shoved me out into the rain and shut the door.

FOUR HOURS LATER I was pounding on the glass door of Kosmos Bakery, desperately trying to catch the attention of a young man in a white apron who was pulling trays from a display case. He looked up, pointed at his watch, and shook his head. Despite my concerns, I'd overslept and arrived too late. Any other night I'd have run into Loblaw's for brownies or a coffee cake, but Mrs. Klein wanted baklava and I couldn't risk disappointing her again. I put my hands together in mock prayer and this time the man came forward and unlocked the door.

"We're closed," he said pointing to the neon sign in the window. He spoke with an accent that evoked images of an older, warmer country. As he leaned toward me, I smelled cinnamon and sugar. It was just after six o'clock, the evening dusk made darker by clouds, a blustery wind, and a spring rain threatening to turn to snow. The bakery's white tile walls radiated light and warmth as I stood shivering in a mini-skirt and thin leather jacket on the damp pavement.

"I promised my boss baklava. She'll kill me if I don't bring it."

"She would kill you for this?" He looked stern, but his eyes crinkled at the corners.

"Absolutely. She's mad at me already."

"Then you'd better come in. I don't want blood on my hands." His body had been blocking the doorway, but now he stepped aside. As I brushed past him, I was unnerved by his physical presence. He wasn't especially tall, yet his broad shoulders and muscular body dominated space.

The shop smelled like home. Not the actual home where I'd grown up with a mother too busy selling real estate to cook, and certainly not the home I'd fled teetering on its foundation. Rather, it smelled like the home I longed for, the one that provides shelter from all adversity and comfort for every sorrow. I closed my eyes, inhaled deeply, and felt my own interminable pain subside for just a moment.

I opened my eyes. The baker was watching me with raised eyebrows and a bemused expression.

"Your shop smells wonderful, absolutely intoxicating," I said, somewhat embarrassed.

"It's not my shop. I just work here at night. During the day I work toward a doctorate in economics." He grinned, pleased at disarming me with this revelation. "My name's Arcas." He held out his hand.

I hesitated for an awkward moment, but how could I insult a man who'd just saved me from looking too incompetent to buy a box of pastry? I took his hand. "Amy."

He smiled warmly as his fingers closed over mine. "Nice to meet you, Amy. Maybe you're a student too."

"Me? No, I used to be a student back in the States, but now I just work in a print shop." For some reason, in a country where I tried to be invisible, I wanted him to see me. "I studied art. I'm an artist," I added much to my own surprise.

He nodded approvingly as he released my hand. "I knew there was something special about you." He assembled a cardboard box and filled it with sticky pieces of nut-filled phyllo dough as we talked.

I cringed. There was nothing special about my mediocre artistic talent. What made me special was the disaster I'd fled my country to escape. It was the reason I kept to myself and avoided idle chit-chat with good-looking men.

I tugged at my short skirt, feeling exposed and embarrassed. Why was I even talking with this man? It was dangerous to forget myself. I made a show of looking at my watch. "Well, thanks for opening the bakery for me. I really appreciate it, but I've got to get going. How much do I owe you?"

"Nothing. We were already closed so this is officially yesterday's pastry."

"No, that's not right. I'm happy to pay whatever it costs."

"Please take it. We would just throw it away." He pressed a box tied up with blue ribbon into my hands. "So, your boss is Greek? Do you have other Greek friends as well?"

"The Kleins aren't Greek. Their son and his wife are just going on a Greek island cruise. This is for their *bon voyage* party."

"So, maybe you've never eaten in a real Greek taverna . . ."

Was he asking me on a date? I was about to mumble an awkward goodbye and run for the door when I felt the little cat pendant hanging from a chain around my neck grow warm. Maybe it was just my imagination, but it felt like a message from my sister. As my hand touched the gold charm I could almost hear her chiding me. "What's with you, Mungo? Don't be such a dork."

I left the shop twenty minutes later with the baklava and an invitation to dinner at The Olive Tree for the following night. My heart pounded and my mind churned as I waited for the streetcar. What had I done? Why had I said yes? Arcus was charming, but that was no excuse. I had to remain inconspicuous and live in the shadows. Would Joanie really want me to go on partying as though nothing had happened when she'd never see the sunshine, never dance again? Mrs. Klein was wrong; something in me *had* died. I was a recluse, and an insomniac. I padded around my apartment at night talking to ghosts. It had been two years since the accident, but I still couldn't look in a mirror because it was always Joanie who stared back at me with hollow, sunken eyes.

I LEFT FOR the taverna directly from work the next day without bothering to change or put on makeup to convince myself I wasn't going on a date. I had to take two buses at the height of rush hour, but then it was only a short walk to The Olive Tree. A welcoming blue awning hung over the front door and the menu, posted in the window, was written in Greek with the English translation in small type added as an afterthought.

Arcas was sitting at one of the tables carrying on an animated conversation in Greek with an athletically built man whose large, soulful eyes and scraggly beard reminded me of a goat. An attractive young woman with straight blonde hair, a wide floral headband and hoop earrings sat beside him playing with the ice in her water glass and staring vacantly around the room. I was surprised to see that the white aproned baker I'd met the previous night was wearing a paisley shirt unbuttoned at the neck. He jumped up when he saw me and gave me an unexpected hug as though we were old friends. Startled, I stiffened and pulled away.

"Amy." He beamed, completely undaunted. "You came. I'm so happy to see you." He smiled triumphantly at the two people sitting at the table. "See, I told you she looked like Nana Mouskouri." Before I could even sit down, he grabbed a carafe of wine from the table and filled my water glass. "This is Greek wine, retsina, have you tried this before?"

"Yes, actually I had some last night at the party." I took a cautious sip to be polite. I already knew it tasted like turpentine. "Who's Nana Mouskouri?"

"A beautiful Greek singer with long, dark hair and glasses like yours. These are my friends, Tom Savas and Nancy Wells." They smiled, sizing me up with unabashed curiosity. "Tom's in economics with me and Nancy's head of the department."

Nancy winced. "That's his idea of a joke. I'm the department secretary." No Greek accent, I noted—a Canadian.

"She's being modest. This woman is absolutely the boss of the department. She runs everything. We have to do everything she says."

"So, what are you studying?" Nancy polished off the retsina in her glass and held it out for Arcas to refill.

I slipped into an empty chair and covered my glass with my hand to prevent him giving me more. "I studied art for a couple years, but I left without a degree. I work in a print shop now, Abbot's Printing on Bathurst."

"You're from the States?" Nancy pulled a package of Belmonts and a lighter from her purse. She lit her own cigarette, handed one to Tom, then held the pack out toward me.

I inhaled the smoke that drifted across the table but shook my head. "No thanks, I'm trying to quit." I moved my hands to my lap to hide my bitten nails and ragged cuticles, evidence of how that project was progressing.

"Yeah, I'm an immigrant like these guys. I've been here about two years now." Should I have lied? Said I was from Ottawa? But what would be the point with an accent that screamed Rochester, New York?

"Why? Is the United States drafting women now?" Tom meant to be funny, but I was sick of that joke.

"Right," I humored him. "Maybe I'll go back when the war's over." His English surprised me. Although he'd been speaking fluent Greek a moment earlier, he spoke English like a Canadian, or someone from the States. "What about you? Are you here dodging the draft?"

"Nope, I'm a legal Canuck, born in Montreal. We moved to Athens when I was two. Anyway, the war *is* over since the Paris Peace Accords. You can go back to the US any time now—unless you want to stay here with my friend." He lifted his fingers in a peace sign and grinned at Arcas. "Make love not war."

I blanched; he had no idea. War or no war I might never be able to go home.

Nancy swatted the back of his head with the laminated menu. "Cut that out. Try to behave like civilized people." She seemed to include Arcas in her rebuke although he was sitting quietly with his arm on the back of my chair and hadn't said a word.

Tom pretended to be indignant. "You're telling Greeks to be civilized? We invented civilization. Arcas, are you going to let a Canadian insult us like this?"

Nancy reached across the table and grabbed my hand. "Don't pay any attention to Tom. He's acting like an idiot because his dissertation committee just turned down his thesis proposal."

"Which I spent months developing and which my advisor thought was brilliant, and which could cost me a full fucking semester, so cut me some slack." Tom downed the last of his retsina and refilled his glass.

Nancy studied Arcas with an appraising eye, then turned to me. "I think you got the better one. He has a much sweeter personality. You might be able to do something with him."

"I'm not sure that I'm ready to take on any new projects at the moment, but thanks for the tip." The evening was getting weird. Had Arcas told them we were dating?

The smell of roasted meat, rosemary, and garlic distracted me. Arcas called the waiter over and began a long negotiation in Greek that ended with platters of roasted potatoes, skewers of lamb, and zucchini cooked with tomatoes and olives being brought to our table along with a basket of warm pita.

We filled our plates, and everyone relaxed as Arcas gave me a culinary tour of Greece beginning with his mother's kitchen in the romantically named province of Arcadia. His family raised sheep. Sheep. I was pretty sure that no one in my family had raised sheep since the Bronze Age.

"This meat is okay"—Arcas waved a fork in front of me—"but not like the sheep my father grows. In Greece they have more flavor. If I was home right now, I'd help my father kill one of the baby lambs, then my mother would take the head and all the inside parts to make the Magiritsa soup for Easter."

I put down my fork. "You kill baby lambs?"

"Of course, so you can eat baby lamb." He pointed to my plate, obviously amused by my squeamishness. He turned to Tom, probably just to goad me further. "Does your mother put the head in her Magiritsa for Easter?"

"Of course." Tom looked insulted that he would even ask such a question.

"I've never cooked a lamb's head, but we always use the whole bird, including the head and feet, whenever we slaughter a chicken." Nancy had ganged up with the guys, enjoying my discomfort.

"Did you all grow up on farms? Am I the only city girl at this table?"

"Actually, I grew up in Peterborough, a small town north of Toronto, but we lived in the suburbs and always kept chickens." Nancy slipped another cube of meat off a skewer and cut it in two.

"And I'm a city boy." Tom stared down at his plate, looking slightly embarrassed. "But we had a summer house in the country where we'd go for Easter."

"And another house outside Montreal where he'd go in the summer." Arcas leaned toward me and lowered his voice. "Tom's mother is Canadian and his father is Greek. He has two passports and lots of money. This makes him a very useful person."

"That's right." Nancy took another helping of zucchini. "Our house revolutionary is the son of a Greek banker and a Canadian socialite, fancy cars and private schools all the way."

"My dad's got a good job, but he's not exactly Aristotle Onassis and my mom's family lost almost everything before I was born. Anyway, I can't help what my family does. I just want to live my own life." He turned toward me. "What about you? Where do you come from?"

I flinched and started to stammer. It was still hard to talk about my family. "I, uh, I grew up in a suburb of Rochester. My father's a dentist and my mom sells real estate, pretty boring really." I examined their faces for a shadow of doubt or suspicion but saw nothing but bland acceptance. Why would I expect anything else? It had happened over two years ago and never made the Toronto papers. They had no idea we'd been the butt of local gossip and lurid stories on the six o'clock news.

"So, another member of the petite bourgeoisie, good for you." Nancy took a puff of her Belmont and blew out a long, thin cirrus cloud of smoke. "Tom doesn't appreciate his luck. He thinks money's a curse, but then he's never had to work for a living."

"Cut it out, Nancy, you know how hard I work." Tom finished his second glass of retsina and poured another into the tumbler almost to the brim. "Her folks can't pay her tuition so she's jealous and she should be. In a just society everyone would earn a decent wage, university would be free and . . ."

"Everyone would have universal health care," I said. The Ontario Health Insurance Plan was a marvel to an American. Not qualifying for OHIP was the thing I regretted most about my illegal status in the country.

"Exactly." He put his hand on Nancy's shoulder. "Nancy can only take one class a semester because she has to work full-time."

"There's nothing wrong with working." Nancy shrugged off Tom's hand. "Not everyone gets a university education handed to them on a silver platter."

Tom raised his glass and intoned loud enough so that everyone in the restaurant turned their heads. "Kill the colonels, burn the prisons. What we need is communism."

"Tom, stop it. You're making a scene." Nancy glared at him, and I could feel a little whoosh of activity under the table as she kicked his ankle.

"Sorry, I forgot, we're in Canada. I have to be polite and keep my voice down." Tom made a pretense of hanging his head in embarrassment.

"What colonels?" I asked.

"The Greek colonels, the junta, please, don't get him started." Nancy held up her hand to stop me and I shut up.

"I'll explain to you later, now isn't a good time." Arcas shot Tom a warning look as he helped himself to more lamb.

"Right, tell her about baklava and rice pudding. She doesn't want to hear about how America is siding with a junta that's torturing students fighting for democracy."

"Please, Tom, stop it. Amy doesn't deserve that. You've had too much to drink."

"You're right. I offer my apologies to the pretty American lady. None of that's your fault. Please, forgive me." He bowed his head in my direction, looking genuinely sorry. "But I've got to go now. I have a paper due on Monday. It was nice meeting you." He stood up, put twenty dollars on the table, and staggered slightly as he headed toward the door. Nancy jumped up and grabbed his arm.

"He can't drive home like this and I don't have a license. Arcas, would you mind driving us?" Nancy reached into Tom's pocket and neatly extracted his keys. Tom made a weak attempt to intercept them as Nancy tossed them across the table to Arcas who made a neat catch.

I looked at my watch. It was only eight o'clock, but the evening was clearly over. "It's time for me to be heading home as well. I think this will cover my dinner and the tip." I pulled a five-dollar bill from my wallet.

"You're my guest, I invited you to dinner." Arcas appeared genuinely shocked at the sight of my money.

"That's not necessary. I can pay for my own meal."

"It *is* necessary. Greeks don't let ladies pay." He was adamant.

I put the bill back inside my wallet. "Well, thank you, I enjoyed the evening. I'll look for you at the bakery the next time I stop by."

"No, don't go, stay with me a while. We'll listen to Greek music after I take these guys home."

Once outside, we walked down Danforth Avenue. The others were arguing about which Greek club had the best music while I was plotting to grab the next bus back to my apartment as we headed toward Tom's car.

I was still walking with them as we neared the parking lot. Arcas and I had just stepped off the curb a pace or two behind Tom and Nancy, when a black car wheeled around the corner and barreled toward us at high speed. It didn't slow down or try to veer away but shot directly toward us like a torpedo. A strong arm reached out and pulled me backward a split second before the impact.

A moment later Arcas was rattled but untouched. Tom was bruised and Nancy lay unconscious in the street, her body floating on a sea of asphalt as I screamed and screamed. Even as paramedics wrapped me in blankets, subdued me with sedatives, and reassured me that Nancy wasn't dead, I continued shaking.

They were tending to Tom's injured arm when another siren and more flashing lights alerted me to an approaching police car. Terrified, I grabbed my purse and bolted without even saying goodbye. I raced down Danforth, ducked down a side street, and kept running. Exhausted and utterly lost, I finally stopped to look around and get my bearings. Well-kept older homes lined both sides of a quiet residential street. There wasn't much traffic but, God bless Toronto, there was a taxi. I clambered into the backseat, gave the driver my address, then started babbling incoherently. I couldn't stop. I told him about the Greek restaurant, the baklava, the print shop, the speeding car, and the injured girl. I told him everything, except I didn't say that for just a moment I'd confused Nancy with my sister, or that I'd heard Joanie call for help from somewhere in the direction of the lake.

Jacob
April 1993

RAIN EXAGGERATES MY tendency to see double. It's difficult to distinguish the reflection of images on water, through glass, or on wet pavement from the blurred images resulting from my weakened ocular muscles. I turn away from the window where rivulets of water are playing tricks with my eyes, melting the pane, and leaving me suspended between worlds. It's been like this for eight years now, ever since Bessie died. On clear days I can tilt my head twenty degrees to the left and bring faces, signs, and scenery into focus, but on rainy days I confuse reflections with diplopia, my double vision, and become perplexed. My thick corrective glasses and cocked head make me look like a myopic spaniel, but they allow me to look people in the face and see just one nose, just two eyes. I can look at my son, Michael, and see a busy man with graying hair and sagging jowls, and not someone who wobbles back and forth between adolescence and middle age every time I blink.

Most people aren't aware of my disability. Sometimes even I forget because there are days, even weeks, when things come into focus. The past and present don't seem so blurred and muddled. Before Bessie died there'd been another kind of doubleness. There'd been two of us, a pair, coupled for nearly fifty years. Double meant increase, abundance, joy. Afterward it meant distorted vision, ocular fatigue, and cold dinners in front of a television with an oscillating horizontal.

There's a brochure on my desk from Bayside Manor Retirement Home. Michael left it for me even though he knows I can no longer read small print on shiny paper. No matter, I know what it says. It says, old man, you've had it. You're done. Pack up and move along, you've outlived your welcome in the world.

A small incident set him off, a minor mishap he's blown out of proportion. I was out walking after dinner a few weeks ago and, preoccupied, I missed my turn. Nothing odd about that, but by the time I realized what I'd done the sun had set and I was wandering around in the dark. With better eyes I could have managed, but, well, I got lost. Whichever way I turned I only got further afield until I was exhausted. I must have been stumbling about because a policeman stopped to ask if I needed help. "I'm fine, just fine," I told him. "But I seem to have misplaced my apartment." It was a joke. I thought he'd laugh and point me in the right direction. Instead, he drove me home then notified my son. Ever since then, all Michael talks about is, wouldn't I be happier living with other people who'd cook my meals and see that I was safe?

If Bessie were still here she'd give him what for. No one ever pushed my Bessie around. I'd like to see anyone try to tuck her away in a warehouse for the doddering and incontinent. Sadly, I don't have my wife's fighting spirit, but I do have all my marbles and a tidy bank account and I'm not going anywhere if I can help it.

Who could have imagined that sweet little Michael would grow up to become my nemesis? I can still see him toddling around our Finchley flat dragging Nimi, his stuffed monkey, behind him by the tail. Whenever I read him a story, I'd have to show the pictures to that monkey, and I'd have to kiss them both good night when he went to bed. My God that was a long time ago.

Lately, I've been thinking more and more about the past and the years I spent growing up in England. I can't remember the last time I went back to Alwoodley, and I probably wouldn't know a soul there now, but in memory I can still saunter down Mount Road, wave at Mr. Friedman, and continue down Goodrick to the reservoir. It's always a perfect morning in late May and I'm always heading for the water. You wouldn't think a Jewish boy from Leeds would have such an affinity for the sea, but there you are. I made small wooden boats and launched them into the reservoir until the momentous day my father bought a Chris Craft runabout, and we began spending weekends on the River Aire.

I don't think he really cared for fishing, but his doctor told him to relax, to get away from the office, and boating appealed to him more than golf. I'd pilot the boat while he sat in the passenger seat reading *The Times*, eating salami sandwiches, and grumbling about Bolsheviks and anti-Semites. Those days were the happiest of my life, at least until I met Bessie and discovered an entirely different magnitude of joy.

I crossed the Mediterranean any number of times when I was younger and working on my doctorate in Classical Archaeology, but after Bessie there was only one great voyage, the passage from Southampton to Halifax just after the war. I was in my late thirties and Bessie in the bloom of early motherhood, that lovely softness belying her genius for organization and efficiency. The woman was a trooper. I'd expected her to balk when I was offered a professorship in Canada. Instead, she packed up for a new life in the Great North without a murmur of dissent. It's embarrassing to remember, but we both imagined Toronto perpetually buried under snow and surrounded by forests teeming with bears, and yet she said yes, just like that, and we were off. The army should have conscripted Bessie instead of me. We would have won the war in half the time.

We booked passage on a Holland America vessel, the Veendam. The ship had been taken hostage by the Germans then bombed half to death by the allies, but by the time we stepped aboard she'd been completely refurbished and was a thing of beauty, the most elegant ship we'd ever seen.

Bess and I both came from hard-working middle-class people. We'd never known hardship, but we'd never been exposed to great luxury either, so the ship was a revelation, a floating palace. Even in Tourist Class we were treated like royalty, allowed access to everything but a few first-class lounges and the first-class dining hall. We were served three meals a day on immaculate white linen by impeccably trained waiters who seemed to have no concern but our comfort. Bessie and Michael spent so much time in the ship's pool that she joked they were swimming to America. Of course, she joked about everything. We were always laughing. There was entertainment every night, then music and dancing and a midnight buffet, and the night Bess dressed up as Carmen Miranda and mamboed with a turban of bananas on her head. My God, that trip was a wonder.

My apartment is pleasant enough, more than large enough for one old man. It's an easy walk to Forest Hills where I buy lunch at the Village Diner and flirt with Kaleisha, the Jamaican waitress who won't serve me corned beef or pickles since learning I'm on a low-salt diet. There's a grocery, a hardware store, and a pharmacy nearby so I rarely go downtown. I have my books, my television, my old recliner, and the chesterfield we brought from the house we sold when Bessie decided we needed to downsize and simplify our lives. As usual, she was right. What would I do all alone in that big house now, and how would I pack it up and move without her?

I don't want for anything. Life is comfortable enough, but lately I've been feeling landlocked. Something's made me restless and I'm remembering sailing trips to Crete, glorious summers boating on the River Aire and that great transatlantic voyage.

So, it's occurred to me that I have options. One of the world's great lakes is only a streetcar ride away. I could buy a small boat and go out fishing or sail to one of the Toronto islands. I can almost feel the wind in my hair and smell the open water. A man who can pilot a boat can certainly manage his own meals, pay his own bills, and is in no way ready for an old age home. Even Michael will have to concede that much. That's why I'm circling ads in the paper. I'm shopping for a boat.

Amy
April 1973

I AWOKE THE next morning exhausted and gasping for air. I'd spent another night thrashing in murky, dream-water, trying to reach the cruise ship that always eluded me no matter how fast I swam. Music pulsing from the ship, some popular song emanating from an upper deck, followed me into wakefulness. "Drift Away," that was the tune. I shook my head to silence the music as I pulled myself from bed. A cold shower, two aspirin, and two cups of black coffee later I left for work, hoping I looked more capable and efficient than I felt.

Mrs. Klein wasn't fooled. She knew something was wrong. "You didn't sleep again last night. You're wandering around like a zombie." She pressed a Styrofoam cup into my hand. "I know what you've been through, and I promised your mother we'd look out for you, but you have to wake up. You have to show us that you want this job."

"I do want it. You know how much it means to me. I've already finished that op art poster. Do you want to see it?"

"Be careful with that coffee, your hands are shaking."

She was right. Small brown waves were sloshing against the side of the cup. I set it down on her desk. There was no concealing the fact I was a mess. "Sorry, you're right. Something happened yesterday, and I can't get it out of my head."

She looked skeptical, probably tired of my excuses, but waited patiently as I decided what to tell her.

"I had dinner at a Greek restaurant last night with some people I met at Kosmos Bakery." That wasn't entirely true, but I didn't want her thinking I'd been on a date. She'd be on the phone with my mother planning my wedding before lunch.

She perked up, nodding her approval. "That's wonderful. I'm glad you're starting to make friends and get out."

"No, it wasn't wonderful. It was awful."

"Why? did you get food poisoning? Is that what kept you up last night?"

"No, nothing like that, the food was great, but after dinner we were walking down Danforth when a car came out of nowhere and hit this girl we were with. I keep seeing her crumpled on the pavement like she was dead."

Mrs. Klein's hand jumped to her chest. "Oh my God, no wonder you couldn't sleep. Is she alright?"

"I don't know. They took her to St. Michael's in an ambulance." I picked at a jagged piece of cuticle on my thumb. "It's not like she's really a friend. I just met her last night, but I can't get her out of my mind." The cuticle began to bleed and I tucked my thumb inside my fist.

Mrs. Klein watched me with an expression I couldn't quite decipher. "Why don't you take some time off?"

"No, honestly, I'm okay." I looked her in the eyes, imploring, afraid she was firing me. "I really need this job." That was the truth, and she knew it. Where would I find another employer willing to pay me under the table and ignore my immigration status?

"Amy, you're a talented designer, but you're not well. Take a long lunch, get your head together, maybe check on your friend at the hospital, then we'll talk."

"Are you sure?"

She nodded, and this time I read affection and concern.

"Thank you, thank you for everything." I was already reaching for my coat. I needed to see Nancy, to know she was alive.

I bought a bunch of daffodils from a sidewalk vendor then caught a southbound subway.

Mrs. Klein was right. I needed to start thinking straight. I needed to start living my life again. The Kleins had given me a toehold in Toronto, and I owed them everything for this second chance. As the train clattered and swayed through the underground tunnel, I realized how much I loved the city and my job. Toronto was a boom town, filled with energy and optimism. I'd arrived like a leaf plucked from a sickly violet hoping that fresh soil and a sunny sill would generate new roots and radiant bunches of purple flowers, but it had been two years, and I hadn't put down roots and I certainly hadn't blossomed. As the car screeched to a stop, I exited to the familiar sound of the subway's door chimes, inhaled its distinctive smell of iron dust, sweat, and vinyl then climbed the stairs to Yonge Street determined to do better.

St. Michael's Hospital was a forbidding structure that covered the better part of a city block. I got so lost in its labyrinthine corridors that an elderly nun had to rescue me. She led me down one hallway lined with vintage photographs of nurses in starched white caps and long white pinafores, then up another decorated with colorful Inuit prints, finally leaving me in front of a bank of intricately etched brass doors with instructions to get off on the fourth floor then turn left. The antique elevator clanked and rattled up four flights and a hundred years to the new wing, a sleek, modern structure awash in fluorescent light.

I followed the signs to the ICU where I was stopped by a kind but determined nurse. "I'm sorry, but flowers aren't permitted in the ICU. You can leave them in the ladies' room or the family lounge, but not in here. Who are you coming to see?"

"Nancy Wells, she was hit by a car last night. The lady at Patient Information told me I'd find her here." I pointed to the erasable white board hanging behind the nurse's station. Nancy's name and room number were clearly visible. "She's in room 416."

The nurse didn't turn around to look, but her expression softened. "Miss Wells is still asleep. The anesthetic they gave her during surgery hasn't worn off yet. You must be her sister. We've been expecting you."

"No, I'm not her sister." Why would the nurse think I was her sister? Could she read my mind? Did she have access to my nightmares? "I'm just a friend. I was with her when she got hit by the car."

The sweet expression faded, replaced by a look of exasperation. "Then I really am sorry, but I'll have to ask you to leave. We only allow immediate family to visit in the ICU. Patient Information should have explained that before letting you come up. We keep telling them family only, but they can't seem to remember." She backpedaled a bit, probably realizing how harsh she sounded. "You could leave a message. I could give it to her when she wakes up."

"She's okay though, isn't she? I mean, she's going to live?"

"Miss Wells's condition is serious, but stable. She's in no immediate danger. I'm afraid that's all I can tell you." The nurse folded her hands protectively over a pile of files on her desk.

"Could you tell her Arcas's friend Amy stopped by and tell her I hope she's feeling better." I retraced my steps down the hall and waited for the elevator wondering what to do with the flowers. The door slid open, and there was Arcas, clutching his own little bouquet of daffodils.

"Don't bother," I said before he even stepped off the elevator. "They won't let you in. Family only, and they don't allow flowers." I was surprised by how glad I was to see him.

He looked startled to see me. "You left without saying good-bye. You just disappeared. I was worried about you."

"I'm sorry, seeing Nancy unconscious in the street like that brought back some bad memories, that's all. I got freaked out and ran away, but that wasn't your fault. I had a wonderful time until . . . well, I owe you an apology."

"I thought maybe you were running away from me, that you didn't want to see me again."

"No, nothing like that, in fact I'm happy I ran into you."

We stared at one another's flowers with amusement as I stepped into the elevator, and stood self-consciously beside him. We descended one floor, two, three. In another moment the doors would open and he'd be gone. *Just as well,* I thought. *It's a risk getting close to other people.* Then the old Amy suddenly emerged from wherever she'd been hiding for the past two years. "Do you want to get some coffee in the cafeteria?" And just like that, I took a first, tentative step toward a new life.

"No, let's go to the diner across the street. It's quieter and they have better pastry."

I looked down at my boots and smiled. He wasn't mad. He still liked me. "How do you know that?" I asked as the doors opened and we stepped off the elevator.

"Because I make it." He smiled at me. "They get their pastry from Kosmos Bakery."

It was the first sunny day in weeks, but I was wearing both a sweater and a raincoat because there was still a chill in the air. Arcas was wearing nothing but a form fitting T-shirt and bell-bottom jeans, yet he seemed oblivious to the cold. We crossed Bond Street and entered a small restaurant on the corner.

I held up my little bouquet of flowers. "What do we do with these?"

He took my daffodils, added them to his, and made a great show of presenting them to the matronly lady in a white apron standing at the register. "Mrs. Panagos, a beautiful lady should have beautiful flowers." He handed her the bouquet, kissing her on both cheeks.

"Arcas, what are you doing? My husband's in the kitchen. You'll make him jealous." She smiled flirtatiously over the yellow blooms.

"Then he should buy you flowers himself. What have you got for lunch?"

We slipped into one of the red vinyl booths, and Arcas ordered a gyro and fries while I had the country salad with warm pita and feta cheese. I tried making mindless small talk, but I couldn't stop thinking about Nancy's accident.

As we finished our meals, I sipped my coffee and picked at the plate of almond cookies Mrs. Panagos had brought to our table *Choris chréosi.* free of charge. "You saved my life last night. Honestly, I froze like a rabbit. I don't know what would have happened if you hadn't pulled me out of the street. Thank you."

"It was nothing."

"No, it was absolutely something. I didn't sleep a wink last night. My eyes must be all red and puffy. They feel like sandpaper." I didn't tell him about my nightmares or that I'd heard my sister scream for help, better to keep those recurring hallucinations to myself.

"No, your eyes are perfect. Even without sleep, they're beautiful."

"Yeah, me and Mrs. Panagos, we're both beautiful, but you can't have us both. You're going to have to choose." How long could I keep up this insipid banter? He was a good-looking guy, and I wanted to be a normal girl again, but I didn't have the patience for this sort of nonsense anymore. My new life would have to be different from the one I'd left behind.

Arcas took a big bite of his gyro and turned to look at Mrs. Panagos whose gray hair was tucked into a net and whose apron strings could barely circumnavigate the equator of her belly. He turned back to me with a perplexed expression. "I'm not sure. This is a difficult decision."

Nancy was lying across the street in the intensive care ward, and we were making jokes. "Seriously, we could have been killed. Whoever was driving that car must have been drunk or high on something. That guy was coming straight at us. He didn't even slow down. Did you know Nancy had surgery last night?"

"No, what kind of surgery?"

"I don't know. The nurse just said that the anesthesia from her surgery hadn't worn off yet. Last night was so scary. I thought she was dead."

Arcas put down his sandwich. "The paramedics told us she has broken bones and maybe a concussion, but she's going to be okay. You don't need to be so frightened."

"The nurse thought I was her sister. Does she have a sister? Has anyone notified her family?"

"Tom gave the police her parents' number, but he was a mess. He could hardly talk." Arcas dropped his voice. "He threw up in the police car when they drove us home."

"I'm not surprised. He'd had way too much to drink. Thank God, Nancy wouldn't let him drive."

"Yes, the drink plus he was afraid the accident was our fault. He felt guilty because he thought that car was meant for us."

"Why in the world would he think that?"

"We got into a fight with a bunch of fascists at our last rally. They threatened us, told us they'd drink our blood, stuff like that, so he thought it could have been one of them."

"Seriously? Is that possible?" I was incredulous but a little frightened. "Could those men have followed us here? Are we safe?"

"Of course, we're safe. Things like that happen in Greece, not Toronto. Tom was just drunk, talking crazy, but still, he blamed himself for Nancy's accident."

We were quiet a moment, staring inward. I was pretty sure we were both reliving the preceding night. "How long have Tom and Nancy been together? I thought I'd see him at the hospital."

"About a year, but it's not serious. Tom's going back to Greece as soon as someone shoots the colonels and Nancy wants to travel and have some big career."

"The colonels?" I felt stupid. I might be living in Canada, but I was still an American. My knowledge of contemporary politics began and ended with Watergate and the Vietnam War.

"You know, the junta. He hates them so much I'm surprised he doesn't go back and shoot them himself."

Arcas clearly assumed that everyone knew about this junta, but I didn't. I'd have to own up or fake it. "OK, I'm stupid. I admit it. I remember reading about some sort of coup, but that's all I know."

"Oh my God, where do I start?" Arcas stared at me, deciding how much history I could take. "Have you heard of King Constantine?"

I nodded. I *had* heard of King Constantine. "He married a Danish princess, right?"

"Right, you used to see his photograph in ladies' magazines because he was this handsome guy who won an Olympic medal for sailing. When I was in high school all the girls wanted to marry him, but he turned out to be an idiot." He ran his fingers through his dark curls and shook his head. "About ten years ago Greece finally elected a decent prime minister, Georgios Papandreou."

Without thinking, I was playing with the pendant I always wear around my neck. Distracted, Arcas lost his chain of thought. "That's a strange necklace. What is it, a cat's head with writing on it?"

I quickly tucked the chain and the small gold charm back into my sweater. "It's nothing, a birthday gift from my parents. So, what happened after Papandreou was elected?"

"Everyone was happy except the military and the monarchists. But then the king forced Papandreou to resign because he wanted to choose his own government. The problem was, Constantine didn't know what he was doing. Every morning we'd wake up and there'd be a new prime minister. Everyone was plotting against everyone. It was like the Middle Ages. The country was a mess, so Papandreou came back, recreated his old party, and planned to run again. This was six years ago—1967. He would have won if the colonels hadn't staged a coup and cancelled the election.

"They told everyone Papandreou was a Communist and threw him into prison. We were supposed to believe they were big heroes for saving Greece from Communism, but only the stupid people believed it. Papandreou, the poor bastard, died in prison a year later, and the colonels are still in power. So that's what happened. My country, the country that invented Democracy, is being ruled by a bunch of fascist pigs."

"Wow." I didn't know what to say. Thank God nothing like that could ever happen in the United States. We were a solid, established democracy, a beacon of freedom for the world. Kings and coups belonged to small, struggling countries without our history of free elections, checks, and balances. "What happened to Constantine? Was he in cahoots with the colonels?"

"Not exactly, but he was the coward who handed them the keys. After they arrested the prime minister and surrounded the palace with tanks, he made them the official government. He changed his mind the next day, but it was too late."

A twisted smile crossed Arcas's lips. "Two days later he jumped into an airplane with his whole family and flew away like a frightened little bird." He made a flapping motion with his hands. "They're in Italy now. They're like Tom, planning to go back as soon as someone shoots the bastards."

"Were you in Greece when all that happened, or were you in Canada already?"

"I was in Greece, at university." Arcas stood up abruptly. "Which reminds me, I have a class in an hour, so I'd better get going. I hope I didn't bore you with Greek politics."

"No, not at all, I'm embarrassed I didn't already know what happened." I stood up and put on my raincoat. "Anyway, I should be getting back to work."

Arcas paid the bill, but neither of us moved toward the door. I thought he might ask me out again, but he just said, "It was a nice surprise seeing you today. Also, it was very nice of you to visit Nancy. I didn't expect to see you there."

"Well, that didn't work out very well, but at least we tried. I thought we'd see Tom, but maybe they don't let boyfriends in either."

Arcas shrugged.

"I'll try sending her a card. Let's hope they allow cards in the ICU." I put out my hand and Arcas took it and squeezed my fingers warmly. Again, I thought he'd say something, but he just studied my face with his beautiful brown eyes. Disappointed, I took back my hand. "Well, good-bye and thank you for the history lesson."

Arcas smiled sadly and brushed a stray curl from my face. "I didn't tell you the whole story. I left out the parts that would make you angry."

"Why would I be angry?"

"Because a nice American lady might not want to hear the whole story. There's a lot I didn't tell you."

"Well, I don't want to hear it now. I've got to get back to work. But you can tell me another time. I'd love to hear the rest of the story."

"Yes, maybe another time." He held the door open for me then jogged off toward the university.

Jacob
May 1993

I'VE FINALLY LOCATED a likely prospect, a 1985 Bass Cat, docked right downtown at Marina Quay. It's only seventeen feet but in mint condition with an upgraded motor. Of course, the seller may be puffing a bit, but he sounds like a decent fellow. It's been years since I've been out on the water and the prospect has taken twenty years off me. I feel as though I've regained the inches I've lost in my old age and stand my full five foot ten again. When was the last time my heart raced with such anticipation? Of course, my son would have me probated if he knew what I was up to, so I'm not saying a word until I have the title safely in my pocket. So what if the boat shaves a few pennies off his inheritance? No, that's unfair, Michael's not concerned about the money, he's worried about me. They both worry, Michael and his wife Sharon. They're good kids, but they're worriers. They'd worry I'd fall overboard, sail off course, or get captured by pirates and shanghaied to Detroit. Who knows what they'd imagine? But I'm not crazy, the Bass Cat's a simple runabout. I've manned sloops twice her size and I can still manage a little putt-putt by myself as long as someone helps me get her in the water.

It's too early to go downtown, but I'm too excited to wait inside, so I decide to treat myself to lunch at the Village Diner. I walk down Spadina, moving pretty briskly for an old guy who can't see straight. Despite the heat I'm wearing a windbreaker and a Greek fisherman's cap which I think project a jaunty, nautical effect.

"Ahoy there," I call out to Kaleisha as I walk through the door.

"Ahoy to you too," she calls back. "Your usual table?"

I order the fisherman's platter even though it's all fried and Kaleisha clucks her tongue at me. "You'll be dying young if you're not careful," she chides me.

"Too late for that," I reassure her, "and bring me a piece of strawberry pie with extra whipped cream for dessert."

She shakes her head disapprovingly but writes it all down. I polish off five shrimp, a piece of halibut, a few chips, and a side of slaw. When was the last time I finished my whole lunch and a piece of pie to boot? I hand Kaleisha a generous tip then leave to catch a streetcar to Queen's Quay.

The journey is easier than I'd imagined. It's a straight shot without any nonsense about transfers or changing cars, but troubles begin as soon as I step off the streetcar. Nothing looks familiar and with my bad eyes I can't even read the signs. But I'm no imbecile. I still know how to get around. I have directions to the Amsterdam Bridge and a boat slip number in my pocket.

A man in a blue uniform is talking to someone just across the street. I pull the paper from my pocket and head in his direction. As I'm almost upon him I stop, alarmed to realize that his uniform is badly ripped exposing a dingy undershirt. His blue pants are denim jeans and his hair is hanging to his shoulders. I squint, wondering if I've got his gender wrong as well before backing away to find someone else to ask for help.

Failing eyesight can lead to awkward situations, but then a real policeman, or rather a policewoman, stops to ask me if I'm lost. This is embarrassing, I had no idea that I was behaving oddly or that anyone would guess at my predicament. Still, it's a relief to see a friendly face, so I show her my paper and explain that I can't read street signs very well. She assures me it's not far off, just over a mile, then asks if I need a cab.

"I may be getting on, but I am still fully capable of walking a few blocks on a lovely day. Thank you very much for your assistance." I tip my hat, a gesture of dismissal more than courtesy, and march off in the direction that she's indicated.

It's only one-thirty and Mr. McClaren isn't expecting me for an hour so I have time to take in the sights as I proceed along the busy water front. It's been years since I've ventured down to the harbor, and I'm surprised by how much it's changed. There are all sorts of galleries and restaurants where there used to be nothing but shipping docks and warehouses. Even the boats look different, mostly impressive yachts instead of fishing boats and trawlers. Their names are printed on the hulls in large black letters that even my poor eyes can read. I shake my head and chuckle as I walk past *For Sail, Cutting Wind, Aqua Holic,* and *Miss Behavin.* I've read articles in the *Globe and Mail* about plans to revitalize the area, but it's something else to see it for yourself.

A group of shirtless punks with long hair whizz past me on skateboards. They look like hooligans, and I feel inside my jacket pocket for the envelope containing the five crisp hundred-dollar bills Mr. McClaren requires as a good faith deposit on the boat. Reassured that the money's safe, I pick up my pace and arrive at the Amsterdam Bridge, our agreed meeting place, with time to spare. I don't recognize Mr. McClaren until he's nearly beside me. He's a nice, clean-cut fellow about my grandson's age, dressed in the Toronto Blue Jays hat and gray sweatshirt he told me he'd be wearing.

I wave him over and we shake hands. "Nice to meet you, Mr. McClaren."

"Bob," he says. "Please call me Bob. I don't think anyone's ever called me Mr. McClaren before."

I start to say, "Well then, call me Jacob," but he's so young and we've only just met so I simply smile and say, "Nice to meet you, Bob."

We exchange a few pleasantries and then get down to business. Bob waxes euphoric about the boat and I'm thinking that if she's half the craft he says she is, he has her significantly underpriced.

He may be aware that he's offering a bargain. "You know, there's been quite a bit of interest in this boat. If you're serious, I'll need a cash deposit to hold her for you."

Not wanting to give my hand away, I nod noncommittally. "You mentioned that on the phone. I have it right here." I pat my jacket pocket. "But let's take a look at her first, don't you think?" He smiles agreeably and I follow him toward the slip where he has her docked. We're not halfway there when he feels inside his pants pocket and comes to an abrupt stop, a sheepish expression on his face.

"I'm so sorry," he apologizes. "I'm a complete idiot. I've left the keys inside my car. Would you mind a little extra walk? I'm parked on a side street just around the corner."

I'm already exhausted, but the poor man is clearly embarrassed, so I assure him there's no problem, that the extra walk will do me good, and we set off in the opposite direction. True to his word, we come to a small side street, an alley really, where he's parked illegally. Parking is scarce and quite expensive in this part of town, so I don't blame him, but I hope he doesn't have a ticket.

He points to a black car parked beside a large trash dumpster. "It's right over there. I'm so sorry for the inconvenience."

Once we're standing beside the car, his whole demeanor changes. "I'm not wasting my time if you don't have that deposit money," he says. "Let's see it."

I'm suddenly aware that we're in a blind alley with no one nearby. "I told you that I brought it, but if you've changed your mind I'd understand. You don't have to show me your boat if you don't want to."

"I just don't want to waste my time if you're messing with me. You brought five hundred dollars, right?"

I nod, dry mouthed. My knees are shaking but I'm trying to keep things normal.

"Show it to me," he demands. "I want to see the money."

I reach into my pocket and pull out the envelope. He grabs it from my hand, slits it open, counts the bills, then gets into the car.

"Wait!" I say stupidly. "I haven't seen the boat."

He slams the door and starts the motor while I stand frozen on the street. As he pulls away, I lunge at his door. "Wait!" I shout as the car peels away, throwing me to the side of the road where my head lands hard against the metal dumpster. I sit there dazed for several minutes. Nothing like this has ever happened to me before. If I were younger, I could have stood up to him, but it's not in me anymore. I'm suddenly glad there's no one around to see me, an old man on his knees in front of a rubbish bin, fumbling for his glasses and blinking back tears.

Some men my age are too weak to pull themselves up from the ground, but not me. I've retained much of my strength and flexibility despite my eighty-three years, except now my legs refuse to hold me up and I'm flailing on the pavement like an old bird with a broken wing or Icarus trying to rise from the sea. It's useless. I'm sitting with my back against the dumpster trying to catch my breath when a car pulls up beside me and a middle-aged woman rolls down her window.

"Are you alright? Do you need some help?"

She's wearing a white nurse's uniform and looks kind, but I'm suddenly wary, certain she must take me for a rummy or a homeless person.

"I'm afraid I've taken a little fall and can't get up. Would you mind giving me a hand?"

"Just give me a minute to park my car. I'll be right with you." She pulls into the spot just vacated by Bob then comes over and crouches down beside me. "Are you in pain? Do you think you might have broken something?"

"No, no, I just need a hand up. Thank you for stopping."

"Are you sure? I work at St. Michael's Hospital. It might be a good idea to get checked out in the ER."

"No, please, just help me up. I'll be fine."

She braces herself, offers me her arm and I'm miraculously on my feet. I do a quick inventory of my various parts and pieces and am relieved to discover that everything seems to be working and intact.

"Can I give you a ride somewhere?" She still has her hand on my arm to steady me.

"Thank you, but really I'm fine."

"Are you sure? It wouldn't be any trouble."

My gaze goes to the end of the alley where the road seems to shimmer like moving water and I remember the long walk back along the waterfront. "Actually, I would appreciate a ride to the Spadina streetcar stop, if that's not too far."

"Not at all, it's on my way. I'll have you there in two minutes." She opens the passenger door and helps me into her car as though I'm one of her patients.

"What in the world brought you down here in the first place? You're lucky I got a bit lost and had to turn around."

"I was going to buy a boat, but it didn't work out." No point in telling her the whole sordid story. I'm humiliated enough as it is.

"A boat? Really?" She looks doubtful. "You know, if you like boats I hear there's a new ship in the harbor offering free rides. They might still have some tickets."

"Thanks, but I've had enough of boats for one day, maybe another time."

"OK," she says, turning toward me with a lovely smile. "Your choice, but they say this boat is something special."

Two minutes later I'm waiting for the Spadina streetcar in the heat of an unseasonably warm afternoon. Streetcars run frequently in Toronto, perhaps that's why the authorities decided we don't need benches and shelters at most stops. Maybe they never considered the possibility of a slightly concussed old man waiting for public transportation after being assaulted and robbed by a violent con artist. I have no idea what they were thinking. I only know that I need to sit down. There's a small coffee shop just behind me, one of those new places that serve continental coffees at exorbitant prices, but it has chairs and air conditioning and looks like salvation at the moment.

As I stand at the counter ordering a small coffee, I realize how fortunate I've been. The thief grabbed the deposit money and ran off without demanding my wallet. I hand over a dollar and a quarter to the clerk gloating at the possibility that I may be able to hide this entire incident from Michael. I don't need him using this as evidence that he should be more diligent about nosing into my private business and scrutinizing my affairs.

I sit in a large leather chair by the front window, although I'm not sure how I'll hoist myself out of the thing. It's a pleasure to sink into its deep upholstered cushion and let my head loll against its back. I take a swig of the hot coffee and close my eyes. Well, perhaps my sailing days are over, but at least I still have my wallet and my dignity. It could have been worse. I consider notifying the police, but then think better of it. What would I tell them anyway? I didn't have the presence of mind to write down the scoundrel's license plate and it's unlikely that his name is really Bob McClaren. Call me Bob, indeed. He ought to be in jail, except if I call the police my son will get wind of my little escapade and and I'll be the one who'll get locked up. Better to keep my mouth shut and kiss my money good-bye.

I take another sip of coffee and brood over this sorry state of affairs when a string of yellow flags flapping from the roof of a small building just across the street catches my attention. Beneath them is a large banner which I can't read given the state of my eyes, but I do see a line of people holding brightly colored balloons, congregating nearby. Probably a promotion for some new shop or condo development I tell myself and look away. But a moment later a brass band marches past the coffee shop leading a small parade toward those yellow flags. Good heavens, the band's playing "The Twelfth Street Rag." Doesn't that bring back memories? I smile despite myself and find that my old, tired feet are tapping along with the rhythm. Energized by the music and the festive atmosphere, I pull myself out of my chair and decide to investigate what all the commotion is about.

As soon as I've crossed the street a man in a sailor suit offers me a red balloon. I shake my head, waving him away, then proceed along a walkway to where a group of people are standing in line, holding balloons, and eating ice cream as though they're at a carnival. The band continues to play, and everyone seems excited about something.

"What's going on?" I ask a young woman pushing a baby stroller.

"It's the maiden voyage of the *Aqua Meridian*." She has to raise her voice to be heard over the tuba that's drowning out the rest of the musicians.

"They're giving away the first fifty tickets for free. If you want to go, you should get in line right now. The free ones are almost gone." She points to a ticket booth where a crowd of people are standing in line.

The sailor with the red balloons seems to have overheard our conversation. "No need to wait." He hands me a ticket. "Compliments of the *Aqua Meridian*, enjoy your trip."

"Well, isn't this your lucky day. I'd go myself if I didn't have to start dinner for my family. Have fun." The young woman wheels off, leaving me holding a ticket and feeling utterly disoriented. What just happened? Am I going on a boat trip after all?

I hear a long blast from a ship's horn and the crowd of people mingling on the street walk toward the water. I walk with them, clutching my ticket and wondering what's about to happen. It's no more than fifty yards to the dock where, what I thought was a small building, turns out to be a ship with yellow flags flying along its top deck. Now that I'm closer, I can read the words, *Aqua Meridian*, painted along her side. She seems to be a pleasure boat designed for short lake cruises. I imagine there's a snack shop aboard, perhaps even a small restaurant serving sandwiches and soft drinks. I look up and see a long row of lounge chairs ringing the main deck. The idea of an hour or two reclining in one of those lounges is suddenly appealing. I can take a nap, enjoy the lake breezes while admiring the city skyline. By the time we return to port I'll have recovered from that unfortunate business and never think of it again. I can tell Michael about the lovely day I had on an excursion boat, and he'll see that I can still get around in the world and manage quite well for myself.

I allow the crowd to push me toward the gangplank where an amiable young woman in a navy uniform festooned with brass buttons takes our tickets and welcomes us aboard. I grab one of the deck chairs before other passengers claim them all and I'm delighted to find myself stretched out with an unobstructed view of the harbor. The ship's horn emits another loud blast, there's a slight lurch, and we pull away from the pier. A moment later we're in open water with the CN Tower and city skyscrapers receding in the distance. I expect we'll just circle the Toronto Islands or wander along the coast a bit before heading back to port, but I feel the expansive exhilaration of someone embarking on a voyage. Although the city remains clearly within view, I feel a sense of adventure as though bound for somewhere new and unexpected. It's a pleasant sensation and I smile to myself as I tip my cap over my face, close my eyes, and let my mind drift off with the little boat.

I may have fallen asleep because I'm startled by a man's voice. "Sir," he says, "excuse me, sir. May I offer you a glass of wine?"

I push my cap back and sit up. A waiter in spotless white livery is standing beside me with a silver tray. It takes me a moment to remember where I am. This is certainly unexpected. The *Aqua Meridian* is apparently pulling out all the stops on its maiden voyage.

"How much for a glass of white?" I ask.

"They're complimentary, sir." He lowers the tray, offering me a drink as though I'm a guest at a cocktail party.

"Well, thank you. Yes, thank you very much." I note that it's real glass, not one of those plastic throw-away things you'd expect on a harbor cruise. I take a sip and squint out toward shore. Is it just my eyes or has the CN Tower really disappeared beyond the horizon?

Amy
May 1973

I DIDN'T SEE Arcas again for almost a month. I sent Nancy a get-well card, care of St. Michael's Hospital, then went on with my life. I stopped at Kosmos Bakery most mornings for my regular breakfast of a Greek biscotti and black coffee, but I never ran into the young baker with gorgeous hair. While I can't say that I never thought of him, I didn't think of him often. A rash of four-color jobs was keeping everyone at Abbot's Printing hopping, and I was enjoying the work, surprisingly happy to be supporting myself by the dint of my own labor.

Spring is a busy time in the printing business as the world gears up for the season of craft shows, sailing regattas, golf opens, and county fairs. Our customers arrived breathless, panicked, and precariously close to deadlines we couldn't control. Canadian civility aside, they were universally disinterested in the fact that there were other customers ahead of them and, no matter how much they whined and carried on, their jobs would still take however long they'd take.

It was Tom, not Arcas, who showed up at the print shop one Friday afternoon in late May. He was wearing the same black T-shirt he'd worn the night we'd met at the taverna, but he'd gotten a haircut and trimmed his beard. Who'd have guessed there was a nice-looking man under all that hair? He no longer resembled a goat, in fact he looked more sheepish, embarrassed to run into me. He'd clearly forgotten that this is where I worked. Frankly, I was surprised he recognized me at all.

I smiled brightly, greeting him as I would any customer coming through our door. "Hello, Tom, what a nice surprise, seeing you again."

"Hi, yeah, nice to see you too, sorry, I don't remember your name."

"It's Amy, don't apologize, we only met the one time, although it was certainly a memorable evening. That car probably knocked my name right out of your head."

"Yeah, I remember now. You were with Arcas that night. Sorry if I was acting like an ass. I'm not a good drinker and I was upset about my thesis proposal. The good news is they're saying they'll accept it now with just a few changes, so I'm okay again."

"Great, that's lucky."

"You two were the lucky ones, that car didn't even touch you."

"No kidding, it missed us by inches." I looked around to see if Mrs. Klein or one of the guys was eavesdropping, but they were all in the back. "How's Nancy? I tried visiting her at the hospital, but they wouldn't let me in. They have some kind of family only rule."

"I know, they wouldn't let me in either, at least not until she woke up and started asking for me. She's still at St. Mike's, but they've moved her to a regular room. You could visit her if you wanted. She might like that."

"Maybe I'll stop by after work one day this week." In reality, I doubted that I'd bother. Nancy had seemed nice enough, but she wasn't a friend. It had taken me weeks to recover from the shock of seeing her struck down in the street and I had no interest in reviving those memories. "That was sure one freaky accident. It happened so fast, one minute we were having a nice evening out, just walking to your car and then, boom. Did they ever find the guy who did it?"

"The police don't have a clue, but we have our suspicions."

I remembered my conversation with Arcas and wondered if there was anything to his story. "If you have information, you should tell the police. Someone needs to pull that guy's driver's license. He's going to kill someone."

"That might have been his plan."

"Are you saying he meant to hit Nancy?"

"No, but he might have meant to hit me or Arcas."

"Wow." I took a step backward. "Arcas told me something like that, but it sounded crazy. I didn't really believe him." I could imagine someone being drunk and reckless behind the wheel of a car, but deliberately pointing two tons of speeding metal at a helpless pedestrian? That didn't happen in my world. At least it had never happened in my old life.

"Well, take anything Arcas says with a grain of salt, but in this case . . ." Tom handed me a large brown envelope. "Look, just forget it. I shouldn't have said anything. I'm being paranoid. Anyway, I didn't come here to talk about the accident. I wanted to know if you could make some posters for us. We need two hundred copies by Wednesday at the latest. It's for a rally in a couple weeks."

I walked over to the counter, slipped the original artwork from the envelope, and laid it on the illuminated glass. It showed a group of people marching and waving their fists beneath an image of a Greek flag. Superimposed over the image was a block of Greek text so dense that, even if it had been in English, I couldn't have read it without a magnifying glass. It wasn't a poster, it was a manifesto. Whatever it said, I'd never seen such terrible design.

Tom must have seen the chagrin on my face because he looked worried and a bit belligerent. "What's the matter? What's wrong with it?"

"I don't want to hurt your feelings. I see that someone spent a lot of time on this, but it's too hard to read. A poster needs to grab your attention with a strong image and just a couple words. The message has to jump out at you."

"It's a complicated subject. You can't explain it in just a couple of sentences."

"You do your explaining at the rally. A poster's job is just to get people to show up." Tom looked annoyed, but then as he studied the poster his face fell, and irritation was replaced by panic. I felt a pang of pity for him. "I could rework this for you, but there's normally a charge for design."

"It's a student organization. We don't have money."

I looked around; my boss and the rest of the staff were still in the back. I lowered my voice. "That's OK, I'll rework it for free if you help me with the Greek, but my boss can't know. There's a Fran's Restaurant around the corner. Could you meet me there at six? I promise, it won't cost you a penny."

"Sure, OK, thanks. I'll see you at six. That's nice of you. I appreciate it." His eyes softened and for the first time I had an inkling of what Nancy saw in the man.

Fran's is always crowded in the early evening. There are young professionals stopping in for drinks after work, golden agers who come for the early-bird specials and the singles who've made it their venue of choice for noncommittal first dates. Tom was sitting at a booth in the back, and to my surprise, Arcas was sitting across from him.

I threw my purse and a bag of art supplies on the floor and slid into the empty seat beside Arcas, trying not to show how unnerved I felt by his sudden reappearance. "Hey, I didn't expect to see you here."

"I just got back. I wanted to see you again, so when Tom said he was meeting you I decided to come along."

"Back? Back from where?"

"Greece, my village, to see my father. He had a stroke, so I had to go home to help my mother."

"I'm so sorry, is he alright?"

"He's getting better, but he can't work. My mother wants me to move back to our village and run the farm. What do you think, should I go home and be a shepherd?"

"I have no idea—" I began.

"If you go home now, you won't be a shepherd you'll be a target," Tom said in a low voice so that no eavesdroppers could overhear him. "They know who belongs to the PAK. I wouldn't go back until the colonels are gone. It's too dangerous."

"I was making a joke. I'm here, aren't I? Let's talk about something else. We have a nice American lady here. She doesn't want to hear about these things." He draped his arm around my shoulder. How long had it been since a man had touched me? Too long apparently, but this wasn't the time.

"Right, we're supposed to be working on your poster. Let's see what we can do with that." I pulled away, glad for an excuse to create some distance before I found my head nestled into the neck of this virtual stranger. I pulled out a sketch pad, a straight rule, and some colored markers and laid them on the table. "OK, now let's see that copy you brought to the office."

As soon as Tom laid his artwork on the table, Arcas threw up his hands and said something in Greek that made Tom turn red. A moment later the two were embroiled in a heated exchange in spitfire Greek that left me feeling awkward and invisible.

Arcas suddenly turned to me and asked, "What do you think? Do we support the junta and abolish the king or stand with the monarchists and spit in the face of the colonels? You can't have it both ways."

He'd asked the question in English, but as far as I was concerned he was still speaking Greek. I had no idea what he was talking about.

Tom, seeing the bewildered look on my face, tried to explain. "There's going to be a vote on whether or not Greece will continue to be a monarchy. It seems our beloved king handed the country to Papadopoulos and his military junta, and now the junta wants to thank him by eliminating his job."

"I thought the king flew off to Italy. Why even bother with a referendum if he's already gone?" I thought I was being reasonable, but both men rolled their eyes. Apparently, I was being stupid.

"Planes fly both ways. Without the referendum, he'll just come back when things calm down," Tom said softly, but vehemently.

"Of course, he'll come back, and we'll deal with him then, but right now the most important thing is getting rid of the colonels and most of the military are royalists." Arcas rose to his feet and towered over Tom. "Do you want to thumb your nose at the crew of the Battleship Velos? Those men may be fighting the junta out of loyalty to the king, but they're still fighting. They're still on our side."

Tom stood up and spit out his words as they leaned into each other, eye to eye. "If Constantine was a real king, if he was a real man, he would have stood up to the colonels. They wouldn't even be there now." They glared at each other, grim and unblinking.

"I could use another beer." I raised my empty glass to demonstrate the gravity of the situation.

Tom turned toward the waitress and motioned her over. "We need another beer over here." He looked at Arcas. "How about you? Should I get a pitcher?"

An hour later the pitcher was empty, my head was swimming, and they were still arguing, but the mood had lightened considerably. Finally, Tom put an end to the debate.

"It doesn't matter what we think, Andreas wants the bastard gone so we hold the rally. Let's just get this poster finished." Tom turned to me. "Design something that will bring every Greek in Toronto to the event. Expats can't vote, but a huge crowd will send a message of support."

I opened my pad of drawing paper, without remembering that I'd been working on a sketch of Joanie. She stared up at me from the open tablet with a look of surprise.

"What's that, a self-portrait? It looks just like you." I tore off the sheet and buried it beneath the pad.

Arcas made a move to retrieve the drawing, but I swatted his hand away. "Sorry, that's private. How about this?" I began sketching with a set of colored pencils. Since the king had fled the country in his private plane, I drew a plane bearing the king's name and a little crown flying off into a blue sky. "How do you say, 'wave good-bye' in Greek, or how about 'and don't come back?'"

Arcas took my pencil and wrote, Και μην επιστρέψετε, Greek for *and don't come back*. I carefully copied the unfamiliar letters at the top of the page.

"And what's the name of your organization?"

"Panhellenic Liberation Movement, but you can just write PAK."

I wrote PAK at the bottom of the page in simple block letters along with the time and location of the rally. Even Arcas admitted the poster looked good even though he was still upset about being overruled. I promised to do a final mock-up at home and have something ready to print the next day.

Tom picked up the check and headed toward the register while Arcas and I finished our drinks.

"You know, I thought of you all the time I was gone," Arcas said, as soon as Tom was out of earshot.

"Then you should have sent me a postcard." I was inexplicably miffed over his unexplained departure. It wasn't as though he owed me anything. It wasn't as though I was in any condition to get involved with a man.

"I don't know your address. I don't even know your phone number."

My hands were shaking. I couldn't even look him in the eye, but I tore off a corner of the placemat as though I were just a normal girl accustomed to casual flirtations. "Well," I said, scribbling down my number, "now you have no excuse."

Jacob
Aboard the Aqua Meridian
Shake Rattle and Roll

TORONTO'S SKYSCRAPERS AND traffic have receded into a foggy blur and all I see are muted shades of blue and gray beyond the rail. I take another sip of my wine, allowing the terrible events of the day to dissolve in the unexpected pleasure of the moment. It's surprisingly good, not that I'm a connoisseur. Something about the wine and the water have put me in a nostalgic frame of mind. My thoughts drift to earlier voyages and I feel my strength returning. I remember my boyhood on the River Aire, idyllic voyages along the coast of Crete, that awful troop ship during the war, and finally the great ocean crossing that brought me and Bess to Canada. But after that, nothing. I can't recall anything but ferry boat rides to the Toronto Islands. Why did I stop sailing with a great lake so close at hand?

Scanning the deck, I realize this ship is much larger than it appeared from the dock, and I'm amazed by the number of passengers strolling by. They're surprisingly well dressed for a lake cruise, and I nod appreciatively as a group of young women in colorful skirts and blouses pass, giggling and chattering the way girls do. There's a little boy in a sailor outfit still holding one of the red balloons they handed out on the pier, and a large man with a tiny dog wearing a nautical scarf around its neck. Very amusing, I'm having a wonderful time. An attractive young woman in a swimming outfit hurries past. I'm not too old to appreciate a shapely bosom and I am delighted by the flamboyant jiggle and bounce even these old eyes can't fail to notice. As she walks past, I salute her with my glass then finish off my drink. Since the nice young man with the wine is nowhere to be seen, I decide to venture inside to see if I can snag another glass.

The ship is now moving at quite a clip and the deck heaves slightly as gentle waves break against her bow. I steady myself by hanging on to deck chairs as I make my way toward the nearest door. Suddenly, a new thought stops me short and I pause, confused. Why was the woman wearing a bathing suit? Surely, there can't be a swimming pool onboard, or am I wrong? The boat is larger than I imagined, but a pool? It's all a pleasant muddle and, for the moment, all I know for sure is that I want another drink.

As I step through the doorway, I find that I've regained my balance but then I'm shaken by the sight of a sumptuous lobby. There's wall to wall carpet on the floor and fancy chandeliers hanging from a paneled ceiling. Not what I'd expected. Apparently, a free ticket on this ship was quite a prize. I hadn't realized.

"May I help you?" A waiter or a steward or whatever is at my elbow, bowing slightly from the waist. He can't be Canadian. Canadians don't bow.

"Yes, I was wondering where I could get another glass of wine."

"Certainly, may I see your ticket?"

He's no less courteous, but I ruffle at a certain officiousness in his tone as I search in my pocket for the ticket. I hand it over without a word and watch as he examines it.

"You'll find the tourist class lounge up the staircase to your right. All food and beverages are included. Enjoy your trip."

He hands my ticket back and I turn toward the grand, open staircase leading to an upper deck. It seems to go on forever. Sighing, I ask, "Is there an elevator? I'm not sure these old legs are up to all those stairs."

He nods sympathetically. "Don't worry, you'll have your sea-legs in no time, but for the moment try the elevator across from the information desk."

I thank him and hurry off in search of another drink. Had he said food *and* beverages were included? Was there food upstairs as well? The display above the elevator door indicates the car is currently on deck four. When number two lights up, the door opens, and I get in. Suddenly, not sure where I'm going, I ask the elevator operator, an older gentleman in a smart uniform and white gloves, where to find the tourist class lounge.

"Smoking lounge or the game room?"

"I'm not sure. The steward said I could get a drink in the tourist class lounge. That's all I know."

"That's the smoking lounge on deck three. It also offers sandwiches and pastries until five." He pulls a large lever, and the doors open to reveal a narrow hallway. "It's just to the right. You can't miss it."

"Thank you. Yes, I see it, thank you very much." A neon sign that reads, GROUCHO'S LOUNGE, in garish blue light is clearly visible. A group of cheerful people pass, smiling and nodding as we all head in the same direction. The lounge, a large room with a low ceiling and simple, modern furnishings, has a beautiful unobstructed view of the water. The room is packed and humming with activity. There are groups seated at round tables, a line of people waiting for their turn at the buffet, and a smattering of loners leaning up against the bar. Nat King Cole is crooning something through the speakers on the ceiling, but it's hard to hear him with so many people talking and laughing all at once. I join the loners at the bar and try to catch the bartender's attention.

He proves to be as friendly and efficient as the rest of the crew, immediately smiling at me and asking, "Hey, Buddy, what'll it be?"

"They were serving a white wine outside on the deck. Do you have any more of that?"

"Sure do, if that's what you want, but how about something a little stronger? Could I interest you in a martini or maybe a scotch and soda?"

I hesitate. It really isn't a good idea to mix alcohol with my medications, but that first glass of wine seems to have done me a world of good. "Are martinis also included in the fare?"

"Yes, sir. Everything's included and I feel obliged to tell you that I make a killer martini."

"Well then, yes please. I'll have one of your killer martinis. Hold the olive. I'm on a low salt diet." The bartender doesn't laugh, but I do. How did such a terrible day end so well? I sip my martini and look around. There are couples standing by the windows looking out at the lake and others talking intimately at some of the smaller tables. It's an international crowd, people of all colors speaking a multitude of languages.

There's a brief lull in the chatter and I can make out the tune playing in the background, an old favorite, "It's Only a Paper Moon." Funny, how the greats never go out of fashion. If only Bessie were here with me now. How she'd have loved this little adventure.

"Excuse me, do you have a light?" A fellow who looks about my son's age is holding up a package of Lucky Strikes. I'm surprised to hear a West London accent. Before I can answer, the bartender hands him a small book of matches. I watch as he taps a cigarette from the pack, puts it between his lips and lights up. "Want one?" he asks, holding out the package.

I haven't smoked in years, but I take a cigarette from the pack. He hands me the matches and I'm amazed by how steady my hands are as I strike one against the box. The almost forgotten taste of tobacco brings back memories of smoky bars in London, tavernas in Athens, and night clubs in Toronto. For once, I'm glad Bessie isn't beside me glaring her disapproval. "Thanks." I blow out a satisfying cloud of smoke and rest my back against the bar. "I'm really enjoying this little trip. Everything's first class all the way."

"Yes," he agrees. "Except we're in tourist class. Makes you wonder what they've got going on upstairs."

"I'm quite happy where I am. Who would have expected free liquor?"

"To free liquor," he agrees, and we clink glasses.

"Nice to find a fellow Brit aboard," I say.

"Indeed," he replies. "To the queen."

"To the queen," I respond, and we clink glasses again.

"Who'd have expected so many Yanks on this ship? I'm from London myself, first time I've ever ventured this far afield. You?"

"Oh, I'm originally from a small town just north of Leeds, but I haven't been back in years. After university I traveled a bit, mostly the Greek islands and Crete. I was in the Navy during the war, and then I sort of wound up in Canada."

The man has kind eyes and an amused expression, and I'm delighted to have found such congenial company. I stick out my hand. "Jacob Kantor."

"Charles Dawson," he says in return.

"Really?" I can't control a little laugh. "Any relation to *the* Charles Dawson?"

"I am *the* Charles Dawson, now that my dad's gone, but no relation to the Piltdown Man, if that's what you're getting at." He takes a sip of his drink and waits for my reply.

"It's probably just as well, *that* Charles Dawson, the one who claimed to have discovered Piltdown Man, turned out to be something of a scoundrel."

"Don't I know it. Thanks to him, I was known as The Missing Link back in grammar school, but most people don't make the connection these days. What are you, some sort of anthropology buff?"

"Archaeology, actually, late Bronze Age for what it's worth."

"Really, what a coincidence." He perks up at once, scrutinizing me with renewed interest. "I teach comparative philology at the University of London, Sumero-Akkadian and Elamite cuneiform primarily. Where do you work?"

"Well"—and here I sigh realizing how long it's been—"I spent most of my career at the University of Toronto, but I retired some time ago."

Mr. Dawson signals the bartender, waving an empty glass in his direction. "Retired at your age? Must be nice. They'll have me chained to my desk another fifteen years."

At my age? Does he think he's flattering me? I'm old enough to be his father. "Time's a funny thing," I say. "You'll be amazed how fast the years fly by."

We exchange wan smiles and then go silent. Strains of Nat King Cole's "Unforgettable" rise above the din, awakening memories that turn my jovial mood into such sloppy nostalgia that I'm afraid I'll embarrass myself by springing a leak and weeping into my drink. I take a last, long swig of my martini and say, "Nice meeting you, Mr. Dawson, but I'm afraid I've got to get going."

"Wife keeps you on a short leash, does she? I remember how that was."

"No, nothing like that." Then, for some reason I tell this total stranger about Bessie. "My wife died eight years ago. Remarkable woman, kind, brilliant, funny, they don't make them like that anymore. I've been on my own since then."

"It's only been four years for me. I still haven't adjusted." There was an awkward silence while I try to think of something to say that won't make the conversation more maudlin. Since nothing comes to me, I nod and am about to leave when he says, "What do you say we meet for supper later, a couple widowers on their own? You can bring me up to date on the Bronze Age."

"Supper? I'm sure we'll be back before supper."

"Back? Back where?" He laughs and pats me on the back. "As far as I know we're only going forward. How about sandwiches at the Sea Breeze Café, much less stuffy than the dining room. Let's say seven o'clock?"

"Yes, fine, seven o'clock. See you then." I set my glass on the bar and leave Charles Dawson and Nat King Cole behind as I make my way out of the lounge, down the hallway, and out onto an upper deck. There's a good wind blowing, and I hang onto the rail for balance as a fine mist wafts against my face. Squint as I may, there's no land anywhere in sight and I swear I smell the sea.

I remove my glasses in the hope that cleaning dust and oily fingerprints from the lenses will make the shoreline reappear. To my surprise, everything comes into focus the moment the specs are off my face. Blinking and rubbing my eyes in disbelief I rotate slowly, taking in details I haven't seen in years: the grain of the wood deck, the slats in the lounge chairs, and the hairy texture of the ropes supporting the lifeboats above my head. I turn back to the rail and gaze out at the water where individual waves peak and break, leaving a trail of frothy foam in their wake. I could count the bubbles if I had the time. Clouds are no longer whitish blotches in the sky, but architectural wonders with heft, dimension, and details I'd almost forgotten. Gaping, infatuated with the floating palaces in the sky, I take out my handkerchief, clean my glasses then put them back on. Immediately, the world's a fog again. I take them off and everything's crystal clear. I put them back on and it's a blur. Strange, very strange. Did that fall jog something back into place? Did a good knock on the noggin correct my vision like when we used to pound on our old Philco to bring the picture into focus? I wrap my glasses in my handkerchief and put them in my pocket. Staring into the distance, as far as my new vision will allow, all I see is water, endless water in all directions. We're very far from shore, perhaps halfway to Rochester. If this boat's some sort of ferry to the US they should have warned me. I would have brought my passport.

I go back inside where I find a small library on the main deck and spend an hour happily perusing old novels and ancient magazines, finally settling on a *National Geographic*. What a joy to be able to read everything, even the captions in small print, without a struggle. By the time I look up it's time to find the Sea Breeze Cafe.

The informal eatery is a large open room with white wicker furniture on blue carpeting with cheesy nautical decorations: an anchor, a life buoy, even a stuffed swordfish, but real candles flicker on each table and the entire back wall opens to additional seating on the deck. I stop at the maître d's station and inquire whether a Mr. Dawson has been seated yet.

"Oh yes," he says, and motions for a young man dressed like an extra in *The Pirates of Penzance* to show me to my table.

Dawson has changed into a dress shirt and navy sport coat, making me feel a bit grubby and underdressed. "Sorry, but I'm afraid this is all I have with me."

"Oh, you're fine, fine. Jackets aren't required out here on deck."

That may be true, but I notice that most of the other passengers have dressed for the evening. There's nothing to be done. I certainly didn't board with dress clothes, so I remove my hat, take a seat, and try to look more comfortable than I feel.

"So, how are you enjoying the cruise so far?" Dawson asks.

"To be honest, it's taken me quite by surprise. I didn't realize the ship was this large and luxurious."

"Yes, they've done a magnificent job restoring her, haven't they? Of course, I've never sailed before so I have nothing to compare her to. You're the traveler so you're the better judge."

"Oh, I've seen a bit of the world, but I'm no expert. I certainly don't have much experience with this sort of thing." I gesture broadly, indicating the entire ship. "As a kid we had a little putt-putt, but that's something else entirely, and you don't want to hear about life aboard a battleship." The waiter comes by with menus and a basket of warm rolls. I take one, tear off a large piece, and slather it with butter. "I'm afraid battleships are a bit short on the amenities. This definitely beats a battleship."

"I don't doubt it. Where were stationed during the war?"

"Greece. The Navy thought I spoke Greek because I could read Aeschylus." We laugh at this common misconception. "Imagine trying to get around modern Athens speaking Attic Greek. Believe me, it can't be done, I've tried it. When I was a student at the British School long before the war, I got lost on my way to some restaurant. The city is a labyrinth, and I was completely turned around when a local gentleman rode by on a bicycle. I flagged him down and asked directions in my best classical Greek. He listened politely, handed me an orange, and rode off."

Mr. Dawson is looking at me expectantly, apparently hoping there's more to the story, so I rummage through a few old memories and come up with something I hope he'll find amusing.

"The Navy was very keen on recruiting young archaeologists for intelligence work because we were supposed to be Cracker Jack cryptologists. They put my wife to work deciphering code at Bletchley Park and sent me off on the *HMS Kipling*. I was presumably an intelligence operative, but my mission was so secret that they never even told me what it was. I spent the entire war waiting for an assignment that never came."

"So, you spent the whole war with your feet up waiting for the phone to ring. You're one lucky bloke."

"Oh no, you've got it all wrong. Without an assignment I was just another poor schmuck in the line of fire. But, in one sense, you're right about being lucky. The *Kipling* was off duty for repairs when the Germans sank our sister ships. The *Kashmir* and *Kelly* both went down. It was an awful thing. We fished Lord Mountbatten and what crew we could out of the Sea of Crete, but of course, we couldn't rescue everyone. There were a lot of casualties." I put down my buttered roll and turned toward the water where the waves were beginning to roil. It looked as though a storm might be brewing. "That was a cruise from Hell. I can tell you that. Do you think it's going to rain?"

Dawson followed my gaze toward the gray clouds massing ominously where there had been blue skies only moments before. "Odd how these storms come up out of nowhere. Do you want to go back inside?"

"No, let's sit here another few minutes. There's something romantic about being out on deck in a storm." I pick up my menu and marvel at how crisp and clear the print appears. It's been years since I've been able to read without my glasses. "I think I'll have The Landlubber's Plate. What about you?"

I notice a young man sitting by himself studying an impressive looking tome. He has a stack of books piled on his table, two more open in front of him and a spiral notebook where he jots down frequent notes. Odd that he's working so hard on a pleasure cruise.

A sudden rush of wind sends menus and napkins sailing in all directions. We all jump from our seats, grab our belongings, and run for cover as the first hard drops of rain pelt us with unexpected force. As I pass the young man's table, I see he's forgotten one of his books. I snatch it up to save it from the rain and hurry back inside with the rest of the passengers. Dawson and I stand panting by the bar grinning foolishly at one another. "Well, that was a surprise."

"Yes," Dawson agrees. "Not very romantic, I'm afraid. Let's see if we can get a table inside."

While Dawson goes off in search of a table, I flip through the book I've just rescued: *Textbook of Physiology*, by Zoethout and Tuttle. The owner's name is penned neatly on the inside cover: Samuel Rabinowitz. So, the young man's a medical student. The name makes me smile. Samuel Rabinowitz I say to myself with a surge of atavistic pride as I look around the room for an industrious Jewish boy who's studying to be a doctor. My search is interrupted by a resonant, male voice broadcast over the ship's speaker system.

This is your captain speaking, wishing you all an enjoyable journey and a pleasant evening aboard Quantum Lines Aqua Meridian. I'm pleased to report that, despite the wind, we remain on course and will continue sailing through the Fabulous Fifties. Please be advised that the Fair Seas Aqua Quintet has been moved from the upper deck to the Grand Foyer due to rain, but the Sock Hop will go on as planned, so put on your dancing shoes and prepare to rock around the clock tonight. Oh, and a word for those with queasy tummies, Dramamine is always available in the ship's dispensary.

Dawson comes back and taps me on the shoulder. When I look up, he points to a small table on the far side of the room, and I follow him to our new seats. The ship is beginning to roll but I keep my balance like an old sailor. I square my shoulders and swagger a bit as we cross the dining room. This trip is making a new man of me. I can feel The Bayside Manor receding further and further into the distance. Our new table is tucked into a cozy corner out of the rain, but with a clear view of the water. A basket of fresh rolls has already appeared and my appetite is picking up.

"A young man forgot this, a medical student. I'll have to find him later," I remark as I put Samuel Rabinowitz's textbook under my chair.

"How will you find him?" Dawson asks.

"He wrote his name inside the front cover."

"Well then, one of the stewards can give you his cabin number. By the way, how do you like your cabin? Mine's clean enough and the bed's good, but it's so small I can practically touch both walls at the same time."

I don't know how to respond. In fact, the question makes me feel more than a little uneasy.

Dawson must see the chagrin on my face because he intuits the problem at once. "If they haven't assigned your cabin yet, we'll just go down to the service desk and they'll sort it out for you. We'll go together right after supper."

"Thank you. I'd appreciate a little moral support." I struggle to ask the next question nonchalantly, so he won't guess the depth of my confusion. "So, just how much longer is this voyage expected to last?"

He looks at me oddly. "Well, there's no land in sight, so I expect we still have a way to go."

Alright. We must be crossing over to the US, but how long can that take? In any case, they might have warned me. I keep those thoughts to myself. "Quite true, I'd better see someone about getting a room."

Once I've finished my hamburger and enough chips to give my doctor a heart attack, and Dawson has polished off a second slice of pie because, well why not, it's all included, we head down to deck one to see about my cabin.

I'm not the only passenger with questions. There's a small queue ahead of me, but the woman at the service desk is personable and efficient and I'm standing in front of her, ticket in hand, within minutes.

"Good evening. What seems to be the problem?" She smiles at me warmly and I relax at once.

"It seems I never checked in properly. This was all rather last minute, and I just went straight up to the lounge without realizing . . ."

"That's not a problem. Are you traveling alone or with your wife?"

"Alone."

She perks up as though this is good news and flashes me that smile again. "Excellent, let's take a look at your ticket."

"Apparently, I'm supposed to be assigned a cabin. I hope it's not too late." I smile back and notice that she's fussing with her hair and leaning forward just enough to give me a quick glimpse of her cleavage. Heavens, is the woman flirting with me?

"Oh no, sir, it's never too late. We can't have our guests sleeping in the lounges, can we?" She studies my ticket for a moment then looks through a large, handwritten ledger. "You've already been assigned a cabin, number 1948 on deck two. It's tourist class, not designed for long-term stays, but I think you'll find it quite comfortable." She takes a metal key off a board and hands it to me. "Will you need a porter to help with your luggage?"

"As I said, this trip wasn't exactly planned. I was offered a ticket at the last moment and here I am, sans luggage." I shrug apologetically. "Maybe there's somewhere on the ship where I can purchase a few things."

"Oh, that won't be necessary. We're accustomed to guests arriving unexpectedly. Housekeeping will see you have everything you need. They're very good about that. Here you go. Take the main elevator off the lobby."

Dawson pats me on the back as we head toward the elevator. "See, no problem at all. Why don't you get settled then look for me in the smoking lounge?"

"Well, that's a relief. I was afraid you were going to invite me to the sock hop."

Dawson's eyes crinkle and the corners of his mouth twitch. "Sorry to disappoint you, but I don't participate much in the theme-night parties. You'll find me sitting with a couple Americans. Do you play bridge?"

"I used to, but it's been years. I'm beyond rusty."

"No matter, we'll get you back up to speed. They don't know Acol, so we play Standard, are you comfortable with that?"

"I'll give it a go, but as I said, it's been years."

"It's just a friendly game, nothing at stake. It will all come back to you." As he exits the elevator I hear strains of "You Make Me Feel So Young" emanating from the lounge.

Amy
May 1973

DATING ARCAS MEANT licking envelopes, putting up notices, and attending meetings in his rooming house on St. George. His room was Spartan, just a bed, a chest, a desk, a couple Theodorakis posters, and an odd bit of pottery he used as a paperweight. I picked it up to examine it more closely.

"What's this?" I asked, pointing to the spiral of hieroglyphics carved into the unglazed clay.

"Just an old relic my father found in Crete when I was a kid."

"Interesting, do you know what the symbols mean?"

"No, I'm not an archaeologist."

I studied it closely, fascinated by the small images carved into the clay. A month ago, the relic would have meant little to me, but now I wanted to know everything about Greece. That small, sunny country full of ancient ruins, was the home of my new friends. I'd been lonely in Toronto, but now I was part of a group. I loved the bull sessions and the rallies, the late nights and the beer and I was gradually and inevitably falling in love with Arcas.

Politics was more than entertainment to the Greeks in our circle. A lot of them, like Tom and Arcas, belonged to PAK, Andreas Papandreou's Panhellenic Liberation Movement, and the restitution of Greek democracy was the focus of their lives. They studied news from Athens, analyzing it and picking it apart for hidden clues like forensic pathologists. Nothing was simple and nothing could be taken at face value. They might have been students of economics, chemistry, or medicine, but defeating the junta was their real occupation, the thing that gave meaning to their lives.

Back in high school, Joanie and I had attended anti-war rallies in Rochester, and we might have gone to the March on Washington if it hadn't been for midterms, but the truth is I didn't care that much about politics. Now, six years later, not much had changed. I was on my way to another demonstration because I thought it was a party and a guy I liked had asked me to go with him.

The rally was being held in the banquet room of a popular Greek restaurant since the Greek church was under the thumb of Papadopoulos and the junta and refused to let the PAK use its facilities. Tom claimed the Greek Church had moved even further to the right since the US had elected Spiro Agnew, a Greek Republican, as Vice President. Luckily, the restaurant's owner, was a passionate anti-royalist, who'd not only provided a room, but urns of coffee and platters of small cookies dusted with powdered sugar. The place was filled to capacity, and the noise was deafening as everyone shouted to be heard over everyone else.

Tables had been removed to accommodate the crowd except for a speaker's table that stood at the front with a Canadian flag on one side and a Greek flag on the other. I'd imagined Arcas and Tom sitting at that table, but they were mere functionaries while older men in suits ran the show. Arcas mingled with the crowd, chatting in Greek and dripping powdered sugar on his T-shirt, while Nancy and I sat on the perimeter speaking English.

It was her first venture out in public since the accident. She looked normal, all the casts and bandages were gone, but I knew she was weak and easily fatigued, so we pulled two chairs into a quiet alcove, sipped our coffees, and gossiped like old ladies, trying to avoid the ruckus.

You look wonderful," I assured her. "You're really bouncing back."

"Not quite, but I'm going back to work on a reduced schedule starting next week."

"Great, the sooner the better. Arcas says they're lost without you. No one else knows how to work the Xerox machine."

Nancy rolled her eyes, "You'd think a bunch of doctoral candidates could figure out where to put the paper."

I grinned in agreement as I surveyed the room. "Quite a good turnout. The guys must be ecstatic."

"Probably, but I'm not surprised. Greeks love politics. It's the national pastime."

I pointed to a young man with unfashionably short hair who was walking through the crowd snapping photos. "Is the *Globe and Mail* covering the rally? It looks like someone sent a photographer."

"I doubt it, more likely a spy for the RCMP or the Greek government."

"The RCMP? That's crazy, why would the Royal Canadian Mounted Police care about the meeting?" I gave her a doubtful look.

"Because they think we're all Communists." She turned away from the man with the camera. "Tom thinks they have files on everyone since Watergate, but he's probably just being paranoid."

That sent a cold breeze whistling down my spine. The last thing I needed was the Canadian government looking at me.

Nancy lowered her voice. "It's probably someone from the Greek government, anyway. They hate the PAK."

"Are you saying the Greek government has men in Canada?" I asked, incredulous.

She looked amused. "It's not exactly a secret. It's called the Greek consulate. They have an office on Bay Street. But they aren't supposed to interfere with fundamental freedoms like free speech and peaceful assembly."

"Is that who Tom thinks ran you over with the car?" I asked in a low voice.

She pursed her lips and shook her head. "Not really, stuff like that happens in Greece, not in Canada. I know he freaked out when it happened, but I don't think he really believed they'd do a thing like that in North America. They wouldn't dare."

I looked around the room where I saw one man after another scowl and turn his back on the photographer. Tom shouted at him in Greek and pointed toward the door. To my surprise, the photographer simply snapped one more photo, closed his camera, and left without a word of protest.

I watched him disappear through the doorway into the outer corridor. "You were right, he's Greek. He sure understood whatever Tom said to him."

"Yep." Nancy was grinning, looking delighted. "Tom's incredible. I know he can be a bit of a jerk sometimes, but he's smart and he has a good heart. He cares about stuff and really wants to make the world better. You wouldn't believe the way he took care of me after the accident."

I put my hand on her shoulder. "That sounds like love."

Nancy shrugged and looked away. "I'm probably in love with him, but there's no point talking about it. He's going back to Greece as soon as the junta's gone. His family wouldn't let him marry me anyway. They're snooty, upper-crust types who've probably got some little virgin from a wealthy family picked out for him already."

I was appalled. "I don't believe it. Tom would never let his family push him around like that. Anyway, he's half Canadian. Why wouldn't he stay here with you?"

"Because he's probably going to be prime minister of Greece someday. Do you see the prime minister of Greece married to a janitor's daughter from Peterborough? I don't think so."

"I can absolutely imagine him married to a janitor's daughter from Peterborough if he loved her." What I couldn't imagine was Tom being the prime minister of anything, but Nancy was smitten. There was no sense arguing that point with her. I looked around for Tom but didn't see him in the room. "The future prime minister seems to be missing. I hope he gets back before the speeches start."

"Don't worry, he's here, he and Arcas are working security. They're probably outside making sure no one tries to shut us down."

Someone flashed the lights, and the room grew quiet as the first speaker took the microphone. The program began without much drama, just speeches, a few whistles, hisses, and rounds of applause, but nothing alarming or out of the ordinary. Of course, they were all speaking Greek so I had no idea what was actually said. Occasionally, Nancy would recognize a speaker and whisper his name in my ear, but since none of the names meant anything to me, I just smiled, went on sipping my coffee and looking around the room.

A mural of the Parthenon was painted on one wall while guilt frames filled with faded photos of the owner's family covered another. There was scuffed black and white linoleum on the floor and acoustic tiles on the ceiling. The food must have been great because I was sure no one came for the ambiance. I turned my attention to the audience, mostly men, seated in closely packed chairs. The older men wore sport coats, the younger ones T-shirts and jeans, but they all leaned forward with the same rapt expressions, nodding in unison when they agreed with the speaker and jeering whenever the words *Vasilia Constantinou* were spoken. You didn't need an advanced degree in Greek to know they were booing the king. It was clear the speakers were preaching to the choir.

A hush fell over the room as the keynote speaker took the floor. Nancy tapped me on the shoulder. "That's Andreas Papandreou. He's a professor at York University now, but his father was the prime minister of Greece. He's the one who started the Panhellenic Liberation Movement. The guys talk about him all the time."

Before I could smile or nod, the room went dark, the mic went dead, and the air-conditioning cut off. There was a moment of confused silence then a murmur, like the buzzing of disturbed bees. I couldn't see a thing, but I could hear the scrape and squeal of metal chairs being pushed against the floor, then the voice of someone, probably one of the organizers, shouting instructions in Greek. There was the sound of feet running and the creak of a door opening, then a moment later the lights blinked back on, the whirr of the air-conditioner resumed, and the former prime minister's son, a nice-looking middle-aged man, returned to the microphone.

Nancy and I exchanged bemused glances then shrugged and listened as Dr. Papandreou gave an impassioned address in two languages that engaged the crowd. There was enthusiastic applause, questions, answers, and more applause. Eventually, everyone but Nancy and I stood up and filed from the room. Tom and Arcas still hadn't reappeared. We waited patiently in our seats, hoping that we hadn't been forgotten. Fifty minutes later there was still no sign of them, and I was about to suggest that we make our own way home on the subway when they pushed open the door and hobbled into the room. Tom's shirt was torn, and his lip was bleeding. Arcas was walking with a bit of a limp and rubbing his arm.

"Where in the world have you two been?" Nancy asked, clearly annoyed. "Everyone else left an hour ago." Then, as she registered their injuries, she let out a little, "Oh, my God."

"Sorry, but there was a problem that needed our attention." Arcas sat down hard in a folding chair.

"Yeah, what do the English say? We regret that we were unavoidably detained." Tom wiped his lip with the side of his hand, then studied his bloodied fingers.

Nancy pulled a package of tissues from her purse and handed one to Tom, softening as she assessed the damage. "What in the world happened? What have you guys been up to?"

Arcas, who'd been sitting with his head in his hands looked up with a wry smile. "Fighting for democracy."

Tom nodded. "Actually, that *is* what we were doing. You know those fascists hanging around outside the building? Well, two of them snuck in and tried to sabotage the meeting. They pulled a couple fuses just as Andreas was about to speak. My job was to keep an eye out for trouble, so I was in the hall and caught them messing with the electric boxes. When they saw me, they ran off with the fuses in their pockets, but I tackled one of them then Arcas showed up and landed the other. After we got the lights back on we had to wait for the police to arrive and file a report. It was all very proper, very Canadian.

"It wasn't actually that easy. Those guys put up a fight." Arcas had his arm extended and was rotating it back and forth, making sure everything still worked.

"No kidding." Tom rubbed his swollen cheek. "But at least we're in Toronto. If they'd caught us holding a meeting like this in Athens, they wouldn't have pulled fuses, they'd have been pulling out our fingernails. The junta's men are monsters."

"Yeah, but the guys who showed up today aren't much better. They're idiots and traitors. How can they support the colonels? How do they sleep at night?" Arcas was livid.

I'd seen the opposition outside the restaurant hawking their fliers and engaging anyone who'd listen in noisy arguments. Arcas had steered me away from their table and crumpled the flier they'd thrust into his hand, making a great show of tossing it into the nearest trash can.

"Were they arrested?" I wanted to know.

"No, but they'll have to show up in court. We'll probably have to go too, to tell the judge what happened."

"You're heroes." I went over to Arcas and gave him a big hug, then pulled him to his feet. "How about pizza and beer at my place tonight? Let's celebrate your victory over the oppressors. My treat." I felt a warm sensation rising through my body. Arcas had jumped on a bad guy and held him by brute force. He was making a difference, standing up for democracy. I pushed aside a dark curl that had fallen across his forehead and inhaled the musky odor of sweat mingled with his usual scent of cinnamon and tobacco. Maybe I'd spring for a couple bottles of wine as well.

Jacob
Aboard the Aqua Meridian
You Make Me Feel So Young

THE KEY I was given at Customer Service opens the door to a well-appointed cubicle with a porthole that looks out on nothing but water. I try the bed and find it more than satisfactory. There's a built-in chest, a comfortable chair, and a bedside table where I place Dr. Rabinowitz's book. I peek into the bathroom and glimpse a walk-in shower, and a vanity supplied with soap and little bottles of shampoo and lotions. There's even a toothbrush and a small tube of toothpaste. Very considerate, they really have made an effort.

When I open the closet to stow my hat, I'm surprised to find a pair of white cotton pajamas and a terrycloth robe all bearing the ship's logo. This is really astonishing. They've thought of everything. Out of curiosity I open a dresser drawer and discover neat piles of sport shirts, slacks, and shorts in various colors. I unfold one of the shirts to check the size and find that it looks about right. Another drawer contains fresh underwear and socks still in their original packaging.

I sit down in the armchair to think about what all this means. It's too extraordinary. It's simply too much. Even the best hotels don't provide clothing for their guests. Or maybe they do. Bess and I never stayed in a truly first-class hotel, so who knows? This might be quite normal and expected in the upper echelons, but I have an uneasy feeling that it isn't. Besides, I'm in tourist class. What do they provide first-class passengers? Ball gowns and evening jackets? I check another drawer where I find a swimsuit and beach towels emblazoned with the *Aqua Meridian* logo. I stare at them for a long minute before reaching out to touch one of the towels. It's a soft terrycloth like you'd find in the best hotels. I close the drawer, wondering if I'll have the nerve to put on the suit and look for the pool tomorrow.

I go into the bathroom, to throw some cold water on my face and comb my hair before joining Dawson in the lounge. I catch sight of myself in the mirror and freeze. The face in the mirror is familiar, but not one I ever expected to see again. Gathering my courage, I lean forward to examine myself more closely. There's almost no light in the bathroom, but still, it's not my imagination. I look years younger than when I woke up this morning. I touch my face and feel the skin, smooth and resilient. It's not just a trick of the light. My eyes are clear, and my hair shows just a hint of gray. Is this the face that Dawson's been looking at all afternoon? I raise my eyebrows, wink, and stick out my tongue. The face works, but my knees have gone a bit wobbly.

I lie down on the bed and close my eyes. I wish Bessie were here with me now, or even Michael. No, not Michael, I wouldn't want him to see me like this. It's not right for a father to look younger than his son. Should I mention this transformation to someone? What would I say? *I may look like a man in his prime, but I'm really an old codger.* How would that go over? Not well, I expect. I open my eyes and examine my hands. They're small for a man, but suddenly well-muscled and strong, not veiny and knobbed by arthritis. They're the hands I remember digging shards of pottery from the ruins of Crete, holding the tiller steady when we sailed, cupping Bessie's breasts at night in bed. They were good hands and here they are again, only now . . .

I stagger to the porthole and look out. There's nothing but rain and endless water in all directions. Where the hell am I? Is this some sort of trick? Someone's idea of a practical joke? An idea strikes me, and I go back to the bathroom to examine the mirror more closely. It seems perfectly normal and besides, what trick mirror would explain my hands? As I stare at the good looking fellow in the glass, my nerves settle and my knees stop shaking. He looks so confident and self-possessed that I have to smile at him. He smiles back and I feel reassured. My initial alarm gives way to gratitude for this unexpected gift. Maybe it's the light, maybe it's my eyes, or maybe my mind's going. It doesn't matter. It is what it is. My heart stops racing, I take a few deep breaths and decide to enjoy this newfound prowess while it lasts. What else is there to do? "Here's looking at you, kid," I say to my reflection. Then I stride out into the corridor to look for Dawson and the smoking lounge.

THE LOUNGE IS crowded and filled with smoke, but I have no trouble recognizing the trio of men laughing loudly and waving cigars as they talk. The atmosphere is decidedly masculine, and I notice that there are no ladies in attendance.

"There he is," Dawson bellows as I approach their table. "We've been waiting for you. Let the games begin."

"Hello." I extend my hand to a lumpy looking fellow with a receding hairline. His face is a florid, purple and he exposes large horsey teeth when he laughs, which he does constantly. Beads of sweat dribble down his forehead. The man is clearly drunk, but I smile amiably. "I'm Jacob Kanter."

"Jacob Kanter," he echoes, laughing, as though my name were the punchline of a joke. "Well, Jake, take a load off and sit down."

"Sorry. Let me introduce you. This is Harvey Newcome." Dawson nods at the fleshy man whose thick, damp hand still has hold of mine. "And this is his brother-in-law, Jack Lewis. They're from New Jersey. Do I have that right? They have a company that manufactures light fixtures."

"Where in New Jersey?" I ask. My wife and I once spent a week at Cape May.

"Trenton," Jack Lewis replies. Like his brother-in-law, he's a hefty guy, but sober. He's managed to button his shirt straight and looks like he may be the brains of the operation.

"Yeah, Trenton." Harvey guffaws as though this news is hilarious.

I extract my hand from Harvey's oversized paw, extend it to Jack, and then take a seat. I feel a surge of energy, the pure animal pleasure of inhabiting a young man's body. "What are we drinking?"

"We're drinking beer, but I hear they make a good Martini," Jack replies, exhaling a plume of pungent smoke.

"Beer's fine." I look around for a waiter, place my order, and grab a handful of peanuts to test the limits of my new stomach.

Dawson puts a deck of cards in the center of the table. "OK then, let's get started. Cut for dealer."

It turns out that Dawson and I aren't a bad team considering we've never played together. At one time I wasn't half bad, and I'm surprised how much comes back to me. The fact is, bridge kept me in pocket money during the war. We wouldn't do well against real competition, but poor Jack is partnered with a drunk and doesn't stand a chance. Too bad we're not playing for money. Dawson and I would walk off with a bundle and apparently our companions have money to lose.

"The thing with light fixtures," Harvey's saying, "is that you can make them out of anything. Not the old-fashioned kind with all those dangly crystal things, but the new modern ones. We've got a whole line made from nothing but scrap metal. We buy old brass pipe for peanuts, drill a few holes, wire them together and voila, I give you our new Serena Series. I'm telling you, we can't keep 'em in stock."

"Give credit where credit's due, Harvey." Jack takes a trick with the nine of diamonds and leads with the King of Spades. I'm not worried since I still have five good trump cards in my hand.

"OK, you're right." Jack takes another handful of peanuts and washes them down with the rest of his beer. "We were selling auto parts until my sister, Harvey's wife, decides to decorate the house. They're short of cash, but she says, don't worry, I'll make everything myself. Next thing he knows, there's a hand-made chandelier hanging from the dining room ceiling, and her friends are swooning over it. They all want her to make them fixtures too. As they say, the rest is history. Now we have a whole catalogue of upscale lighting for the modern home. She does the little drawings and artsy stuff. Jack and I run the business, and a sweet little business it is. It's paid for a ten-bedroom house in Essex Falls, a Porsche turbo, and a Cessna Citation."

"We should never have bought that plane." Harvey throws away the queen, making his brother-in-law wince." You're no pilot. What made you think you could fly that thing?"

"Hey, I took lessons. I would've had my license in another month if we hadn't run into weather."

"Too late now. That plane is toast. I don't know how we're even sitting here. So, what do you guys do for a living?"

I catch Dawson's eye, and we exchange wry smiles as he takes the trick with his king. "We just met this afternoon, but it turns out we're both professors. I'm a linguist, he's an archaeologist."

"Whoa, we better be careful what we say around these guys. I don't want professors flunking us for bad grammar."

The waiter returns with my beer as I lay my hand face down on the table. "You're safe," I reassure him, before taking a long, satisfying swig. "Academics aren't the strait-laced prigs you imagine. We're actually a pretty disorderly bunch. Believe me, if I could put up with Christopher Hollis all those years, I can certainly—"

"You knew Hollis? I worked with him on the Kish Tablets. His name is on three of my papers, but I couldn't agree more. He was a pain in the ass."

"You must have been with him at Tell Uhaimir. I'd love to know what he was like back then. I knew he'd done a lot of work on Sumerian cuneiform, but we never discussed it. My work was mainly in Crete."

"At Knossos? You knew Pendleton?" Dawson's eyes gleam with excitement.

"Hey, it's your play." Jack blows a cloud of smoke in my direction. "Could you guys talk shop another time? I don't want to be here all night."

"Sorry, of course." Dawson examines his hand and tosses out the two of clubs.

Jack follows with the four of clubs. I'm about to play the jack when a woman walks into the lounge. She's wearing a green cocktail dress like the one Bess used to wear and she has dark hair bobbed the way Bess wore hers when she was young. I watch, waiting for the woman to turn around so I can see that she's a stranger. This happens to me all the time. The year Bess died every woman with short, gray hair, every woman wearing a red coat or carrying a large tapestry bag would make my heart stop for one hopeful moment until I saw she was no one that I knew at all. This woman is different. She doesn't look the way Bess did in her old age. She looks like the young Bess in our wedding album. She never turns, and I continue to stare as she orders a glass of wine and walks away.

It's crazy, but I jump up from the table. "Excuse me, I think I see someone I know. I'll be back in a minute." I sprint into the hallway, hoping to catch her, needing to see her face, but all I see is a flash of green as the elevator doors close. It's a stupid thing to do and I feel foolish as I rejoin my companions. "False alarm. A case of mistaken identity." I play the jack, take the trick, and wonder how Bess is getting on wherever she is now.

It's dark outside, but I can see the rain as it continues to fall relentlessly through the beams of the ship's running lights. We're rocking a bit, but the motion is soothing like being in a massive cradle, although my own equilibrium is utterly shaken. The woman couldn't have been Bess, yet I can hardly control an impulse to jump up again and search for her.

"Wake up. It's your turn. You've fallen asleep at the switch." Jack sounds more amused than annoyed. "Thinking about that woman, aren't you? I've never seen a man move so fast. Too bad it was the wrong one."

"Yes, it is too bad. Are there any peanuts left?"

Two hours later we're tallying up the final scores and saying our good-byes. It's been a pleasant evening and it's taken my mind off more disturbing thoughts. I really should get out more. Maybe I'll join a bridge club and start playing again. The rain hasn't let up, but no one seems to mind.

"I'll look for you tomorrow," Dawson says, shaking my hand. "It seems we have a lot to talk about. Will you be coming down for breakfast?"

"Yes, I suppose so."

"Well, then, I'll see you in the morning. Good night."

"Good night." As I turn to leave the lounge, I notice the young man who'd forgotten his textbook standing by the window. I walk over and tap him on the shoulder. "Excuse me, but I believe I have something of yours."

"Oh, please tell me it's a physiology textbook."

"You left it beside your table when it started to rain. I picked it up so it wouldn't get ruined. It's in my cabin if you want it."

"That's wonderful, but would it be okay if I pick it up tomorrow? It's been a long day and I'm exhausted now."

"Of course, I'll bring it down to breakfast in the morning."

"I can't thank you enough. I have a big exam coming up and I really need that book." He holds out his hand to me. "Samuel Rabinowitz."

"I know. It's written on the inside cover. Jacob Kanter," I say as I take his hand. "I'm glad I could rescue it for you. It would have been soaked in this downpour." We turn toward the window where the rain continues to come down in sheets. "This rain just won't let up. It's hard to believe it was sunny all afternoon."

"Yeah, it's been the oddest day," he says.

"It certainly has," I agree. "Well, I'll look for you at breakfast."

"Thanks again, I feel as though I've been forgetting things all day."

"Really?" I'm already heading toward the exit, but I turn back to see him still standing by the window. "It's been just the opposite for me. All I've done is remember."

Amy
June 1973

ARCAS WAS A busy man. His studies, his job, and his political involvement didn't leave much time for a social life, but we couldn't bear to be apart. As a solution, I began working at the bakery, not officially, but I'd show up most evenings after work, put on an apron, and make myself useful. At first, Helen and Petra, the other bakers, were suspicious of me, but they figured it out quickly enough and welcomed me with warm smiles and little pats on my cheeks. They were kind women who enjoyed seeing young people happy. The romantic atmosphere put everyone in good spirits, and they appreciated the extra help.

Even though Kosmos was a busy, commercial bakery, most of the work was done by hand and I discovered that patting and rolling, turning, and shaping sweet, yeasty dough was sensual and strangely arousing. The odors were intoxicating and the heat from the ovens, combined with the sultry night air that wafted in through the back door we kept propped open with a wooden chair, made us shed layer after layer of clothing until, once Helen and Petra were gone, we worked in nothing but our aprons, our hot, sweaty skins and, of course, the little gold necklace I never took off.

"I see the dough is rising," I teased as I leaned into his erection.

"No, it needs more kneading. Knead it a little more," he breathed into my neck.

So I did. We kneaded and kissed and rolled and rubbed and steamed in our own heat until we lay sated on the sacks of flour that cushioned our after-hour's labors and for a moment I could almost forget everything and imagine that I was the carefree girl Arcas imagined that I was. I ran my fingers through the dark tangles of his hair and closed my eyes.

"You are crying again, *koritsaki*." Arcas leaned over and licked the tears trickling down my face. "Do I make you sad?"

"Oh no, you make me happy. It's something else." I lay very still, listening to the thrum of traffic on the street.

"Then tell me what makes you sad. I want to know everything about you. I want to know about your family, the house where you grew up, where you went to school, why you always wear this little cat necklace and why you cry when we make love."

I didn't open my eyes. "Arcas, let's pretend that I was born here, fully formed like Athena. Don't ask me about anything before Toronto. I have a family, my parents are great, but I don't want to talk about them. Is that OK? Can we still be friends?"

"Of course, *koritsaki*. I understand. Everyone has secrets."

He was right, we all had secrets and I wasn't ready to share mine. I was just happy to feel myself coming back to life, to be his *koritsaki*, a Greek term of endearment that means "little girl."

That was our personal summer of love. Passion ran rampant and we fucked like gods in bed, in empty classrooms, in the ravine behind Winston Churchill Park, and of course at the bakery. Arcas was delicious and I couldn't get enough of him. I don't think either of us slept that entire summer. We were at Kosmos Bakery when the sun went down late in the evening and we were still there, sneaking out the back door laughing, talking politics, and leaning into one another's exhausted bodies when the first pink glow of daylight rose over the roofs of the Indian restaurants, and small Korean groceries down the street.

Since Tom, Nancy, Arcas, and I all worked near one another, we met for lunch several times a week. Our favorite haunt was Spiro's, a hole in the wall diner run by a PAK sympathizer. It had only four tables but the best gyros in the city.

Nancy arrived a few minutes late. "Have you been watching the Watergate hearings? There's no way Nixon wasn't involved. I don't see how he can worm his way out of it."

Tom crushed his cigarette in an ashtray that had a photo of Geórgios Papadopoulos, the junta's leader, pasted beneath the glass. "He'll never admit it. He'll mount a coup of his own before he gives up power."

"No," I protested. "That's not how things work in the US. We don't do coups. We're a democracy."

Three sets of eyes turned to me with varying degrees of incredulity and pity. Arcas sighed but took my hand. "Germany was a democracy. Greece was a democracy, Chile was a democracy. Don't kid yourself, *koirtsaki*. There are fascists everywhere."

"Exactly, so you need to help with our newsletter, or do you two have other plans?" Tom grinned, wiggling his eyebrows suggestively like Groucho Marx. He and Nancy teased us incessantly like an old married couple amused by a pair of love- struck teenagers.

"Count me in if you need help with layout and printing," I volunteered, glad they were done ragging me about my political naivete.

Tom took a big bite of his sandwich, dribbling tzatziki sauce onto his plate. "What about you? Can you help with distribution?" He turned to Arcas who was admiring the portrait of Nancy I'd scribbled on his napkin.

"Sure, of course."

"OK, then, and as our reward, we're all invited to go sailing on a yacht next Sunday. It belongs to one of Andreas's supporters. Cool, huh?"

I blanched and put down my sandwich. Tom didn't notice and Arcas was focused on his napkin, but Nancy didn't miss a thing. She studied me with an expression of concern.

"I don't know, what time are we going?" Arcas responded without looking up.

"Andreas just said Sunday. We'll sail around the harbor and then over to the islands. It'll be fun."

Arcas handed the napkin to Nancy. "Amy really got you. She's wasted in that print shop." He squeezed my knee and turned to Tom. "Sailing sounds great, as long as we're back by five. I have to work this Sunday."

"I'm sorry, I can't go." My mouth was so dry that I could hardly spit out those few words. I picked up my glass and sipped iced tea in silence as the others waited, expecting an explanation.

"Sure you can," Arcas cajoled. "You don't work on Sundays. Besides, I want to see you in a bikini."

"No, honestly I can't go."

"Why, are you afraid of the water?" Arcas was teasing me.

I stared at him open mouthed and speechless. There was no way to explain.

"Don't worry, you're with a bunch of Greeks. We invented sailing. I promise you won't drown." He grinned at me.

I could feel a tear wending its way down my cheek. I turned my head, brushing it away, but then there was another and another. I willed the tears to stop, but they kept coming.

"Shhh, shhh, it's okay." Arcas was no longer smiling. He pulled my chair toward his and put his arm around my shoulder as I tried to regain control.

Biting my lips, holding my breath, thinking of ice cream, nothing worked. Crying in public was humiliating and, of course, now they'd want an explanation. Arcas rubbed my back and sang something in Greek, probably a children's song. Tom joined in and the two of them serenaded me as I continued to snivel. Nancy held out a tissue so I could wipe my eyes. If I could have crawled under the table and never seen any of them again, I'd have been gone in a minute.

I didn't want to look into their concerned faces or answer stupid questions. "What's the matter? What did we say? Are you all right?"

I ignored Nancy's tissue, picked up a paper napkin, and blew my nose. "I'm sorry, but I've got to go." I stood up, walked out of the diner, and headed south on Spadina, away from Spiro's, away from my friends and away from Abbott's Printing. I could hear Arcas close behind me and doubled my pace. All I wanted was to be alone, preferably invisible. It was stupid, I couldn't outrun him, but I didn't stop until I felt his hand on my arm. He fell into step beside me as I continued walking.

We were all the way to Dundas before I could speak. "You know there's a reason I moved to Canada, and it wasn't to avoid the draft."

Arcas didn't say anything. He just kept pace as I tore down the street as though I knew where I was going. His silence was infuriating, worse than a lot of intrusive questions. Was he waiting for an explanation? Did he think I was going to tell him the whole goddam story? Couldn't he tell I didn't want to talk? The strap on my platform sandal snapped and I stumbled toward the pavement. Arcas caught me, breaking my fall, and held me in an awkward hug until I pulled away.

I croaked out a small, "thank you," without looking at him. Taking off the broken shoe, I saw that the strap had ripped in half. There was no saving it, just one more thing I'd ruined. Too bad, it was a good sandal that deserved a longer life. I tossed it into the trash can on the corner and hobbled down the sidewalk in one high heeled sandal and one bare foot for another block. We eventually came to a bench where I sat down, took off the remaining sandal and cradled it like an orphaned kitten.

"OK, we can talk now?" Arcas sat stiffly, a safe distance away. He seemed to be afraid of me.

"I'm not going sailing, not next Sunday, not ever. Do you understand?"

"Yes, you don't go sailing. I understand." After several long, silent minutes, Arcas asked, "Are you very afraid of boats?"

I shook my head. "No, not exactly."

"Maybe you get seasick?"

"Stop it. I'm not playing twenty questions. Look, I'm sorry for making a scene. I'll try not to do that again, but please, just let it go. I don't want to talk about it."

"Like not talking about your family?"

"Yes, like that. Maybe I'll explain someday, maybe I won't. Just trust me, it hurts a lot and it makes me crazy, so please stop prying, OK?"

"OK." He took my hand, and I scooched over so I could put my head on his shoulder.

We sat quietly, ignoring the traffic, the streetcars, and the Chinese merchants hawking plastic toys and packaged snacks from sidewalk tables.

"Can I ask what you're thinking?" Arcas asked.

I stared down at the lone sandal cradled in my lap. "I was thinking about this sandal. I was wondering if she's lonely without her sister."

That night, in bed with Arcas, I swam toward the dream ship, drawing closer and closer to the lights guiding me forward. I got so close I could hear music playing from an upper deck. I could almost touch the side of the boat when a great wave washed over me, and the ship suddenly disappeared. The alarm sounded and I awoke, trembling, to feel Arcas rubbing my back and whispering, "You're OK, I'm here. It was just a bad dream."

MY PARENTS CALLED every Sunday, but they rarely visited. Rochester was only a few hours away, but I hadn't seen them since Christmas, so I was delighted when they offered to drive up for a few days in June.

The last time they'd visited, my mother had sighed over the dilapidated state of my apartment, my abysmal housekeeping, and the thread-bare furniture I'd bought at the Salvation Army Thrift Store. I decided to redecorate before their visit to console her with the knowledge that her surviving daughter lived in clean and cheery rooms. Although I was the artist, Nancy was the decorator. She kept up on current trends, had a great sense of style, and an eye for a bargain so I recruited her to help me with the project.

Her enthusiasm surprised me. Apparently, she'd been waiting for the chance to move my furniture around and to rearrange my knickknacks. She pulled the sofa away from the wall, swung my chairs around, and angled my desk beneath the window. Within minutes the living room appeared cozier and significantly larger. She regarded my couch with a disapproving eye. "Your Chesterfield's too big for the room and it throws everything off balance. You need something smaller, preferably in red or orange to coordinate with the chairs."

"But I need a big sofa," I protested. "I sleep on it when my parents visit."

"Buy a small sleep sofa. Then all you'll need is a rug and some throw pillows to pull your color-scheme together. I bet you could find something in Simpsons bargain basement."

I looked around at the mismatched thrift store pieces I'd acquired because they cost next to nothing. They'd been chosen for function not aesthetics. "I don't have a color scheme."

"Well, you would have a color scheme if you got a sofa that picked up one of the colors in those chairs. She turned to the canvases I had propped against the wall. "And let's get some of your artwork framed. These are beautiful. What are they? They're kind of mysterious, like you're looking at a sunset through a mirror or through water"

I didn't answer. She didn't need to know they depicted the world through Joanie's eyes, looking up from the lake floor.

"Trust me, this place could look like something in *Toronto Life*."

I didn't particularly want an apartment that looked like a page from a glossy magazine, but I agreed to dip into my savings if we could find something decent for the right price. So, the following Saturday we caught the subway downtown and set off on a hunting expedition. Nancy's mood was, typically, brighter than my own, but I was happy enough, enjoying her company and imagining my parent's approval when they discovered that I was finally taking an interest in my surroundings. The sky was blue and cloudless as we got off at Yonge Street and walked the rest of the way, sipping cups of Orange Julius and window shopping as we headed south.

We tossed our paper cups in the trash then pushed our way through revolving doors into a perfumed world of cosmetics, hosiery, silk blouses, and costume jewelry. She wanted to try on hoop earrings and check out the new lipstick colors but I'm not a shopper. I just wanted to find a sofa and go home.

It turned out that Simpsons bargain basement sold dining room tables, recliners, sectionals bigger than my living room, and an odd assortment of chairs, but no sleep sofas. It took about two seconds to figure out this trip had been a waste of time.

"Come on, let's go home. I think there's a subway entrance on this level." I scanned the room for a sign pointing to the subway.

"No, wait. I want to look around." Nancy loved department stores.

"OK, you look around while I find a ladies' room. I'll meet you back here in a few minutes." I made my way through hardware, auto parts, and the garden center before I found a toilet. There was a line of women ahead of me, so it was awhile before I retraced my steps back to the marked down furniture. Nancy was nowhere to be seen, so I stretched out in one of the recliners and waited for her. A few minutes later, she showed up with a gray-haired man in an ill-fitting suit.

She was negotiating for something, and she sounded pretty persuasive. "There's no way that thing is worth a penny over two hundred dollars. The legs are scratched and there's a stain on one of the seat cushions."

The clerk looked tired but resigned. He clearly wasn't interested in debating the issue. "I'm sorry, but that's the price. If you think there should be an adjustment, you'll have to take it up with the manager."

"OK, then, where's the manager?"

I couldn't see anything worth haggling over but didn't say a word until the clerk trotted off in search of his superior. "Nancy, what's going on? I don't want any of this shit."

Nancy didn't flinch. "Look at this. You won't believe it. I told you to trust me." She led me toward the toy department where a little domestic tableau on a raised platform featured a mother mannequin knitting on a red couch while twin daughter mannequins played a game of Candy Land at her feet. "What did I tell you? It's perfect." She pointed to a brown smudge on the sofa and lowered her voice. "That's just dirt on the cushion, not a stain. It will wash right off."

"Nancy, it's a display piece. It's not even for sale. Anyway, I thought we were looking for a sofa bed."

She pointed to a tag pinned to the seat cushion. "Read that. It *is* a sofa bed and it's half price. It originally sold for four hundred dollars, but we're going to get it for two hundred, maybe less."

I tried to focus on the sofa, but my eyes kept returning to the little girls playing on the floor. Joanie and I had played like that when we were small, dressed in identical outfits like the ones in the display. I felt queasy and overheated. One of the fiberglass girls seemed to be eyeing me accusingly. An odd buzzing sound set my teeth on edge. Was it one of the fluorescent lights or something inside my head? I had to leave. I turned to Nancy who was grinning smugly, delighted by her find.

"Come on," I said. "I don't want a red sofa. Let's get out of here."

Her expression turned to shock. "Of course, you want a red sofa. There's red in the floral fabric on your chairs. It will absolutely make your room. This sofa's perfect."

I looked at the sofa a second time and could sort of see her point. Maybe in my other life, the one where I still had a sister, I could have managed a red sofa, but not now. It was too loud, too cheerful, too fashionable.

"No, really. I just want to go."

It didn't matter. It was my money and my apartment, but Nancy was adamant. I had to have it.

There was no fight left in me. "OK, then, can we just buy it and go home?"

The man in the gray suit reappeared with a man half his age, presumably the manager. Nancy whispered, "Let me do the talking," as she stepped forward to greet them. No wonder the guys claimed she ran the department. Half an hour later she'd debated, negotiated, and flirted the price down to two hundred dollars including delivery.

Nancy was ebullient. "We need to celebrate. I'm treating you to lunch at Swiss Chalet and then we're shopping for accessories."

My ears were still buzzing as we stepped off the escalator. Nancy was babbling about Marimekko something or other when we nearly collided with two men carrying a female mannequin in a blue bikini. Long dark hair concealed her face, but I knew she looked like my sister. The buzzing in my ears grew louder until it resembled the roar of an outboard motor or the sound of rushing water. Then, above the din I heard a familiar cry for help.

Joanie's shouts rose above the wind as she struggled to keep her head above the waves. I put my hands over my ears and closed my eyes, but she was still there, still struggling to stay afloat, the panic in her eyes a mirror of my own, her pale, freckled skin, her green eyes fraught with horror, identical to mine. I watched helpless, my heart pounding until she disappeared, as she always did, beneath the roiling waters of Lake Ontario.

A minute later Nancy was patting my shoulder and asking, "Are you OK? What just happened?"

I stood there disoriented, breathless, adrift in time, hostage to the dream or hallucination that had loomed up like a tsunami and washed away the escalator, the racks of dresses, the very walls. There was no way to explain that I'd just been transported to a small boat on a turbulent lake at dusk where my sister's calls for help rose above dark water.

"Did you change your mind about the sofa?" She produced a nervous laugh, but I knew I'd frightened her. I shook my head and tried to respond with some sort of joke, but found I couldn't talk. Shoppers rushed past, annoyed that I was blocking the escalator.

"You'd better sit down." Nancy led me over to a chair that was probably intended to relieve bored husbands while their spouses shopped. I sank into it without a word of protest while trying to come up with a plausible explanation for my implausible behavior. Nancy stared at me with an expression of genuine concern. She was a nice person. I didn't put enough value on her friendship.

"I'm OK, I just get these dizzy spells sometimes. Give me a minute to pull myself together."

"OK, wait here while I get a glass of water."

"Thanks, then how about if I buy you lunch? You deserve a reward for putting up with me."

MY MOTHER'S REACTION when she walked into my apartment exceeded all expectations. The red sofa, a few accessories, and the framed paintings had converted my old rooms into a trendy showplace that charmed the real estate saleswoman in my mother. She appraised the room with a professional eye as though she saw a fat commission in her future. No, I'm being unkind. Despite all the pain I'd caused them, she was genuinely glad that joy and color were returning to her daughter's world.

"Oh, my darling, it's beautiful. I can't believe this is the same place we visited last Christmas. Seeing what you've done here was worth the hideous drive in this awful heat."

I exchanged a sympathetic look with my father. The temperature was quite moderate for August. In fact, people with cottages were complaining that it was too cold to swim in the lakes north of the city. There was a window air conditioner in the bedroom, but I never turned it on.

"How about some iced tea? I only have instant, but it's not bad."

My mother made a face. She didn't approve of instant anything. "How about if we unpack and then go out for lunch? Henry, bring the luggage in here." She disappeared into the bedroom and my father obediently followed carrying two large suitcases. A moment later I heard the air conditioner click on, then the loud thrumming of the fan.

Whenever my parents visited, they took me to restaurants I could never afford on my own. The first time they'd driven up we'd gone for drinks on the rooftop of the Park Plaza Hotel and my mother wanted to go back there. We could have saved time and money by taking the TTC, but my mother didn't do subways, so my father dropped us off on the corner of Bloor and Avenue then set off to find a place to park that would probably cost more than our meal.

It was past the usual lunch hour, but too early for supper, so the restaurant was nearly deserted as the waiter showed us to our table. There was a pleasant breeze and a lovely view of the city from the terrace, and I could see my mother starting to relax.

I squeezed her hand and smiled. "It's so good to see you. I never realize how homesick I am until I see you and Dad. Have you heard from any of my old friends?"

Her face darkened slightly. I'd forgotten how much my friends reminded her of everything she'd lost. I should have asked about her sister in California or the dog or pretty much anything else.

"No, I don't hear from any of them." There was a note of bitterness in her voice. "But I do hear *about* them from time to time. There's not much to report. They're all off living the lovely lives they planned. I try to be happy for them." She took a cigarette from her purse. "Do you want one?"

"No thanks, I quit a while ago, but you go ahead."

She lifted a silver lighter to her Raleigh. "Elsie got married last month."

"I know, she invited me, but of course I couldn't go."

"How could she invite you? No one knows you're here."

I was embarrassed to admit that I'd broken our cardinal rule. "I called her a couple months ago. She's sworn to secrecy, and I absolutely trust her. I had to talk to someone. The loneliness was getting to me."

"All right, but for God's sake don't mention that to your father. He's nervous enough about you being here as it is." She closed her eyes and exhaled an elegant plume of smoke. "Are you sleeping better these days? No more nightmares? You're not still hearing voices, are you?"

"I'm fine, practically back to normal." I was playing with my necklace, a nervous habit I've had since childhood. "How about you?"

"There are good days and bad days, you know how it is." She took a sip of coffee from a gold rimmed cup and stared out over the roof of the Royal Ontario Museum.

"I sent Elsie a pair of Dansk candlesticks in her China pattern."

My mother smiled weakly and nodded her approval. "Did you know that Stephen just got engaged?"

"Joanie's Stephen? No, I didn't know that." The truth was he'd never really been Joanie's Stephen. They'd just gone out a few times that last summer. "I guess that was bound to happen eventually."

My mother put down the coffee and patted my hand. "So, are there any candlesticks in our future? We'd love to meet this Greek god that you've been dating."

"Not this trip. He's back in Greece helping his mother with some family business."

"Oh, that's too bad. What's he like?"

My father's timely arrival saved me from having to unpack my love life for my mother.

He was out of breath and out of sorts. "I should have just left the car in Rochester and walked to Toronto. It couldn't be much further, and it would have saved a bundle."

"My God, Henry, your face is bright red. Sit down and drink some cold water." My mother signaled the waiter who'd been hovering nearby. "And let's order a bottle of wine with lunch. You look like you could use a drink." Our attention turned to the menus, and we were soon happily sipping chilled Chablis and murmuring appreciation for our salads and the pasta with grilled shrimp and vegetables.

Even my notoriously critical mother seemed satisfied with the meal.

"That was wonderful, and it's so good seeing you again. I wish that you lived closer."

"It's good to know you miss me. I sometimes wonder if you shipped me off to Canada just so you wouldn't have to see me anymore." I'd never said that to them directly, but I'd wondered. Maybe they really couldn't bare the sight of me. I wouldn't blame them.

My mother startled me by slapping the table. "Don't you ever say anything like that again. It was an accident, a horrible, tragic accident that changed all our lives, but we still love you. You're here for your own good, not because we don't want you with us."

My dad's eyes were tearing too. "It cost us a fortune to protect you, but we spent that money gladly because you're our daughter and we love you. You can make a good life here in Canada until it's safe to return home, but believe me, this isn't what we wanted."

"Well, this was your idea. I would have . . ." I didn't know what else we could have done.

Jacob

Aboard the Aqua Meridian

What's Going On

GOOD MORNING, THIS is your captain. I'm pleased to announce that we've left the rain behind as we sail into the Psychedelic Sixties. Expect all your funkadelic favorites in the lounges and at pool side. Groove to the beat of the Beach Boys, the Beatles, and the Rolling Stones. As a special treat we've scheduled a Happening in the Grand Foyer at nine o'clock this evening featuring fondue fountains that are out of sight. Twist the night away to the captivating voice of Lauren Wyland, the Barbara Streisand of the seas. So, get down and get funky. This is your captain wishing you another magical day on the Aqua Meridian. Peace out.

My God, I feel good. I can't remember the last time I bounced out of bed without an ache or pain ravenous for breakfast. Could lack of stress and a hearty dose of fresh air make such a difference? I brush my teeth, marveling at the dashing fellow who looks back at me. He isn't quite as young as I'd first imagined, but good looking none the less. I shave with the razor and one of the fresh blades from the medicine cabinet then smooth down my hair with an *Aqua Meridian* comb fresh from its plastic wrapper. My youthful appearance is a mystery, but no longer a surprise. Could poor eyesight have led me to believe I looked older than I do? Doubtful, but then what? I flirt a bit with my image in the mirror. It's unmanly, but I'm besotted with the young fellow who winks back at me, an old love I never thought I'd see again.

I wander down to breakfast freshly showered and wearing one of the sport shirts housekeeping provided. I'm not sure if the shirt is a gift, on loan, or if I'll eventually receive a bill, but it doesn't matter. I'm glad for the change and delighted by how well it fits. The smell of hotcakes, bacon, and eggs greets me as soon as the elevator door slides open. The jovial chatter and clatter of diners already at their breakfasts makes me smile. This is going to be a very good morning. I approach the hostess at reception and ask if Mr. Charles Dawson has been seated yet.

She consults a printed seating chart and a small handwritten list then shakes her head. "I'm sorry, sir, but I have no record of a Mr. Dawson. Perhaps you'll find him in the first-class dining room."

"No, I'm quite certain he said to meet him here. We're both traveling tourist class. I'm sure of it."

"Well, people do come and go from tourist class. He may have disembarked. You could check with customer relations at the information desk. I'm sure that they could help you."

"Yes, I see." I thank the woman but make no move to leave. This makes no sense. Dawson wouldn't have made plans to meet me if he were going to disembark. Disembark where? Had we pulled into a port in the middle of the night? I stare at the hostess with suspicion. "Are you sure? Would you mind checking one more time?"

She obligingly goes through the motion of rescanning her list before shaking her head in defeat. "I'd suggest you try the first-class dining room. If he's not there, the information desk is in the Grand Foyer. I'm sorry that I couldn't help you."

My good mood dissolves into anxiety and confusion. What the deuce is going on? First class is just one deck up, so I race up the stairs, hoping to find Dawson polishing off a plate of eggs Benedict with truffled something or other, whatever people in first class eat, but I'm stopped by a large man in an odd uniform.

"Your ticket, please." He smiles agreeably as he holds out his hand. He isn't going to let me pass. His hair is cut in a long, incongruously feminine bob that's jarring on someone with such a burly frame. His trousers flare at the ankle in a style I haven't seen in years. I hand over my ticket and wait for the verdict.

"The tourist class dining room is one deck down." He hands me my ticket back with a sympathetic smile. "I'm afraid the Marlin Deck is first class only."

"Yes, I know, but I was sent up here to look for a Mr. Dawson, a Mr. Charles Dawson. The hostess downstairs thought he might be having breakfast in this dining room."

"No problem, I'll be happy to check for you. Would you mind waiting here for just a minute? I'll be right back. Mr. Charles Dawson, is that right?"

He returns with the news that there is no Mr. Dawson in first class. "He may be at poolside or in one of the lounges. It's easy to lose someone on such a big ship. Of course, tourist class passengers do sometimes disembark. I'd try customer relations."

"Yes, thank you. Maybe someone at the information desk can help me." I wander back down the stairs totally flummoxed and less enchanted with the *Aqua Meridian* than I was half an hour earlier. I pass a schedule of onboard activities decorated with large flowers that look as though they were drawn by a child. I'm intrigued by how much there is to do. Most of it is silly cruise fare: bingo, a twist contest, cooking with gelatin, learn the Watusi and the Mashed

Potato, that sort of thing. But there's a lecture on northern shore birds I might attend, especially if Dawson will go with me.

The woman at customer relations is the same one who gave me my key last night. I recognize her even though she's poufed up her hair with so much hairspray that the smell makes my eyes sting. She smiles when she sees me. Apparently, she recognizes me as well. Good, maybe I'll finally get some answers.

"Excuse me, I need some help finding a passenger, a Mr. Charles Dawson. You may remember him. He was the gentleman who was with me when I checked in yesterday."

"Yes, of course I remember you both. Are you enjoying the cruise? Is your cabin comfortable?"

At last, someone who knows her business. "Yes, everything is perfect, better than I'd expected, except that I don't know how to locate Mr. Dawson. We were supposed to meet for breakfast, but the dining room doesn't have any record of him."

"Was he traveling first class?"

"No, no I'm quite certain he was tourist class, same as me. We had dinner together last night in a tourist class lounge."

"I'm afraid that doesn't tell us anything. Tourist class passengers aren't allowed in first class, but first-class passengers have the run of the ship. They can eat wherever they like, but I'm sure I can track him down in the guest register." There's a large credenza against the wall that holds a leather-bound journal. She turns and peruses its pages. A moment later she looks up smiling triumphantly. "Ah, there he is. He disembarked unexpectedly due to a medical emergency, but I'm sure he'll be fine. These things happen."

"Disembark? Where? Where are we anyway?"

"Well, we're not in any port at the moment, but I promise we're right on schedule. Is there anything else I can do for you?"

This evasiveness annoys me and I'm about to question her further when I notice the woman in green from last night, the woman who looks like Bess, only now she's wearing a sundress that strikes me as too short for such a distinguished woman. I stare at her hard, waiting for her to transform into a stranger, but she doesn't. She remains Bess as she leans against the railing one deck above me, staring down into the Grand Foyer.

"I'm sorry, I've got to go. I've just seen someone." I don't wait for the elevator but race up the grand staircase two steps at a time, but I'm not fast enough. By the time I reach the top she's gone. I feel ridiculous chasing after a strange woman and walk back to the tourist dining room embarrassed, panting and out of breath. All the joy of the early morning is gone, and I feel despondent and out of sorts. The fact is, I was looking forward to breakfast with Dawson. I've only just met him, but we had so much in common. I feel as though I've lost a friend and the cruise has lost much of its allure.

I return to the dining room where I sit alone sipping a cup of coffee while I wait for my breakfast. The coffee revives me and by the time I finish a plate of scrambled eggs, toasted bagel, and bacon the world's come right again. I'm just settling back to enjoy a second cup of coffee when Samuel Rabinowitz slides into the chair across from me.

"There you are. I've been looking all over for you. I was afraid you'd disappeared."

"No, I'm right here, but a friend of mine has gone missing. He was taken off the ship last night due to some sort of medical emergency. I was running around trying to find him while you were looking for me."

"What sort of medical emergency?"

I shake my head irritably. "I have no idea. I didn't even know we'd dropped anchor last night. This whole cruise is a mystery to me. You're going to think I'm addled, but honestly, I thought I was going on a harbor cruise. Now it seems we're sailing to Kingdom Come. I don't even know how long this thing lasts."

Dr. Rabinowitz looks at me with satisfying concern. He's a nice boy. "Well, that depends on your ticket. What sort of ticket do you have?"

I shrug, embarrassed that I can't answer such a simple, straightforward question. "A clown with a balloon just handed it to me. It was a gift or a prize or something. No one ever explained the rules." I know I sound unpleasant and ungrateful, so I try again. "Actually, it was a much bigger prize than I realized. This ship is much larger and more luxurious than it seemed when I saw it at the dock, but still they should have given me some instructions, some time to prepare."

"No kidding. That's where the *Aqua Meridian* totally misses the boat, no orientation. The same thing happened to me, but if you show your ticket to someone in customer relations I'm sure they'll explain everything."

An uncomfortable thought crosses my mind. "This is a round trip cruise, isn't it? They won't just drop me off in some strange city?"

"Oh, they'd never do a thing like that. The *Aqua Meridian* has an excellent reputation."

My ear isn't that good for accents, but the young Dr. Rabinowitz doesn't sound quite Canadian. "Excuse me, Dr. Rabinowitz, I don't mean to pry, but where's home for you? Did you board with me in Toronto?" It dawns on me that the inaugural cruise of the *Aqua Meridian* didn't necessarily originate in Toronto.

"Please, call me Sam. I'm from Cleveland, but I moved to Chicago to attend medical school. That's where I came on board, which reminds me, I really need that book you saved for me."

My God, Chicago? If this ship can navigate the St. Lawrence Seaway we could be anywhere. I may not be imagining salt air.

"You do still have my book, don't you?"

"Oh, I'm sorry, yes, your book, of course. It's in my cabin. Wait here while I run down to get it."

"Don't make a special trip." He reaches into the breadbasket and helps himself to a bagel. "Do you mind? I never got breakfast." He tears the bagel in half and stuffs a piece in his mouth. "I'll be in the library later. We could meet there. Let's say . . ." He looks at his watch then frowns. "This thing's useless, it keeps losing time. Anyway, how about two o'clock?"

"Very good, I'll meet you in the library at two o'clock, assuming they don't kick me off the ship before then. To be honest, I hope my ticket's good for another day or two. I'd like to take a dip in the pool and there's a lecture that interests me. I might even attend the party this evening."

"The Happening? I don't normally attend the theme-night parties, but the food's always good and the music's first rate. Personally, I think they overdo the costumes and decorations."

"Well, then, I'm going. As long as I'm here I may as well enjoy the ride. In fact, I'm going to learn the Mashed Potato and the what? The Whatsit?"

"The Watusi?"

"Yes, I'm going to learn the Watusi. Why don't you come? Don't be such a wall flower."

"I'm not a wall flower, more of a nerd actually. They're different. Maybe if I had a girlfriend or someone to dance with, but I'd feel stupid dancing by myself."

"Come on, we'll just eat fondue and listen to the music. You don't have to dance."

"Sure, why not? It's a Happening. Maybe something will happen."

Amy
July 1973

BECAUSE I HAD long dark hair and sometimes wore glasses Arcas thought I looked like Nana Mouskouri, which flattered me. I started wearing red lipstick and parting my hair in the center to enhance the illusion, but where Mouskouri's hair was sleek and straight, mine frizzed and curled.

I was jealous of Nancy's long, silky hair so one afternoon, while we were sitting on my couch leafing through the fall *Vogue*, I asked how she got it to hang so straight. I told her I'd tried everything: oversized rollers, sprays, and gels to no avail.

"Oh, for heaven's sake, there's nothing to it. Go wash your hair and I'll style it for you. You just have to know how to blow it dry." It seemed there wasn't anything Nancy couldn't do.

I was sitting at the kitchen table a few minutes later while she sectioned my hair and styled it with a round brush and the small blow dryer I'd purchased, but never mastered. I was skeptical but showed her a photo of Nana Mouskouri and told her that was the look we were shooting for.

"I know what she looks like. Nothing to it," she assured me. "Things are getting pretty serious when a woman changes her hairstyle for a guy. When's Arcas coming back? I thought he'd be home by now."

"His father had a relapse, and his mother needs help with the dairy. The university gave him a leave of absence, but he has to be back soon or he'll lose the semester."

"Tom's worried about him being gone so much." Nancy spritzed hairspray on another section of my hair then rolled it onto her brush. "He thinks it might be dangerous for him in Greece right now. The military's arresting students right, left, and center—well, mostly left."

I laughed. "I'm not really worried about the military. I mean, he's on a farm in some remote rural area, not fomenting an insurrection. But he's only sent one postcard in three weeks. That's what I'm worried about. Do you think there's something he's not telling me?"

"I hope not, I hate secrets. I had a friend back in Peterborough whose husband sold their car and wouldn't tell her what he did with the money. He said it was none of her business."

"You're kidding? Of course, it was her business."

"Exactly, it turned out his brothers knew what was going on, but none of them would talk."

"Did she ever find out what he did with the money? Ouch, you're pulling too hard."

Nancy eased up the pressure on my hair. "It wasn't that much money, the car was an old junker, but I told her I'd get to the bottom of it. I'm good at asking questions and getting people to talk, so I just kept asking around until one of her sisters-in-law spilled the beans. It turned out her husband had knocked up a girl, one of our good friends actually, and he needed the money for an abortion."

"Well, you'd make a great investigative reporter, but that doesn't exactly make me feel great."

"I'm just saying I don't like secrets. That's one thing I love about Tom. He tells you exactly what's on his mind, whether you like it or not."

The conversation was making me uneasy. "The postcard said he loves me, but I have a feeling there's something I don't know. That whole crowd is full of secrets. They're always plotting something. Of course, with those guys, it's usually something political.

Nancy unplugged the hairdryer and returned it to its box. She was smart and unusually perceptive, so her opinion mattered.

"Do you think there's something going on?"

"I think we should go shopping. You need something cute to wear when you meet him at the airport."

I smiled, grateful she was trying to buoy my spirits. "Did I tell you how much my parents loved what you did with this apartment?"

"You did, but you can thank me again. It really turned out well, didn't it?"

"You're a good friend."

"And that's a good hairstyle." She handed me a mirror and I was astounded by the smooth dark hair parted smartly down the middle. No one would ever mistake me for Nana Mouskouri, but Arcas would love it—assuming he came back.

A postcard arrived the following Monday. The gorgeous stamp in the upper right-hand corner bore the figure of a Greek man in a traditional costume. I turned it over and read, *Returning on schedule. Olympic Airlines Flight 270 5:57 pm. Miss you, Arcas.* It wasn't the love letter I'd been hoping for, but at least he missed me, and he was coming home.

I met Arcas at the gate with flowers and balloons as though he'd come back from the war or a year in prison. I anticipated a passionate kiss and a joyful reunion, but something had changed. There was a crankiness to him, a distracted irritability that I'd never seen before. He gave me a cursory peck on the lips then stared stupidly at the small bouquet I offered him. He finally thanked me, but left it in my outstretched hand, without even noticing my new hairstyle.

I carried the gifts back through the terminal and to the bus stop where we stood side by side without touching. A chill went through me, but I decided the problem was anxiety about his father and I chided myself for being so frivolous, so self-centered. His father might be dying and I, of all people, should know what it meant to lose someone you loved.

I'd planned a romantic candlelight dinner followed by a night of passionate love making at my apartment, but Arcas begged off, claiming jet lag and exhaustion. He got off the bus at St. George and returned to his rented room, leaving me alone on the bus with a bouquet of lilies in my lap and a stupid balloon bobbing against the ceiling.

Then, unbelievably, weeks passed without a word, weeks spent staring at the phone, weeks without eating and weeks without sleep. For three weeks the world stopped spinning, the sun didn't rise and even my sister's faint calls for help, always audible just beyond consciousness, went unanswered. Nancy was no help. She had no idea what was going on, except to say that he looked awful and wouldn't tell anyone why he was avoiding me.

There's a story about a genie trapped in a lamp. He yearns for freedom and swears to reward whoever saves him with a palace made of gold. When a hundred years go by and no one comes the genie swears he will reward his savior with a palace made of gold and a harem of women, each more beautiful than the moon. After another hundred years have passed, he promises a golden palace, a harem of beautiful women and the gift of eternal youth. But no one comes. The genie sinks into despair and stares ruefully into the dark cursing his lot and nursing his grief into a tsunami of rage. Then one day, after endless time has passed, a young man finds the ancient lamp, takes the curio home, and polishes it. The genie, finally freed from his long imprisonment emerges like a thundering storm and strikes the young man dead.

I was that genie when I finally heard a timid rap at my door one Saturday morning in late September and found Arcas, pale and downcast, standing on my doorstep. He was holding a small box from Kosmos Bakery tied up with blue ribbon. "I brought you some loukoumades. They're still warm."

I slammed the door in his face, ran into the bedroom, and hunkered down under the duvet waiting for the knocking to stop. But it didn't stop, and each knock made me angrier and angrier. Finally, I ran back, threw open the door, and yelled, "I don't want your damn donuts. I didn't order any pastry."

"I had to see you."

"Well, take a good look, because it's going to be a long time before you see me again."

"No, please, I'm so sorry. We have to talk. I need to explain." He pushed past me into the apartment before I could slam the door a second time.

"OK, so what is it? You've been on a secret mission to overthrow the junta? You were abducted by aliens? You got amnesia and forgot that I exist? What?"

"No, no, it was nothing like those things. It was something different." He looked into my eyes with the passion I'd expected at the airport. "I was going to tell you that it was wrong for us to be together. I'm like Tom. I need to go back to Greece when the junta falls. My mother needs me. I have family there and . . ." He paused. "I've made promises to people in Greece, but that doesn't matter now. What matters is that I can't stand another day without you. I need to see you, I need to be with you, so I'm asking your forgiveness."

"Seriously, that was your plan? You were just going to stop seeing me? No letter, no phone call, nothing. Didn't you think I deserved to know why you decided to stop seeing me?"

He put the bakery box on the table and came toward me with open arms. "Believe me, If I could, I would see you forever. I love you. No matter what happens I will always love you, *koritsaki.*"

I took a step backward then stopped, agitated and confused. "What do you mean, no matter what happens? What's going to happen?"

Arcas dropped his arms. "OK, sit down. I can't tell you everything, but I will tell you what I can."

I sat down in an armchair and Arcas sat across from me on the sofa. "You know that Tom and I and some of the other Greeks in Canada are working with Papandreou to do whatever we can to overthrow the junta."

I nodded, although I'd never imagined any of them actually overthrowing anything.

Arcas looked deadly serious. He covered his mouth with his fist as though trying to hold back whatever he was about to say. I leaned forward and braced against some awful news. He lowered his fist. "What if I tell you that I really *was* on a secret mission? It's true that my father is ill, but that's not why I went home."

A secret mission, seriously? Did he take me for an idiot? I almost said something cutting and sarcastic but looked into his eyes and saw a sea of misery and fear. Despite my native skepticism, my heart raced with alarm.

"I can't tell you anymore because there are dangerous people who don't like what I'm doing. You know what happened to Nancy. Do you understand? That's why I thought I should stop seeing you."

He looked at me as though I were a child, a *koritsaki*, someone to be placated and protected. It had to be a lie or some sick joke, but he looked so distraught, so conflicted, that I started to believe him. "So why did you come back? What are you doing here in my apartment?"

He sank his head into his hands, hiding his face. "I don't know what I'm doing here. I don't know if I should ask your forgiveness for staying away or for coming back." He looked up with eyes glistening with tears he hastily blinked away. "I'm not thinking right. I'm sorry."

I got up and sat beside him on the sofa. "Arcas, I don't like secrets. How can you say you love me and then keep me in the dark about whatever's going on? I need to know the truth."

"No, no you don't." He took both my hands and held them as he shook his head. "You have your secrets and I have mine. Too many questions will ruin everything."

"I don't care." I pulled my hands away. "No more secrets. What the hell is going on?"

Arcas looked ill, and I thought he might get up and leave. Instead, he asked to use the bathroom. When he came back, he was a shade paler than usual, but his face was washed clean and he looked more composed. "OK, I will tell you more, but you can't tell anyone else, not even Nancy. Do you promise me?"

I wasn't sure what I was promising, but I nodded.

"Things are going to happen in Athens very soon, big things." He paused. "Do you still have the ouzo that I gave you?"

"In the cupboard next to the fridge." I grew increasingly irritated and impatient as he disappeared into the kitchen, but I was glad when he returned with two glasses.

He handed me one then perched on the arm of the sofa, as though he didn't want to get too comfortable in case I threw him out. "There are people with money and power who want the colonels gone. They plan to smuggle guns into Greece to arm the resistance and I am helping these people. Now, do you understand?"

No, I didn't understand. This was beyond anything in my experience. My heart pounded as though the colonels' thugs were coming after me. I took a sip of the ouzo and waited for my heart to slow down. The cold liquor warmed and chilled me at the same time while my mind replayed scenes from an old action film recast with Arcas clinging to the mast of a wind tossed ship at night. "What does that mean exactly? How are you helping them?"

He pursed his lips, and I didn't think he was going to answer me. "There are cargo ships that go back and forth between Montreal and Athens and if you know people who work on these ships it's possible to do things. I know these people."

"How do you know people who work on ships? You're a student. Your family raises goats."

"Yes, but . . ." He hesitated and looked away. "My father was in the Navy during the war and . . . No, that's not the truth. The truth is that two of my friends from school went to sea after they graduated. We are still very close, like brothers. They'd risk anything to bring down this government."

"So, you just connect the guys with the money and the guys on the ships. Is that right?" Somehow, that didn't sound so scary. He'd make a phone call or pass along a letter of introduction, no hanging from the rigging with a dagger clenched between his teeth.

"No, there's more." He hugged himself and rocked back and forth. "I've made promises that will take me back to Greece and I have to keep those promises. Believe me, I'd rather stay here with you, but I don't have a choice." His voice sounded uncharacteristically high pitched and whiney.

I put down my glass and leaned forward. "You do have a choice. You always have a choice. If you don't want to go, don't go. It's that simple."

"No, it's not." He put down his glass and raked his fingers through his hair. "Maybe in America everything is simple, but I don't live in Disneyland. My world isn't like that." His voice broke and he looked away. When he turned back to me his eyes had lost their light and the skin beneath his chin seemed to sag. "Listen, I've made real promises to real people and terrible things will happen if I walk away. People I care about would get hurt and they wouldn't forgive me. I can't tell you more, but I want to be with you now. I want to stay with you as long as I can even if I can't stay forever. Please let me be with you."

The past month's emotional roller coaster ride had exhausted me. I didn't have the energy for a fight. "When it's over, will you come back to me?"

"I can't make promises because I don't know what will happen. But if it's possible to come back, I will." Arcas put his arm around my shoulder and let me bury my face in his neck. It felt so good to melt into his body, to feel him beside me once again that I ignored the alarms going off inside my head and simply basked in his heat and the familiar smell of his skin as he patted my back and made Greek cooing sounds in my ear.

As my crying subsided, I realized that he wasn't just murmuring nonsense, he was trying to tell me something. I finally heard "I might not be able to come back. What I'm doing is dangerous and terrible things could happen."

"What could happen? Please, don't do anything crazy. I need you to come back."

"Let's not think about that now. Let's enjoy this time while we're together." He lifted my face to his and kissed me on the lips.

I opened my eyes and he was staring at me. I held him close and whispered, "You know I'd go with you. I'd move to Greece. I'd do anything."

"Yes, yes, I know *koritsaki*, but I can't take you with me, not now. Maybe someday after the junta falls you will come to Arcadia and meet my sheep and go to the beach and swim in the Aegean Sea like a naiad, but not now. These are dangerous times, and you need to stay here where you're safe. Do you understand me? Do you hear what I'm saying?"

I unbuttoned his shirt and kissed his chest when a new thought struck me. "What about Tom and the others? Is Tom in danger too?"

"No, no, he's safe." Arcas stroked my hair. "He doesn't know about these things I'm doing. He's a politician, not a soldier. It's better if he doesn't know. You can't say a word to him or Nancy. Do you understand?"

"What could I tell them? I don't know anything."

"You know much more than you should. Let the others think I went to Greece to help my mother. Only you and I know there's more. Is that a promise, *koritsaki*?" He pulled me up from the sofa and held me close. "Do you promise that whatever happens you'll never say a word?"

I nodded my consent, feeling confused and a little frightened.

"Good." He kissed me again. "Lives depend on this promise."

The threat of danger, and a long separation gave a desperate edge to our love making. Part of me felt disembodied, floating, flying through space while another part responded to every touch of his hands, every kiss, every lick, every bite. He took me with passion that bordered on violence, and I clung to him, shivering and moaning until the sun had set and hunger finally lured us from my bed.

Neither of us wanted to leave the apartment so I threw on a robe and went into the kitchen to see what I could put together for our supper. There wasn't much, but a quick inventory revealed the makings of an omelet. While Arcas showered, I took out a frying pan and watched a large pat of butter sizzle and dissolve as I tried to make sense of the past twelve hours. What was I doing? I adored Arcas. I was terrified of losing him and wanted nothing more than to wake up beside him for the rest of my life. He loved me enough to tell me about his political work and yet I still hadn't told him about my sister. What was I afraid of? Why was I keeping my past a secret from the man I hoped would return to Canada and make me his wife? I took the pan off the heat and went into the dining room where I opened the bottom drawer of the buffet and took out a shoe box that held my most valued treasures.

Arcas walked out of the bedroom dressed and smelling faintly of my herbal shampoo. He kissed me on the cheek as I slipped a mushroom and Cheddar omelet onto a plate, added two slices of hot toast and a grilled tomato. Before he'd even sat down, he noticed the small, framed photograph in the middle of the kitchen table. It showed two identical young women flashing identical toothy smiles from the hood of a bright red Chevy Camaro.

He examined it a moment then turned to me with a puzzled expression. "You're a twin? You never told me you had a twin sister."

I poured two glasses of wine from a bottle of Chardonnay and sat down next to him at the table. "Her name was Joan." I pointed to the girl on the right. "That was taken on our twenty-first birthday, three weeks before she died."

"She was very beautiful, like her sister. What happened to her?"

How much did I intend to tell him? He might never look at me the same way again, but what choice did I have? If we stayed together he'd find out eventually. I began cautiously. "She drowned."

Arcas put his hand over mine, lacing our fingers together. "I'm so sorry. What a tragedy. Why didn't you tell me about this before?"

"Because I killed her. That's why I can't go back to the States. There's a warrant out for my arrest."

Arcas moved his hand away and my heart stopped. He was going to make some lame apology and leave. Who could blame him? It's what any normal person would do.

"No, you didn't kill her. That's not possible." He sounded both angry and confused. "Why would you say this to me?" Various emotions played across his face in quick succession: doubt, irritation, sympathy, concern. His changing expressions reminded me of the weather in Rochester that could turn from hot to cold, sunny to rainy in an instant. They reminded me of the weather on Lake Ontario the night my sister died.

"I didn't kill her on purpose. It wasn't murder, it was an accident, but it was my fault. I made every boating mistake in the book even though I'd been raised on the lake and knew all the rules." I put my hands in my lap so Arcas wouldn't see them tremble.

"What happened?" Arcas pushed his plate aside and looked at me intently.

It took me a full minute to find my voice, when I did it seemed to come from some other place, and I listened in horror along with Arcas as the story unfolded.

"My dad owned a speedboat, and we went to the lake almost every weekend during the summer. A couple weeks after our twenty-first birthday, we were allowed to take the boat out by ourselves, and we invited a boy we knew, Stephen, to go water skiing with us. He'd gone on a few dates with Joanie, but we both had a crush on him. Everything was friendly, although there was a kind of tension about which one of us he liked the best. Sometimes we got competitive like that. Anyway, Joanie and I brought beer and he showed up with a couple joints and two bottles of tequila. It was a gorgeous evening in late August, about six o'clock but still light. The temperature must have been in the nineties, but we could get a great breeze by running the boat at full throttle. We burned a lot of gas and laughed ourselves silly seeing how fast we could go cutting across our own wake to make the boat jump. I was the pilot. It was my job to stay sober and get us home safely, but we were finally of legal drinking age, so I felt obligated to get totally wasted. Joanie warned me to slow down on the tequila shots, but I ignored her. She was always the voice of reason, and I was the wild one in those days. That's how you could tell us apart. I figured Stephen would be impressed by my crazy, free spirit and choose me over my boring sister. Stupid, huh?"

I took a gulp of the wine. "I never saw him again, except for the day he was called to court as a witness."

Arcas hadn't stirred, he'd hardly blinked as I unwound my confession. His face barely moved as he asked, "Witness to what? What happened?"

"We were having a wonderful time, so we stayed out too late and went out too far and I broke every rule I'd ever been taught about piloting a boat. We started out wearing life jackets, but they were hot and bulky so we took them off. That actually worked in my favor at the trial since it meant Joanie was partly responsible, but it wasn't enough to get me off." I looked out the window. My eyes traveled from the red brick wall of the building next door to its shingled roof, then past a tangle of electric wires to the sky, a sea of dark clouds in a rising wind.

I turned away and stared into my half empty glass as I went on. "Joanie wanted to ski one more time before we went in. It was already dusk, and we should have been making a beeline for the harbor, but we were all high and not thinking clearly. She was a strong skier, so I wasn't worried about her. Someone's supposed to keep their eyes on a skier at all times, but I was more interested in flirting with Stephen and finishing off the tequila. Anyway, she was already up on her skis when we heard the first clap of thunder. I turned to let her know we were going to go in, but she wasn't there, just the rope dragging behind us. I scanned the lake as far as I could see, but it was already dark, and I didn't know how far back we'd lost her. I shut off our engines and heard her calling for help from somewhere off on our starboard side, but I couldn't see anything but water. We drove slowly in the direction of her voice, but then it seemed to be coming from a different direction, so we changed course and tried again, and again, and again."

I took another large sip of the chardonnay to steady myself. "After a while I wasn't even sure I was hearing her voice. It might have been the thunder, the rain, or the water crashing against the side of our boat. Even when I knew I couldn't hear her anymore, I kept driving in circles all over the goddamn lake trying to find her in the dark. Stephen finally had to wrestle the tiller from my hand and drive us back to port.

"I begged the police to send the Coast Guard out to find her, but they just took one look at the empty cans and bottles in our boat and arrested me for boating under the influence and involuntary manslaughter. That's how the night ended. They arrested me for killing my own sister."

"Did they ever find her?" Arcas asked.

"No. We had a memorial service with an empty casket. I get the willies whenever I think of her body at the bottom of the lake." I looked directly at Arcas. "Sometimes, I can still hear her calling for help. It's like an auditory hallucination or something. It scares me every time it happens."

"I'm so sorry." Arcas took my hand and kissed my fingers, one after the other. I hadn't scared him away. He was still sitting beside me. "How did you come to Canada? What brought you to me?"

I twined my fingers between his and squeezed his hand, grateful for his presence. "There was terrible publicity after the accident. The local papers went wild with the story, 'Drunken boater kills identical twin sister' with lots of photos of the two of us in bathing suits. It was all over the six o'clock news. Journalists stood outside the house for days ringing our bell and demanding interviews. It was a nightmare. My lawyer said I had about a fifty percent chance of getting off, which meant I had a fifty percent chance of going to prison for up to fifteen years. My folks paid a small fortune to bail me out prior to sentencing, knowing they'd never see that money again because they arranged for me to skip bail and leave the country. They even helped me get my job off the record with Abbot's Printing. So here I am."

"But Canada and the United States help each other in these matters, don't they?"

"Sure, the US and Canada have an extradition treaty, but I'm small potatoes. No one's looking for me. As long as I don't go back to the States, I'm safe." I picked up the framed photo of two laughing girls and stared at it, trying to remember being that happy and that innocent. "So, now you know. That's my story."

Arcas took the photo from my hands. He put it face down on the table and stood up, pulling me toward him. "I wish I could make you promises, *koritsaki*. I wish I could take you away where bad memories would never find you."

Jacob

On Board the Aqua Meridian

Love is Alive

It's Happening! Be there or be square.
Eight o'clock on the Janus Deck
Dress: Hippie chic.

I REREAD THE invitation affixed to the door of my cabin, *Hippie chic*, now there's an oxymoron for you. The *Aqua Meridian* hasn't provided a costume and I don't own anything remotely chic, hippie or otherwise. I tie the sash from the complimentary bathrobe around my forehead, but the effect is ridiculous, and I toss it on the bed. Maybe I'll filch a flower from one of the bouquets in the lobby and then . . . what? Pin it to my hair? How many would I have to steal to make a garland?

There's a knock at the door and I'm afraid it's the steward coming to politely throw me out of my room so housekeeping can come in, but no, it's Sam wearing a tie-die T-shirt. How did he know to pack a thing like that?

I'm a bit annoyed since I'm nowhere near ready and have no idea what to wear to this shindig. "What time is it? I wasn't expecting you this early."

"I came early because I thought you might need this." He walks past me carrying a plastic bag and sits on the bed. He pulls a wadded bundle of denim from the bag and hands it to me with a wide smile, clearly delighted with himself.

I unfold the material and find that it's a sort of vest. Did hippies wear vests? It looks more like a cowboy costume.

"And love beads." He hands me the bag with a flourish. I look inside and see about a cup of children's breakfast cereal. My confusion must be visible, because he says, "Here let me show you." He reaches into the bag and pulls out a length of twine beaded with the colored cereal and hangs it around my neck. "They're Fruit Loops. The steward got them for me. Creative, huh?"

"Absolutely. Far out." I put on the vest and check the effect in the mirror. I look like an overgrown five-year-old dressed for Halloween. "Are costumes really required? I'm not sure I'm the costume type." I hate to disappoint the young man, but I'm not going out in public in this get up.

"You look great. Way to go." He pulls another chain of Fruit Loops from the bag and strings them around his own neck. "OK now. We're ready to par-tee."

I can't tell if he's joking, but I laugh amiably while handing him back the necklace. "Maybe I'll just wear the vest."

"Alright, if you're sure." He loops the second strand of cereal around his own neck then pulls a pair of sunglasses with round frames and colored lenses from his pocket. "Here, I was going to use these myself, but if you're not wearing the beads you should wear the granny glasses."

The glasses make everything look slightly pink and out of focus. They make me a bit dizzy, but I hate to disappoint him again. "Thank you. How do I look?"

"Out of sight. Come on. The first ones there always get the best food."

The pulsing sound of rock music grows louder and louder as the elevator ascends to the Janus Deck. By the time we step off the elevator it's so loud I can feel the floorboards vibrating beneath my feet. Attending this event was clearly a mistake. I steal a glance at Sam, but I can't read his expression. Maybe he's enjoying the throbbing bass that's giving me a headache. I was expecting a guy with a guitar singing about free love or hitchhiking to San Francisco. Isn't that what hippies did? I don't remember this noise.

The air is thick with incense and something that smells suspiciously like pot. You can't teach university for forty years without recognizing that sweet, pungent odor. The deck is already crowded with passengers in bell bottom pants, long skirts, bare feet, flowers, and tie dye everything. Nearly everyone has long hair. Where did all this hair come from? Are they wearing wigs? A smattering of young people, both boys and girls, are completely topless apart from the garlands of flowers around their necks. I'm not a prude but I look away. This isn't the party I was expecting.

Sam steers me over to the bar where we grab a couple cold beers and sip them self-consciously like a pair of spinsters at an orgy while everyone else undulates and spins to the deafening music. A beautiful young woman in a sort of sarong grabs my arm.

"May I paint your face? You could use a little color."

Before I can answer she's dabbing my cheek with a small brush. "You too." She paints a red heart on each of Sam's cheeks then kisses him on the lips before moving on to paint blue waves on the belly of a fat man, I think it's Harvey Newcome, dancing alone in a joyous trance.

"This is quite a party," I shout in Sam's direction. "I think that girl's taken a shine to you."

"What? I'm sorry. What did you say?" Sam leans down from his lofty height of six foot whatever to hear me better.

"I said you ought to ask that girl to dance. I think she likes you."

"Not likely." Sam reddens slightly. "She probably has an ugly friend she wants to set me up with. That's what usually happens."

"Then go dance with her ugly friend. You're only young once." I take a swig of the beer and look up at Sam. He looks okay to me. I can't see why he'd have trouble attracting a girl.

"I can't dance. I look like I'm having an epileptic fit. Why don't you ask her? She drew flowers on your cheek too."

Flowers? I touch my cheek and laugh. If Bess could see me in this getup she'd wet her pants. "I've already got a girl." I'm not sure if I'm lying or not.

"You do? Is it serious?" Sam looks surprised. I guess I don't look like a lady's man.

I don't want to explain that I'm widowed, and that Bess has been gone for eight years, so I just say, "Very serious," and leave it at that. Sam bobs awkwardly to the music for a moment, then gives it up. He's right. He can't dance. "How about if we grab something to eat then blow this joint? We could sit out on the lower deck and watch the sunset."

Sam, bless him, looks relieved. We elbow our way to the front of the fondue table where we dip squares of bread in bubbling cheese and strawberries in melted chocolate then take the elevator down to where the music is just a soft murmuring in the distance. The lower deck is a vast expanse of empty lounge chairs that recline companionably in the twilight. Sam and I sit at a small plastic table and gaze out at the water. It's almost nine o'clock but the sun is still visible just above the horizon.

We eat in silence, enjoying the relative quiet until Sam asks, "Where were you born? You said you came aboard in Toronto, but you don't sound Canadian."

"Yorkshire, near Leeds in the north of England, but I've lived in Toronto a long time now."

"Do you ever get homesick?"

"No, not really. I used to go back every few years, but I don't anymore. Not much point now, everyone I knew is gone."

Sam nods as though he understands, but he can't be thirty yet and I doubt that he's experienced much loss in his young life.

"I grew up in Cleveland, but I never go back there either." He takes a swig of his beer. He looks as though he wants to tell me more but hesitates.

"Why's that?" I encourage him.

"Bad memories. I was engaged until my fiancé dumped me. You don't want to hear about it."

"Sure I do. What would make a girl walk away from a great catch like the handsome young Dr. Rabinowitz?"

"It wasn't like that. She wasn't some gold digger who wanted to marry a doctor. She left me for an unemployed actor. You can't get less mercenary than that."

"Probably not," I have to agree.

"We had a ring, a date, a hall, a band, the whole megillah, and then she meets Frankie and practically leaves me standing at the altar."

"Frankie? That's a child's name."

"Being childlike was his attraction. Frankie was spontaneous and knew how to have a good time. It seems I'm too serious and a tight ass."

"No, I wouldn't say that," I reassured him. "You're responsible and mature, but that doesn't mean you can't have fun."

Sam gave me a wry smile and gestured around the empty deck. "Right, I'm the life of the party."

"Maybe she was just the wrong party."

"No, Veronica was fantastic. She was a talented musician, funny, pretty, smart. She'd get jobs playing in the orchestra for local musicals. That's where she met Frankie. He was auditioning for the lead in *Bye Bye Birdie*. You know, the greaser in tight pants who keeps combing his hair."

I'm afraid I don't know that show."

"It doesn't matter. The point is we'd been dating for three years and I was crazy about her. I was the happiest guy in Cleveland and then, Bye Bye Birdie, it's over.

"I'm so sorry, but I'm sure you'll find someone else. There must be a lot of girls who'd love to meet a guy like you," I say.

"Well, you'd be wrong. I went two years without a date. I tried losing myself in my studies and my work at the hospital but that just made me more isolated. It was awful, a classic case of depression. I wasn't eating or sleeping. I wasn't thinking clearly. I was terrified I'd screw up and kill somebody by mistake and then, like that wasn't bad enough, my Aunt Rose called to say my parents were dead, carbon monoxide poisoning from a faulty furnace."

"Oh my God, how awful."

"No kidding. I packed a suitcase full of books and a few shirts and started to drive home for the funeral, but I couldn't force myself to go. I looked in the mirror and thought, what's the point? What's the sense of even being alive? Anyway, I don't know why I'm telling you this, but I went down to the harbor instead, intending to jump off the Skyway Bridge."

"Thank God you did no such thing." I couldn't imagine the pain that would drive a healthy young man to such an act.

"Yeah, I guess I was lucky. I was standing on the bridge thinking it would all be over in a minute when the *Aqua Meridian* sailed by. I could hear the band playing as she headed into port. I think it was the music that saved me. Something about that music told me that everything would be alright if I could just get on board that boat. I turned around, drove to the port, and bought a ticket just like that. What did I have to lose? Why not do something spontaneous, be the kind of wild and crazy guy Veronica wanted?" He gestured around the empty deck where we were sitting quietly by ourselves. "So, are we a couple of wild and crazy guys or what?"

We clink bottles and I finish off the last of my beer, ruminating on Sam's sad story. The sun is low in the sky. It will be gone in another minute. I can hear the band playing faintly above us and I'm thinking about going back for more fondue when something makes me pause and cock my head.

Sam's heard it too. He's on his feet and leaning out over the rail. "Did you hear that? It sounds like someone's out on the water."

"It's probably coming from the upper deck," I reply without conviction. But he's right. There's something chilling about the sound, a human voice that seems to be coming from somewhere outside the ship, somewhere closer to the bow.

Sam runs along the deck in the direction of the voice, and I follow close behind him. It's the voice of a woman in distress. I can hear it clearly now.

"Help!" she calls. "Help!

Amy
August-October 1973

HOW COULD I remain angry with Arcas while Toronto shimmered in the last golden light of August? How could I deny the bond that had grown between us or the passion he aroused? I knew there was something reckless about our time together. I knew the man had secrets and that he might slip away again at any moment, but I never again doubted that he loved me. He'd listened to my confession about the guilt and shame that followed me to Canada, and he hadn't recoiled or run away. Instead, he'd held me in his arms, trying to console me. My defenses had toppled, and, despite his warnings, I dreamed of a shared future stretching out to grandchildren and our dotage.

Toronto is beautiful in late summer. Crowded streets thin and the pace slows as workers take their vacations and the well-heeled leave for cottage country. University buildings, devoid of students, enjoy an interval of silent contemplation. Leisurely lunches become leisurely afternoons at the outdoor tables along Yorkville. Canopies of old maples shade the sidewalks in front of stately Rosedale mansions and lush urban ravines come alive with the songs of birds. Men in suits, who normally race head-down toward endless appointments, look up to discover the sun is shining. They pause to let the heat unknit their brows and relax their knotted shoulders. Farther to the south, beyond their mirrored office towers, white sails dot the lake between Queen's Quay and the Toronto Islands.

Tom and Nancy had been invited to a friend's cottage on Lake Muskoka. Kosmos Bakery was closed for the owner's annual holiday in Greece, and Arcas's classes wouldn't start for another week. I'd taken a week's vacation from Abbot's Printing, so we were both at leisure and had the city to ourselves that last luxurious week of summer.

We hadn't made any plans and didn't have money for expensive trips or trendy restaurants, and I still wouldn't go near the lake, but Arcas surprised me with tickets to a Santana concert at the newly renovated Maple Leaf Gardens. The sun was still shining when we arrived following supper at a small Mexican Restaurant. The crowd was massive and bent on recreating Woodstock right there on the corner of Church and Carlton in the middle of Toronto. Those polite Canadians had a dark underside the band exposed. Despite tight security and a visible police presence, the air was heavy with weed and the crowd was buzzing, wired with excitement.

Maybe it was the tequila, maybe it was simply that I hadn't been to a concert since coming to Canada, but I felt an unreasonable level of anticipation, an almost altered state of consciousness. I hung onto Arcas as we pushed through a throng of excited young bodies and found our seats. Arcas must have been feeling the energy as well because he put his arm around me and pulled me into a long kiss as soon as we were seated. Other couples were also discarding their inhibitions, kissing and fondling one another even before the lights had dimmed.

Santana appeared as if by magic in a pool of purple light and the hall rocked to a percussive Latin beat. The music and the crowd merged into one throbbing, pulsing organism that grew with the rising decibel level until it filled the old ice hockey rink, pounding on the walls and stomping on the ceiling. When the final encore was over, and the lights came back on my ears were buzzing and my heart was pounding. We were all filled with a wild energy that we carried out into the night. The sun was gone, but the street was bright with flashing neon signs, traffic lights, and the lights from cars and taxis that passed us as we headed toward the subway.

"Arcas!" A male voice boomed above the chatter of the crowd. We turned to see a short man with a thick moustache jogging toward us.

Arcas smiled, but I could feel his body stiffen. He wasn't happy to see this man who was plainly delighted to see him. He reached us, nearly out of breath, and clasped Arcas around the shoulders drawing him into a manly hug. The two of them had an animated conversation in Greek while I smiled inanely at nothing, waiting to be introduced. I noticed Arcas's eyes wander nervously along the street as he spoke as though he was expecting someone or something to appear. He looked at his watch and shrugged then turned and walked back toward the concert hall. I gave the stranger an apologetic smile and turned to run after Arcas who was disappearing into the crowd.

"Nice to meet you. Sorry I can't stay to meet your husband," the short man called after me in heavily accented English.

My husband? Why did he think I had a husband? I caught up with Arcas and took his hand. "Who was that? Why are we running away from that guy?"

"He's a jerk, someone with a big mouth from my village. You don't want to know him." We were standing inside Maple Leaf Gardens again, staring through the glass doors at the short man who was hailing a taxi. We waited until he was gone before venturing back onto the street.

"Why does he think I have a husband? What did you tell him?" The whole episode had me confused and a little upset, destroying my post-concert euphoria.

"He wanted to share a taxi, so I told him we were waiting for your husband. It was the first thing that came into my head. *Malakas*, the bastard's going to tell everyone he knows that he saw us together."

"So what? What's the problem?"

"I don't like him. He's the sort of idiot that supports the junta. Let's get out of here." He pulled me toward the subway, hunched over and scowling, but once we were on the platform his whole demeanor changed and he was his usual charming self again. He bought me a bag of warm cashews from a candy vendor and fed them to me on the subway as we headed back to my apartment.

September brought more blue skies and warm afternoons as our romantic idyll continued into the fall. Arcas and I didn't officially live together, but he slept at my apartment almost every night. We'd fallen into a comfortable routine of work, shopping, cooking, evenings out with Tom and Nancy, the occasional movie and constant sex. His presence was insulation against the homesickness I felt for Rochester and the incapacitating waves of guilt and depression that still came over me without warning.

The Greeks continued to foment as much resistance as they could to Papadopoulos's fascist regime, but I had no sense of imminent danger. Arcas's warnings about our future were stored in a back closet of my brain where they gathered dust undisturbed by any present fear, and yet there were signs, signs I shouldn't have ignored.

I came home late one Tuesday afternoon to find Arcas sprawled barefoot on my sofa engrossed in a Greek language newspaper, a cold Molson's balanced precariously on the arm of the couch. I picked up the beer and moved it to the coffee table. "Aren't you supposed to be in class? I thought you taught econometrics on Tuesdays."

He turned with an expression that confounded me. He looked belligerent, as though I'd said something to offend him.

"Look at this, your damn CIA engineered the whole thing," he shouted, poking a finger at an article. "The colonels are nothing but American puppets. Here's proof, how are you going to defend them now?"

I'd never defended the CIA, in fact I had little interest in politics, so I just stared at him not knowing how to respond.

He stood up and shook the paper in my face. "Is this your idea of democracy? Is this how you lead the free world?"

Four empty Molson's bottles were lined up on the floor beside the sofa and a bottle of scotch sat open on the kitchen table. He wasn't normally a big drinker, but he'd clearly had about three too many. I picked up the empty bottles and eyed him warily, frightened by his behavior. "What's the matter? Are you OK?"

"No, I'm not okay." He shook the paper again. "Are you OK? Is anything OK?" He picked up the remaining beer and drained it dry. The drink calmed him, at least he stopped shouting. "I've withdrawn from the university. Maybe I'll go back next semester, or maybe I won't."

"Why? What are you going to do?" I dumped the bottles in the trash and poured myself a small shot of scotch, completely rattled.

"I'm going to fix this. I'm going to force those fascists to give me my country back and I can't waste time at some Canadian university."

"But you have a class to teach this evening."

"I'm not the professor, I'm a graduate assistant. Anyone can cover for me." He started to put his shoes on, but the look on my face seemed to stop him. "Don't look so worried. I dropped out before the fifteenth so they'll refund my tuition. I'm not crazy."

"Do Tom and Nancy know?" I was still trying to make sense of the sudden detour his life had taken.

"Not yet, maybe Tom will drop out too. Maybe all the Greeks will drop out. This is war."

"Arcas, what's changed? Why now? I don't understand."

"Miss America doesn't understand? Ask the CIA, maybe they'll explain it to you."

I recoiled at this unsolicited attack. "That's not fair. Why are you being like this?"

He finished tying his shoes without looking at me. "Let's go out to dinner. I need some air."

"Not so fast, you owe me an apology."

"You're right. I'm sorry." He looked up with an ingratiating smile. "I should show Miss America more respect."

"Yes, you should." I wasn't sure if he'd apologized or not.

"Come on, let's go. I want to get out of here." Arcas started for the door. I downed the last of my scotch and set the glass on the coffee table beside an open envelope with a Greek stamp made out to Arcas in a woman's flowing hand. I picked it up and handed it to him. "What's this?"

"A death sentence."

"What?" I did a double-take and stared at him.

"That was a joke. It's nothing, a letter from my mother." He tore the letter into pieces and shoved the scraps into his pocket as we headed out the door.

He didn't return to the university after that, but he didn't seem to spend any time overthrowing fascists either. He picked up some additional hours at the bakery. He talked politics with friends at the tavernas on Danforth Street, and drank a little more than he used to, but he showed up with wine or a box of pastry most evenings and he was as attentive and affectionate as ever. I chalked up the unaccustomed outburst to the beer and guessed the real reason he'd dropped out of school had something to do with money. I didn't ask too many questions because I was young and blinded by love. No, that's a lie. It was because I was dependent and frightened he'd leave me. The demons that had followed me from Rochester still peered in my windows at night and howled for me out on the lake. Arcas kept them at bay and I needed him, no questions asked.

So, our relationship remained outwardly the same. We kissed and cuddled and held hands as the leaves changed color and the windows were reluctantly closed against the cold. The biggest difference was that we no longer saw Tom and Nancy. Tom had stormed over to my apartment when he heard that Arcas was taking a leave of absence. I don't know what he said since the argument was entirely in Greek, but things got so heated that Tom shoved Arcas into a wall and Arcas came back swinging. The two of them were on the verge of an all-out fist fight when I yelled at Tom to get out of my house, threw his jacket at him, and pushed him toward the door. To my relief he put on the jacket and left, but not before turning to me and saying, "You're sleeping with a traitor. Don't believe a word that guy says."

Arcas was rubbing his shoulder. He looked concussed even though he hadn't hit his head. I put my arms around his waist. "Wow, Tom's really got a bug up his ass. Doesn't he understand that you dropped out so you'd have more time to fight the junta?"

Arcas pushed me away. "Who the hell is he to call me a traitor? The stupid bastard's only half Greek. Fuck the *malakas*."

"Hey, I'm on your side. Relax, he'll probably call to apologize in the morning."

"If he calls throw the phone out the window. I'm finished with him. I already know too many idiots."

"Tom's not an idiot, he's your best friend. I don't know what you two were arguing about, but I'm sure you'll work it out."

"If you like him so much, maybe you should fuck him. I'm going home."

"No!" I panicked, frightened that if he left he'd never come back. "Who cares what Tom thinks? He doesn't matter. The only thing that matters is for us to be together. You're the only one I care about."

He pulled me close and kissed me hard, too hard. His teeth bruised my lips as he held my head back by the hair. I tried to struggle loose, but he picked me up and carried me into the bedroom where he tore off my pants and mounted me like a wild animal without foreplay, without the usual precautions. When he was finished, he turned away from me and I could hear him crying into his pillow. I took his hand and kissed the back of his neck.

He turned and held me close. "I really do love you." He stroked my back and smoothed back my hair. "You have to know that. Whatever happens you have to know that I really love you."

"Yes, yes. I love you too." I kissed his neck and ran my fingers through the hair on his chest as we fell asleep in one another's arms. The next morning, I got dressed and went to work, Arcas went to the bakery and that evening we walked downtown and shared a pizza and a bottle of wine as though nothing had happened. So, once again the storm passed, the water receded and all I saw were lovely lights twinkling along the shore.

Tom never called, but Nancy wrote to say she missed me but that we'd better not see each other until the guys worked out their problem. Then my parents called to say they were driving up for Thanksgiving, the Canadian Thanksgiving in October, not the American holiday a month later, and they were looking forward to finally meeting my new boyfriend.

Arcas surprised me by saying that he'd love to meet my parents. He even offered to prepare a Greek style turkey and an assortment of sweets. His interest in my family filled my heart with such joyful anticipation that his earlier warnings were forgotten. Our lives resumed their comfortable routine, I felt increasingly secure and looked forward to a holiday dinner with the three people I loved most in the world.

I was sitting at my kitchen table on a glorious October morning leafing through *The Joy of Cooking*, searching for recipes that were impressive without being intimidating. I'd already earmarked several good prospects when I heard Arcas at the door. We were planning a fall hike through Crothers Woods and then a quick shopping expedition to purchase a big roasting pan, since my kitchen wasn't equipped to deal with twelve-pound turkeys. He was early, but that was fine with me. I jumped up and ran to greet him with a kiss.

He never looked more handsome than he did that morning with his dark curls disheveled by the wind and his cheeks glowing from the cold. He was carrying flowers, a bouquet of white lilies he must have bought from one of the small florists along Bloor.

"Thank you, they're beautiful." I took the flowers with an appreciative smile, although something inside me buzzed with alarm. He never brought me flowers. "What's the occasion? I know it's not my birthday."

"No, it's not your birthday." He threw his jacket across the back of a chair and sat down. "Do you have coffee? "I watched as he crossed and uncrossed his legs and looked around the room with eyes that never settled on anything.

I arranged the flowers in a pitcher and put them on the table, then poured the last of my morning coffee into a mug and carried it to the living room. "Here you go. I think it's still hot. What's going on?"

"Sit down. I need to tell you something."

I sat, holding my breath.

"You know that I promised to do certain things for certain people. I told you that I might need to go back to Greece. You knew that. I didn't lie to you. Well, now they called and said it's time. No, don't ask me any questions." He held up his hand before I could utter a word. "I can't tell you anything. I don't know how long I'll be gone. I don't know if I'll be back and if I knew I couldn't tell you."

"But."

"I'm sorry. Those are good-bye flowers. I'm leaving tomorrow. Do you understand?"

"No, you need to tell me more. I deserve to know what's going on. Can we write? Can I call you on the phone?"

"No, nothing. What I'm doing is very dangerous, that's all I can tell you. I have a friend who has your address. If something happens to me, he promised he'd write to let you know. I'm sorry, *koritsaki*."

I was too shocked to cry, paralyzed by disbelief. This couldn't be happening, not now, not when we were both so happy. He stood up and put his hands on my head, then bent over and kissed me. "You know that I love you. I wouldn't go if I had a choice." He reached into his pocket and took out a small box and pressed it into my hands. "Something to remember me."

I opened it, crazily hoping for a ring, but of course it wasn't. It contained the old paperweight he kept on his desk, the one with the spiral of mysterious hieroglyphics.

"You always asked about this relic whenever you came to my room. I can't tell you much except it's very old. I've always kept it with me because it was a present from my father, but now I want you to have it. Think of me when you look at it. I really did love you, koritsaki." Then he stood up and left without another word.

Jacob
Aboard the Aqua Meridian
River of Dreams

"I CAN'T SEE anything, but someone's out there." Sam is leaning over the rail, straining to make out a form in the darkening water. "Someone must have fallen overboard."

"I'll go for help." I'm about to sprint back toward the elevators when Sam grips my arm and pulls me back.

"There's no time, we're losing her." Sam is suddenly the man in charge. He puts his hands to his mouth and bellows into the void. "Hello, can you hear me?"

Old memories come flooding back. I pulled bodies, some living, some dead, onto the deck of the *HMS Kipling* during the war. It isn't an experience I want to repeat.

"Help!" The shouts fade until they are almost inaudible above the sound of the waves slapping against the side of the boat and the thrum of the motor. Either the woman is growing weaker or she's drifting farther from the ship.

"Help!"

"Hang in there. We're sending help." Sam is wild eyed, scanning the deck like a madman, then he pitches plastic chairs overboard. I can see their white forms bobbing in the water. He shouts into the abyss, "Swim over to one of those chairs and hang on. We're going to get you out."

At first all I see are chairs drifting away from us, but then a form takes shape, the silhouette of a woman struggling toward the ship. As she gets closer, the red running lights illuminate her body and I can see that she's young with a mass of long wet hair hanging around her face. She tries to grab one of the chairs, but she's weak and disoriented and the waves tear it from her grip. We lose sight of her as the ship continues its journey forward.

Sam rips off his shoes and shimmies out of his trousers. "Get help. Tell them to lower a lifeboat. I'll keep her head above water as long as I can." Then he's gone, just like that. As I stare overboard, I see his head surface, then his body. He's alive and swimming. I take off running, screaming as I go, "Man overboard. Man overboard."

Most of the other passengers are unaware of the drama unfolding just beyond the ship. The music and dancing continue unabated while I pace grim-faced, hugging myself against an odd chill despite the warm weather. There are only a few of us, a half dozen crew members and a handful of curious bystanders on the lower deck waiting for the lifeboat to return. The rescue effort doesn't take long, but I've lost all sense of time and it feels as though years have passed before I see Sam, wrapped in a warm blanket, step off the tender. He's followed by two uniformed crew carrying a body on a stretcher.

I run to him and clasp him around the shoulders. "Thank God you're alive. What were you thinking? That was the craziest stunt I've ever seen." He's shivering and seems to be in shock. A few soggy Fruit Loops still hang from the string plastered to his chest. The man is a hero. Who would have guessed he had it in him?

"She's going to be okay," he manages to say through chattering teeth. "They got us in time."

"What the hell happened? How did she manage to fall overboard?"

He pulls away from me and runs after the stretcher. "Sorry, they don't have a real doctor on board and she needs immediate medical attention. See you tomorrow."

So, I'm left standing by myself again. This certainly isn't the little harbor cruise I'd envisioned when I boarded the ship, but what a story I'll have for Michael when I get home.

THE SUN HITS me full in the face and I turn to bury my eyes in the pillow when I remember Sam and the half-drowned woman. I reach for the bedside clock and see that it's almost eight. How long have I been asleep? I remember wandering around the ship at loose ends after Sam ran off. I'd paced the ship for an hour or so, then sat by myself nursing a drink before returning to my cabin. Could I have slept ten hours? Time is a slippery commodity on this ship. Who knows how long I've slept?

I wash, dress quickly, and head up to the dining room, hoping to find Sam when a new thought hits me. Maybe he was evacuated with the woman during the night. I turn and run down the stairs toward the customer relations desk on the lower level. There's a new clerk on duty. Maybe it's her impeccable uniform or the gray hair with every lacquered strand in place, but I'm put off and hesitate before approaching. She's on the phone and holds up a long, polished fingernail indicating that I should wait. As other passengers queue up behind me, she turns her back on us and continues her conversation.

She finally hangs up and turns to me without a word of apology. "Do you need something?"

Of course, I need something. Why else would I be standing here? But I don't say what I'm thinking and smile pleasantly. "There was an incident last night. A woman fell overboard and was rescued by one of your lifeboats. Do you know how she's doing? Is she still aboard?"

"Of course, she's on board. We didn't throw her back."

"No, of course not, but I thought . . ."

"She's in sickbay. Are you a relative?"

"No, but I was with the fellow who dived in to save her, a Dr. Rabinowitz. Do you know if he's with her now?"

She looks at me as though I'm an idiot. "I have no idea."

"Alright then, can you tell me how to get to sickbay?"

She sighs and purses her lips. "Access to sickbay is restricted to family and medical personnel. Is there anything else? There are people waiting behind you."

"Yes." I decide to stand my ground. "Please call sickbay for me and ask if Dr. Rabinowitz is there."

She reaches for a notepad and a pencil. "You can call yourself. Here's the number. Use the phone to the left of the grand stairway. Next." She hands me a slip of paper and turns her attention to a young woman holding a squalling child by the hand.

I hadn't noticed the phone booth before. It's one of those sumptuous little padded cells that are in the lobbies of opera houses or fancy hotels. I slip inside and dial the number. To my surprise, Sam answers on the first ring.

"Sam? It's Jacob. I've been worried about you. How's the girl?"

"I'm fine now that I've dried out, but the girl . . . um. How about if we meet in the dining room? I didn't sleep a wink last night and I could really use coffee."

A few minutes later we're carrying coffee and cheese Danish out of the dining room, away from the hubbub of the breakfast crowd, and into a small interior room furnished with rows of chairs, a small lectern, and a portable movie screen. The room is set up for meetings or lectures, but now it's perfectly quiet. The lights are turned off and, as if by agreement, neither of us switches them on. The dim light is a balm to our jangled nerves. I settle into a chair in the back row and motion for Sam to join me. "So, what's the story? Last night you said she'd be fine. Has anything changed?"

"Not really, she's young and strong and should be back to normal in a couple of days. I expect she'll make a complete recovery."

"Well, good then, that's wonderful."

Sam nods, giving me a tentative half smile. There's clearly more to the story than he's telling.

I wait, but he doesn't say anything more. "If the patient's making such a splendid recovery, why the long face?"

"She's fine physically, more than fine. She's in remarkable shape under the circumstances, but she can't tell us what happened. She doesn't remember anything, not even her own name."

"Well, I'm no doctor, but I'm pretty sure retrograde amnesia is pretty common following a big accident, especially if someone's hit their head."

"Yes, of course, but no one knows who she is. They checked the ship's manifest and everyone's accounted for. They're wondering if she fell off some other ship. Isn't that weird?"

I nod in agreement. It is weird.

"She's clearly from a nice family, educated, well-spoken, and really sweet. Do you know what she said when she woke up this morning? She said, "Are you alright? You could have gotten killed jumping off a ship like that." He took a bite of his Danish. "Isn't that amazing? She calls me Dr. Mark Spitz."

"Like the Olympic swimmer?"

"Yeah, she's got a sense of humor. Wouldn't you think a girl like that would have family desperate to find her? But the captain hasn't received any missing person notices and there's no request for search and rescue from any other ship. It doesn't make sense."

"Maybe she's a stowaway. That would explain why she doesn't want anyone to know her name or where she's from." I can see that Sam doesn't like this idea, but it's all I can come up with.

"She was wearing a bikini for God's sake. Who stows away in a bikini?" He dunks his Danish into his coffee before polishing it off. "Anyway, if you talked to her, you'd see that she's not the sort of person who sneaks onto ships without paying."

I can see that Sam has taken a shine to this girl. "What happens to her now? They can't just dump her at the next port without a name or a toothbrush."

"I'll keep her in sickbay as long as I can and hope her memory starts to come back. Most people recover in time, but not everyone. Some people never remember who they are."

"That must be awful, like someone with dementia finding themselves in an institution surrounded by strangers." The thought brings back recent memories of my own.

"She's very confused right now. I mean, who wouldn't be? Thank God, we heard her when we did. Another few minutes and she'd have drowned." Sam turns and stares out a porthole at the water reaching to the horizon.

"That's true, and you saved her. You're quite the hero. Seriously, you deserve a medal. When did you learn to swim like that?"

"I'm not a swimmer, not really. I just jumped in without thinking about it."

"Well, you saved her life, but you almost gave me a heart attack." I smile at our local hero and pat him on the back. "When can I meet this mermaid you pulled from the sea?"

"If she feels well enough, I guess you could meet her tomorrow. I'll ask if she's up for company." Sam stands up and brushes the crumbs from his slacks. "I better get back to my duties as the volunteer doctor."

"What do we call this naiad with no name? We can't keep calling her the girl."

"I don't know. If she doesn't remember her name, I guess she'll have to choose something." Sam is already halfway out the door.

"See if she likes Clio or Doris. They're Greek sea nymphs." I'm not sure if he's heard me. The door slams shut and I'm all alone with a cup of cold coffee.

It's still morning and I have no idea what to do with the day. I could go to the library. There's nothing wrong with passing the day with a good book, but as I wander from the meeting room past a bank of tall windows, I see the sun is shining and decide to go for a swim. It doesn't take long to change into the swimsuit the cruise line's provided. The air is warm, the sun is bright, and the pool is quiet and uncrowded. I pound my belly for the simple pleasure of hearing a resounding thud, then do a racing dive into the water. It's colder than I expect, but I was a good swimmer in my day, and I have no problem finding my rhythm and completing several laps of the Australian crawl. I'm barely winded, but I switch to a breaststroke just for some variety. Stroke-inhale, glide-exhale, stroke-inhale . . . I lift my head and catch a glimpse of a familiar pair of legs at the far end of the pool. I stop swimming and tread water to get a better look as the woman attached to those legs hurries past in a modest swimsuit and wide brimmed hat. It's her again. It's Bess or Bess's double. I swim faster but every time I come up for air she's closer to the exit. It's hopeless. By the time I reach the edge and pull myself from the pool, she's gone again.

I'm standing at the shallow end of the pool, dripping and confused, when a waiter with a tray of drinks walks by. "Excuse me. I'm sorry, but I was wondering, do you happen to know the woman who just left, the one in the big hat?"

"I'm sorry, I don't know her name, but she is very good at crossword puzzles. She finished this before I could bring her coffee." He hands me a magazine he has tucked under his arm. It's turned to the puzzle page. Every square is neatly filled with a simple printed letter. They are just simple block letters, but my heart stops. It's Bess's handwriting. I'd swear it is.

"Does she come here often?" I ask. "Would I see her if I came tomorrow at this time?"

"I couldn't say sir, but I've seen her before. She usually sits just there." He indicates a lounge chair beneath a yellow umbrella. "She does a puzzle or reads a book, always by herself. She comes and goes. I couldn't say when she'll be back. I'm sorry, sir." He smiles and I wonder if I should tip him, but he doesn't wait and hurries off with his tray of drinks.

I want to go down to the customer relations desk to ask about the woman, to learn her real name and put this nonsense to rest, but what would I say? Could you tell me the name of the lovely lady who looks remarkably like my late wife?

Not likely. All the air has suddenly gone out of the morning, and I no longer feel like swimming. I return to my cabin, change back into street clothes, and wonder if Sam will meet me for lunch. Odd that my only friend on this cruise is a fellow young enough to be my grandson, but I like the boy, in fact, I'm in awe of him. Imagine, jumping off a ship to save a girl. That Veronica he was engaged to made a big mistake. If there's one thing I've learned about Dr. Sam Rabinowitz it's that he's not boring.

"So, how's the mermaid?" I ask Sam who's wolfing down a corned beef sandwich in the Sea Breeze Café. I'd like to tell him about the woman who looks like Bess, but he doesn't know I'm married or widowed or whatever, and it would be too hard to explain. He looks remarkably well for a young man who might have been paralyzed or dead if things had gone the wrong way last night. In fact, he's glowing. God bless the young. I fish around in my bowl of clam chowder for a bit of potato, but I'm not hungry.

"She's remarkable. I've never met anyone like her. She nearly drowns, can't remember a thing about what happened, not even her own name, and yet she keeps asking about me as though I'm the patient. She's already up and walking around, although I'd really like to keep her in bed for a day or two, just to let her recover from the shock."

"So, can I hope to meet her sometime soon?" I take a spoonful of soup, but it's gone cold, and I push it away.

"Sure, she wants company, but you can't mind if she doesn't make a lot of sense after what happened." He lowers his voice as though he's telling me a secret. "I brought her a mirror this morning so she could clean up, but also because mirrors sometimes trigger memories in amnesiacs. Seeing themselves sometimes helps them remember who they are. Anyway, she looked in the mirror a long, long time and I expect her to say, "Oh yes, now I remember. My name is Sally Smith and I'm from Buffalo, but she doesn't say anything. She just keeps looking and looking. So finally, I say, 'What is it? What are you looking at?' And she turns to me and says, 'That girl looks just like my sister.' It was kind of *Twilight Zone*, but like I said, she's not thinking straight."

"Well, that's a clue. She has a sister. I bet a lot of stuff will come back to her over the next few days. How old would you say she is?"

"Young, probably in her early twenties and really good looking."

I raise my eyebrows and smile. "So, you did a thorough examination?"

Sam blushes. I'm really growing fond of this boy. Not many young men these days have the modesty to blush.

"A doctor has to be observant in a case like this. Everything's a clue, like her teeth for instance. They're perfect. She's had orthodontia and ongoing dental attention so she must come from a family that could provide all that. Oh, and they pipe classical music into sickbay to calm the patients. When the nurse turned it on, she sat up and said, 'Dvorak's cello concerto. That's one of my favorites.'

Anyway, she's not just some random stowaway. She's an educated girl from a family that took good care of her. I don't understand why there aren't helicopters and search boats out looking for her. The captain made inquiries and there isn't so much as a missing persons bulletin."

"I expect someone will come forward to claim her in a few days, but it is odd." I push my chair back from the table and stand up. "Let me know when she's well enough to leave sickbay. I'm not allowed down there family and medical personnel only."

"You won't have to wait long. She hates being a patient. How about if we all meet in the dining room for breakfast tomorrow? But let's make it on the late side, say ten o'clock, after the crowd's had a chance to thin out."

"It's a date, ten o'clock tomorrow. I'll get a table by the window."

Sam shakes his head. "Actually, it would be better if you asked for an inside table with no view. It's going to be awhile before she wants to look at water again."

I nod. "Wish her a speedy recovery from me and tell her that I'm looking forward to making her acquaintance." I give Sam a little nautical salute then wander up to the library to look for a good book.

THE YOUNG WOMAN isn't quite what I was expecting which isn't surprising since I've been picturing a mermaid. She's tanned, with dark curly hair, a slender figure, and large, green eyes. Those eyes are her best feature. She leans on Sam who keeps a protective hand on her arm as he leads her to our table.

I stand to greet her. "How do you do, I'm Jacob Kanter. Sam tells me you're quite the swimmer."

"I'm not that good, in fact, I couldn't have held out much longer. I'd have drowned for sure if you two hadn't rescued me." She tilts her face toward me, and I'm treated to a wan smile that's all moonlight and shadows. No wonder Sam is smitten. "How do you thank someone for saving your life?"

"Oh, it's Sam you need to thank, not me. I just alerted the crew. He's the one who jumped off the ship to haul you in."

"I know." She turns her smile toward him, but this time I detect a hint of starlight. "It's a miracle he wasn't killed in the process. That was a stupid thing to do, Dr. Spitz."

"Well, I hate losing a patient." Sam pulls out a chair and eases her into it before taking a seat beside her.

The girl sags like a rag doll propped against the back of the chair. The poor thing's clearly weaker than she looks. Like me, she's wearing a shirt with the *Aqua Meridian* logo embroidered on the pocket. There's a gold bauble hanging from a chain around her neck. It's engraved with a few words that I can't read. Thinking they may be a clue to her identity, I say, "That's a pretty necklace you're wearing. What does it say?"

She reaches behind her neck, takes it off and hands it to me. "It's nonsense. Sam and I have been trying to figure it out, but it's just gibberish. What do you make of it?"

There are five short lines engraved on a cat's face, or rather half a cat's face. It's been cut along a jagged line like one of those friendship necklaces girls used to exchange. Presumably, someone else has the other half. I hold it up to the light to read the small letters.

> errie &
> leteazer
> derful
> king
> ether

"I can't help you. It doesn't make any sense to me either. You've only got half of each word here."

"Exactly, king is the only real word, and even that one might be wrong." She fastens the chain back around her neck. "It feels like a clue, but I don't know what it means."

I hand her a menu. "Let's get some breakfast into you. We can decipher your necklace later."

She studies the menu, then looks up in alarm. "I don't have any money. I can't pay for anything."

"No one pays for their meals on this ship. Everything's included in the cruise," I reassure her.

"But I didn't pay for the cruise. I'm not a passenger or . . ." Her lovely, young face is contorted by confusion and despair. "Or am I? I don't know."

Sam takes her hand. "All the *Aqua Meridian* passengers are accounted for, so you probably weren't booked on this ship, but for now the captain says you're his guest. You're not to worry about a thing. Order whatever you want. Go wherever you want. As long as you're on board you'll be treated the same as all the other passengers."

"That doesn't sound right. They ought to put me to work swabbing the decks or something."

"You can swab some decks when you're feeling stronger. Right now, you're my patient and I prescribe a cheese omelet with toast and strawberry jam."

I fill her cup with hot coffee from a carafe on the table. "This is the ship's maiden voyage and quite a number of passengers, myself included, received free tickets, so don't feel bad. There are a lot of freeloaders aboard. You're in good company."

She looks at me with interest. "Are you from England?"

"I am, but I've lived in Canada for many years now. Where are you from?" I'm hoping the answer will simply slip out and that we'll have another clue to her identity, but she looks at me with chagrin.

"I don't know. I don't have an English accent, so I must be from the US or Canada. Can you tell from the way I talk? Do you know where I'm from?" She's sincere. She'd really like us to give her a home, to place her on the map.

"Sam, do you have a pen? I'll only need it a moment." He hands me a ballpoint and I write the letter Z on a corner of the menu then show it to the girl. "What's this? What do you call that?"

She looks at me bewildered. "Zee, it's the letter zee. I can still read, thank God."

I click the pen shut and hand it back to Sam. "She's a Yankee. A Canadian would have said zed."

The nameless lady stares at me dumbfounded. "Really? I'm an American? That helps, it really does. Thank you."

"I'm not great with accents," Sam says, "but I'm pretty sure you're not from Texas or the deep south if that helps."

"That narrows it down, but not by much." Tears are glistening in her eyes.

What would it feel like to forget your own name, your home, your family? I'd been heading in that direction myself before this trip. Maybe the cruise will work the same magic on her. She wipes at her eyes with her napkin. "I'm sorry, this is so weird. I remember everything except who I am and where I came from. I want to hit my head against a wall to shake things loose. I mean, I could be anyone. I could be a bank robber, or a murderer and I wouldn't know it. My God, I hope I'm not a criminal."

"You're not a criminal. Don't upset yourself with such ugly thoughts. It's more likely that you're a mermaid. Do you know the story of the little mermaid?" I'm desperate to distract her, to cheer her up a bit.

She shakes her head. "Not really, I've heard of it, but I can't remember how it goes. I guess that's one more thing I've forgotten."

"Well, then, let me tell you." To be honest, I don't remember most of the story either, but I improvise. "Once upon a time there was a beautiful mermaid who lived in the sea. She lived with her father, the King of the Mer-people and she had everything a mermaid could want, except for one thing." *What was the thing?* I search my memory and come up blank. *What would a mermaid want? She falls in love with the prince, but that isn't it.* Then I remember. "Mermaids live a long time, but she'd heard that humans have immortal souls and that's what she yearned for beyond all else." The girl is listening with the upturned face of a small child, so I go on, hoping the story will help her forget everything she can't remember. "Her grandmother tells her to be happy because mermaids live a thousand years while humans rarely live a hundred. But the mermaid refuses to be consoled. She goes to an old mer-witch, a water sorceress with special powers, and she begs her for an immortal soul. The witch laughs at her and says that the only way she can get a human soul is to fall in love with a human who loves her back. 'But,' she cackles, 'mermaids can't live on land and humans can't live in water, so it's never happened, not once since the beginning of time.'"

"So, it's just an unproven hypothesis," the doctor interjects. "No one knows if it would even work."

"Exactly," I agree. "It's an unproven hypothesis that's never been put to the test. But the little mermaid doesn't care because she's seen a young prince sailing on one of his father's pleasure boats and she's already fallen in love with him."

Our patient is looking inward, mulling something over, so I stop the story and wait patiently.

"Love at first sight isn't very realistic, is it?" She sneaks a quick peek at the young doctor. "Do real people ever fall in love that fast?"

"I did." I almost tell her the story of how I met Bess, but then I remember that things are complicated here and bite my tongue.

"So," I go on, "the mermaid dreams that someday the prince will fall in love with her and that they'll spend all eternity together. But years go by, and he never even sees her when she swims to the surface to watch him sailing or swimming in the sea with his royal friends. Then one day while he's out sailing the sky turns dark, a great wind begins to blow, and a storm overturns the prince's boat. The prince is borne away by a wave. No, wait a minute, that's not right." *What the hell happens?* I don't remember, but I soldier on hoping that something will come to me. "He begins to sink to the bottom of the sea where the mermaids live. The little mermaid sees him and quickly takes him in her arms and swims with him to a beautiful island where she lays him gently on the shore. The prince opens his eyes and . . ."

"He's like Snow White. Her kiss wakes him up and they live happily ever after," the girl says, sounding delighted.

"Yes exactly," I agree. "She kisses him and he instantly falls madly in love with her and asks her to marry him."

"Wait a minute," Sam says. "She still can't live on land, and he can't live in the water, so how does that work?"

"It's a magic island. As long as they live on the island the mermaid can walk on land and the prince can breathe in the water. I thought that was obvious." I give Sam a look that says the story's over and no more questions. "And they lived happily ever after."

"Did the mermaid have a name?" the girl asks.

"If she did, I don't remember it. What should we call her? What's your favorite name?"

The girl thinks a moment, and then laughs. "Oh, you mean me. You want me to choose a name for myself."

"You really do need a name." I notice Sam's hand is resting over hers. "Is there some name you particularly like? Maybe a name that feels like it belongs to you?"

I can practically see her running through a list of names and discarding them one after another. The haunted look returns to her eyes and she shakes her head.

"I can't think of any name that feels like it belongs to me. They're all just names. I guess any old name will do for the moment. Ellen? Barbara? Susan? Just pick something. I don't care."

I'd been thinking of names and was going to suggest Clio, Doris, or Melia, names of sea nymphs with venerable histories, but Sam blurts out, "Josephine, it's sort of old fashioned, but it was my grandmother's name and I've always liked it."

"Josephine is a good name," I concede, although I would have preferred something classical. "We could call you Josie, that's kind of cute."

"Yes, Josie or no, not Josie, how about Joanie? I like that one. It feels good."

"OK, then. We'll call you Joanie until you remember your real name." Sam takes her hand and gives it a squeeze. "If that's okay with you, Joanie."

I sense the beginning of a romance and hope it's for the best. Sam is on the rebound and the girl, Joanie, is recovering from exhaustion and whatever trauma she suffered out there on the water. It's not really my concern, but I can't help thinking that this could go badly if the girl suddenly remembers she's married or something of that sort.

I fell in love with Bess the first time that I met her, but our love wasn't blind. We were at university together and shared a lot of friends. We both knew what we were getting, but these two? Well, God protects fools and the very young. I can only pray He'll look after them.

The food gives Joanie strength because when Sam offers to take her back to sickbay, she says she wants to go somewhere livelier where she can see people and not feel like such an invalid. So, after breakfast the two of them go off to one of the lounges and I return to my book.

When we meet for supper later in the evening Joanie is visibly improved and she and Sam make no effort to hide their growing attraction. By the next day Joanie feels well enough to sit by the pool sipping something pink garnished with maraschino cherries on a frilled toothpick, and by the day after that she's been moved to her own cabin, outfitted I'm sure, with an *Aqua Meridian* wardrobe similar to mine.

How many days have I been aboard this ship? I've lost all sense of time, but I suspect Michael must have the police out searching for me by now. I'll owe him an apology when I get back, but won't he be amazed by his old dad? I imagine him telling an officer, "My father seems to have wandered off. The poor thing's feeble and half blind. Treat him gently if you find him. He's not playing with a full deck." Well, he'll sing a different tune once he sees how a little salt air and a good vacation have transformed me.

When I arrive in the dining room there's no one at our table. Sam and Joanie usually arrive ahead of me, so I'm surprised to find myself alone. I flag down a waiter, order a dry martini, and sip it while keeping an eye on the door for my tardy friends. There's no sign of Sam and the mermaid, but I blink my eyes in disbelief as Charles Dawson saunters through the door. The man looks in the peak of health without a sign of whatever ailment took him from the ship. I jump up and wave him to my table.

He smiles broadly and takes a seat beside me. I pat him on the shoulder. "Good to see you again. I was worried. They said you were taken off for a medical emergency."

"Yes, heart problems I'm afraid." He thumps his chest. "They rushed me to hospital, but I'm fine now. It all worked out for the best. The *Aqua Meridian* sent a driver to pick me up and then they bumped me to first class, isn't that something?

"The ship sent someone to bring you back? That's incredible."

"Yes, isn't it? I got a call yesterday morning asking if I was ready to come back on board. I was at my daughter's house by that time, so God knows how they found me, but I said, 'Sure, that would be great.' They sent someone around for me later in the day and here I am."

"So, what's it like in first class? They won't let us peons up there."

"Beyond belief and not arrogant at all. I've already met the loveliest people. Too bad they won't let me show you around."

"Well, I'm happy for you and I'm glad to have you back. How about a game of bridge this evening? Are Jack and Harvey still around?"

Dawson shakes his head and chuckles. "I'm afraid not. They were being escorted off the ship just as I was boarding, and I can tell you they weren't happy. Such language." He emits a few tsks in mock disapproval.

"Why? Do you know what happened?"

"Oh yes, the porter gave me an earful. They got drunk and barged into the first-class dining room waving fistfuls of money around and demanding to be seated whatever it cost. When that didn't work, they tried bribing the maître d who explained this is a cashless cruise, and you can't pay for an upgrade once aboard. Instead of apologizing and backing down, they began shouting and hurling abuse at the other diners. 'You're all a bunch of arrogant assholes. We could buy and sell the lot of you,' that sort of thing. So, the dining staff called security, security called the captain, and the captain pulled their tickets. I don't know where they went next, but I know they're no longer aboard."

"Lucky he didn't make them walk the plank." I fish the olive out of my martini and pop it in my mouth. "Too bad though, now we'll need two new players to make a foursome."

"Well, if we can't play bridge, maybe we can have that chat about your work in Crete." He signals for the waiter. "I'd love your thoughts on the Sumerian influence on Minoan cuneiform."

"Absolutely, that would be a pleasure. How about meeting in the library after dinner?"

He looks a little surprised. "Why not talk right now while we eat?"

I shake my head. "Sorry, but I'm waiting for two young friends who aren't much interested in archaic languages. In fact, here they are now."

Two ebullient young people practically skip through the door. Joanie has recovered her beauty as she's grown stronger, and they make a handsome couple. Heads turn and smile as they make their way through the dining room toward our table.

"You're late," I admonish them, smiling. "What was more interesting than your supper?"

"Lots of things." Sam is grinning, and Joanie is looking at him with an expression of open admiration. She's wearing a black dress with a neckline that shows off her gold necklace. We still haven't deciphered what it says, but she never takes it off. It shines brighter than usual this evening.

Sam is radiant. "The ship's purser called me into his office this afternoon and offered me a job. You're looking at the *Aqua Meridian*'s new chief medical officer."

I'm surprised they'd offer the position to someone so young, but I smile and shake his hand. "Chief medical officer? That's an impressive title. Congratulations."

"He's a member of crew now and gets an officer level cabin in first class with all sorts of perks." Joanie is beaming. "They only had nurses in sickbay before, but they really need a doctor and they could see that Sam was perfect, so they offered him the job."

"When do you start?" I ask. "There must be a lot to get in order before you sign on."

"Yes, but they're taking care of everything." Sam shakes his head in amazement. "They supply uniforms and if I need any books or equipment, they'll supply those too. I can't believe my luck. I'm getting paid to live on a cruise ship."

"That's remarkable. I had no idea you were interested in a life at sea." I give him my most encouraging smile, although I'm confused by this sudden turn of events.

"To be honest, I never thought about it, but when I was offered the job, it was like my whole life just fell into place. I realized that this is exactly what I want to do. It's like being the head of a small hospital. I'll be in charge of everything. It will never be dull or routine. There will always be new ports and new patients and I never have to cook. What could be better?"

"Won't you miss your friends?" I'm concerned he's making an impulsive decision he may regret, although I've never seen anyone so happy.

"There isn't anyone to miss. My parents are gone, and I've never been close to other family. I know a few people at university and the hospital, but no one special, no one who'll really miss me. There was Veronica, but you know how that turned out."

Joanie takes his hand and kisses it. "I'm going to be his family now. We haven't known each other long, but when something's right you know it right away. I guess people do fall in love at first sight."

"I guess so." I hoped my smile doesn't radiate the concern I'm feeling for them. "But . . ." I hesitate, not wanting to cast a shadow over their newfound joy. "Wouldn't it be better to wait until you've recovered from the accident? There's so much you don't know about yourself."

"Of course, it would be better, but it wouldn't make a difference." Joanie is unflappable. The same determination that kept her alive in the water is now focused on this new relationship. "Whoever I am, I'll love this man." She gives Sam's hand an affectionate squeeze then turns to look me in the eye. "All the time I was in the water and for days afterward I felt weird. It wasn't just the amnesia. It was like part of me was missing, literally missing. It was terrifying."

"People hallucinate when they're stressed and suffering sensory deprivation. The brain creates its own reality when there's not enough external stimulation," Sam explains.

"Maybe, but it felt real." Joanie shudders. "I know I was scared and kind of half in and half out of my body. I can't explain it. It was a nightmare. But then this guy showed up and things came back into focus, and I started to feel whole again. Is this making any sense?"

"It sounds like love. You may be made for each other, but I think Dear Abby would advise giving it more time." I'm a complete hypocrite. I asked Bess to marry me on our third date. But would I have proposed if neither of us knew her name or where she was from? Probably, a rose is a rose is a rose. She would have still been Bess and I would have still been head over heels in love with her.

JOANIE HAS JUST been released from sickbay and issued a room of her own, however, from what I can see the cruise line is wasting its money since she's effectively moved in with Sam. Officers' quarters aren't huge, but I understand they're a big step up from a standard passenger cabin. It's got sleeping quarters, a sitting room and a tiny kitchenette with a fridge, an electric kettle, and a microwave oven. It's all very compact, but comfortable, just big enough for a pair of love birds. They want to invite me over to show it off, but of course they can't. First class only on those upper decks, but Joanie is in high housekeeping mode. I hear she's cozied up the place with a pot of yellow hibiscus and a floral tablecloth snagged from a recent luau. I expect she'll be putting up chintz curtains and knitting doilies next. I wonder where she comes from. There must be people trying to find her, and yet the captain claims there hasn't been a word. It doesn't make sense. What would I have done, what wouldn't I have done, if Michael had gone missing?

It's sweet to see the two of them so happy, but we're all ignoring a lot of unanswered questions that could swamp this little love boat. What happens if the ship just dumps her at the next port? I can't believe they'd abandon her without a nickel or a name, but she's over twenty-one, or is she? What's the law is in a case like this? Who's responsible for looking after her? Maybe I can take her home with me. She could sleep in the TV room until she gets things sorted out.

IT'S NINETIES NIGHT on the ship, which is odd since it's only 1993. They're serving dinner in the lounge this evening, so I head up to Seinfeld's, previously known as Groucho's, where a black vocalist is singing a pop song I've heard on the radio. It's not loud and raucous like the music at the seventies party. It's a love song and the black vocalist has a beautiful voice with a warm vibrato that warms my heart. I'd worried about not having anything appropriate to wear, but they've relaxed the dress code. There are women in cocktail dresses studded with rhinestones sitting next to youngsters with torn jeans and pierced noses who look like the hooligans I saw at Queens Quay. It's like being back on shore, anything goes these days. The last time Michael took me to Bardi's for my birthday, they were serving a hundred dollar a plate steak dinners and no one was wearing a jacket. It was all sweaters and jeans as though we were at McDonald's.

Sam is wearing his new white officer's uniform and looks quite dashing. He's sitting in a corner with his arm around Joanie's shoulders. The two of them are beaming like a pair of Cheshire cats. Dawson's sitting beside them nursing a whiskey and looking utterly beatific. Something's afoot.

"Did you order my martini?" I ask, slipping into a vacant chair.

"Better, we ordered champagne." Sam is absolutely glowing, and I wonder if he's about to announce an engagement.

"And what, may I ask, are we celebrating? It must be something spectacular from the look of things. Were you just awarded a Nobel in medicine?"

Before he can answer the waiter arrives with a chilled bottle of Tattinger. We wait while he makes a great show of presenting the bottle, "Compliments of the captain," uncorking it, and pouring a taste for Sam's approval. Once he's taken his bows and departed, Sam lifts his glass. "To the *Aqua Meridian*, the kindest and most generous cruise line on the water."

I lift my glass. "To the *Aqua Meridian*, for whatever it's done to deserve this honor."

"They're going to let me stay on board while I figure things out. I have to share Sam's cabin, but that's what we want anyway, so it's perfect. I love this ship." Joanie takes a sip of the champagne and Sam and I follow suit.

So, I wasn't far off, the lovebirds are going to share a nest. I look around and the entire room seems illuminated by the golden glow emanating from this young couple. As with most cruises, there aren't that many young people aboard, so Sam and Joanie always elicit special smiles and attention. I take another sip of champagne and lean back, breathing a sigh of contentment. This unexpected trip has been a godsend and I feel utterly at peace.

"How much longer does this cruise last? Does anyone know?" I ask Sam.

"Well, it depends on your ticket. Tourist class passengers don't usually stay as long as first-class, but we'll be docking soon. We're coming into port."

The waiter returns with menus, and I open mine, hoping to find a good steak with all the trimmings only to discover that the print is blurred. I move the card back and forth trying to focus, blink and try again. It's no use. I can't read a thing.

"Is there something wrong with these menus? The print seems off," I ask Sam.

"No, they look fine to me," he answers.

"Damn, it's me then. You'll have to excuse me for a minute while I get my glasses." As I stand my knees give way. I catch myself on the back of the chair, straighten up, and hope that no one's noticed, but Sam looks at me concerned. "I guess I haven't got my sea legs yet. Did we just hit a bump?" I try to deflect his anxiety with humor. "Go ahead and start without me. I'll be back in a minute." As I turn, wobbly on legs that don't want to hold my weight, I notice the woman again, the one who looks like Bess. She's staring at me from across the room. I take a step toward her and feel a pain in my hip, take another step, collapse against a table, and crash to the floor in an avalanche of cutlery and china and then the room goes black.

When I finally open my eyes, the world is a blur and I'm strapped to a stretcher carried by two burly porters. They transport me across the deck toward a gang plank that's been lowered to the dock. A group of curious passengers huddles nearby, watching as we go. As they carry me from the ship a familiar face leans toward me. The porters don't stop, but our eyes meet for one fleeting moment. I can't turn to look back, but as they transfer me to a waiting ambulance I can hear her calling, "Jacob!"

Amy
October-December 1973

I DIDN'T CRY or scream or howl as Arcas said good-bye and shut the door. Stupefied, I sat motionless for several minutes then got up, tucked the old paperweight he'd left me into a drawer, then stood staring at the dogwood trees across the street. I could hear my sister calling for help in the distance, in the distance, but I ignored her. For once, I was the one who needed help. Finally, I picked up the phone and dialed Nancy's number. If she refused my call and abandoned me as well, I wasn't sure I'd make it through the day. My hands were shaking but my voice was steady when she answered.

"Nancy, I know you said we shouldn't talk until Tom and Arcas patched things up, but things have changed, and I really need to see you."

To my surprise, she didn't ask a single question or hesitate a moment. She simply said, "Things have changed here too. I guess it's time we talked. Where do you want to meet?" I was so relieved I could have kissed her.

We agreed on Mars, a little dive on College Street where the four of us used to meet for Mars muffins, greasy potatoes, and fried eggs on Sunday mornings. Nancy was already waiting in a small booth when I arrived. As we hugged, I felt the first real wave of grief swell within me. I blinked away the tears and tried to look like someone who wasn't about to make a scene in public.

Nancy looked me over with an expression of alarm. "What's going on? Where's your coat? Hell, where are your clothes? You can't walk around like that."

She was right. I'd run out of my apartment wearing nothing but a T-shirt and a pair of sweatpants. The temperature was barely above freezing, but I hadn't even felt the cold. "I'm OK, but I could use a cup of coffee." I slipped into the booth and realized I was shivering.

Nancy draped her coat around my shoulders and pushed her cup of coffee toward me. "You're not okay. What happened? I've never seen you like this."

I sipped the hot coffee without talking, determined not to cry. Finally, I managed, "Arcas is going back to Greece, and I don't think he's coming back. He's on some sort of secret mission that might get him killed and that's everything I know."

"Wow, when did all this happen?" Nancy took my hand across the table.

"This morning, right before I called you. It came out of nowhere. I was happy, planning a nice Thanksgiving dinner and then . . ." That did it. The dam broke and I heard a loud thin wail echo through the diner. Nancy came and sat beside me with her arms around my shoulders.

"Oh, you poor thing," she cooed. "Don't cry, he'll be fine, and he'll come home. He's crazy about you. Everyone knows how much he loves you. Did he really say he wasn't coming back?"

I shook my head and blew my nose into a paper napkin. "No, but it felt final, like he might die or go to jail for years." Nancy's face twisted with concern as I choked out, "I might never set eyes on him again."

"A secret mission? Really? Our guys don't go on secret missions, that sounds like crazy talk." Nancy shook her head in disbelief.

"That's what he said but if you'd been there you'd believe him. I think it's true." An idea popped into my head that gave me a sliver of hope. "Could Tom talk to Dr. Papandreou? I bet he knows what's going on."

Nancy looked doubtful and I could feel the small swell of optimism collapse inside me. "I can ask, but I don't know what good it would do." She let go of my hand. "If Arcas is really on a secret mission then it's secret, Papandreou wouldn't tell us." She paused. "But honestly, there's something fishy about this story. Arcas stopped working with us a month ago. He hasn't handed out a flyer or put up a notice since he got back from Greece. That's why Tom was so mad. Arcas dropped the ball on a bunch of things he was supposed to do, and now he's risking his life for the cause? I don't get it."

Nancy was a good friend, but she was useless. Her loyalty belonged entirely to Tom and Tom wasn't part of whatever Arcas was involved with. Papandreou might know, but not the students attending rallies and arguing politics in the tavernas. They were pawns. Arcas was a knight. If he'd stepped back from the small efforts being made by expat students in Toronto, it was because he'd been recruited by someone or something bigger and more dangerous. I remembered the dark car careening toward Nancy the night we met and the stories about Greek military police imprisoning, torturing, and even murdering members of the resistance. I pulled Nancy's coat tighter and slumped against the wall. I wanted my sister. I missed her more at that moment than I had in all the time since she'd been gone.

Joanie would have known what to say. Her simple presence, even without a word, would have reassured me, but she was dead, and now Arcas was gone too. This wasn't the way my life was supposed to go. I was one of the Adler twins, pretty, popular, and over-indulged by doting parents. I was supposed to grow old with Joanie delighting in loving husbands, precocious children, fulfilling careers, and long vacations on sunny beaches. What the hell was this misfit of a life? I glared at Nancy, angry that she was not my sister, and that Canada was not my country.

"You poor thing," Nancy continued to coo, oblivious to my irrational anger. "Let's get some breakfast into you, or are you ready for lunch?"

"I'm not hungry."

"Well, I've already ordered, so why don't you just share my muffin and then I'll call Tom to bring his car and drive us home."

I nodded morosely. It wasn't Nancy's fault that my life was shit. I tried to smile, but my face had frozen into a glum scowl. She continued looking at me with kind eyes glistening with sympathetic tears.

"Thanks for the coat. It's really helping."

"Good, do you want more coffee?"

"Sure." There was an awkward silence and then I remembered our earlier conversation. "On the phone you said things were changing with you too. What's going on?"

"Oh, it doesn't seem that important now. It can wait until we've got you sorted out."

"No," I insisted. "I'm OK, what did you want to tell me?"

"It's about that application I sent to UBC."

"UBC, what's that?" I asked. I couldn't recall her applying for anything.

"University of British Columbia, you're such an American. I told you about it. At least I told you that I was applying for a journalism scholarship."

That jogged my memory, but I was still confused. "I thought you were applying for a scholarship here, at the University of Toronto."

"I applied to a bunch of schools, but UBC is the only one that's offered me a free ride: tuition, room and board, a work-study stipend, plus it has the best journalism program. The thing is, it's on the west coast."

"Wow, well, congratulations. Are you going to take it?"

"I don't know. I mean, Tom can't go with me. He has to stay here to finish his degree in Toronto, but when am I going to get an opportunity like this again? The way things are now, taking one class a semester, I'll be ancient by the time I graduate."

A dull throbbing made its way up my neck and settled in my temples. "My losses were really adding up: Joanie, Arcas, and now Nancy. "Do you have an aspirin? I'm getting a headache." While Nancy sifted through her purse looking for some Anacin, I tried to be happy for her, but I only felt abandoned and betrayed. "What did Tom say? Does he think that you should go?"

"He won't tell me. He says it has to be my decision, but he looks miserable, and he's been extra sweet ever since I got the offer. I feel guilty leaving him, but I'd feel worse giving up this chance. What do you think?"

"You might never get another scholarship this good, but you might never meet another guy like Tom either. It's up to you, but I'd think twice before leaving my boyfriend. I would never have left Arcas."

Nancy shook her head. "You're such a damn romantic, standing by your man, but Arcas is gone, and Tom will disappear too as soon as they throw out the colonels. Honestly, hearing about Arcas leaving makes me think. We have to look out for ourselves." She handed me two aspirin then sat back in her chair, a resolute look on her face. "I'm taking that scholarship."

I was too stunned to respond. I swallowed the aspirin with the last sip of coffee and calculated my options. For a moment, I thought of moving to British Columbia so I wouldn't be left in Toronto by myself, but then I'd be thousands of miles away from my parents and finding another job, given my illegal status, wouldn't be easy. So, there I was, living a life with no escape, no friends, no lover, and no sister.

The waitress came by with a cheese omelet, bacon, potatoes, and a large bran muffin. The smell of the food repulsed me. Even the sound of the plate being pushed across the table rattled my nerves. At least Joanie had the decency to be quiet and stop her incessant calls for help. I closed my eyes and held on to the table, afraid I might faint as the restaurant whirled around me.

A familiar voice whispered in my ear. "You're going to be OK, just keep breathing. There you go. Everything's going to be fine. Exhale slowly, that's it. You're strong and your life is going to be wonderful. Trust me. You're not alone." I couldn't tell if the voice was Nancy's or my sister's, but I started to relax.

When I opened my eyes Nancy had her arm around my shoulders. "I've called Tom. He'll be here in ten minutes. I'm so sorry. I shouldn't have dumped my problems on you at a time like this."

"No, that's okay. I'm alright now, but I think I'd like to go home. Could Tom drop me off at my apartment?"

"Of course, he'll take you wherever you want to go, but I have to get to work. We've got an accreditation review coming up next week so it's all hands on deck, but I'll be back by six if you want to come for dinner. It'll just be takeout, but I'd love to have you join us."

"Not today, Nancy, but I'll call tomorrow, and thanks for meeting me on such short notice—and for your coat." I handed the coat back and gave her a hug." You're a good friend and I'll miss you to pieces if you leave."

Tom and I drove back to my apartment in virtual silence. Nancy had told him about Arcas, but what could he say? He mumbled something about being sorry to hear the news and I mumbled something back then turned and looked out the window at shoppers going about their business, each engrossed in their own little dramas and oblivious to mine. I wanted to ask Tom what he knew, but I'd promised Arcas not to tell anyone about his mission, and I'd already said too much.

Tom pulled up in front of my building and I started to open the car door when he cut off the motor and said, "Wait a minute, there's something I need to ask you."

I kept my hand on the door handle, but I turned back, hoping he knew something that would make sense of all this.

"Listen, Arcas lost all interest in our work. He dropped the ball on a couple big events, stopped returning our calls, and wouldn't even meet for drinks. That's why we had that fight, I thought he'd lost all interest in the cause, and now Nancy tells me he's risking his life for the resistance. I don't get it."

I opened the door without saying a word.

"But we've heard that something's about to happen," he continued.

I paused, half in and half out of the car.

"Frankly, I wouldn't think he'd even know about it. I sure wouldn't think he'd be involved. All we've heard are rumors, but now I'm wondering. Are you sure he didn't tell you anything? If he did, I'd really like to know."

My God, this was too much. Tom was pumping *me* for information. "No, he didn't tell me anything. Maybe your friend, Dr. Papandreou knows. Ask him and then tell me." I got out and slammed the door.

The cookbooks were still spread out on my kitchen table when I got back to my apartment. All those recipes, all those happy plans . . . I cleared the table to hide the evidence, poured myself a glass of chardonnay, and called my mother.

"Hi, Mom, listen, I can't do Thanksgiving this year. Arcas had to go back to Greece and I'm just not in the mood. No, I'm fine. He didn't say, some kind of family thing. He doesn't even know if he'll be back. Sure, I'd love to see you, but I'm not cooking. No, please don't bring anything. We'll go out or eat scrambled eggs and toast. Sorry, I'm just not feeling very festive. No, I'm not crying. Maybe I'm coming down with something and I guess I'm kind of shell shocked. Please, stop worrying. I love you too and tell Dad I'm sorry about Thanksgiving."

My parents arrived with a carload of groceries: turkey, sweet potatoes, cranberry sauce, the whole shebang. There was no stopping them. I sat sullenly on the sofa while they diced and spiced, basted and whipped. There was too much food for three people, so we invited Nancy and Tom to join us.

They arrived in good spirits which only annoyed me further. Tom, who'd recently shaved off his beard, turned out to be unexpectedly good looking. Who could have guessed he was hiding a strong jaw line beneath that scraggly beard? I figured he'd spruced himself up as a ploy to keep Nancy in Toronto, but the only ones he was charming were my parents. So, there I was, sitting at a table covered with festive food trying not to barf. I smiled and nodded until nine o'clock when I couldn't fake it any longer.

"Sorry, I don't know why I'm so exhausted, but I need to crash. The party's over and I'm officially throwing you out."

"But it's only nine," my mother protested. She loved parties and came alive in company.

"I know, but I can't stay awake another minute and you're sitting on my bed." This was true since I slept on the sofa when my parents were in town.

Nancy was on her feet in an instant. "No problem, I completely understand. It's been a long day for all of us." She gathered up plates and glasses and carried them to the kitchen. "You've been tired a lot lately. Could you be coming down with something? There's a nasty flu going around."

"Nah, I'm just pooped." I watched as Nancy filled the sink with soapy water and rolled up her sleeves. "Hey, you don't have to do the dishes, you're my guest."

"How about if I wash and you dry?" She tossed me a towel then returned to scraping and stacking. "I wanted a few minutes to talk with you in private anyway."

I turned and saw my parents and Tom still engrossed in an animated discussion of the scandal surrounding Spiro Agnew, the first US vice president of Greek heritage. No one but Nancy seemed to have noticed that I'd thrown them out. "OK, my mom will stay up all night doing them herself if we don't wash them first." I took a dripping platter from Nancy and began drying.

Nancy lowered her voice, although no one in the living room was paying any attention to us. "Tom doesn't know it yet, but I've officially accepted that position at the University of British Columbia. I'll be leaving right after Christmas."

The serving dish nearly slipped from my hands. "Why so soon? Doesn't the program start in September?" *Right after Christmas?* That was only two months away. I saw the silhouette of my sister slipping beneath the waves. Everyone I loved was disappearing.

Nancy handed me another dish. "The program starts in September, but I'm missing a bunch of prerequisites. If I go now, I can make them up then start with everyone else in the fall.

"Leaving Tom is going to be hard, but we're talking about the rest of my life and well . . ." She lowered her voice to a whisper. "I never thought Tom was forever."

The sound of running water merged with the whooshing static inside my head. I was speechless. There were no words, only white noise, and a growing queasiness. I stood frozen for a long minute then my stomach heaved, and I ran for the bathroom.

MY PARENTS STAYED for a week. They asked a few discrete questions about Arcas but didn't push for answers. In fact, they were nothing but solicitous and kind while I was moody, sullen, and uncommunicative. They deserved better, but I couldn't pull it off. Abbott's Printing had given me two days off for Thanksgiving and I'd taken additional vacation days imagining dinners at my favorite restaurants, trips to the theater, and hikes through the park. I'd pictured my parents laughing with Arcas, discussing politics, economics, and his childhood in Greece. Instead, we mostly hung out in my apartment reading, napping, and watching old movies on TV.

Arcas's absence was so sudden and so absolute that it felt unreal. I startled every time the telephone rang and waited for the mail, hoping for a Greek postmark that never appeared. My mother treated me like an invalid. She made me shower, forced me to eat, and took me out for air despite my protests. It wasn't the trip any of us had imagined. Finally, she'd had enough.

As she stared at me over the *Globe and Mail,* I could see the disapproval in her face. It was nearly noon, and I was still in my pajamas. She tried to maintain a pleasant tone, but I knew she was teetering somewhere between sympathy and disgust. "Well, if you don't want to go shopping and you don't want to go out to lunch and you don't want to go to a museum, what do you want to do?"

I turned off the TV and sat up. "Why don't you and Dad go somewhere by yourselves this afternoon? How about Casa Loma? It's this castle some crazy guy built in the middle of Toronto. I've been there a half dozen times, but you'd love it."

"Amy, we came here to be with you. The whole point of the trip was spending time together as a family. Isn't there anything you want to do?"

I did an inventory of all the sites and attractions Toronto had to offer. It was a long list, but none of them appealed to me. "All I want to do is sleep. Maybe I'm coming down with something."

My mother pressed her cheek against my forehead the way she'd done when I was small. "You aren't running a fever, but you certainly haven't been yourself. You should see a doctor. Do you have a doctor here?"

"Not really, there's a family practice near where I work. Mrs. Klein knows a doctor there who'd see me without insurance, but honestly, it's probably just a stomach thing. I'll be fine in a day or two."

My mother raised her eyebrows. "I certainly hope so, but promise me you'll see a doctor if you're not better by next week. We're concerned about you."

She was right. I needed to shape up and stop making other people miserable. I hoisted myself out of the sofa cushions. "Look, I'm standing up. I'm going to get dressed and then I'm taking you to Casa Loma, OK?"

I showed them around the monstrous hundred room mansion some warped megalomaniac had built just before the First World War, and then I heroically attempted lunch in China Town. The won ton soup stayed down, but I couldn't even look at the sweet and sour chicken. The point is, I made an effort. I tried to be pleasant and to salvage our last few days together. They deserved that much from their sole surviving daughter.

By the time they left, I'd put their minds at ease and had begun imagining some sort of post-Arcas life for myself. Tom, on the other hand, was coming apart. His behavior was totally unexpected and out of character. Of the four of us, he'd always been the most self-assured and self- controlled. His passion was politics, not women. He rolled his eyes at couples like me and Arcas who made a public display of their affection. I never expected to find an utterly bereft, half crazed man standing at my door. Maybe I'd misjudged him.

"Tom, it's seven-thirty in the morning. What are you doing here?"

"Nancy says she's leaving in two weeks. You've got to talk to her." He walked past me without an invitation and stood vibrating in my kitchen.

"Are you sure? She told me she wasn't leaving until Christmas." I buttoned my robe then filled the coffee maker with water from the sink.

"She was invited to spend the holidays with family in Alberta, so now she's leaving November first. She says she hasn't had a real vacation in three years." He threw himself into one of my kitchen chairs. His eyes were red and his hair looked like Medusa's. "Why is she doing it? What's the point?"

The coffee machine hissed and gurgled while my stomach roiled. Frankly, I was almost as shocked as he was. "Is there any chance she'll change her mind?"

"Not for me, but maybe if you talk to her. Tell her she can be a journalist in Toronto even without a degree if that's what she really wants."

I poured two cups of coffee and sat down beside Tom. I pushed a cup in his direction. "Here, drink this. It might help you think straight. You look as if you haven't slept." We sat without talking, staring at our coffees, bleary eyed and desolate. Finally, I said, "She doesn't want a job on some neighborhood newspaper, she wants The *Globe and Mail, The New York Times, The Washington Post*. This is her big chance. It's not fair to make her stay. You're going back to Greece and then what will she do?"

"But that's just it. I'm not going back." Tom stood up and paced. "I just got a great job offer here in Toronto. I told her, but it didn't make a difference." He sat down, hugged himself, and rocked in his chair. "She doesn't care."

"You'd give up going back to Greece for Nancy?"

"Not just for Nancy. It's a really good job, not just good money, but an opportunity to do important work. They want me part-time now and full-time when I finish my degree. I love Greece, but who knows when the junta will fall, and I thought I had a life here with Nancy."

We both had tears in our eyes, orphans abandoned by the ones we'd loved and trusted most. Nancy wasn't going to change her mind, and who knew if Arcas was ever coming back.

"She was my first real girlfriend." Tom cradled the cup of coffee against his chest. "I never dated before moving to Toronto. In Greece we hung out in groups, there was never anyone special. Then, as soon as I arrived, I met Nancy. We hit it off right away, even though we didn't have that much in common. She's never traveled outside Ontario, but she had my number from day one." He looked at me with a sad, resigned, half smile. "I thought about moving out west to be with her, but that would mean walking away from my degree and this great job. I can't do that." He sat back in his chair and looked at me with an appraising eye. "What keeps you here? You could go back to the States any time."

"No, I can't. I really can't go back." Tom's eyes widened. "It's a long story, but trust me, I never meant to live here, but I don't mind it anymore. Toronto's incredible and it's starting to feel like home."

WHEN THE NAUSEA and fatigue didn't subside and my period was two months late I made an appointment with the family practice down the street, paying for the visit out of pocket as Mrs. Klein suggested. I already knew that I was pregnant, but I needed to hear it from a doctor. She confirmed my diagnosis. I was due in early July.

That night, alone in bed I howled in terror. I couldn't have a baby, it was impossible. I wouldn't be able to work for months, and then I'd need to pay for childcare. How would I pay for everything, for anything, with no job and no insurance? I couldn't even apply for welfare without risking deportation and arrest. What if I were sent to jail? What if they took my baby?

"Help!" I screamed into the night. "Help! Help!" But Joanie couldn't save me any more than I could rescue her, and Arcas was a million miles away. The little life inside me whispered, "Shh, shh, shh." And I saw her, alive in the water of my womb floating peacefully, alive, not drowning.

I desperately wanted Arcas. I needed to tell him he was going to be a father. I needed to see his face, to know that he was happy. I wanted him to take me to prenatal appointments, to make sure I took my vitamins, to hold my hand when I was scared, and to help hang curtains in the nursery. But you don't always get what you want, not even what you need.

The other person I needed desperately was Joanie. How many years had we played with dolls, imagining our babies growing up together? Now, she'd never be a mother and she'd never know this child, her niece or nephew, and my baby would never know her. This was simply wrong. My life was all off script. Where was the devoted husband, the cozy house, the ecstatic family? Where was Arcas? Where was Joanie?

It was another week before I found the courage to telephone my parents. They were devastated by the news. Apart from the shame and embarrassment they struggled to conceal, there were a million practical objections. I couldn't move back home. I couldn't even cross the border. I didn't have health insurance. My apartment was too small and how could I care for a baby and keep my job? There was nothing they said I hadn't already thought of. I closed my ears to their sensible concerns, terrified but undaunted.

This was Arcas's baby, and we'd be waiting for him when he returned. If he came back, he'd love us both and we'd make a life together. Women through the ages had babies while their partners were at war or working far from home. There was no reason I couldn't do it too. With luck, Arcas would be back before the little one was even born. Without luck . . . my heart sank. Without luck the future looked bleak, and I didn't know how I'd manage.

But I did have luck and it came from an unexpected source. The bright light was Abbott's Printing. The Kleins received my news with good humor and congratulations, then made plans for me to work from home. They promised to send a drafting table and supplies to my apartment so that I could cut and paste while caring for a baby, and then they offered me the chance to earn more money selling on commission on the phone.

Knowing I could support myself put my parents' minds at ease. They began suggesting baby names, they ordered a crib from Simpsons, promised to visit me at Christmas, and to stay two weeks in July. I looked forward to seeing them but held on to the delusion that Arcas would be back and looking after us by then.

Nancy was already gone, and Tom was moping around, miserable without her. Neither of them knew about my pregnancy. I'd have to tell them soon, but I put off the inevitable, hoping for a miracle.

Within days extraordinary news from Greece destroyed that fantasy. Greek students protesting the junta had occupied the Polytechnic in Athens and thousands of people were pouring into the streets supporting them. Fires were being set, bombs were being thrown, military snipers had already killed twenty-four civilians and injured hundreds more. I was sure Arcas was in the middle of the fray, and that he wasn't coming home to hold my hand.

Tom began dropping in to visit unannounced. We'd sit in front of the television, eating takeout and watching news from Greece. As we watched horrific footage of a tank ripping through the Polytechnic gate with students still clinging to its bars, I clutched the necklace that I always wore and prayed to Joanie, as though she were my patron saint, *please keep him safe, please keep him safe.*

A week later it seemed my prayers had been answered. It was a Saturday and Tom and I were going out for lunch when the mailman passed us in the hall. "Amy Adler?" He held out a small pile of envelopes. I saw a Greek stamp and my heart all but stopped. He'd written. He was coming home. I tore the envelope open and unfolded a single sheet of typed print with trembling hands. It wasn't from Arcas.

My Dear Miss Adler,

I am sorry to tell you that your dear friend, Arcas Vasiliou, has died a hero. I cannot give you more details, but he knew he was putting himself in danger and instructed me to write you if he did not survive. He was a brave man who will be remembered as a martyr to a noble cause. He said to tell you that he loved you very much. Please accept my sincere condolences.

May you have a long life,

Someone who wishes you well

I was sure I'd misread it. I tried reading it again, but the letters were spiraling around the page like cut glass in a kaleidoscope. Then one word emerged, pulsing from the page: died, died, died. I ran out the door and gyrated dizzily outside the building not knowing which way to turn until I finally collapsed, holding my belly, and rocking on my knees. Tom wrapped his arms around me asking, "What happened? What's the matter?" I handed him the letter then doubled over again until Tom lifted me up and carried me back inside the building.

He sat beside me on the tattered sofa in the lobby, rubbing my back as I wept uncontrollably. "I'm so sorry, I'm so, so sorry. I can't believe we doubted him. He was the best of us, the only one who really made a difference."

I caught my breath as the convulsive sobs subsided. "What happened? How did he die? That stupid letter doesn't tell us anything."

"I don't know." Tears brimmed in Tom's eyes. "People doing that kind of work keep a low profile and cover their tracks. They don't want their identities exposed."

I picked up the envelope from the floor and turned it over, hoping for a clue, a name, an address, anything. But there was nothing but my typed address and two Greek stamps. I handed the envelope to Tom. "Where's it from? What's the postmark say?"

"Athens."

I nodded, wiping tears from my eyes. "That doesn't tell us much. What do you think happened? Is there anyone who'd know?"

He shook his head. "I'll ask around, but I don't think so. We aren't involved in stuff like that." He held me to his chest and stroked my hair. "We should have a memorial service for him. He's a hero and we should honor him. I'll let Nancy know—unless you want to call her yourself."

I sat up and swallowed hard. It was difficult to talk. "No." Tears crept down my cheeks. "You call her—and tell her I'm pregnant with his baby."

Tom flinched, dropping his hand from my hair as he jerked away from me. "I'm sorry, this is too much. You need your mother. I can't . . . Are you sure?"

I nodded and crossed my hands over my belly. "I've been to the doctor. I'm due in July."

"Do your parents know?"

"Yeah, they'll help me as much as they can, but I can't go back to Rochester."

"Why not? They love you. They'd take care of you."

"I can't go home. Trust me, there's a lot you don't know." I felt as though I'd been knocked down and beaten up, but I managed to stand, find my balance, and make my eyes focus. I looked at Tom. "I'll be okay. I have to be okay for this baby, but right now I'm going upstairs, take two aspirin and lie down."

He stood trembling in front of me, as shaken in his way as I was in mine. "Do you need anything? Is there anything I can do?"

"No, I just want to be alone for a while."

"OK, I'll call later to see how you're doing, and I'll let Nancy know about Arcas . . . and the baby." He kissed the top of my head. "You're going to get through this."

As I leaned into him and closed my eyes, he whispered in my ear, "Don't be afraid. It's a blessing you're carrying Arcas's baby. It means a part of him is still alive."

THE NEXT FEW months were a blur, but Tom never left my side. It wasn't love exactly, but it was safety and comfort. We were both desperate for an intimate human connection and turned to one another. It seemed natural and inevitable, and it solved all my most basic problems. We married in March to the delight of my parents who'd fallen in love with Tom before I did. As the legal wife of a Canadian citizen all the doors previously closed to me swung open. I still couldn't cross the border, but I no longer had to hide in the shadows and my daughter was welcomed into the world by two doting parents.

Part Two

Jacob
July 1993

"WHAT WERE YOU thinking? If you wanted to go on a ferry ride you should have told me. I'd have gone with you. You're in no condition to be wandering around Queen's Quay by yourself. How did you even get down there?"

I want to glare at Michael and say, "How do you think? I took the streetcar," but every bone in my body aches and the diplopia is worse than ever. I turn my head away from the angry blur that is my son and close my eyes. The pillow is cool and soothing against my cheek, and it muffles his exasperated pleas for an explanation. Why did I go down to the lake after all these years? I'd simply wanted a boat, or rather I wanted the freedom and exhilaration that comes from piloting a small boat across a lake in summer. I wanted to feel young again, but now I only feel embarrassed and confused, mostly confused.

It was a mistake saying I'd fallen in a cruise ship's dining room. Apparently, the harbor isn't large enough for a cruise ship and now everyone thinks I'm senile, *non compos mentis, meshuggah*. Maybe I am, but I'm sane enough to understand their indulgent smiles and sidelong glances. Sam should have accompanied me to the hospital. He's the ship's doctor. He could have corroborated my story. I close my eyes. But what if they're right? What if Sam, Joanie, Bess, the ship, all of it, was some sort of hallucination? My God, I hope I didn't tell Michael that I saw his mother. He'd have me locked up in the loony bin for sure. A sharp stabbing sensation jabs me in the groin.

"Michael, call the nurse. I need something for the pain." My voice is so soft I'm not sure he can hear me.

"Of course, is there anything else? Do you want water or juice, another blanket?"

"Would you turn out the light? I'm going to take a little nap."

"OK, I'll be back later, and I'll ask the nurse to give you something for the pain."

The room goes dark, and I relax a bit. "You're a good son."

"Dad, I'm sorry, I didn't mean to lecture you, but you had us worried. We just want to keep you safe."

"The desire for safety stands against every great and noble enterprise," I whisper into the darkness.

He's still there. He's heard me. "Oh, for heaven's sake, which one of your Greek philosophers said that?"

"Tacitus, and he wasn't Greek. He was Roman." I smile, pleased with myself. Maybe I'm not so far gone after all.

"Good night, Dad." I hear Michael chuckling as he shuts the door.

They must have laced my pain medication with sleeping pills because the next time I open my eyes a nurse is fussing with a breakfast tray. Sun is streaming through the window, I need to pee, and my leg hurts like the devil. The nurse looks vaguely familiar, robust, and competent, but I can't quite place her. She puts the tray on the dresser and hands me a urinal, asking if I can manage by myself. This is the ultimate indignity of old age. I take the plastic contraption and glower at her until she leaves the room. I never urinated in front of my wife of forty-five years, and I have no intention of sharing that intimacy with a stranger.

I'm looking for a place to set down the filled urinal when I see another one of those damn brochures on my bedside table. I can't read it without my glasses, but I recognize Bayside Manor's cheery blue and yellow lettering. Now that I've proven myself incompetent to manage a short trip downtown, Michael's more determined than ever to consign me to an old folk's home. I put the urinal on top of the brochure and feel around for my glasses.

The nurse pokes her head back inside. "Ready for your breakfast?"

She looks so familiar, but where have I seen her? "Just some coffee and a newspaper. Do you have newspapers here?"

"We always have copies of the *Globe and Mail* at the nurse's station. I'll nab one for you, but you need to eat something. If you don't like scrambled eggs, I could bring you oatmeal."

She looks so genuinely concerned that I hate to disappoint her. "How about a slice of toast? Would that do?"

"That's a start." She hustles over to my bedside, inspects the urinal with a satisfied nod, then empties it into the toilet. A moment later she has me sitting up with a full breakfast tray laid out in front of me: eggs, bacon, orange slices, toast, and coffee.

"Eat whatever you can manage. I'll have a volunteer stop by with your paper. I must say, I didn't expect to see you again."

I stare at her, feeling embarrassed and confused. Again? Had she been on the boat with me? Had she seen me fall?

"Oh dear, you don't remember, do you?" She fills my coffee cup from a small metal pot. "I helped you up after your fall in that alleyway. I was the one who drove you to the pier. Do you remember now?"

"Yes, of course, of course I remember." So, that's why she looks so familiar. She was the good Samaritan who scraped me off the pavement after I was mugged. "You were very kind. I don't think I thanked you properly."

"Oh, it was no trouble, no trouble at all."

The eggs don't look half bad for hospital food and the coffee is steaming hot. I pick up my fork and take a bite. "They gave me a free ticket on that boat you told me about, the *Aqua Meridian*. It was quite the adventure."

"Was it now?" Isn't that wonderful. I'd love to hear about it when I have more time, but at the moment I have eight patients needing morning meds. Press the call button if you need anything."

I'm pouring myself a second cup of coffee from the little pot when there's a knock at the door. "Come in," I call out as loudly as I can. My voice feels stronger today and I'm pretty sure it carries.

An attractive girl with an astonishing profusion of dark hair appears, pushing a book cart. She's wearing a green pinafore over a plaid shirt, blue jeans, and army boots. The pinafore must be some sort of hospital uniform since it's too large by a mile. She looks both ridiculous and endearing. I can't help but smile. "Have you brought my paper?"

"Yes, and I also have some books from the hospital library if you're interested. Are you a reader?"

"I was definitely a reader at one time, but my eyes aren't what they used to be. Do you have anything with large print?"

She hands me my newspaper then rummages through the stack of books on her cart. "How do you read the newspaper? It has really small print."

"Good question. When I'm at home I use a magnifying glass, but here I'll be sticking mainly to the headlines, which means I'll miss a lot—but I see you don't miss much."

"How about these?" She hauls a couple large print volumes to the top of the pile. "*Texas, Part Two* by James Michener, but we don't have Part One, so probably not." She tosses the book aside and reads the next title, *Lonesome Dove* by Larry McMurtry. "Wow, I didn't know that was a book. I just knew about the film. Did you see it?"

"No, I don't see many movies these days."

"Oh, it's old. It came out when I was just a kid, but if you didn't see the film you might like the book since you won't know how it ends."

She was adorable, a little younger than my grandson, Peter, but without his studied nonchalance. "Maybe I would. What else have you got?"

"This has big print, but it's for kids and, my God, here's a math textbook. How did that get in here?" She's obviously new at her job and unfamiliar with her inventory. I watch her digging through the books like a puppy tearing up a garden. "Wait, here's a large print book by P.D. James. He writes mysteries."

"P.D. James is a woman, Phyllis Dorothy. Which one do you have there? I've read most of her work."

"*The Black Tower*, have you read that one?"

"Probably, but I don't remember it. Let's give that one a try. How do I sign it out?"

"You don't do anything. It's not like a real library. Just leave it on your bedside table when you're discharged, and someone will pick it up. Do you want *Lonesome Dove*, too? You can keep up to three books."

"Just the P.D. James mystery."

She obligingly places the book beside my breakfast tray. As she bends over my bed, I get my first good look at her face.

"Joanie?" It's a ridiculous question. Why would Joanie be pushing a book cart in this hospital, and yet who else could it be?

"No, I'm sorry. My name is Arcadia, Arcadia Savas. I should have introduced myself."

"You look just like another young woman I know. In fact, the resemblance is quite remarkable. What did you say your name was?"

"Arcadia, but everyone just calls me Cady."

"Arcadia? That sounds Greek. I spent a lot of time in Greece when I was young." I continue to stare at her, astounded and unnerved. A moment ago, I was a man in control of his senses and now I'm not sure if I'm awake or asleep, conscious, or hallucinating. I can't take my eyes off her. What is Joanie doing here? Why doesn't she know me?

"Did you?" She plops herself down in the chair reserved for visitors. Apparently, she's planning to stay awhile. "I've been there six times, but the first two times I was so young I don't remember anything. My father's half Greek and he has a ton of family outside Athens. Well, technically he's my stepfather, but I mean he's my dad. He's the only father I've ever known. My real father was killed in Greece before I was born so I never met him."

I feel a chill run through me. Something is completely off, and I can't explain it. "You weren't recently on a cruise ship, were you? The *Aqua Meridian*?"

"No." She laughs. "I've never been on a cruise ship. Why would you ask me that?"

"It's nothing, I'm being silly. You just remind me of someone."

"Why were you in Greece? You sound like you're from England."

"I am. I studied archaeology at the British School in Athens and then I worked with a man named John Pendlebury excavating a Bronze Age site in Knossos."

"Wow, you're an archaeologist?"

"Yes, but I've been retired for a long time. I stopped doing field work years ago. I mostly taught at the University of Toronto."

"U of T? That's where I go to school, but I'm pre-med, all math and science, not much time for the classics."

This naif is going to be a doctor? I'm surprised, but why not? I've often wondered what Bess would have become if she'd been given half a chance. Prime minister, I imagine. My earlier burst of energy is starting to fade, but I defend the old philosophers. "You'll swear the Hippocratic oath one day. You ought to know what Hippocrates had to say. He might surprise you." My lids have drooped shut, but I suspect she's rolling her eyes. This generation doesn't read anything older than yesterday's newspaper. "Thank you for stopping by, but I need a little nap right now."

"Sure, do you want me to bring you a paper every morning while you're here?"

"Yes, thank you, Joanie. That would be very nice."

I FEEL A slight tickle along my arm and awake from a dream of grilling sardines on the pink sands of Crete's Elaphonisi Beach and flirting with a pretty girl named Bess. I'm disoriented for a moment until the smell of alcohol and bleach brings me back to Toronto and St. Michael's Hospital.

"Mr. Kanter, are you awake?" A nurse I haven't seen before is shaking my arm.

"I'm uh, yes, of course, do you need something? I must have dozed off for a minute."

"Sorry to disturb you, but we have to get you down to Neurology. Dr. Mendoza is expecting you."

I don't know this woman but she's very efficient. She has me tucked into a wheelchair, covered with a skimpy hospital blanket, and handed off to an orderly before I'm fully awake. The man pushes me toward the elevator at such a clip that I'm afraid of adding whiplash to my other injuries.

"Wait, slow down. Why am I going to neurology? I broke my hip not my head. What's this about?"

The man is what the Canadians call a visible minority, probably Jamaican judging from his accent. He's affable enough, but as clueless as I am. "I don't know, you better ask the doctor."

"You bet I'll ask him. They can't cart me around like a sack of potatoes without telling me where I'm going." The elevator door opens, and I find myself in a basement hallway. It's cold and one of the fluorescent lights is flickering.

"Dr. Mendoza is a lady doctor. She's very nice," the orderly reassures me.

"Mendoza? That's a pretty name."

"She's a pretty doctor." The orderly winks at me, then leaves me shivering outside the doctor's office.

I'm not wearing a watch and there's no clock in the corridor, but it feels as though I've been sitting here for ages. A woman in a white uniform emerges from the elevator and disappears behind a frosted glass door before I can ask the time. An orderly pushes an empty gurney past my chair, but pretends not to see me. Apart from their brief appearances I'm completely alone, cold, hungry, and increasingly irritable. From the pain in my groin, I'd guess it's half past time for my medication. I'd wheel myself back to my room if I knew where it was.

I'm wondering if I can turn myself in to the Lost and Found when the office door opens and an attractive brunette pops out, smiling apologetically. "I'm so sorry to leave you waiting. We had a bit of an emergency, and I couldn't get away. Jacob Kanter, right?" She pretends to shake my hand while actually checking the ID band on my wrist, very smooth. "Can I get you anything, a glass of water, some ginger ale?"

What I'd like is my pain medication, but that's not her fault so I'm polite. "No, but if you have something hot, tea or coffee, I'd like that."

"I do have coffee. In fact, I'll join you if you don't mind. How do you take it?"

The warm coffee is a comfort, and I can feel my ruffled feathers settle down. She pulls up a chair and sits beside me instead of taking her rightful place behind a large, imposing desk. She smiles so sweetly as she gathers up her pen and a manila folder that I feel myself relax. Even the pain in my groin seems to diminish slightly.

She does a quick perusal through the file then looks up with an expression of concern. "Mr. Kanter, I see that you fell and broke your hip. Can you tell me exactly how that happened?"

The last few days are pretty hazy, but I try to reconstruct events as best I can. "I was at dinner with some friends when I realized I'd forgotten my glasses. When I got up to get them the boat must have lurched because I lost my balance and went down. The next thing I know I'm in the hospital with a broken hip."

"My notes say you were on a cruise ship, is that right?" She leans forward encouraging me to tell her more.

I'm a bit wary, but nod in the affirmative.

"How interesting, what else do you remember?" A small silver cross sways on a chain between her breasts. She looks too young to be a doctor, but everyone looks too young for everything these days.

I'm not sure that I can trust her, but her sweet smile persuades me to go on. "It was called the *Aqua Meridian*. At first, I thought it was just a harbor ferry, but it was bigger than it looked."

"Really? How was that?"

"It was quite remarkable really. They were giving away free tickets to celebrate the ship's maiden voyage and they gave me one. I thought we'd just sail around the harbor and be back in time for supper, but it turned out to be a longer trip than I'd expected. It really took me by surprise."

"My goodness, how long were you gone?" She's still smiling her sweet smile, but I begin to suspect a trap.

"I'm not sure, time is different when you're at sea. I'm afraid I lost count."

"What did you do for clothes? You didn't have a suitcase with you."

"No, I didn't." My memory's distressingly disordered with disconcerting gaps, but I tell her what I remember, knowing how odd it sounds. "The cabin was equipped with complimentary shirts and toiletries, even a bathing suit." I stop myself midsentence. Is that what happened? Did the ship really provide clothes for its passengers? That doesn't sound right. My story dissolves as I tell it. Nothing holds water. I become agitated and start choking on my coffee.

Dr. Mendoza hands me a tissue. "Are you all right Dr. Kanter? Do you need a minute to catch your breath?"

I wipe spittle from my mouth while she gathers up some papers. I was an idiot for talking to her. She's going to use it all against me.

She opens a spiral notebook. "Are you up to answering a few more questions?"

"Not about the ship, I don't want to talk about that anymore."

"No, we're done with that. Now I'm going to say three words. I want you to remember them then say them back to me. Are you ready?" She pauses then over-articulates, "Lemon, baseball, antelope."

This is insulting, but I repeat, "Lemon, baseball, antelope," like a trained parrot.

"Very good, perfect. Now I'm going to ask you to draw the hands on three clocks."

She hands me a clipboard holding a paper showing three clock faces without hands. "Can you make the first clock say six o'clock?"

I've never been a great artist and it's hard to read the small numbers even with my glasses, but I manage well enough. I complete the other two clocks according to instructions and hand them back.

"Very good." She looks pleased and I assume I've aced the test. "Now, do you remember the three words I gave you earlier? Can you repeat them back to me?"

My mind's a blank. What happened to those words? I try to stay calm, but I begin to panic. "Orange, I think. I think one of them was orange and—and I can't remember the others. The clock thing knocked them out of my head."

"Oh, that's perfectly all right, don't worry about it. You got them all the first time. Now can you tell me the name of the prime minister?"

When she's done peppering me with inane questions, she sends me off to another department for a CT scan without a break for lunch. I could kiss the orderly who finally arrives to take me back upstairs, starving, desperate for my medications and a nap.

I'M SITTING IN bed, sipping beef broth from a cup when Michael arrives carrying a large potted plant. A toy bird perched on a stick above the foliage is clearly intended to cheer me up.

"Thank you, very thoughtful. Put it on the windowsill, would you?"

"Absolutely, how's your day been? They tell me you've been sleeping quite a lot." It's odd that he's here in the middle of the afternoon when he should be at the office. A moment later his wife, Ellen, bustles in with a box from Harbord Bakery. I know it's full of rugalach even without looking. They're both smiling broadly and talking much too loudly. The hairs on the back of my neck prickle.

"What are you doing here at this hour? Who's minding the store?"

"Michael just decided to take a couple hours off. There was nothing so urgent that he couldn't take some time to see his father." Ellen makes a show of opening the bakery box and offering me a small crescent of sweet pastry filled with raisins and chopped nuts.

I brush the box aside. "Thank you, but I'm drinking this right now. I'll have one after dinner. Michael, what's going on? Why are you both here?"

Michael is standing at the end of the bed shifting from one foot to the other. I recognize the expression on his face. It's the one he wore when explaining a bad mark or why he couldn't make it home by curfew as a boy. He's about to tell a lie.

"Well, we got some wonderful news today. There's an opening at Bayside Manor. One of their premiere rooms just opened up."

"You mean that someone died." I stare at him with the fiercest expression I can muster.

"Well, I suppose that's possible. We don't know why it became available, but we need to decide right away. I'd hate for you to lose a chance like this. Honestly, the place is spectacular. The residents all love it there. They even have their own Rehab Department so you could go there directly from St. Mike's and get therapy right where you live."

"That's not where I live."

"But you *could* live there, we could have you moved in within the week. You could go right from the hospital to your new apartment. You wouldn't even need to pack. We'd take care of all that for you. It's a corner unit with a bedroom and a nice sitting area with a little table where you can eat if you don't want to go down to the dining room."

Was that supposed to be an enticement? I'd never go home again, and strangers would pack all my things. How did this boy survive as a lawyer if he couldn't make a better argument than that? I wasn't buying it. "We've discussed this before, Michael. I'm not ready for one of those places. They have an excellent rehab department right here at St. Mike's, then when I'm ready I'll go back to my own place. Moving would be too upsetting right now. Thank you, but I'm just not interested."

"Oh, for heaven's sake, be honest with him. Tell him the truth." Ellen plunks her oversized frame into a small metal chair and takes a large bite of one of the rugalach.

I cast a stony eye at my son. "So, tell me, what's the truth? What don't you want me to know?"

Michael comes around to the side of the bed and takes my hand. "Dad, we got a call today from one of your doctors, a neurologist. She did some tests and, I'm sorry, Dad, but she says you're showing signs of dementia."

"Don't be ridiculous, my memory's fine. Maybe I didn't remember all the words on her little test, but ask me about the Palace at Phaestos. Ask me about the Dorian invasion."

"You're right, Dad. Dr. Mendoza said your memory's pretty good, but your judgement's impaired and well, you're hallucinating. There's no brain tumor, so she thinks it's some sort of dementia. Whatever it is, she says your hallucinations are so vivid you can't tell what's real from what you're imagining. It's just not safe for you to live alone anymore."

I feel as though I've been cast overboard with a pocket full of rocks. "I see." I swallow hard. So, this is how it ends, eating with strangers in a home for the terminally old. I muster the strength to protest. "But I've been doing fine. I haven't had any problems. My bills are paid. I eat my vegetables."

"Dad, you're in the hospital because you got confused and wandered off to the lake by yourself. You had no business getting on a boat with your poor balance and double vision."

"I didn't wander off. I went down to the lake on business. It was a perfectly rational decision. A man can go down to the harbor if he wants to."

"Not at your age, not in your condition. You should have called me first. We could have gone together. Oh, don't look at me like that. I'm not punishing you. I love you and want to protect you."

Michael keeps hold of my hand while I silently say good-bye to my sofa and chairs, my papers and books, the framed family photos, the moth-eaten rug from Morocco, and the familiar view of the courtyard.

"You're still not being honest. Tell him the whole thing. It will be worse if he's not prepared." Ellen's a trained therapist and very big on honesty, but I'm not sure I can take any more. She stops gobbling down cookies and stares at me with a forlorn expression as though I'm already the dearly departed.

"Not now, Ellen, give him a break. Can't it wait?" Michael lets go of my hand and runs his fingers through his thinning hair. His eyelids sag and his jowls wobble. It suddenly strikes me that my son is old.

"Tell him, Michael. You can't wait until he moves in."

"OK, OK, just give me a minute." Michael pours some water from the carafe on my tray into an empty glass and slugs it down like a shot of vodka. "OK, Dad, there's more. That very nice apartment at Bayside Manor is in the Security Unit. There'll be an alarm on the door so you can't wander off again. There's a call button you can use when you want to go out, but you'll be under supervision. I'm sorry, Dad, but it's for your own good."

Amy
July 1993

I WAS IN an especially good mood when the phone rang with bad news. For the first time, my recurring nightmare had surprised me with a happy ending. It had started out as usual, with me swimming against the waves, struggling to reach the lights from a passing ship. But this time, a lifeboat suddenly appeared, and kind hands reached out, hauling me to safety. That had never happened before, and I'd awakened happy and refreshed.

I put down the phone and braced myself, waiting for the distant calls for help that always followed bad news or an unexpected trauma. Even after twenty years I still heard Joanie's voice whenever I was stressed. But today, nothing, only the sound of my own heart pounding as I picked up the receiver again and dialed my husband. "I just got a call from the ER at St. Mike's. They think Nick has a broken leg. They're waiting for a report from radiology. I'm heading over there right now."

"Wait a minute, what happened?"

"He fell off his bike. Thank God, he was wearing a helmet or this would have been a lot worse. Apparently, he and a friend were racing down Brimley Road out by Scarborough Bluffs."

"Scarborough Bluffs? That's suicide, what was he thinking?"

"He wasn't thinking. He's seventeen, but that's a good question. You can ask him when we get to the hospital. I'll be there in about twenty minutes."

I was breathing heavily as though I'd been the one careening down that steep hill instead of my idiot son. It had only been a few months since we'd rushed him go the ER with a concussion. I shook my head, muttering, "Boys." Cady had never caused us this kind of grief. I paused again, listening. Not a word from Joanie. No calls for help, no heart rending screams, just unending silence. The absence of her familiar voice made me strangely uneasy as I shut down the printer, grabbed my purse, and headed out the door.

TOM WAS STANDING at the information desk talking to the receptionist as I burst through the doors of the Emergency Department. "Has he been admitted? Can we see him?" I leaned into Tom, taking comfort in the heat radiating from his sweaty body. He must have run the six blocks from his office on Jarvis Street.

"Relax, he'll be okay." Tom handed me a visitor's pass and guided me toward an unmarked door that clicked open to admit us to a brightly lit room full of small, curtained partitions. We made our way to a central counter where six or seven people in white uniforms were talking on phones, filling out forms, and comforting distraught relatives. Tom caught the attention of an elderly woman working at a computer. "I'm looking for Nick Savas. Can you tell me where he is?"

She pointed to a curtained stall to the left. "Number 8A, but I need you to fill out some forms." I hurried off, leaving Tom to deal with the clerk.

Nick was sitting up on a small cot, holding an ice pack to his left arm. An ugly purple bruise ran from his chin to the corner of his eye.

"Oh, you poor thing, look at you."

Nick flinched and pulled away as I went to embrace him.

"Don't, Mom, you'll hurt me. They think my leg's broken. I may need surgery."

"Oh no, are you in much pain? Can I get you anything?"

"They already gave me *Tylenol*. I'm not supposed to eat or take anything else until they decide what to do with me."

I bent down and gave him a very gentle kiss on his forehead. "You know you could have broken your fool neck. No one in their right mind races down that hill."

"Bikers do it all the time and nothing ever happens."

Tom pulled back the curtain and stepped inside the cubicle. "Well, something happened today. They tell me you've shattered your left tibia in two places. They're going to have to put in a plate to hold it together."

Nick slumped against the pillow. "How long does that take to heal? Will I be able to play hockey in the fall?"

"It's too soon to tell, but you're going to have to stop being such a daredevil. This is our third trip to the ER this year."

I was standing by his bed with a brave smile on my face, but my insides were churning. "When are they scheduling the surgery?"

"Today." Tom shot me a commiserating glance. "Someone will be coming in to start prepping him any minute now." He put a hand on Nick's shoulder. "Don't worry, they're going to take good care of you. We'll be here the whole time."

Of course we'd stay, but I had a huge print order to get out by morning. It was for my biggest account, and I couldn't afford to screw it up. I'd started a desktop publishing business when the Kleins retired, but it was still a start-up and every job mattered.

I smoothed Nick's hair out of his face. "I'll be back in a minute. I need to make a call." I gave him a peck on the forehead and set out to find a payphone.

"Cady, your brother's at St. Mike's with a broken leg. No, this time he fell off his bike. Don't worry, he'll be okay if I don't kill him, but he needs surgery. They need to put a plate in his leg to hold it together. No, please don't come down. I need you at home to help with a print run that has to be done tonight. You know how to use the new LaserWriter, don't you?"

IT WAS TEN o'clock by the time we returned to the cottage we'd bought the year Cady was three and Nick was still a bulge in my belly. I threw my purse onto a chair and opened the refrigerator. I hadn't had anything but waiting room coffee and powdered creamer since lunch and I was starving.

"Come in here," Tom called from the dining room. "You've got to see this."

The dining room was set with our best company China. A warm quiche, a large salad, and a bowl of strawberries waited on the sideboard. "I love that child. Where is she?" I started up the stairs to look for Cady, but Tom stopped me.

"She's not here. She left this note:

> *Dear Mom and Dad,*
>   *Sorry you had such a tough day. Hope this helps. I'm staying with Jackson tonight. See you in the morning. Cady X*
>   *PS The print run's finished and stacked in boxes in the office. XX*
>   *PPS. Aunt Nancy called, but she's on assignment so you can't call her back. She said she'll call again tomorrow. XXX*

I filled a plate with a large slice of quiche and a heaping mound of salad. "I wonder what Nancy wanted. She never calls when she's on the road. Do you think she's OK?"

"She's fine. She's the Bionic Woman. Remember when she was covering that conference in Baghdad and an Iranian general crashed his plane in front of her hotel? It practically landed on her head, but she walked away without a scratch. She's indestructible."

"I hope you're right. I've had enough drama for one day." I was suddenly so overcome with exhaustion I could barely lift my fork. Nick would need a lot of attention over the next few weeks, and I had a load of print jobs to get out. "I didn't need this right now. How am I supposed to juggle everything?"

"Eat your quiche and stop worrying."

I dutifully took a bite of the cheese pie. It was delicious. I gobbled down the rest and took a second slice. "I guess we won't be going to the cottage. Do you think we can get our deposit back?"

"Don't be such a pessimist. I'm betting we still go, as long as Nick doesn't break anything else in the meantime."

"Maybe." A disquieting memory suddenly came back to me. "Tom, you know how I hear my sister's voice whenever I'm stressed or something bad happens?"

"Uh huh, I bet your sister really chimed in this afternoon when Nick broke his leg."

I shook her head. "No, she didn't. I was plenty upset, but I didn't hear a thing, no cries for help, nothing."

"Well, that's good, isn't it? Maybe you're finally letting go of the past. It's about time."

"I know, but it feels odd, kind of lonely. I know it's weird, but I missed hearing her voice."

"Sweetie, it's been over twenty years. Do you really want to relive that nightmare forever?"

"No, of course not, but I've gotten used to hearing her, like she's still out there somewhere."

"Well, you may miss her, but I'm sure your therapist will be thrilled to know that Joanie's finally moving on."

"I guess so, but twin bonds are really strong. Even after all this time I feel her presence, like we're still connected." I wondered if I should tell him about the dream, but decided to keep that to myself. "I'm sorry, I'm being silly." I took one more bite then put down my fork. "It's been a long day. Would you mind clearing up? I'm going to bed."

"Sure, should I wake you if Nancy calls?" Tom finished his quiche and polished off the bite I'd left on my plate.

"I don't think she'll call tonight. She's in Greece covering the elections and it's what, five in the morning over there?"

Tom looked at his watch, "Five-thirty. You're right. She won't call until tomorrow. Sweet dreams, Sweetheart."

"Sweet dreams."

BY MID-MORNING I'D loaded five thousand advertising circulars into my minivan and dropped them off at The Shoe Box's corporate office and was mentally designing a new brochure for Maple Leaf Rags, a trendy dress shop catering to tourists. As I started down the steps to my basement office the flashing red light on the kitchen answering machine caught my eye. Worried that something had happened to Nick, I raced into the kitchen and pushed the button for new messages.

Hi, it's Nancy. It looks like I missed you again. I'm in Athens at the Plaka Hotel, but don't call because I'm never in my room. Everything's fine, but something incredibly weird's happened. I'll try you again later.

Love to Nick and Cady. Oh, and tell Tom that it looks like Papandreou has a lock on the election.

What could be so important that Nancy would call from Greece? I headed back to the basement and turned on my computer. Before it even had time to boot up there was another call, this time from my daughter.

"Cady, I'm glad you called. I wanted to thank you for dinner last night. It was so sweet of you to have a meal waiting for us."

"I figured you'd be hungry. The quiche came out really well, didn't it? Listen, I saw Nick this morning. He's on the same ward where I volunteer. He's OK, but his leg hurts more than he's letting on."

"I'll talk to his doctor when I visit later. Does he need anything from home?"

"Yeah, he wants food. He says they aren't feeding him enough. If there's any quiche left, he'd like some of that."

"I'll wrap it up and bring it to him. Are you still at the hospital?"

"No, I'm back at Jackson's place, studying for a chem exam. I'll probably stay here again tonight, so don't wait dinner for me."

"You're not planning on moving in with him, are you? You're way too young for that sort of commitment."

"No, Mom, I'm not moving in with him. But honestly, you weren't much older than I am when you met my father. Oh, that reminds me. I met an English guy at the hospital who's a retired archaeologist. You should show him that old paperweight Dad gave you before he died. I bet he'd know what it really is."

"Really? I'd love to know what all those symbols mean, but it seems rude to impose on someone in the hospital."

"I don't think he'd mind. He's a sweetheart and he knows ancient Greek so he might be able to read it for you. Honestly, you might never get another chance like this."

"It's tempting, let me think about it. I'd sure like to know how old that relic is." I opened the top drawer to my desk and removed a small white box. "When are you coming home? I owe you a big hug for running off that print job and making dinner for us."

"I'll see you tomorrow. Oh, and bring socks. He says they keep the air conditioning too low and his feet are freezing."

"OK, see you tomorrow and thanks for telling me about that archaeologist."

I lifted the lid from the box to reveal the ceramic disc, safe on its bed of cotton. I touched it to my lips, glad that Tom wasn't home to catch me in this small infidelity. Tom was a wonderful husband and I loved him dearly, but Arcas . . . I closed my eyes and allowed myself to travel back in time to Kosmos Bakery. I'd been a troubled girl, frightened and heartsick, exiled from family and friends until Arcas had taken me in his arms and made me believe life could be good again.

But in the end, it wasn't Arcas who saved me, it was Tom. What had begun as a marriage of convenience, a ticket to legal status and insurance, had grown into the marriage I'd always dreamed of. We were a perfect match, better suited to each other than either of us would have been to our lost loves. A photo taken on Kavouri Beach near Athens glowed on my computer. The scene, my screen saver, was as blue and white as the Greek flag: blue sky, blue water, white sand, and my family smiling in the foreground. My life had turned out just fine despite everything. Those years with Arcas felt as distant as the time when the disc in my hand was new.

IT WAS THREE o'clock by the time I got to the hospital. I've never been a fan of hospitals, but I'd spent more than my share of time at this one. Both my children were born there, and my daredevil son had brought me back time and again with numerous breaks and bruises. I stepped off the elevator, grateful to be visiting Orthopedics and not the ICU. As I bustled past closed doors and navigated around a nurse's cart I felt a pang of guilt, wondering if Nick had inherited his impulsive streak from me.

I remembered myself at twenty-one, a bottle of tequila in one hand, the throttle of a speeding motorboat in the other, laughing wildly at a boy who was standing on his seat shouting some nonsense to the wind. Leaning against the wall, I closed my eyes and breathed a prayer that Nick would never have to pay as steep a price as I'd paid for youthful recklessness.

When I entered Nick's room, Big Bird and Elmo were having a serious discussion about how to cross the street. Embarrassed, Nick switched off the television.

"A little old for *Sesame Street*, aren't we?" I raised my eyebrows in mock disapproval.

"At least Big Bird isn't pregnant by the ghost of her best friend's husband. That's what's on the other channel."

"Is Big Bird a girl? I always thought Big Bird was a boy."

"I don't know. It's hard to tell what's going on under all those feathers. Did you bring food? Lunch was a sandwich with like one slice of turkey and half a lettuce leaf. I'm absolutely famished."

As Nick polished off the quiche, I arranged two pair of socks, a box of cookies, and a copy of *Snow Crash* by Neal Stephenson on his bedside table. "You didn't ask for the book, but it was on your desk, so I figured you'd want it."

"Thanks, it's got to be better than *Sesame Street*." He pushed his empty plate aside. "How long do I have to stay here? This place sucks."

"I don't know. The nurse doesn't have discharge orders yet, and I haven't been able to reach the doctor, so we just wait." Nick tapped the cast on his broken leg.

"I didn't think it would hurt this much. The physical therapist almost killed me this morning. The whole summer's shot."

I patted his shoulder. "You'll be out of here in a few more days and Dad thinks we'll still make it to the lake in August—although you can't go swimming. You'll have to stay high and dry on the beach with me this year."

"It could be worse. I met an old guy in PT today who's going to have to live in a nursing home for the rest of his life."

"Oh, how sad. The poor man."

"No kidding. Can you imagine having to live in a nursing home? He taught archaeology and traveled all over the world. I bet he never expected to end up like that."

"No one does. He sounds like the man Cady was telling me about. She wants me to show him that old piece of pottery her dad gave me."

"That's a good idea. Did you bring it with you?"

"No, I'm not sure I should ask him. Doesn't it seem rude to ask a favor like that from someone who's in the hospital?"

"Nope, he'd love talking with you. I think it would cheer him up, but you'd better hurry before they ship him out to that nursing home."

I started toying with the little cat pendant I still wore around my neck, a sign that I was feeling anxious. All this talk about the relic was bringing back old memories of Arcas and my sister. "Really? You don't think he'd mind?"

"He's just down the hall. One of the nurses will give you his room number."

"I've always wondered about that old curiosity. It would be nice to know what it really is and where it came from."

"Tell the nurse you're looking for Jacob. I don't know his last name, but he has an English accent. They'll know who you mean."

After arranging Nick's books, putting his snacks within easy reach, fluffing his pillow, and kissing him good-bye, I went off in search of the archaeologist. A clerk directed me to a room halfway down the hall. Through the open door I saw an elderly man holding a book he didn't seem to be reading. I watched as he rubbed his eyes, looked away, put the book down on his chest, picked it up, turned a page, then put it down again. His white hair was thinning and his boney hands trembled. He seemed so frail, but archaeologists had to be tough. They spent months in remote locations excavating ruins buried under layers of dirt and hot, unforgiving rock. He must have been strong and athletic once. A potted plant sitting on the windowsill made me think he couldn't be as lonely as Nick imagined. Someone had brought him a gift.

"If you need something, just come in, I'm awake." He turned and looked directly at me through thick lenses that magnified his eyes making him look like a blue-eyed owl.

I blushed, embarrassed that he'd caught me staring. "I'm sorry, I just wanted to ask a favor. I could come back later if this isn't a good time."

"Ah, then you're not a nurse."

I hesitated, not sure if that was an invitation or an accusation.

"Come in. What can I do for you?" He put the book on his bedside table and gestured for me to come closer. "I'm afraid I can't see you very well if you stand so far away."

I took several steps into the room.

He removed his glasses then put them back on as though he was having trouble focusing his eyes. "Cady?"

"No, my name is Amy. Cady's my daughter and my son is Nick. They thought that I should talk to you."

"Yes, I know them, very nice youngsters. You should be proud of them. Too bad about Nick's leg, but young people bounce back. He'll be healed up in no time." He pointed to the chair beside his bed. "Please, have a seat, my eyes aren't what they used to be. I'm afraid you're a bit blurry over there."

"Oh, of course." As I moved closer, I felt him studying me intently.

"You look just like your daughter. The resemblance is remarkable."

"I know, my mother always says that if my sister were still alive we'd be triplets."

His eyes softened behind his thick lenses. "You've lost a sister. I'm so sorry. She was a twin sister?"

I nodded. "It was a long time ago. Cady looks just like her, and like me, of course."

The man rubbed his eyes and looked at me again. "It's so odd. I don't know what to think. When Cady first arrived I was sure I knew her. I thought she was on the ship where I had my accident, but maybe . . . No, it couldn't have been you either." He paused, shook his head, and looked away. "They say my mind is going and I'm afraid they may be right." His smile took on a wistful quality.

We sat in an uncomfortable silence while I searched for something comforting to say. "I see someone's brought you a plant. It's quite attractive. Do you know what kind it is?"

"It's from my son and his wife. My wife would have known what it is. She was the gardener in the family, but I don't know one plant from another. It could be poison ivy for all I know."

I laughed. "I'm like that too. My sister loved flowers and she'd always help my father with the garden, but I'd go deaf and run away if he asked me to weed or water anything."

"You were a naughty girl. Now, what can I help you with, young lady?"

"My kids tell me that you're an archaeologist and that you worked in Greece when you were younger."

The old gentleman shifted in bed, trying to sit up. "That's true. I worked in Crete under Pendlebury back in the thirties. I'm so old that I can remember meeting Sir Arthur Evans, can you imagine that?" I shook my head in feigned amazement. The name meant nothing to me, I assumed Evans was a famous archaeologist, but I'd never heard of him.

"Of course, it won't be long before some young fellow is digging up my bones and dragging them back to his lab."

I stared at the old man's wasted body and was tempted to agree with him, but I just responded with a weak smile. "My kids say you speak ancient Greek and can decipher old Greek writing."

"Well, there are a lot of languages that might be called ancient Greek. Which one did you have in mind?"

"I have no idea. That's what I was hoping you could tell me. Cady's father gave me an old relic. It might be a coin or some sort of decoration, we don't really know. It has writing on it that's definitely not modern Greek. My husband speaks Greek fluently and it's Greek to him."

"Old Greek coins are quite common. A lot of them were minted, so it's probably not valuable, but they're all fascinating. Each city-state produced its own coins with its own symbols. The image should tell us where and when it was minted. What do you see on yours?"

"There are a lot of little pictures. It's like some sort of hieroglyphics that go around in a spiral, only it's nothing like the Egyptian hieroglyphics you see in books."

"I see. And how big is this coin?" I didn't like the way he raised his eyebrows and smirked slightly as though I'd just told a bad joke.

"It's big for a coin, five or six inches in diameter. Maybe it isn't even a coin. We don't know what it is. Cady's dad used it for a paperweight."

"Well, I think I know what it is, but bring it in anyway. I'd be happy to look at it."

"Thank you. I'll bring it tomorrow when I come to visit Nick. What do you think it is?"

"I can't say for sure, but frankly it sounds like a copy of the Phaistos Disc. No one knows how to read those images. Those hieroglyphs predate Linnear A and we still haven't broken that code. All we know is that Linear A is the alphabet of a pre-Hellenic Minoan language and that the Phaistos Disc is even older than that. I spent the larger part of my career trying to figure it out."

"How would my boyfriend have a copy of something like that?"

"He'd have bought it from the gift shop at the Heraklion Archaeological Museum. They're popular souvenirs. I have one on my desk at home."

My heart struck a resounding clang, the sound of a heavy coin hitting a metal trash can. My great treasure, Arcas's last token of love and devotion was a gift shop souvenir. The dark clouds quickly receded, but I knew Dr. Kanter could see the disappointment in my face.

"I'm so sorry to disappoint you. I didn't realize how much it meant to you. I could be wrong. I'd have to actually see it to be sure."

"That's very nice of you. I'll bring it tomorrow when I visit Nick. Thank you for your time and please don't feel bad if it's just a replica of something. I was just surprised."

"Of course. Say hello to Cady and tell her I'm enjoying the book she gave me."

He wasn't enjoying the book, but he was a kind man. "I'll be sure to tell her." I paused at the door. "Are you sure you want to see me tomorrow? It seems pointless if it's just some hunk of clay made in China for the tourist market."

The old man did a sort of double take and leaned toward me. "Did you say clay? When you called it a coin I assumed it was made of metal. The replicas are almost always made of a cheap alloy finished to look like bronze." His eyes took on an unexpected gleam. I'd apparently piqued his curiosity. "What color is the clay? Was it fired? Is it glazed?"

As many times as I'd looked at the old paperweight, I didn't know the answers to his questions. "It's just clay colored, kind of a yellowy clay. It's not shiny so I don't think it's glazed. Of course, I don't know much about clay. I'm a printer not a potter."

"Please, promise you'll come back tomorrow. I want to see whatever it is you've got there. It might be something interesting—especially to a printer."

I brightened a bit. Maybe it would turn out to be something after all. "OK then, see you tomorrow."

"Please close the door on your way out. I'm going to take a nap and thank you for stopping by. I'm looking forward to tomorrow."

AT SUPPER THAT evening I wanted to tell Tom about my encounter with the archaeologist, but he was in a nasty mood, preoccupied with troubles at the office. His company had just released an analysis of the economic impact of new, non-traditional immigrants moving north of the city. It showed these immigrants fueling the economy by starting new businesses at a higher rate than existing residents and filling many essential bottom-rung jobs other Canadians didn't want. The results should have been good news, but the study had enraged the Heritage Front, a white supremacist group opposed to immigration. Tattooed skinheads and swastika toting neo-Nazis had turned up with signs and banners while counter protesters had shown up with their own placards. The whole thing had erupted into a brawl outside Tom's office. He'd run a gauntlet of catcalls and threats when he'd left the building and his nerves were on edge.

I bided my time, listening patiently to the tale of his harrowing day while he finished his dinner. He was talking fast, agitated by his encounter with the Fascists. "That group is awful. They hate immigrants, Jews, blacks, Asians, pretty much everyone. I didn't approve the ARA ransacking one of their houses, but someone needs to stand up to them."

"The ARA?" I didn't recognize the name.

"Anti-Racist Action something. They're a fringy group that really pushes the boundaries. I think they were involved in the riot outside my building. You must have read about them. They were in the paper last month for tearing up a house in the east end."

I shook my head.

"It belonged to a National Front guy who was broadcasting hate speech from the basement." Tom tore into a last bloody bite of steak as though he was sinking his teeth into one of the racists. "You should have seen their signs. They aren't ashamed to spew actual Nazi slogans in the original German. God, I hate fascists."

I refilled Tom's glass with the last of the Cabernet. "You and Arcas did your bit to fight them back in the day. You have nothing to be ashamed of on that account. The colonels are gone, and Papandreou is prime minister of Greece. It's not your fault if new fascists just keep coming."

"I handed out leaflets. It's guys like Arcas who were the real heroes." He took a sip of the wine and reached for my hand. "It's ironic that my happiness is the result of Arcas's sacrifice. You'd have never looked at me if Arcas hadn't died."

I squeezed his hand. "But things worked out for us, didn't they? We have great kids, good jobs, a nice house. Oh, and I met a retired archaeologist who's going to tell us about that old relic Arcas left me."

"Where in the world did you meet an archaeologist?"

"At the hospital, just down the hall from Nick. He's offered to look at it tomorrow."

I stood up and began to clear the table. "I almost hate to share it with him. It's the only thing I have from that chapter of my life. It's always been kind of sacred to me. You don't mind, do you?" I kissed Tom on top of his head on my way to the kitchen.

"No, of course not, we all have our memories, which reminds me, Nancy called again. She left another message that she really needs to talk with you."

Jacob
July 1993

SO, IT'S COME to this, I'm an old man shivering beneath a thin blanket on a narrow bed waiting to be shipped out to a home for the feeble minded. What time is it anyway? The large clock on the wall seems to say 1:45, but that can't be right, or is it? Who knows? My eyes are bad, and time's gotten slippery lately. I used to be able to count on days and hours to behave themselves, to line up in an orderly queue and wait their turn, but now? The only thing I know for sure is that I'm cold and that my hip is killing me.

How did I wind up in Canada anyway, so far from Alwoodley and the Humber, another wandering Jew cast out on a foreign shore? My parents must have been just as surprised to find themselves in Great Britain. Thirty years after emigrating from Odessa, my mother, may her memory be a blessing, could barely speak English. Yulia Kanter was a sturdy soul with a kind heart and an unwavering devotion to her family, and here I am, an old man still yearning for the comfort of her arms.

There, you see, time's slipped again and I'm ten years old waiting for her to take a honey cake from the oven. I fidget in my chair, fingering the slick silk of the hand embroidered tablecloth, hoping she doesn't see the soup I've dribbled on the fringes. Time means nothing. I can still smell the garlic she hung around my neck to prevent colds in winter and the thread she made me bite while sewing a button on my shirt to ward off the *malakh ha-movet*.

Bess nearly wet herself when she heard that one, the bit with the thread. Her parents were enlightened Jews from Germany who'd cast off old superstitions even before they arrived in London a generation before my folks fled the Odessa pogroms of 1881. The memory of my mother hanging garlic around my neck makes me laugh out loud. The sound echoes eerily in the empty room and makes my fractured hip bone ache.

"My God, I've become a sentimental old fool. Bess would give me what for if she caught me wallowing in such nostalgic muck. I need hot tea and my medication. Where's that call button they claim will bring a nurse? For God's sake, they've pinned it to my pillow. They really do believe I've lost my marbles.

If Bess were alive, she'd never put up with this. She'd be sitting right there in that chair beside the bed reading something by Gabrielle Garcia Marquez and stopping every few minutes to share a passage with me. She'd make sure I had something to drink and that the nurses were looking after me. Where is she now? That's what I want to know. Well, I'll have the answer soon enough. How much longer can I cling to this leaky old skiff of a body? That woman on the ship was so like Bess, and she seemed to know me. I wonder if she had Bess's childlike laugh. One more thing I'll never know.

Everything's *farmished*, I'm in a constant state of confusion. Cady, her mother, and Joanie are all mixed up in my head to the point where I don't know what to think. Considering my mental state, it was a surprise when that Savas woman showed up yesterday asking for a consultation. I didn't think anyone would want my opinion about anything anymore, although I'm still remarkably clear about the distant past. Its recent memories that fade like dreams.

Wouldn't it be funny if she actually had something, a second Phaistos disc? I smile, imagining a groundbreaking article in the *American Journal of Archaelogy*. "Ancient professor uncovers new Rosetta Stone." What do you think, Bess? Do you think the Archaeological Institute of America would give me a gold medal? Of course, I've been out of the game for a while, but a second Phaistos Disc, imagine.

"Mr. Kanter, do you need something? You pressed the call button." It's the nice nurse who came to my rescue the day that huckster took my money. I'm delighted to see she's back on duty.

"Yes, thank you, I could use another blanket and a pain pill, and maybe a cup of tea." I try to roll over to face her, but a sharp, shooting pain stops me cold. "Damn. How long do these hip fractures take to heal, anyway?" I try not to sound too plaintive, but I can hear a faint, childish whine in my voice.

She's immediately at my side pretending to take my pulse, but I think she only means to hold my hand. I pull away, appalled to be seen as so pathetic. "Would you mind getting that blanket? This room is freezing, or am I already in the morgue?"

"Good heavens, no. You're quite alive, but I'm afraid they keep the air conditioning too low for many of our patients. I'll be right back with a hot cup of tea and some Demerol."

"And a blanket," I remind her.

She leaves as quickly as she arrived and I'm left staring at the ceiling wondering if my old friend, Izzy is still alive. How old would he be now? A year older than me, that's how old. He was a nice boy, good at maths, but we lost touch after grade school even though he lived just a few blocks away. I can't think why we stopped being friends. It's strange how people appear and disappear. I hope he had a nice life. There's a knock at the door to my room, even though it's standing wide open.

"Come in, don't be shy."

"Hi, it's me, Amy Savas. I brought you that clay disc we were talking about. Is this a good time?"

Before I can answer, the nurse bustles back into the room. "Here you go, Mr. Kanter." I feel the weight of a proper blanket settling over me and my shivering legs relax. "Now, let's see if we can get this bed cranked up a bit so you can drink your tea."

"I see you're busy now. I'll come back another time. Sorry to disturb you." The woman is about to leave with her small treasure.

"No, please don't go. I want to look at whatever you've got there. Can you wait just a minute?"

The nurse empties a large pill from a frilled paper cup into my hand then notices my guest. "You're Nick and Cady's mother, aren't you? I didn't know you were friends with Dr. Kanter."

"We're not really friends, in fact we just met. My daughter introduced us because he's an archaeologist and I have an artifact I'd like him to look at."

She hands me a glass of water and waits while I swallow the tablet. "I'll leave you to your discussion then. It's so nice the two of you have finally met. I know you have a lot to discuss." She gives me a beatific smile, pats me on the leg, and leaves the room.

The warm blanket and hot tea work their magic even before the Demerol kicks in. The young woman, I've already forgotten her name, is still standing just inside the door. It's hard to make out details with my bad eyes, but she resembles both Joanie and her daughter from this distance. They all have the same compact shape and disorderly black hair. I blink and squint, trying to focus, trying not to see Joanie in this woman. Was Joanie even real? The question gives me a cold shiver.

"Come in, I've been hoping to see you again. Let's see what you've brought me."

"If you're sure I'm not disturbing you."

"No, not at all, you're a welcome distraction. I'm glad you're here." Now that she's closer, I can see she's older than Joanie, but those eyes, the resemblance is remarkable. She hands me a small white box, the sort of thing you'd get from a jeweler. I take off the lid and try to make my eyes focus. If it's supposed to be a copy of the Phaistos Disc it's an obvious fake. The real disc is just shy of six inches in diameter and marked with a spiral of hieroglyphic shapes on either side. This thing can't be more than five inches across and it's a tad thicker than the original.

I struggle to make out the markings on the piece. I know the symbols on the Phaistos Disc as well as I know my own name, but my eyes are useless. I run my finger over the surface, trying to read the piece like Braille. Even with my bad eyes I can tell it's not a copy, it's something else. There aren't enough spirals, and the central medallions are like nothing I've ever seen before. I move my glasses up and down on the bridge of my nose, trying to make out the images pressed into the clay. This one could be the plumed head, this one the eagle, and those might be the beehive and the ship, but these others are completely unfamiliar. It's all a bit of a blur although I recognize the diagonal lines separating groups of images. Similar lines on the Phaistos Disc have always fascinated me. Are they some sort of archaic punctuation? Symbols in their own rite? Are the glyphs between the lines meant to be read as a single words or as full sentences?

"What do you see? Do you know what it is?" The young woman is hovering over me, attentive and expectant.

"I told you this might be of particular interest to a printer."

"Yes, I was wondering what you meant by that."

"Well, if I'm correct, this is one of the first examples of printing ever created in the world. It precedes Gutenburg by thirty-five hundred years. Look closely and tell me if you see the same glyphs repeated at intervals, like this one here that looks like a little boat."

She bends over the disc and examines it closely with her excellent young eyes. "Yes, it's kind of sidewise, but it does look like a boat. I see one here and here and two more here."

"Exactly. Those boats weren't carved into the clay the way someone would write on a clay tablet with a stylus. They were printed. A Bronze Age Minoan carved a set of movable symbols and used them to stamp or print this disc. It's extraordinary, isn't it? The art of printing was invented four thousand years ago and then was lost again for eons."

My mind is racing, and my heart is beating too fast for someone my age, but this is remarkable. If this is real, it's the only other example of late Bronze Age Minoan writing apart from the Phaistos Disc. It might even hold the clue to its translation. I try to keep my voice steady as I look up at the woman standing expectantly by my bedside. "Where did you say you got this?"

"From an old boyfriend, my daughter's father actually, he gave it to me just before he went back to Greece."

"And where did he get it?"

"His father brought it back from Crete a long time ago. I don't know if he found it or bought it as a souvenir. Arcas just used it as a paperweight."

My palsied hands are trembling so badly that I'm afraid I'll drop the piece, shattering a four-thousand-year-old relic on the floor of a twentieth century hospital. I place it back in its cotton nest and replace the lid. "So, your boyfriend's father wasn't from Crete. Was he there on holiday?"

"No, he was just there for the summer working as a cook. He went back to his village in Arcadia after that and raised sheep and made cheese for the rest of his life. That's pretty much everything I know."

"Could he have been working around a place called Phaistos? Does that name ring a bell?"

"I'm sorry. Arcas just said Crete. He was working for some Italian professors if that helps."

It does. The penny drops. "And this would have been, when?"

"In the fifties, I don't know when exactly, but Arcas was old enough to remember his father being away, so maybe the late fifties. Do you know what this thing is?"

She continues talking, but I can barely hear her. I'm back in Crete at a small cafe on Chandakos Street sipping Turkish coffee with Bess who's polishing off a cream-filled bougatsa. The sky is that impossible blue you only see along the Mediterranean. We have the day off so, once we've finished our small repast, we hold hands and stroll down Heraklion's old stone streets gawking at Ottoman mosques, Venetian fountains, and the dome of a Greek Orthodox church. Our walk ends at the port where small fishing boats cast off into the sea and we can just make out the silhouette of the Rocca a Mare Fortress protecting a thin peninsula to the east.

It's Arpil of 1935 and we're in Crete working with Pendlebury to excavate the ruins at Knossos. Most of our time is spent classifying shards of Minoan pottery, but we have ample time off to explore the island. The Phaistos site, just thirty-five miles to the south, has been abandoned since Luigi Pernier left in 1929, but Bess and I have been there numerous times, poking around, imagining what we'd do if we had the resources to complete the project. I imagine coming back one day and making my name uncovering its treasures. I'm in love with Phaistos. It's as remarkable as Knossos, nearly as large and, of course, it's the place where the mysterious Phaistos Disc was discovered. Like many diggers of my generation, I'm convinced that other examples of the strange hieroglyphics must be buried in the ruins. A second disc or tablet is the holy grail we're all searching for. Without more examples we'll never solve the riddle inscribed on that old clay disc.

I never did get back to Phaistos, but Doro Levi, an Italian Jew, excavated the site with a team from the Italian School in the fifties. I'd have given anything to join them, but I was teaching in Toronto by that time and well, I missed my chance. By the time I showed up with a group of Canadian students the work was finished. We were little more than tourists gawking at the excavation of the ancient temple, but this woman's boyfriend's father was there in the fifties, working at the site with Levi and his team. He'd probably noticed a curious engraved rock, picked it up, and brought it home as a souvenir for his young son. Security wasn't as stringent in those days. Even so, it would have been a crime. He must have known he was compromising his employer's work and appropriating an ancient treasure for himself. Do I tell her that her boyfriend's father was a thief?

"Dr. Kanter, are you alright?" I feel a small hand on my shoulder and see the woman staring at me, a concerned expression on her face.

"Please, forgive me, I'm alright. The pain in my hip sometimes gets the better of me, but the spasm has passed." I start to refresh my cup of tea, but my hands are shaking. I put down the cup. "What were you saying?"

"I just wanted your opinion. Do you know what this thing is? Can you read what it says?"

"Oh, my dear, don't I wish that I could read it. That would be the dream of a lifetime. It seems to be an example of the earliest known Minoan writing that no one has deciphered yet. We don't even know if these symbols are true hieroglyphics or if they represent the sounds and syllables of a pre-Hellenic language. I can't say for sure, it would take a team of experts to authenticate, but if I'm right, it would be the second example of late Bronze Age Minoan writing, ever found."

"Wow." She steps away from the small box, apparently impressed by what I've told her.

"How would Arcas have a thing like that?"

"That's what I was wondering. The only other example is inside a bullet proof case in The Museum of Archaeology in Heraklion." It's an effort to keep my voice steady. My heart's pumping faster than can possibly be good for a man my age, and I'm hiding my trembling hands beneath the bedcovers. I need to show this relic to someone at the university, but the new department chair doesn't know me from Adam. Who might still remember me? What strings can I still pull? MacComber? No, he resigned and moved to Florida. Tinsley? Dead. Grunberger? Senile and living with his daughter. What about my students? My God, it's been almost twenty years and I've lost touch with everyone.

"Forgive me, I've forgotten your name."

"Amy."

"Yes, Amy, this could be an important find. I can't authenticate it by myself. It will take a team of experts to tell us what we have here. Would you trust me to show it to some of my old colleagues?" It's vanity, but I want to be the one to bring this marvel to the attention of the world. If I live long enough, I could even work on the translation. What an achievement at the end of a long, but undistinguished career, the Kanter Disc, just think of it.

"I don't know." I can see the wheels in her head turn. "If it's real, I assume it would be quite valuable. Forgive me, but we don't really know each other." There's a long pause while I hold my breath as she weighs her options. "How about this, once you feel better, you can call your department and make the arrangements, and then we'll take it there together. Would that be alright?"

I nod. She's quite correct. She doesn't know me. I have no intention of stealing from her, but she has no way of knowing that. The university doesn't have the budget to purchase such a thing, but the Royal Ontario Museum might. Of course, if all she wants is money, she'd do better selling to some billionaire who'd just throw it in a drawer with his other baubles. The thought gives me the shivers.

My mind is suddenly clear. The excitement has deadened the pain in my leg, and I'm determined to see this through to the end. "You do understand that the piece is of no value, it's just a lump of old clay, until it's authenticated." A few moments ago I was ready to give up the ghost, but now I'm alive with anticipation. I turn to her with my most ingratiating smile. "It will need a champion, someone who believes in its potential, to present it to the world. I'm only asking to be that advocate. I completely understand your reticence. Of course, we can go together."

"I'll look forward to it then, just as soon as you're back on your feet." She's smiling as she tucks the jewelry box into her large handbag, but I'm afraid she's humoring me, that she'll simply walk away and disappear with that precious relic.

"Wait, before you go, I'll need photographs of the disc, both front and back, taken against a plain background. Do you have a camera?"

She smiles at me as though I'm simple minded. "I'm a printer. I work with commercial photographers all the time, and I do some photography myself. I can get a set of prints to you in a day or two. Will you still be here?"

"I honestly don't know." It's the truth. I have no idea where I'll be two days from now. "You'd better jot down your contact information so I can find you if I'm transferred to another facility." She hastily writes down her phone number and disappears into the corridor.

The sound of her heels clicking down the hall is audible for a moment and then fades into the general cacophony of a hospital at work in the late afternoon. I lay in bed, listening to the squeal of wheeled carts, the murmur of a distant television, the beeps, and thrums of medical machines with a smile on my lips. It's all music to my ears. I cling to the shred of paper in my hand as though it's my ticket back to a world I'd almost forgotten. Doors open in my mind and possibilities present themselves. Articles appear in respected journals under my name. I'm on a stage lecturing to an audience of my peers. I almost feel like the man I was on the *Aqua Meridian*. I feel that good.

Michael doesn't show up until long after they've cleared away my dinner dishes and given me my evening meds. Despite the late hour and my flagging energy I am still riding a wave of ebullient joy. I can't wait to share my good fortune with my son, although he's in one of his moods and it's hard to get his attention.

"Michael, something happened today that's quite remarkable, almost unbelievable." He's just arrived, but he's already pacing and checking his watch as though it's time to go. "Sit down, for heaven's sake. You need to hear this." He takes a seat, but his feet continue tapping beneath his chair. His agitation is contagious, and I lose my train of thought. "Michael, what in the world? What's going on? You look as if you're about to jump out of your skin."

"It's Peter. He went and got himself arrested. He's spending the night in jail because they can't schedule a bail bond hearing until tomorrow."

I'm dumbfounded by the news. It's not possible. Peter's never been in any sort of trouble. "I don't believe it. The boy's never done anything out of line."

"Oh, believe it. He turned up at a white supremacist rally with a group from the Anti- Racist Action Committee and beaned some Nazi with a wooden pole."

Ah, now, this makes sense. I brighten considerably. "Did he kill him?"

Michael presses his lips together so tightly that they disappear altogether as he glares at me with bulging eyes. He looks like an oversized carp. "This isn't funny. The man needed stitches and he's pressing charges. Peter says it was an accident, but who knows?"

"Well, I'm proud of him. If there'd been more Peter's back in the thirties we might have avoided the Holocaust."

"I doubt it. More likely he'd have been the first one thrown into the furnace. What was he thinking?"

"Michael, stop that, he was doing the right thing. You have to nip Fascists in the bud. You can't give them an inch."

"Of course, you're right. I am proud of him. He's got more guts than I do, but this could cost him his scholarship. I was really enjoying not paying his tuition." He leans forward and puts his head in his hands. "His mother was on the phone sobbing to her sister when I left the house. I've never seen her so torn up."

"Tell her not to worry. He'll be fine. It's good to be passionate and idealistic when you're young. In fact, if I were younger, I'd be out there with him."

Michael stands up and paces again. "Don't be ridiculous. You're not interested in anything that's happened since Alexander the Great conquered Thebes."

Is that what my son thinks of me? I'm surprised. I've always imagined myself a man of the world, someone interested in the events of the day. "Not true. You should have seen me during the war. No one accused me of being a dusty academic when I was fishing Mountbatten's men out of the drink."

He runs his fingers along his balding pate, and I take an odd satisfaction in knowing that I have a better head of hair than my middle-aged son. He shakes his head. "Sorry, Dad. I didn't come here to dump on you. You're right. Peter will be fine. You'll be fine. We'll all be fine as soon as we get things sorted out. Now, what were you starting to tell me?"

I struggle to pull myself to an upright position, but an awful pain runs down my leg and I collapse back into my pillow, but my excitement must be evident because I finally have Michael's full attention. I grin at him, anticipating his amazement. "You know the Phaistos Disc? I have a copy of it on my desk at home. You used to play with it when you were little." He nods, but I can see that he's already losing interest. "It's one of the great archaeological mysteries. I've spent years of my life, many of us have spent years of our lives, trying to decipher it, but without more examples it's impossible. We've always needed more and then today, well, you won't believe this, a woman shows up with what I'm almost certain is a second disc from the same site, a disc that was stolen from Doro Levi's dig forty some years ago."

Michael stares at me, mouth agape, utterly flabbergasted. It's satisfying to see that he's grasped the magnitude of the news. "The woman is going to bring me professional photographs of this new disc so I can present them to my old department, although I expect the ROM will be in a better position to purchase such a thing. Early Minoan artifacts don't just walk into your hospital room every day, now do they? Can you believe my luck?" Michael is still staring at me with bulgy fisheyes. "Well, what do you think? Amazing, isn't it?"

"Oh, Dad." He comes to my bedside and takes my hand. I think he's congratulating me, but then I see tears in his eyes. "This is too much. How much can I take in one day?"

"What? What do you mean? It's wonderful news."

He pats my hand in an utterly patronizing way. "Sure, Dad, it's wonderful news, but would you do me a favor? Please, don't call anyone at the university for a while. Maybe we should do a little research first, make sure this disc's the real deal. Can you promise me that?"

He thinks I'm daft. Well, it *is* hard to believe, but I'm not an idiot. I spent fifty years studying late Bronze Age artifacts and I know a genuine article when I see it. I remove my hand and glare at him. "No, Michael, I'm sorry, but this is too important. The disc may have shown up in an unorthodox way, but I believe in it. A disc like that could be another Rosetta Stone. It could unlock mysteries surrounding Bronze Age culture." He opens his mouth to protest. "Don't try to talk me out of this. I am going to alert my colleagues. It would be irresponsible not to."

He closes his eyes and takes a deep breath. I can see he's deeply troubled, but his misgivings aren't going to deter me from what I have to do. "Go home, Michael. Look after Peter and your wife. Get some sleep, bail your son out of jail, and stop by again in a day or two. Don't worry about me. I promise I won't bother you about the disc again."

"So, you won't call anyone at the university?" He opens his eyes and looks at me with a hopeful expression.

"No, I said I won't bother *you* again. I'm afraid I can't promise more than that."

He shakes his head and sighs. "Oh, Dad," he mumbles. "Oh, Dad, I'm so sorry."

Amy
July 1993

AS SOON AS I got home, I took the box from my purse and put it back in the desk where it's lived for the past twenty odd years. I was suddenly afraid of it. What if the professor was right and the disc was as important as he said? Of course, it was more likely that he was delusional, but what if? What if indeed? I half expected whirling emanations, awakened spirits, and ancient spells to begin seeping through the drawer. The whole thing creeped me out. I couldn't wait for Tom to get home from work so I could talk with someone sensible and grounded.

I had work to do, but I couldn't concentrate on layouts and copy edits, so I went into the laundry room and sorted sheets and towels. Still feeling unfocused and overwrought, I cleaned out the refrigerator. The remnants of an old casserole, some slimy greens, and a half-eaten apple went into the trash. I was about to discard an open bottle of Chardonnay, well past its prime, when I had second thoughts and poured it into a water glass instead. I was sitting at the kitchen table drinking awful wine and listening to *All Things Considered* when I heard Tom come through the door.

He picked up the pile of mail I'd dropped on the kitchen counter then came and sat beside me at the table. "So, how's Nick? Any idea when he'll be discharged?"

I took a swig of the wine and made a face. "They're only keeping him a few more days, but he'll need months of therapy. With luck he'll be in good shape by hockey season."

"Poor kid, there goes his summer. I don't know what he's going to do with himself until the fall."

"He's bummed out, but he'll be OK, and we can still spend August at the cottage. I have him signed up for out-patient therapy in Kingston."

"Good work." He tore open an envelope containing an advertisement for replacement windows and threw it in the trash. "So, how'd it go with the professor? What did he say about your relic? Does he think it's real?"

"Oh, yeah, he thinks it's real all right. In fact, he thinks it's the second Rosetta Stone. He wants me to photograph it and then, after he shows the photos to some other archaeologists, I'm supposed to go to the university with him to let them examine it in person. It needs to be authenticated before we can sell our house and move to a mansion in Rosedale."

"A mansion in Rosedale? Well, then, we're set for life." Tom was grinning as though I'd just told a good one.

"No, seriously, that's what he said. Well, he didn't mention mansions, but he did think it was valuable. The question is whether he's in his right mind. I mean Arcas used the thing as a paperweight. If it's that extraordinary, wouldn't someone have noticed it before now?"

"Maybe not, we never thought it was anything but an old curiosity. If he's right, that was some going away gift Arcas left you. What are you going to do with it?"

"Wait and see. Part of me thinks there might be something to it, but another part is saying, 'Don't be a schmuck. The old guy's demented.'" I got up and poured the rest of the wine down the sink. "What do you think?"

"I'd give him the photographs. If he's off his rocker, it doesn't cost us anything, and if he's not, things could get very interesting."

"OK, I'll set up the lights and take a few shots later tonight. But the poor man's so frail he could be in a nursing home before the film gets back from the lab."

Two hours later I was in the basement snapping photos of the disc against a black velvet cloth that would have made a bent fork look like a museum piece. I was thinking of framing a couple of the prints even if the thing turned out to be a hoax when the phone rang.

A moment later Tom called down the stairs, "Amy, it's Nancy, she's calling from Greece."

I glanced at my watch. It was just passed seven in Toronto, so it was two in the morning in Athens. I ran up the stairs and grabbed the phone from Tom's hand. "What's wrong, Nancy? Are you alright? Why are you calling in the middle of the night?"

"I'm fine, I just couldn't sleep, and I figured this was a good time to reach you."

I relaxed a bit as I stretched the cord over to the kitchen table and sat down while Tom hovered behind my chair. "It's good to hear your voice, but what's up? This call must be costing you a fortune."

"It is, but something really weird happened a couple days ago and you need to know about it." There was a long pause. I heard her swallow and then she said, "I've seen Arcas."

"What?" I covered the mouthpiece on the phone and whispered to Tom, "She says she's seen Arcas." He rolled his eyes, but I was worried. Nancy wasn't the type to see ghosts. Was she tripping on something? Was she having some sort of break down? "Oh, sweetie, that's not possible. You must have seen someone who looked like him. I know how that can happen. For years after Arcas died

I imagined that I saw him everywhere: on busses, in cafes, walking into shops. Your mind plays games with you like that. Being in Greece must have triggered a lot of old memories and—"

"No, Amy," she said. "He turned up at a political rally I was covering for the paper. You should have seen his face when he realized who I was. He tried running away, but there was a crowd, and he couldn't push through fast enough, so I caught up with him. He's been living on his family farm all these years."

Tears pricked my eyes, but I didn't know if they were tears of joy, or sorrow or rage. I literally couldn't talk. I handed the phone to Tom who listened with a clenched jaw. He didn't have much to say either. We were both in shock.

"Why? Why would he do a thing like that?" he asked. There were a few mumbled comments punctuated by long silences as he listened to Nancy's story. "That's no excuse . . . the bastard . . . serves him right . . . what about the note? Unbelievable . . . what did you tell him? OK, we'll talk when you get back. Thanks for letting us know."

"No, let me have the phone." I grabbed the phone and asked the one question that really mattered. "Did you tell him about Cady? Does he know he has a daughter?"

Nancy hesitated a moment. "I told him you had two kids, twenty-one and seventeen. I didn't say that Cady was his, but I'm sure he did the math."

"Damn." I didn't mean to swear at my old friend, but I was enraged. "No, no, Nancy, I'm sorry. I'm not mad at you, it's just that . . . oh my God. I could kill him. I think I could actually kill him."

Nancy tried to calm me, but what could she say? We'd taught Cady to idolize her heroic, martyred father, and now this. It was too awful. I hung up the phone and stood staring at the wall barely able to contain my rage.

For once, I was glad that Cady was staying with her boyfriend. I couldn't lie to her, but how could I tell her the truth? Tom was all for forgetting the whole thing. Why rock the boat? If Arcas wanted to be dead, let him be dead. The deader the better. At last, I conceded that Tom was right. What was the point in telling Cady that her father was a bastard? How would that make anything better? I went back to my office and put the disc back in its box. It was suddenly just a lump of old clay. All the magic had gone out of it. If it weren't for the professor, I'd have smashed the thing against the wall. The archaeologists could have it. I didn't want it in my house.

That night I lay in bed trying to reconstruct every moment I'd spent with Arcas. There must have been clues I'd been too stupid or naive to pick up. There were those trips back to Greece to visit his sick father. Those were probably a cover for whatever he was up to—or maybe he wasn't up to anything. Maybe he'd just gotten tired of me, or maybe it was Karmic retribution for what had happened to my sister. I turned over in bed and looked at the clock. It was almost one in the morning. Tom was snoring happily, untroubled by nagging doubts or a guilty conscious while I was obsessed with the idea that every bad thing that happened was a just punishment for killing my sister.

"Oh, Joanie," I murmured as I touched the small pendant I'd worn since I was twelve, the talisman of our eternal twinship. "Where are you? I really need you now." But she didn't answer.

The following afternoon I drove back to the hospital with a container of fried chicken for Nick on the seat beside me and the clay disc for the archaeologist tucked into my purse. I was in a terrible mood. After so many years, why did I even care whether Arcas was alive or dead? But I did. I cared a lot, both for myself and for my daughter. Poor Cady, what could we tell her to soften the news? I pulled into a parking space still feeling dazed and angry. The only thing I knew for sure was that the son of a bitch might have hurt me, but he wasn't going to hurt my daughter.

I put on the cheeriest face I could muster and walked into Nick's room, waving the Tupperware container in front of me. "Meals on Wheels. Hope you're hungry."

"What's the matter? You look awful." He furrowed his brow and examined me closely. "Did something happen?"

"No, why would you ask that?" I wondered what had given me away.

"You just don't look right. Your hair's a mess and you . . . I don't know. You look kind of wild eyed. Are they going to have to amputate my leg or something?"

"Of course not, it's nothing like that. In fact, you're being discharged in a couple days." I put the food on his bedside table and kissed his cheek. "I didn't sleep very well last night, that's all."

I sank into the chair beside Nick's bed. It was only three-thirty in the afternoon, but I was exhausted. Arcas must have cost me more sleep than I'd realized. I kicked off my shoes and put my feet up on Nick's bed. "Did Dad tell you what happened at his office two days ago? He practically got mugged by a mob protesting his agency's immigrant impact report. Who knew being an economist could be so dangerous?"

"You're kidding, who cares about some agency report? It's just a lot of statistics."

"A bunch of white supremacist thugs, that's who. I doubt they even read the thing, but they heard it says immigrants are an economic driver and a net benefit to the province. They wanted a report that said immigrants are all on welfare or in jail. That would have made them happy."

"Did they actually get violent?"

"Mostly they just screamed ugly things at people coming out of the building, but there was a physical confrontation between the racists and some counter-protesters. Dad was pretty shaken when he got home."

"I'd have been there if I'd known about it." Nick was suddenly animated.

"And if you weren't seventeen and laid up with a broken leg. You were better off safe in this bed. Those things can get ugly."

"Why didn't you tell me about it yesterday? Was it on the news?"

"I meant to tell you, but I was too preoccupied with this." I took the box holding the clay disc out of my purse and put it on the bedside table beside the fried chicken. "Your archaeologist friend thinks my little gift from Arcas might belong in a museum. He wants to show it to some people at the university."

"Wow, aren't you glad I made you talk to him? I bet it's worth a mint."

"I wouldn't count on it. It's more likely that he's confused and imagining things, but I'm going to leave it with him anyway. It means more to him than it does to me at this point." I bit my lip. That wasn't what I'd meant to say.

"What do you mean? I thought it meant a lot to you. I know it means a lot to Cady."

"Well, the other possibility, the one that's more likely, is that it's a replica from a museum gift shop. Dr. Kanter wasn't sure which, and frankly I don't know how much we can trust what Dr. Kanter says."

"He seemed fine when I saw him in PT. I don't know why everyone thinks he's senile."

"I had a nice conversation with him too, but I guess these things can be subtle. We're not doctors so we don't know what to look for." I picked up the box and put it back in my purse. "Why don't you work on that fried chicken while I talk with Dr. Kanter."

"OK, let me know what he says."

Nick pried the lid off the Tupperware, and I watched as he devoured a drumstick in two bites. This was the boy I had to coax to eat by making faces out of raisins and bananas in his oatmeal. I kissed him again then headed to the door.

"Mom," he said, his mouth full of chicken. "Can I really go home in a couple days? I'm going crazy in this place."

"That's what they tell me," I assured him, then headed down the hall to Dr. Kanter's room.

His door was wide open, but his bed was empty. I felt foolish for expecting him to be available whenever I stopped by. Then I had a new thought and something inside me lurched. Was he already gone? Had he been moved to a nursing home overnight or worse, had he died?

I was standing in front of his door clutching my purse and staring stupidly at his empty bed when I felt a hand on my shoulder. "Don't worry, he'll be back shortly. He's just gone down to radiology."

The touch startled me, and I turned to see who was there. It was the nurse I'd met on my first visit, the one who knew Cady and Nick. "Thank you, I just came by to show him that piece of Greek pottery I mentioned yesterday. I can come back later."

"No, no, please have a seat. He'll be back in just a minute. I know he wants to see you."

"Really?" Had Dr. Kanter told this nurse about the disc? I looked at her more closely. She looked back at me with a warm, sympathetic smile.

"Maybe I'll go back to my son's room and wait for Dr. Kanter there."

She beamed broadly when I mentioned Nick. "Now that's a fine boy you have there. We'll miss him when he leaves us. Not many boys would take time to talk to an old man, but Nick's special. You should be proud of him."

"Yes, we are, although I don't think talking to Dr. Kanter is all that remarkable but thank you."

"Trust me, I know a good soul when I meet one and . . . oh, here comes Dr. Kanter now. Why don't you wait out here while we get him settled? I'll call you the moment he's ready for visitors."

I stepped aside as an orderly pushed Dr. Kanter's wheelchair past me. The professor smiled and gestured for me to wait. He looked tired and somehow smaller and thinner than the day before. Simply going for x-rays must have exhausted him. I waited in the hallway until the nurse opened the door and invited me inside.

"Well, what a pleasant surprise. I didn't expect to see you back so soon. Please, have a seat." Dr. Kanter gestured to the chair beside the bed. I sat down as he adjusted his thick glasses and focused his gaze in my direction. There was something disconcerting about his stare. It wasn't lascivious or suggestive, and yet I felt uncomfortable, as though he were examining me. His expression turned quizzical. "Do you have the photographs already? Can you get them that fast?"

"Oh, better than that." I opened my purse and pulled out the box. "I decided that you might as well have the real thing. Why don't you take it and show it to your colleagues at the university? There's no sense my going with you. I don't know anything about Bronze Age artifacts. I'd just be in the way."

Dr. Kanter looked genuinely surprised. "Well, that's very generous of you. Are you sure? To be honest, it will take time to get a definitive opinion on the piece. They'll need to keep it for quite a while."

"That's OK, just let me know what they say once they've had time to study it." The memory of Arcas handing me the disc with fake solemnity roiled my stomach. It had all been an act. The fantasy of a financial windfall suddenly seemed stupid. I couldn't wait to wash my hands of Arcas and his Minoan tchachka. "If it's real, maybe I'll donate it to the university. I haven't decided yet."

Dr. Kanter looked surprised. "Now, that really would be generous, but there's no hurry. In the meantime, let's store this little treasure someplace where it can't be lost or stolen. There's a safe at the back of my closet." He gave me a sly smile. "Can I trust you with the code?"

I'd never thought about security. I'd always kept the thing in an unlocked desk drawer. Maybe I was being foolish. Maybe I should have consulted a lawyer and gotten reams of signed documents before handing the disc over to this man, but a quick consultation with my gut informed me that I didn't care. I was glad to be rid of it. "I work undercover for the Mossad. No one will ever get it out of me."

"Well, then . . . " Dr. Kanter paused, looking puzzled. "It's . . . wait a minute, I'll think of it. It's my birthday. I was born in May on the . . . How old am I?" He lay back against the pillow and closed his eyes. "I'm sorry, I don't remember." An expression crossed his face that I hadn't seen before. It might have been fear or confusion or both. "Can you believe that? I don't know what year I was born." He tapped his forehead with one finger. "The old noggin seems to have slipped a cog."

"We all forget things. It'll come back to you."

He took off his glasses and rubbed the bridge of his nose. "Would you call the nurse for me? She can check my chart. How could I forget a thing like that?"

I pushed the call button that was pinned to his pillow. "You look tired. We can deal with this another time."

"No, please, wait just another minute. She'll get this sorted out. She's very good."

I didn't know what he thought the nurse could do, but I remained standing awkwardly at his bedside. "Is there anything I can do for you? Would you like a glass of water?"

"If you wouldn't mind, I'd like to sit up a bit higher. Could you put another pillow behind my head? There's one in the closet."

I'm not a natural nurse and repositioning a strange man felt uncomfortably intimate, but I couldn't refuse such a simple request. I fetched the pillow and helped him sit up enough to slip it under his head. As I was leaning over him, the small cat pendant I always wore slipped out of my blouse. To my chagrin, he reached up and grabbed hold of it.

"Where did you get this?" he asked, looking more alarmed than when he couldn't remember his own birthday.

I pulled it out of his grasp as gently as I could. "It's just something my parents gave me when I was a kid." I tucked it back into my blouse and stepped back from the bed. The way Dr. Kanter was staring at me gave me the creeps. "Why? Is there something wrong with it?"

"No, no, it's just that I know someone who has a necklace just like that. It's so unusual . . . or maybe it's not. Maybe it was common at one time?"

"As far as I know there are only two in the world, this one and my sister's. Our parents made them for us when we turned twelve. They had a cat pendant engraved with a line from a poem we liked, then they had it cut in two and gave us each half. You probably saw one of those friendship necklaces girls used to wear. They look very similar."

He didn't take his eyes off me as he recited, "errie and eazer had ful way of gether."

I stared at him, fear and confusion rising within me. "I'm sorry, what did you just say?"

"It was written on that other necklace, the one that looks like yours. Do you know what it means?"

"You didn't see that, you couldn't have."

"There was a young woman wearing it on the ship where I had my fall. She looked remarkably like you, only younger."

I've never fainted in my life, but my vision was suddenly pricked with stars, a black cloud washed over me, and I began to hyperventilate. The next thing I remember the nurse was shaking my arm and calling my name. I opened my eyes and saw her concerned face shining down at me from beneath a halo of gray curls.

"There now, just sit quiet a minute. What in the world? Have you eaten anything today?" She crooned as I struggled to regain my senses. I shook myself awake and tried to stand up but a small, plump hand held me firmly in place. "Not so fast, young lady. How about some juice? You aren't pregnant, are you?"

That almost made me smile, but then the memory of Dr. Kanter reciting the words from my sister's necklace made me woozy again and I doubled over, putting my head in my lap.

"That's a good girl. Sit just like that while I get you some orange juice." The nurse patted me on my shoulder and left the room.

Dr. Kanter and I sat in silence for several minutes.

"That other girl, we called her Joanie," Dr. Kanter said. "She didn't know what the words on the necklace meant. We spent a lot of time trying to solve the puzzle. It was sort of a game we played."

"It's a line from a poem by T.S. Eliot. We . . . Wait, you called her Joanie?"

Dr. Kanter looked as shaken as I was. I could see the Adam's apple in his thin neck move up and down as he swallowed. "That's what we called her, but it probably wasn't her real name. She had amnesia and couldn't remember anything before coming on board the ship, not even her name. We had to call her something, so we suggested names at random and she liked that one."

How could a strange woman named Joanie be wearing my sister's necklace? I searched my brain for a plausible explanation but came up blank. I'd always imagined the necklace around my sister's neck at the bottom of the lake.

"Do you know who she is?" he asked after a long pause.

"My sister," I whispered.

"What? I'm sorry I couldn't hear you." Dr. Kanter leaned toward me expectantly.

"My sister's name was Joanie. It's an incredible coincidence, but I don't know the woman on the ship. I have no idea who that woman was. I'm sorry, but this is scaring me. I really need to go."

"She looks exactly like you, or perhaps more like your daughter. Could she be a cousin or some other relative?"

I was rocked by another wave of vertigo. Reality suddenly seemed fluid, floating, receding into the distance. I half expected the walls to dissolve or Dr. Kanter to levitate above his bed. I needed to escape. "I'm sorry about the poor woman with amnesia, but that has nothing to do with me. I really must go."

"Please, wait." His voice became softer, more plaintive. "I'm so confused about everything on that ship. If you know anything, please, I need to know."

I was saved by the nurse barging back into the room with a little box stuck through with a straw. "Now what are you doing standing up, young lady? You were told to stay put until I came back with this juice."

"Thank you, but I'm feeling much better. I was just leaving."

"No you don't. You sit down and drink this first. We can't have people fainting away in our hallways. Low blood sugar is usually the culprit in these things. I bet you're dieting, tiny as you are."

"No, honest, I had a good lunch. I don't know what came over me, but I'm fine now." My protests were useless. The nurse somehow maneuvered me back into the chair and stuck the juice box in my hand.

"Now, what can I do for you?" She adjusted Dr. Kanter's pillows and straightened his bedclothes. "Would you like me to raise the bed a bit, you don't look comfortable like that."

"Yes, thank you, but there's something else. That's not why we called you."

The nurse pressed a button on the side rail of Dr. Kanter's bed, and he was smoothly elevated to an upright position. I felt foolish for fussing with his pillows. If I'd simply pressed the stupid button, he wouldn't have seen my necklace and I wouldn't be having a panic attack.

"Why did we call the nurse? What was it? Do you remember?" Dr. Kanter turned to me.

"You wanted the combination to the safe. It's your birth date. You said she'd have it in your chart." I sucked on my straw and stared sullenly at the nurse who was holding me hostage.

"Why would I do that? I know my own birthday, May 4, 1908. The combination is 5-4-0-8."

I slurped up the last of the juice and threw the box in the trash. "Thanks, I'm sorry to have crashed like that, but I have to get home." I stood up, relieved to find the room had stopped spinning.

"Wait, before you go, may I see that pendant one more time? It's so strange that you and Joanie would be wearing the same necklace." Dr. Kanter looked at me with imploring eyes.

I unfastened the clasp at the back of the chain and handed it to him. He held it close to his face and then at arm's length trying to make out the words. "I'm sorry, can someone read this for me?"

He handed my necklace to the nurse who read, "Mungoj/ Rump/ had a won/ way of wor/ tog." She shook her head and gave it back to him. "Now that's an odd inscription if I ever saw one, but it reminds me of something." She closed her eyes and dropped her head as she tried to solve the puzzle. A moment later her head snapped back up and she turned toward me, a wide smile brightening her face. "It's Mungojerrie and Rupelteazer, isn't it? That's why it's shaped like a cat. I love that show."

Dr. Kanter was nodding. "I've heard of them, Mungojerrie and, uh, the other one. But you said it was from a poem not a theatrical production."

I sighed as I retrieved my necklace from the professor. "It was a poem first, now it's a musical too. *Cats*, I'm sure you've heard of it." Dr. Kanter shook his head, still bewildered. "Anyway, there's this one poem about two naughty cats who are always getting into trouble, Mungojerrie and Rumpelteazer. It was a family joke. They used to call me Mungo and my sister became Teazer. Actually, we called her Rump for a while, but she didn't like it, so we switched." I refastened the clasp behind my neck and tucked the pendant into my blouse.

"Mungojerrie and Rumpelteazer . . . something, something. What's the rest of it?" The nurse was still trying to solve the riddle.

I sighed then begrudgingly recited, "Mungojerrie and Rupelteazer had a wonderful way of working together." That line had been a secret bond between me and my sister. I didn't like sharing it with strangers.

That's it. I know that line. I know all the lines from the show." The nurse beamed. "*Cats* is my absolute favorite musical."

Dr. Kanter seemed to be reconstructing the verse in his head. "errie and eazer had ful . . . Yes, of course, it works. Now I know where it's from, *Old Possum's Book of Practical Cats*. I read it to Michael when he was small."

"Isn't that lovely?" The nurse looked pleased. "You'll have to explain it to Joanie when you see her again."

My stomach lurched and I needed to leave. I couldn't even wait for the elevator. I picked up my purse, said a hasty good-bye and raced toward the stairs. I didn't stop running until I'd left the hospital and was halfway to the parking lot. It had started to rain, but I didn't slow down or take cover. I would have kept running but I tripped over a curb and went sprawling on the pavement. A nice man with an umbrella stopped to help me, but I assured him I was fine, and he hurried off. I was fine, apart from a rip in the knee of my slacks and bloody scrapes on both my palms. I listened for my sister, expecting to hear her calls for help, but she'd gone silent ever since the dream where I'd been rescued from the water. There was no sound but the pelting rain, the rush of afternoon traffic, and the pounding of my own heart.

I was spooked by the thought of Joanie's doppelganger aboard a ship somewhere in the middle of the lake. The dead were coming back to haunt me, first Arcas and now my sister. No wonder I was freaking out. *Calm down. You never have to think about Arcas again, and whoever Dr. Kanter met out on the lake, it certainly wasn't your sister.* I touched my pendant through my blouse and wondered how Dr. Kanter could have known what was engraved on the other half. Nothing made sense. If there was a logical explanation, it eluded me completely. Tom would know what to make of it. He was solid and sensible. He hadn't let his sister drown or fallen in love with a liar. His head wasn't clouded by muddy water.

As I limped the last block to the parking lot, my equilibrium returned and felt like a fool for running into a summer storm without an umbrella or a coat. I brushed a lock of wet hair from my face, got into my car, and started the motor. Nick would be discharged from the hospital in a few days. He'd come home, we'd go to the cottage, and I'd worry about my real, substantial family and forget about old ghosts.

Jacob
July 1993

"WOULD YOU MIND putting this in the safe? The combination is 5-4-0-8." I hand the box to the nurse who secures it with my other valuables. My head is swimming, In fact I'm entirely at sea. Nothing's made sense since I stepped onto that strange ship, and yet I miss it. Have you ever awakened from a vivid dream and wished that you could close your eyes and return to that receding world? You had a life in that other realm as rich and complex as the one you've just awakened to. Such an odd sensation, the buildings, the landscapes, the people are so real and then they vanish like images on overexposed film that fade in light. But what if they're not really gone? What if they're waiting patiently while you dream that you're awake?

Michael thinks I'm no longer *compos mentis,* and perhaps he's right. My memories of the *Aqua Meridian* don't make sense, not even to me. I'm an empiricist by nature, a modern archaeologist trained to seek laboratory-based physical, chemical, and biological evidence from an excavated site. I seek facts and solve puzzles, wary of anything that shows up in the wrong strata, misplaced in time or space. So, considering the unlikely events I've recently experienced, I must consider Michael's diagnosis. My brain may be going soft, but if it was all a delusion then how . . . ?

"Nurse, what was the line on that cat pendant Mrs. Savas was wearing?"

"Mungojerrie and Rumpelteazer had a wonderful way of working together."

"No, just the words on her half, the part she was wearing."

"Oh, I don't know. It started Mungoj and Rumpel. That's how I figured it out, but I can't remember the rest. But you know what the other half says, don't you?"

"Yes, there was a young woman on the *Aqua Meridian* wearing the other half of that pendant who looked exactly like Amy Savas, only younger. She might have been her daughter or a younger sister, but Mrs. Savas claims she doesn't know her. It doesn't make any sense, no sense at all." My teeth chatter and my skin breaks out in goose bumps. "Nurse, am I losing my mind? Please, be honest, I need to know."

As she turns, the late afternoon sun illuminates her face and hair. Her white uniform glows in the light streaming through the window. I take a deep breath then exhale slowly, unclench my jaw and wait, trusting that she'll tell the truth.

"Your chart says you're suffering from dementia, most likely Alzheimer's. Symptoms include delusional thinking, poor short-term memory, and impaired judgment."

Tears well in my eyes.

She steps closer and gives me a conspiratorial smile. "But sometimes doctors miss the big picture. They've never sailed on a ship like the *Aqua Meridian*, so they assume it's a hallucination, but we know what we know, don't we?"

"No, I don't know what I know at all. I mean, I know I was on a boat where I fell and broke my hip. Everyone agrees about that, but beyond that, it's a blur. One minute we were in the Toronto harbor and the next we were at sea without passing through any locks or canals that I recall. How could we have reached the ocean? And I felt younger there, or I was younger, it's hard to explain. Seriously, do you think I'm going mad?"

"Nurses aren't allowed to make those kinds of diagnosis, but you seem okay to me."

"Thank you." The usual hubbub in the corridor is strangely silent. I can hear the wall clock tick. The nurse stands at the foot of my bed without making any move to leave. You'd think she had all the time in the world. "They're going to lock me up in some sort of loony bin. They're trying to put a good face on it, but that's what it is."

"Humph." She makes a dismissive sound and shakes her head. "Well, you don't have to go, you know. You have other options."

"Really?" I stare at her incredulous. "I do?"

Just then an alarm goes off and the quiet hallway is instantly transformed into a busy thoroughfare. People in white coats, pushing carts and gurneys, stream in the direction of the noise while a loudspeaker screams, "Code blue." Like that, the nurse is gone, swallowed by the throng racing down the hall and I'm left wondering what my other options are.

Does she know about the disc? Does she imagine I'll be working with the university again? Maybe she figures Michael can't keep me under lock and key if the Canadian Archaeological Association is asking for articles and inviting me to speak. Or is there something else, something I don't know about?

In any case, I need to contact the department straight away to let them know what's in my safe. My time as a free man is running out, and yet I hesitate, afraid they'll dismiss me as a crank. I decide to proceed cautiously, make some notes, and write out my talking points. As I twist to reach the pen and paper on the bedside table a shooting pain nearly knocks me out, so I ring the button for assistance, but everyone's busy rescuing some other poor soul down the hall and no one comes. I wait patiently for a quarter hour and then, exhausted by the afternoon's events, I fall asleep.

MICHAEL ARRIVES WITH Peter just after supper. I'm usually delighted to see them, but this evening they've interrupted my preparations for the call I need to make tomorrow. I hide my notepad under the bedclothes and welcome my errant grandson who's just been sprung from the hoosegow. His hair is too long, his T-shirt's too small, and his ball cap's on backward. He looks like a hooligan, but his face lights up the moment he sees me, and he throws his arms around me like a child.

"So, the jailbird's flown the coop." I kiss him on the cheek. "I hear you've been standing up to racists and anti-Semites. Good for you."

"Dad, please don't encourage him. He's out on personal recognizance. They'll throw him back in jail if he pulls a stunt like that again. I couldn't take it. I'm living on antacids as it is." Michael rubs his belly and emits a sour smelling burp. My son, for all his bluster, collapses under stress.

Peter is a warrior like his grandmother. "Your father's right," I admonish him. "You can't go about beaning Nazis on the head in Canada. There are other, legal ways to bring them down."

"We *were* protesting legally. There was a lot of shouting on both sides, but I swear, I didn't mean to hit anyone."

"Then what happened?" I'm trying to look stern, but I'm secretly relishing the image of my grandson whacking the thug with a wooden post.

"One of the skinheads grabbed my placard, and I was trying to yank it back, but he outweighed me by like fifty pounds. When I finally let go, he flew backward and the pole whacked his ugly tattooed head. It wasn't my fault, it was pure physics, an equal and opposite reaction. Served him right, anyway."

"Great, we'll call Sir Isaac Newton to testify in your defense." Michael isn't amused.

I take a sip of cold tea from my supper tray so they won't see the grin spreading across my face. "Well, be more careful in the future. You can't set the world right from the inside of a jail cell."

"I will be more careful, but the Heritage Front is sponsoring a speech by a big Holocaust Denier, Ernst Zundel, next week and I'm going to be there. I'm not letting them spread their lies without pushing back."

I'm no longer smiling. "Peter, those people are violent and dangerous. Your protest could turn into a street brawl, and they won't fight fair."

"Don't worry, I'm going with a group from B'nai Brith. They'll keep it under control. Anyway, someone has to stand up to the Fascists."

I nod, but the joy's gone out of me. Peter's right, of course. Someone does need to fight the Nazis, but I thought we'd already won that war.

Michael pulls a pillbox from his pocket and downs a small pink tablet with the last of my tea. "Well, on a happier note," he begins, but he doesn't look happy. He's smiling too broadly, and his eyes are blinking as though he's just walked into a bright light. I'm immediately on guard. "The hospital's discharging you to Bayside Manor at the end of the week."

"No, they're not. I'm going back to my own apartment."

"Be reasonable, Dad, you have a broken hip. You need someone to look after you." He turns to Peter as though I'm not within earshot. "Do you see, this is exactly what I'm talking about. He's not in his right mind. He can't be left alone."

Peter, bless him, comes to my defense. "People go home after breaking their hips. He just needs to heal up a bit more. Can't he just go to a nursing home for rehab until he gets better? It doesn't have to be permanent."

Michael brightens immediately. "How's that for a compromise? You go to Bayside Manor for a few months and then, if you're able to look after yourself, we can talk about other options. What do you think?"

I think he thinks I'm an idiot. No one over four years old would fall for such an obvious trick. But, on the other hand, he's right, I do need assistance. I can't even get to the toilet by myself. I look toward the closet where the disc is hidden and wonder how I'll negotiate the future of a valuable artifact from a locked ward. My fantasy of belated acclaim begins to fade. I'm not going to be taking any bows. At best I'll hand the disc over to a younger, more vigorous man and hope he remembers me in a foot note.

". . . and you can take some of your furniture and personal belongings, so you'll feel right at home." Michael is pitching the place like one of those sleazy guys selling payday loans on late night TV.

"How much can I take?" The move is beginning to feel inevitable, the beginning of the end.

"They provide a bed and chest, but you could bring your recliner and your TV and some pictures for the walls. We'll make it real cozy for you."

I can bring a chair and a few tchotchkes. My heart sinks, but then I feel the hidden paper crinkle beneath the sheets and realize that I still have one avenue of escape. I can write. I can still write the articles I've been planning. "I'll need my desk and books. I'm not going anywhere without them. And my papers, I'll need my files."

"Dad, it's a small apartment. Your desk is huge. It would take up the whole room."

"Then we're done here. I'm not going." This is pure bravado, and he knows it, but I'm desperate.

"How about if we bring your papers and say, one box of books, and set up a small table where you can work. Would that do it?"

I nod, it will have to do. Then I have another thought. "Wait, one more thing. I want the framed photo of your mother and the copy of the Phaistos Disc that are on my desk. Could you bring them the next time you visit?"

"Sure, Grandpa," Peter answers. "I'll bring them tomorrow."

He's such a good boy.

I NEED TO gird for battle, but I'm not the soldier I once was. I tried doing a thorough reconnaissance of the archaeology department but couldn't remember how to locate directories or track down faculty. My nurse, bless her, called the library and verified that Ianni Stournaris is chairman, and got his number for me. I have his number and personal extension jotted down on the back of my breakfast menu, along with my own personal history, including the years I taught in the department and the time I spent in Greece. The phone is beside me on the bed. My only reservation is how to explain the improbable story of how I came into possession of the disc. Well, there's no help for that. It is what it is. I pick up the phone and punch in the numbers.

A pleasant-sounding woman answers. "Good morning, Dr. Stournaris's office. May I help you?"

"Yes, I'd like to speak with Dr. Stournaris, please."

"I'm sorry, but he's out of the country until August. Is there anything I can do for you?"

"No, I need to speak to him directly, or to whoever's covering for him while he's gone."

"That would be Dr. Jordan Mansour."

"Fine, then, may I speak to him."

"She's in a meeting at the moment. May I take a message?"

She? Times have certainly changed. Bess would have been happy. "This is Jacob Kanter. That's Kanter with a K. I used to teach in your department, but I retired a while back. I've come into possession of a remarkable artifact, possibly a second Phaistos Disc, and I need to speak to someone right away. Please have Dr . . . what did you say her name was?

"Mansour."

"Yes, well, have her call me as soon as possible." I leave my number and hang up. Adrenaline is coursing through my system and my heart is beating fast. I was expecting to change the course of ancient history. Simply leaving my number and waiting for a return call is a complete letdown. I console myself with the thought that Dr. Mansour will call back later in the day. I just hope she doesn't call when I'm in therapy or asleep.

PETER AND MICHAEL surprise me by showing up again just after lunch. I'm a bit on edge since I'm still waiting for Dr. Mansour's call, but I'm glad to see them. Peter's carrying a plastic bag that he empties on my bed. There's my replica of the Phaistos Disc and the picture of my wife. I pick up the framed photo and look into Bess's eyes. I could swear she looks right back at me. "You old fool," she seems to say. "How long do you plan to keep me waiting?"

I had a professional photographer take her portrait as a gift when she turned forty. He caught her Ava Gardner looks, but the black and white photo couldn't capture her chestnut-colored hair, peach complexion, or those gray eyes that always saw right through me. Who could have imagined cancer would transform that beauty into a bald skeleton with sunken eyes? Poor Bess, you were a trooper to the end. You didn't deserve that last year. Neither of us did.

"Grandpa, what are all these papers on your bed? What have you been working on?"

"Oh, top secret stuff." I gather my scattered notes into a pile and tuck them into the mystery I've been reading. "Speaking of secrets, I bet you'd like to know what I have hidden in my safe."

"Dad already told me. He says you found a second Rosetta Stone."

"Did he say *I found* or that *I imagine that I've found*, as in the old guy's addled and doesn't know what he's looking at?"

Peter looks a little sheepish, but nods. "Yeah, more like that."

"What I said is," Michael says, "I hope whatever he's got is worth a fortune, because Bayside Manor costs a bundle. Dad, you have no idea the sacrifices we're making to take care of you. A priceless artifact would really help pay all those bills."

"Are you out of your mind? It's not for sale. It's going to the university."

"Yes, of course," he says in a smarmy tone, intended to console me I suppose. "But there's no reason to simply give it to them. If it's worth something, why not make them pay for it? I'm sure they have a budget for things like that and we could use your share to cover the cost of Bayside Manor."

"I don't have a share. The disc belongs to a Mrs. Savas who's donating it to the university."

"Then she needs an attorney to negotiate on her behalf. Maybe I should talk to her." I can see the wheels turning in Michael's head and I don't like the direction they're going, but I don't have the energy to fight him.

"That will be up to Mrs. Savas, but it's irrelevant until we get the piece authenticated."

"Grandpa, can I see it?" Peter's never been interested in archaeology before, but talk of a fortune seems to have piqued his curiosity.

"It's in the back of the closet. There's a little safe back there. The combination is 5-4-0-8." I can hear him push aside the hangers holding my shirt and trousers.

"This thing is a joke," he calls over his shoulder. "I could pry it open with a butter knife."

A tall orderly appears in the doorway. "It's time for PT, Dr. Kanter." He pushes an empty wheelchair in my direction.

"Would it be alright if I skip therapy today? I'm expecting an important call."

"Sorry, my orders are to have you in therapy by two o'clock, but don't worry, the nurses will take a message while you're gone."

Peter backs out of the small wardrobe. "Is it okay if I go with you? I have the afternoon off."

"Sure, you can come," the orderly answers for me. "Family's always welcome in PT." It's amazing how quickly I've become invisible since being admitted to the hospital, but it will be good to have Peter with me for another hour. The orderly may have spoken out of turn, but he knows his business and gets me into the chair with a minimum of fuss.

Michael waves us off. "Go ahead without me. I have some errands to attend to. See you later."

Peter stays by my side as the orderly wheels me down the hall, into the elevator and down another corridor until we reach the rehab waiting room. A few other patients have family with them, but none as young or vital as my Peter. I feel a surge of pride in the handsome young man sitting by my side.

I pat his hand. "Would you like a cup of coffee or some soda? There are free drinks at the nurse's station."

Peter shakes his head, and then bends to whisper in my ear. "Everyone's so old. Don't young people ever come for therapy?"

As if in answer to his question, an orderly wheels in the young Nick Savas. I smile when I see him and he smiles back, directing the orderly to park his chair across from mine.

"Hello, young man. Good to see you. Let me introduce my grandson, Peter." The boys look at one another, sizing each other up. "Peter, this is Nick, he's a daredevil cyclist who took a nasty spill and broke his leg."

"Too bad about your leg. Will it take long to heal?"

"They say it'll be back to normal in time for school, and there's nothing wrong with my arms. I don't know why they need to push me around in this thing." He pounds the arms of his wheelchair. "It makes me feel stupid."

"Yeah, that would annoy me too."

Nick points to Peter's T-shirt with approval. "You're into Barenaked Ladies. I love those guys. I heard them at Ontario Place a couple years ago."

Peter grins. "That's pretty precocious for a high school kid. I didn't get into Indie rock until I was in college. Where do you go to school?"

"Malvern Collegiate, it's my last year."

"No kidding? That's where I went. Does Mrs. Norton still make you dissect cats in biology?"

"No, we do frogs now, that's gross enough."

"Yeah, that's probably why I'm majoring in poli sci, no blood and guts."

"Oh, there's blood and guts in poli sci the way you do it," I tease. "Just ask that fascist you whacked upside the head."

"What?" Nick did an amusing double take. "You actually hit a fascist?"

Peter looks embarrassed. "It was an accident. I was with a group standing up to a bunch of Nazis from the National Front. He got hit by a pole I was carrying."

Nick's eyes widen. "That happened outside my father's office. He was there and told me about it. I wish I could have been there with you."

"We can always use more volunteers. In fact, there's another rally coming up . . ."

I'm relieved when my therapist emerges from behind a pair of double doors and cuts this conversation short since I doubt Nick's mother would appreciate having her son recruited by the ARA.

The therapist is very pleasant, but all business. She gives Peter a quick smile as she waves us in.

Peter stands up to follow me into the therapy room. "Nice meeting you. Hope your leg heals up fast."

"Wait, I'd really like to talk with you about that rally. Will you be around later?" Nick calls after us.

"No, but I'll be back tomorrow afternoon. My grandfather's in the South wing, room 918."

"I know, he's right down the hall from me. See you tomorrow then."

"Right on!" Peter pumps his fist in Nick's direction and Nick pumps his arm in return, as though they're already comrades in arms.

I'm exhausted by the time the orderly wheels me back to my room. The therapist was merciless and my poor leg aches from being tortured by the iron maiden. Peter's already left and I'm looking forward to a good nap. However, as the orderly pushes me into my room, I find Michael poking through my papers.

"Find anything of interest?" I inquire.

"Sorry, just tidying up." He doesn't even look embarrassed. He picks up the menu I've scratched up with notes and phone numbers and holds it out accusingly. "Look at this." He waves the paper in my face. "Dr. Stournaris on Sabbatical until August. Dr. Mansour will call back later. What were you thinking? Didn't I ask you not to call the university?"

"And didn't you say you'd be out running errands? What are you doing here?" I'm surprised and upset, but I keep my cool.

"I came back to check on a few things, and I'm glad I did. Why wouldn't you listen to me? You're going to embarrass yourself with the university."

I'm dumbfounded, my son has absolutely no faith in me. "You don't understand how significant this object is. The university will be calling any minute."

Michael presses his lips together and looks away, shaking his head. "I'm sorry, let's not talk about it. I didn't come here to argue, I came to make you an offer. You know that old recliner in your living room? It's in terrible shape and I can't see the point of moving it. How about if I treat you to a comfy new chair with fresh fabric and good springs? Simpsons could have it delivered to Bayside Manor before you move in. What do you say?"

I don't say anything. I polish my glasses with the end of my hospital gown to buy some time. It's just a chair, I tell myself, man up. But that chair is one loss too many and I can't find the strength to let it go. Michael promised I could bring a few things from my apartment. He promised me that chair.

"No, Michael. Your mother picked out that chair. I've sat in it for twenty years. It fits me like a glove and that's the chair I want. Certainly, one chair isn't too much to ask."

Now, for the first time, he looks embarrassed. "Well, actually that's a problem. I'm afraid there was a miscommunication and the guys I hired to clear out your apartment took it by mistake."

Amy
July 1993

IT WAS LATE afternoon when I got home, stripped off my damp clothes, and took a hot shower. I longed for a nap, but there was a print job to complete and a deadline to meet so I got dressed and went back to work. Tom must have heard the exhaustion in my voice when I called to tell him I was too tired to cook. He brought in carry-out from Lichee Garden, cleared up, and washed the dishes while I sat in a dumb funk staring at a small stain on the wallpaper.

"You need to get some sleep." Tom rubbed my shoulders as I sipped a cup of jasmine tea. "I think the thing with Arcas has you completely rattled. He's a liar and a coward, but so what? We've had twenty-one good years together. Frankly, I'm grateful he disappeared and left you here with me." He kissed the top of my head and I leaned back into his warm hands.

My husband was right. I wasn't cut out to be a Greek shepherdess. I had the life I wanted, but my memory of a great romance with a star-crossed lover was now ashes. Arcas had come back from the dead destroying my fantasies and injuring my self-esteem in the process.

I closed my eyes and let Tom knead the aches and tension from my neck. I tried to relax. but there were too many unanswered questions playing through my head. "It isn't just Arcas, it's that woman on the boat. Doesn't that story give you the creeps?"

"Coincidences happen, although this one does seem improbable. Are you sure he had the inscription, right? Maybe he just said some mumbo-jumbo and you heard what you wanted to hear."

"No, there was a nurse there and she heard the same thing and . . ." I turned around to look Tom in the face. "He said she looked just like me, only younger. I can't get that out of my head."

Tom shrugged. "There are more things in heaven and earth, Horatio."

"Seriously, it doesn't freak you out?"

"A little, but weird things happen. We can't know everything. How's this for a guess? The necklace lay at the bottom of the lake for many years until a big carp came along and, mistaking it for a worm, devoured it whole. Then, one day the carp is caught by a kid fishing off Queens Quay pier. He brings it home, slices it open and, *voila*, your sister's necklace. The little boy gives it to his incredibly beautiful mother who has dark, curly hair just like yours. She wears it when they go out on a harbor cruise the following week and meet a nice old professor. What do you think? Would that do it?"

I laughed. "Not bad, not likely, but not bad." I finished my tea and stood up. "I'm turning in. I'm short of sleep and the last twenty-four hours have exhausted me." I started upstairs then turned back. "Don't tell Cady about Arcas. Let her be the daughter of a hero a while longer."

I hoped that when I woke the next morning the sun would bring clarity and light to the dark muddle inside my head, but it didn't. Arcas was still not dead, and some unknown woman named Joanie was still wearing my sister's necklace. I decided to call my mother.

She answered on the first ring. "What happened? Is Nick alright?" She'd become an alarmist since Joanie's death, always expecting bad news. On the other hand, she didn't panic in water deeper than a bathtub, while I still suffered from debilitating aquaphobia. It was a family joke that we'd rented a cottage at the lake every August since Cady was ten, but I'd never gotten my feet wet.

"Everyone's fine, Mom, relax, I just wanted to ask you something. Do you have a minute?"

"Of course, I'm all ears." The tension disappeared from her voice as she settled down for a chat.

"You know those cat pendants you gave me and Joanie? I always thought they were one-of-a-kind, but could there have been others?"

"That's an odd question." My mother paused for several moments. "The cat medallion was something the jeweler had in stock, but the engraving was custom, and he cut it in half specifically for us. Why are you asking about that now after all these years?"

"I met a professor at the hospital when I was visiting Nick, and he claims he met a girl on a harbor cruise who was wearing a medallion just like Joanie's."

"Well, she might have been wearing the same cat pendant, like I said, it was a regular stock item."

"It was more than that. It had been cut in half and had the same inscription. Are you sure there weren't more made? I've had the willies ever since I heard that story."

"The same inscription?" I could almost see my mother's jaw drop.

"He knew exactly what it said, even the words that had been cut in half."

"That's not possible. You're giving me goose bumps."

"There's more. He said she looked like me and they called her Joanie."

My mother gasped.

"It isn't our Joanie, obviously. It can't be. It's someone Cady's age, but it's so strange."

"It certainly is, my hands are shaking."

"I didn't mean to upset you, but I had to know if there were other pendants like the ones you gave us."

"There aren't, at least not as far as I know."

I didn't know what to say and let the silence go on for too long.

"Was Joanie wearing it that day, the day she died?" she asked in a very soft voice.

I nodded as though she could see me. My throat was dry, but I managed to swallow. "We never took them off, but it was a long time ago. Memory's a funny thing so maybe I'm confused. Maybe she took it off and left it somewhere and another woman found it."

"Maybe," she replied. But neither of us believed it.

BEFORE VISITING NICK that afternoon I finished a print run, threw in a load of laundry, cleaned the bathrooms, and vacuumed the living room carpet. When I began to defrost the refrigerator, I realized I was procrastinating. All I had to do was visit Nick, something I'd done every day for a week. Why did the thought of walking into the hospital make me cringe? I turned off the vacuum and sat down with the sudden realization that I was afraid. The professor had evoked Joanie's ghost and an irrational part of my brain was terrified that I'd walk into his room and find her sitting on his bed. My rational self knew this was nonsense, but another part of me kept wondering, what if the lady from the boat shows up at St. Michael's and what if she's Joanie and what if she's still angry that I let her drown? I put the vacuum away, washed my face, brushed my hair, and took two aspirin. As I got into my car and drove toward the hospital, I touched the pendant around my neck. "I'm sorry," I whispered to the air for the gazillionth time. "Please forgive me."

I arrived to find Nick in a good mood, in fact, he was his old self again, full of plans and limitless energy. He was excited about protesting a speech by a holocaust denier with Dr. Kanter's grandson. His fervor reminded me of the time Arcas and Tom couldn't talk about anything but bringing down the junta. I smiled at the memory of Arcas and his youthful passion until I remembered his lies, but there was nothing dishonest about Nick's enthusiasm. His eyes glowed as he recounted the sins of the fascist Heritage Front and why they had to be held in check.

Once he'd finished recounting the sins of the infamous Ernst Zundel he told the story of the heroic members of the ARA who'd confronted white supremacists on Parliament Hill. His new friend had given Nick a blow-by-blow description of everything that had happened. I remembered watching the confrontation on the six o'clock news. I'd recoiled at the sight of angry men snarling and spitting through barred teeth, but Nick couldn't wait to enlist, broken leg and all. I worried about him, but I knew Tom would be proud.

When he finished regaling me with his plans to right the world, he asked, "Mom, I never got Peter's phone number. Would you stop by his grandfather's room and get his number for me?"

"No," I wanted to scream. "Absolutely not, I will never walk back into Dr. Kanter's room." I felt my face flush with embarrassment. I was being a coward and utterly irrational. How could I explain my anxiety without sounding completely unhinged?

I fished the little medallion from beneath my T-shirt and held it out for him to look at. "You know how I always wear this necklace in memory of my sister?"

"Sure." He looked understandably puzzled.

"And you know how it's inscribed with a line from a poem that Joanie and I loved when we were children."

"Yeah, 'Mungojerrie and Rumpleteazer worked very well together.'"

"Exactly, and the words were cut in half so they don't make sense unless you put the two pieces together."

"So?"

"So, the professor claims he saw someone wearing Aunt Joanie's half of the pendant on the boat where he fell. He knew exactly what it said, nonsense half-words and all. And . . ." I tucked the pendant back into my shirt. "He said she looked exactly like me, or maybe more like Cady since she was about Cady's age, the age my sister was when she drowned."

Nick looked at me as though he were the parent, and I was a silly child. "So now you think he saw your dead sister and you're completely freaked out."

I nodded. "Yep, I get the heebie-jeebies whenever I think about it. I mean, how could he know what was on her half of the pendant?"

"Mom, what did Dr. Kanter do for a living?"

"He was an archaeologist."

"Right, and not just any archaeologist, he specialized in decoding ancient languages. That's why he wants the disc, so he can figure out what those odd inscriptions mean. Deciphering your necklace was a piece of cake for him."

"But he only saw half the inscription and he'd have had to know the poem." Then I remembered, he *had* known the poem. He'd read it to his son when he was little. I let out a breath I hadn't realized I was holding in. Nick's explanation certainly made more sense than Tom's. "You know, I bet you're right. I hadn't thought of that. Thank you."

"No problem, but I can ask the nurse to get Peter's phone number if you're still spooked."

"No, that's OK, I'll get it for you." I opened my purse, took out my wallet, and found the photo of Joanie I kept tucked in a little plastic sleeve behind the photos of Nick and Cady. "You know, I sometimes wonder what I'd say to her if we met again. We were identical twins, but we were different in a lot of ways. You won't believe this, but I was the wild one."

"Oh, I believe it. You may be afraid of boats and water, but I've seen you on the ski slopes and you're the only mom I know who subscribes to *Mother Jones*."

He was right. He got his daredevil streak from me. "I wasn't afraid of anything when we were kids. All I wanted was travel and adventure while Joanie dreamed of nothing but a husband and kids. It's funny how things turned out. Sometimes it feels as though I'm living her life instead of mine."

"Mom." Nick's face clouded with concern. "Aren't you happy? Do you wish you'd had a different life?"

"Oh no, your dad and I were just saying how glad we are that things worked out the way they did, but still, I got the life that Joanie wanted. She missed so much."

"Yeah, that's sad," he agreed. "It makes me realize that you shouldn't waste your life. I'm going to make sure mine counts for something. That's why I'm going to stand with Peter and the ARA at that Rally."

"Go for it," I said despite my trepidations. "Just be careful. You'll be on crutches, so you won't be able to run if things get nasty."

"Don't worry, I don't want to die a martyr like Cady's dad, but I don't want to live my life on the sidelines either."

"Right." I pressed my lips together. I wasn't ready to tell him the truth about Arcas. I put Joanie's photo back in my wallet and stood up. "You know, maybe I'll go pay a visit to our friend down the hall."

Dr. Kanter was as white and wrinkled as his bedclothes when I peeked in on him. I might have missed him in the tangle of sheets if he hadn't turned his head and looked at me. "Is that you, Joanie? Is it time for supper?"

"Dr. Kanter, it's me, Amy Savas. Did I wake you?"

"What? I'm sorry. I must have drifted off. I thought I was back on the ship."

"No, you're in the hospital, St. Michael's." He looked confused as he struggled to sit up. "Would you like me to call a nurse?"

"No, that's not necessary." He felt around for his glasses buried in the blanket and put them on. "You're the woman with the disc. I thought you were someone else for a moment there. Forgive me, I'm still half asleep, please, come in."

I wasn't convinced, but I took a few tentative steps into the room.

He kept looking at me and shaking his head. "You and your daughter look so much like Joanie it's uncanny. It's hard to believe you aren't related."

"A lot of what you've told me is uncanny. To be honest, your story about the woman on the ship brought back a lot of memories. You really had me going, the way you figured out what was written on the other half of the pendant. That's quite a stunt you pulled."

"I'm sorry? I'm not sure what you mean."

"The way you deciphered the other half of the poem. That was really clever. You archaeologists are even smarter than I thought."

"Oh, my dear, I wish we were that intelligent. I remembered the inscription because we spent a lot of time trying to figure it out. It was a parlor game we played to amuse ourselves, but none of us ever came up with a good solution. It really bothered Joanie, poor thing. She was sure it was a clue to her identity, but we could never solve the puzzle. Are you sure there weren't more of those necklaces made?"

His denial had me spooked again. "I was wondering that too, so I called my mother and asked where she bought it. Apparently, the cat medallion was a stock item, but the engraving was a custom job. I suppose, if the jeweler liked it, he could have made more of them." I was desperate for a logical explanation. "Was your Joanie from Rochester by any chance?"

"She doesn't know where she's from. She can't remember a thing about her past. I was hoping that you knew her."

My hands were trembling as I pulled Joanie's photo from my wallet and showed it to him. "This is Joanie, my sister."

"Yes, that's her. She looks just like that."

"Joanie died twenty years ago. She drowned in a boating accident."

"No, no, she's . . . I don't know. I'm confused."

I turned and looked out the window at a small silver plane passing through a cloud. "It was my fault. I was charged with driving a boat under the influence and involuntary manslaughter. That's why I came to Canada."

"How awful."

"So, you can imagine how disturbing I find your story. It's almost as though you saw Joanie's ghost or something."

"I can assure you that the Joanie I know is very much alive. In fact, she's just fallen madly in love with the ship's doctor. I expect they'll get married soon."

I was inexplicably pleased by this news. It's what Joanie would have wanted. "I'm happy for her, whoever she is."

"She's a domestic little thing, rather old-fashioned that way. I wish I could see her again, let her know what the other half of her pendant says."

"Yes, I wish you could tell her that, and what it meant to us, I mean to me and my sister." I was embarrassed to ask, but I had to know. "Is she happy?"

Dr. Kanter looked at me, surprised, but nodded. "Yes, she's very happy now that she's found Sam. They're in seventh heaven, but that's the way with lovebirds, isn't it?" As I put the photo back in my purse he asked, "Why the unexpected visit? You haven't changed your mind about the disc, have you? You haven't come to take it back?"

"No, you can keep it. I stopped by because Nick wanted your grandson's phone number. It seems they've really hit it off."

"How nice, hand me my notepad and a pen, they're in the bedside table." He jotted down the number in an old man's jagged scrawl. "I'm relieved about the disc since I've already contacted my department. I haven't heard back yet, but I'm expecting a call any time now."

"There's no hurry," I assure him.

"Frankly, the person I'd really like to talk to is Charles Dawson. He teaches comparative philology at The University of London. He'd be just the man for the job, but he's aboard that ship where I took my fall, and I don't know how to reach him."

"He was aboard the ship with you and Joanie?"

"Yes, we were all having supper together that last night. Everyone was happy. Joanie was absolutely glowing since she and Sam were moving in together. Dawson was toasting them with a glass of champagne. He's a lovely fellow, brilliant mind. I don't know why I didn't think of him sooner."

"I suppose a couple good minds could have the disc sorted out in no time."

"Oh no, it takes an eternity to decipher a lost language, but the fun is in the process, and it would be a pleasure working with a man like Dawson."

An unaccustomed sense of well-being settled over me. The room felt awash in light as I stood up. "It was wonderful talking with you. Let me know if you hear anything about the disc." I picked up my purse and turned to go. "And I'm glad to hear that Joanie is so happy."

On the way home, I bought a bouquet of yellow hibiscus that I arranged in a pitcher on the kitchen table. They looked like a party, a celebration of sunshine and summer. I turned on the radio and there was Whitney Houston singing, "I Will Always Love You." I turned up the volume and was singing along at the top of my voice when Tom appeared in the doorway between the kitchen and the dining room. He must have thought I was singing for him, and maybe I was, but mostly I was singing for Joanie and the Arcas I thought I knew when we were young.

Tom took me by the hand and pulled me close. He began the slow foxtrot that was the only dance step he knew. I shut my eyes but kept on singing until the song was done and the station cut to a jingle for a local amusement park. I gave my husband an affectionate hug before breaking away to switch off the radio. "I didn't expect you home so early. It's not even five o'clock."

"We had a power failure, no lights, no computers, no AC so we called it a day. I've been home for two hours. I didn't know you were back until I heard you singing. That was quite a performance."

"I don't know why, but I feel wonderful. By the way, your son is planning to join the resistance."

Tom raised his eyebrows.

"Dr. Kanter's grandson convinced him to protest a speech by a holocaust denier a couple days after he's discharged from the hospital. Apparently, he's feeling much better."

Tom grinned. "And you're okay with this?"

"What can I say, it's in his blood. There was no stopping you when you were his age."

I stepped closer and put my left hand on his shoulder and took his right hand in mine. "Let's dance some more. That was fun. Why don't we ever go dancing?"

"Because we're a couple of klutzes who trip over each other's feet." He held me close anyway and we swayed without music.

I lifted my face to his and he kissed me and then he kissed me again and I suspected that dinner might have to wait while we took a detour to the bedroom when I heard the doorbell ring. We exchanged quizzical looks as I pulled away to see who it could be. I opened the door to find Arcas standing on our doorstep.

He'd put on some heft over the years and his dark, curly hair was cut short and shot through with gray, but it was Arcas. He was wearing a black button-down shirt open at the collar. A bouquet of red roses bloomed optimistically from his right hand. My first impulse was to shut the door and lock it.

"Tom, come here. You'll never guess who's paying us a visit."

Tom ambled up beside me then did a double take when he saw who it was. "My God." He took a step forward to stand between me and the man at the door. "What are you doing here?"

Arcas held up the flowers. "These are for my daughter."

Tom didn't miss a beat. "You don't have a daughter. There's nothing for you here."

"That's not what Nancy tells me." He sounded confident, but his shoulders drooped, and I could see he was exhausted. He looked past Tom to me. "Are you going to ask me in?"

I stepped aside to admit this ghost from my past, while Tom held his ground and didn't move. Arcas pushed past my husband and stood awkwardly in our small living room. My heart was pounding, but I smiled cordially as though this was a normal visit. "Cady isn't here. Do you want me to put those flowers in a vase?"

"No." Tom was adamant. "He takes the flowers with him when he goes. He has nothing to do with Cady."

Arcas rubbed his neck with his free hand and looked around the room. "I never imagined you and Tom together. I pictured you back in the States with your parents all these years."

"And I pictured you dead." I wasn't as angry as I thought I'd be, although Tom was turning red. He looked as though he'd like to take our visitor outside and beat him to a pulp. I asked the question that had been haunting me since Nancy told us Arcas was alive." Who the hell sent that letter telling us you'd died? Did you write that yourself?"

Arcas dropped his belligerent pose and nodded sheepishly. "My wife was pregnant, and I didn't like to tell you that."

"Your wife! You had a wife?"

"It was an arranged marriage, but then I came to Canada and fell in love with you, but then she got pregnant and . . ."

I was outraged. "So, the whole story about smuggling weapons and risking your life for democracy was a set-up? You planned this all out?"

"I didn't want you to hate me. I made up a nice story so you'd always have good memories."

"Thanks, very considerate of you."

"I didn't know you were pregnant too. Why didn't you tell me?"

"I didn't tell you because you were dead!"

"She didn't tell you because it was none of your business." Tom's voice was low but I could see the muscles in his neck stiffen. "Cady's my daughter, not yours."

Arcas looked Tom straight in the eyes and smirked. "No, she's mine. You may have raised her, but she's my blood."

Tom put his arm around my shoulder and shook his head. "That's where you're wrong. We'd been sleeping together for months before you disappeared. Why do you think Nancy left? She knows everything, just ask her."

Now Arcas looked confused. He clearly didn't know what to believe. He turned to me. "Is this true? You and Tom were sleeping together? I don't believe it."

Tom squeezed my shoulder and I moved closer to him. We were in this together. "Didn't you see how Tom and I looked at one another? Didn't you wonder about all that overtime at Abbott's printing?" Lying was easier than I thought.

I didn't expect him to believe a word, but to my chagrin Arcas's face crumbled.

"Oh for God's sake, pull yourself together," Tom said. "You have your own children. You don't need mine."

"No, we never had children. My wife was pregnant when I left. That's why I had to go back, but she lost the baby, and we couldn't have children after that." Arcas sat down on the sofa, threw his head back, and closed his eyes. Maybe it was grief, maybe it was just exhaustion, but he couldn't seem to stop the flow of tears trickling down his face.

He was little more than a stranger after all these years, just a large, middle-aged Greek weeping on my couch. I didn't need this relic from the past barging into our lives, but there he was. "Do you want a glass of water?"

"Thank you." He dried his eyes on his shirt sleeve. "I'm sorry. This isn't what I came for. It's not what I expected."

"What the hell *did* you expect?" Tom was furious, but I don't know what he said next because he lapsed into rapid fire Greek while I went to get the water. Once in the kitchen, a glass of tap water seemed inadequate. I pulled a bottle of ouzo from the cupboard and put it on a tray with three glasses of ice, a pitcher of water, crackers, and a hunk of Brie. My pulse was still racing, so I made a detour to the bathroom where I peed and ran a brush through my hair before returning to the living room.

"I figured we could all use a drink."

Arcas poured a good shot of ouzo into his glass then added a splash of water. Tom and I followed suit, raised our glasses, and mumbled a half-hearted, "Yamas." The licorice flavored liquor gave me a jolt, but that was what I needed. Seeing Arcas again had me completely rattled.

I stared down at the man slumped on my couch. "So, bring me up to date. What have you been doing for the past twenty years?"

"He's been making cheese," Tom said.

"Yes, I make a lot of cheese, but that's not all I do," Arcas said. "I'm also a member of the Arcadian prefectural council. Papandreou recommended me for the position."

I could see that Tom was impressed, but he didn't want to give Arcas the satisfaction. "Really? He didn't mention you the last time we spoke." Tom was trying to one-up his old friend, but his boast wouldn't have held up under scrutiny. He'd spent all of five seconds congratulating Andreas at his first post-election party a decade ago and hadn't spoken with him since. I blushed, embarrassed for my husband. I'd never heard him brag like that before.

"So, you're married and you make cheese," I interrupted. "Do you still raise sheep?"

"No, we got rid of the sheep after my mother died. Kula couldn't stand the smell of them."

"Kula? Is that your wife?" I asked.

His face darkened. "She's my wife for another two weeks, then she's going to marry a naval officer like her father."

"You married a woman whose father was a naval officer while we were trying to take down the colonels?" Tom was livid. "What sort of man are you?"

"I'm a man who loved my family, maybe too much. You wouldn't understand, but I wouldn't dishonor them. Our grandfathers fought together against the Turks."

I felt bad for Arcas, even after all the pain he'd caused, but I wasn't giving him Cady. I took another sip of ouzo and looked at him over the rim of my glass. He was practically doubled over with his head in his hands. I picked up his empty glass and refilled it with another shot. "Here, drink this."

He shook his head and waved the drink away. "Do you have retsina?"

"No, sorry. If you'll recall, I can't stand the stuff." I put the drink back down. "So, what's your plan? How long will you be in town?" I was hoping he'd say that he was taking the next plane out, but he just studied the empty space between me and Tom without answering.

"Arcas?"

"I don't know. I have no idea." He looked up at me with a sad half-smile. "I thought maybe my daughter would want to live in Greece and help me run the business. It's a big cheese factory, *Arkadiko Tyri*. She'd be a rich woman."

Had Arcas really thought Cady would move to Greece to make cheese? He'd apparently been spinning happy fantasies ever since Nancy made him believe he had a daughter. "First, she's not your daughter and second, she's going to be a doctor."

"That's nice. Your daughter will be a doctor. You must feel very proud." He stood up and bowed slightly from the waist. "I'm sorry for disturbing you. I'm sorry for everything and I'm very tired. Would you mind calling a taxi for me? I'll wait outside."

"No, don't be silly. Tom will drive you to your hotel, won't you, Tom?"

Tom gave me a dirty look, but said, "Sure." He reached into his pocket for his car keys. "Where are you staying?"

"The Four Seasons, it's not far away."

"I know where it is. You must be selling a lot of cheese." The Four Seasons was the priciest hotel in the city.

"Yes, I sell a lot of cheese. I should have brought you a wheel of Graviera. It's our signature product."

"You know, Tom still has family outside Athens. We go there every couple of years. Maybe we'll call you the next time we visit." I was trying to end this on a less tortured note.

"That would be nice. I'll give you a tour of my factory." He paused, looking around our house, taking in the well-worn furniture, the books, the piano, the framed photos of our kids. "I'm glad you're happy. You deserve a good life. It was nice seeing you again."

Tom and Arcas were halfway out the door when I remembered something. "Wait a minute, there's something I need to ask you. Do you remember that clay paperweight thing you gave me when you left? What do you know about it?"

"Just that my father brought it back from Crete when I was a kid. Do you still have it?"

"Actually, I gave it to an archaeologist who's interested in things like that. He'd love to talk with you if you have the time."

"Sure, I don't have anything else to do."

"Great. I'll let him know that you're in town. He's in the hospital at the moment, so you'd have to meet him there."

"No problem." Arcas pulled a business card out of a sleek leather cardcase and wrote a number on the back. "You can reach me here. As I said, I have nothing scheduled for the next few days. Good night."

"Good night, I'll be in touch."

Tom and Arcas left me examining the card. It was in Greek, but I could make out *Arkadiko Tyri* and there was a logo of Pan playing his flute to two identical women with long curly hair. I stared at it, wondering if one of them was me.

TOM RETURNED AN hour later, tired, hungry, and out of sorts. He kicked off his shoes and stretched out on the couch with a plate of left-over brie and crackers. "Well, that was surreal. What do we tell Cady?"

"Do we have to tell her anything? Can't we pretend this never happened?" I knew that wasn't an option, but I was afraid the truth would damage her. She'd always been the child of a hero, martyred to the cause of democracy. I didn't want her redefined as the child of an adulterer and a liar. I didn't want her tainted by that man.

"She's not a child, Amy. She's twenty-one. It has to be her decision. Who knows? Maybe she wants to be the child of a Greek cheese mogul."

I doubted it, but I wasn't sure. Arcas wasn't the man I'd imagined, and I didn't know what Cady would make of him. "Well, at least she wasn't here tonight. That gives us time to think. We'll have to break the news to her tomorrow."

Cady was spending less and less time at home and more and more time with her boyfriend. I had my reservations, but she was twenty-one years old. Twenty-one, the number reverberated in my brain and made me shudder. That's how old I was, we were, when Joanie died. Whenever I thought of my long dead sister I was overcome with regret for all that she had missed. I didn't want Cady to miss anything. If she was ready for a serious relationship, then I could only wish her happiness, the happiness that Joanie never had. "Carpe diem, gather ye roses, go for it, Sweetie," I whispered to my absent daughter. "Live your life."

It was almost noon, so Cady was probably at the hospital. She usually stopped by her brother's room when she finished her shift, so I could catch her there. But what would I say? Tom and I had argued into the wee hours about what to tell her. I was in favor of delay and deceit, but my husband was an honest man. He wanted to present her with the whole, ugly truth. Why couldn't we just let her be happy? Why did we have to complicate her life? I dialed the hospital and asked for Nick Savas's room.

"Hi, Nick, is your sister there? Good, can I talk to her?"

"Hi, Mom, what's up?" Cady was her usual perky self.

"Something unexpected happened and we need to talk about it. Can you be home for dinner tonight? It's important."

"Sure, I was coming home anyway. It's Jackson's poker night so he'll be out with his buddies. Are you OK? 'Something unexpected' sounds kind of ominous."

"We're fine, it's nothing like that, we just need to talk. Tell Nick I'll stop by later with a care package. Love you, bye." I hung up before she could ask another question. I still didn't know what we'd tell her, but the truth would be out.

I hesitated before picking up the phone again. I pulled the card Arcas had given me from my pocket and dialed the number, half hoping that he wouldn't answer, but he picked up on the first ring. The voice on the other end of the line was so familiar that I found myself momentarily tongue-tied, tangled in time, twenty-four again. "Hi, hello, I wasn't sure you'd be in. I was wondering if you'd have time to stop by the hospital later."

"Sure, what time do you want me? I'm free all day.

Jacob
July 1993

IT'S BEEN OVER twenty-four hours and Dr. Mansour still hasn't called. I don't understand it. You'd think she'd be falling all over herself to get a look at a second Phaistos disc. I stare at the number scrawled on yesterday's menu wondering if it's too soon to call again when my phone rings. It's beside me on the bed and I pounce on it immediately.

"Hello, Dr. Kanter, it's Amy Savas."

My heart sinks, but I try not to sound disappointed. "Good afternoon, nice to hear from you."

"It's about the disc."

Damn, she's changed her mind. She wants it back.

"Something unexpected happened last night. The man who gave me the disc showed up at our house. He just rang the bell out of the blue. It's a long story, but he's willing to tell you everything he knows about where it came from and how he got it. Would you like to meet him?"

My mood brightens immediately, but I'm puzzled. "Of course, I'd like to meet him, but I thought you told me he was dead."

"Well, it seems we were wrong about that. He's alive, in good health and visiting Toronto. Cady doesn't know about her dad yet, so please don't tell her."

"No, of course not, mum's the word." I'm astonished, imagining, Cady's long-lost father returning from the dead. For years I'd fantasized about coming home and finding Bess in the kitchen putting away a bag of groceries. I'm always surprised and say, "Bess, what are you doing here? I thought that you were dead."

"Oh no." She turns to me with her angelic smile. "I was just away visiting my mother."

So, miracles do happen. This man has returned from wherever he was just when I need him most. I can't wait to meet this resurrected ghost. "When can he stop by? I'd like to see him before they move me out of here."

"He could see you this afternoon if that's alright. I don't know how long he'll be in town so the sooner the better."

"How about three o'clock? I should be back from therapy by then." The rusty old cogs in my brain start to churn. There are so many questions I want to ask. Knowing the story of the disc's origins will give it a patina of credibility, although the disc will have to speak for itself. I'm the one whose credibility is in question. No one will do business with a man locked inside the memory ward of Bayside Manor. Michael may be well-intentioned, but he underestimates me. I'll have to slip his leash before he ruins everything.

Amy arrives promptly at three. There's a man with her, a bit overdressed for Toronto in the summer. Beneath his tailored jacket is a shirt unbuttoned halfway to his navel. I've never been a fan of jewelry on men, so I'm instantly put off by the gold chain he's clearly showing off. I try not to be judgmental, but I wonder what a nice woman like Amy ever saw in him.

"Dr. Kanter, this is my old friend, Arcas, the man who gave me the clay disc."

Introductions are awkward when you're in bed and can't even sit up properly. I extend my hand. "Jacob Kanter, thank you for stopping by." His grip is firm, and he looks intelligent enough. Perhaps I've been too hasty.

He hands me a business card that I can't read because the print's too small. "Amy tells me you're an archaeologist. My father worked for a group of archaeologists when I was little. That's how he got the disc. We always knew it was old, but no one ever thought it was particularly valuable."

"Please have a seat." I realize there's only one chair, so I ring for the nurse. "If you wait a moment someone will bring in another chair. Tell me, how old were you when your father brought home the disc?"

"Just a kid, maybe eight or nine. I'm not really sure. He used to bring us all sorts of little things he'd pick up on those digs."

My eyebrows nearly hit the ceiling. "He brought home other 'little things'? Was your father an archaeologist?"

Arcas laughs. "No, he was a cook, but he'd find odd bits of pottery and bring them home. He always said the Italians didn't mind as long as he didn't take anything valuable." He suddenly stops and looks away. When he turns back to me two lines crease his brow. The penny's dropped. He's just realized a cook couldn't know what was and wasn't valuable. "He was an uneducated man. He didn't know a piece of broken pottery could be worth anything."

Maybe, but I have my doubts. "So, where are the other bits of pottery? Does your family still have them?"

A cloud passes over Arcas's face. He clearly understands the implication of my question. "I don't know where they are. Like I said, I was just a kid. Maybe he gave them away. Maybe he threw them out. I know we don't have them anymore. My parents are both gone, so there's no one to ask. Is there anything else you'd like to know?"

"Yes, do you know why your father kept this one old relic when he apparently discarded all the others? Was there something special about it?"

A faint smile crosses Arcas's face and I can see he's remembering something. "I don't know if he thought it was special, but he thought he had to keep it. It's a strange story."

"I'd love to hear it."

"It's nonsense, but he used to tell this story about something that happened on the ship crossing from Crete back to Athens. He was standing in line at the snack bar looking at the disc when a woman in a white uniform, probably a nurse, came up to him and said, 'The disc belongs to another man in another time. Keep it safe for him.' That's all she said. Then she touched his shoulder and disappeared into the crowd. But after that he wouldn't part with it." Arcus chuckles and shakes his head, looking embarrassed. "I told you it was a weird story."

"It is. Yet you parted with it. You gave it to Amy."

"Why not? I'm not superstitious and it seemed like a nice gift. I thought the disc would be happier with her."

I've made him uncomfortable, and he won't tell me anything else if I don't lighten up, but I'd bet money those other bits of pottery were sold on the black market. Security was looser in those days and a smart cook could get away with archaeological mayhem. Doro Levi's team never even produced a definitive pottery report, so who could say what was there and what went missing? God knows what was lifted from the site. "Does the name Doro Levi mean anything to you? Was he one of the Italians?"

"Levi? That sounds Jewish, not Italian."

"Yes," I agree. "He was Jewish, an Italian Jew. He was head of the Italian School of Archaeology at that time. Do you remember hearing his name?"

"No, but my father used to talk about a Jew who ran the operation. He just called him, the Jew. That could have been him."

I bristle, but try to maintain a neutral expression. "And do you know exactly where your father was working? There were several active sites in Crete at that time."

"I don't know the exact location, but they were excavating a palace, not the big one at Knossos, a smaller one somewhere else."

"Could it have been in Phaistos? Does that ring a bell?" I was leading the witness, but I needed to tie the disc to Levi's excavation.

"Yes, that's it, the palace in Phaistos."

I let out a sigh of relief. One man's story wasn't proof, but it certainly supported the idea that we had a second Phaistos disc. "That's very interesting. It seems your father may have picked up a valuable clue to unlocking a lost language. It may change history, or at least our knowledge of ancient history. Did the Italians know about the little things your dad brought home?"

Arcas maintains his composure, but he's clearly annoyed. "I doubt it. They were just souvenirs, and he figured they belonged to us, the Greeks, not the Italians anyway."

Before I can respond the nurse is at the door. "You rang. Is there something I can do for you?"

"Yes, please. Could you bring in an extra chair for my guests?"

Amy looks out the window at a patch of dark clouds gathering to the east. "Please don't bother, we won't be staying long. It looks like rain, and I don't want to get caught in another downpour." But the nurse has already disappeared.

"Yes," Arcas agrees. "I don't think I have any more to tell you."

"There is something else." I want them to stay. There's more I need to know. "What did you think the disc was? Did you ever wonder what it was for?"

"Not really, it was just a curiosity. We used it for a paperweight." He shrugs, indicating that he's never given it any thought, and then he unexpectedly smiles, remembering something else. "My mother used it as a cheese press for a while. The customers liked the designs it made on the cheese, but it didn't fit our molds properly, so she gave it up. Did the Minoans make cheese?"

"I'm sure they did." I smile back at him, but I'm appalled. The disc had no doubt withstood worse than being pushed into cultured sheep's milk over the course of its four thousand years, but the idea of it being used as a cheese press, my God.

The nurse returns with a chair from the waiting room. "Here you go. Is there anything else I can do for you?"

"Yes, would you mind taking that clay disc from the safe? I'd like to show it to my visitors."

She hesitates, looking at her watch. "A patient down the hall is due for an infusion. Could we do that later? I don't want to keep her waiting."

Amy turns from where she's been looking out the window. "Go ahead, we've both seen it. There's no need to take it out."

"Good then, no need for me to get it now." The nurse turns to go.

"I'd like to see it. I haven't looked at it in years." Arcas addresses the nurse, but she must not hear him because she continues out the door.

"Well, then, if you don't mind giving me the combination to your safe again, I could take it out," Amy says. "But I really do want to leave before it starts to rain.

"It's 5-4-0-8. We'll just give Arcas a quick peek before he goes."

Amy disappears into the closet then emerges a moment later, absolutely stricken. "It's not in there. Are you sure that's where you put it?"

I struggle to sit up in the bed so I can see her better. "Of course, I'm sure. The nurse put it in there for me. Look again. It has to be in there."

She comes back with my watch, my wallet, my house keys and two quarters and lays them on the bed. "This is it. This is everything that's in there." We stare at each other, speechless. Then it comes to me. My son took it. Michael must have stolen a priceless artifact and sold it for a few dollars to subsidize my nursing home. I feel dizzy. Fireworks go off inside my head. There's a vast array of exploding stars and then the screen goes blank.

"Dr. Kanter, are you alright?"

I feel a small hand on my shoulder. The Savas woman is standing beside me, a concerned expression on her face. "Yes, yes," I start to tell her. "I'm fine, it was just the shock of finding that the disc is gone." But not a word comes out, just a strange gurgling sound I've never made before. Her face comes into focus, and I can see that her eyes are wide with fright. "It's all right," I want to say. "No need to be alarmed." But all that emerges is a hideous rasp. Is this how my story ends, babbling strangled sounds to a woman I barely know, the disc gone and betrayed by my own son? I close my eyes and wait while Amy calls the nurse.

Moments later all hell breaks loose. White coats surround my bed, needles are stuck in my arm, electrodes are pasted to my chest and a large machine begins beeping and blinking cryptic messages I can't decipher. I try to swat away a woman covering my mouth and nose with a plastic mask, but my right arm won't move. I'm too old for all of this, but I can't get up and run away, so I do the only thing I can. I shut my eyes and go to sleep.

"DAD, ARE YOU awake? Blink if you can hear me." Michael is sitting by my bed patting my leg with one hand and dabbing at his runny nose with the other. Tears are running down his great, ruddy cheeks. I haven't seen him cry like that since his mother died. I blink and he grabs my hand. I want to rock him on my lap like I did when he was a little boy, but then I remember the disc and turn my head away.

"You were a wonderful father," he whispers in my ear.

Were? Am I already dead?

"You were the man I wanted to be, but couldn't. I was never as smart or brave or generous as you, but I tried. I wanted you to be proud of me."

Bess and I were always proud of him. He'd been a good boy. He'd done well in school, and he'd grown up to be a good father and provider. Who'd have guessed he'd betray me at the end? I'd never have suspected my Michael capable of such treachery.

"It was awful watching you fail these last few years. I wanted you to be strong and independent forever, but what could I do? Your mind started to go, your brilliant, curious, questioning mind that was so full of facts and stories. I had to protect you. I didn't want people laughing at you. I didn't want you to be the butt of mean-spirited jokes."

What is he talking about? Why would anyone have laughed at me?

"I know you didn't want to go to Bayside Manor, who would? I didn't want to send you there, but you were falling apart, and I didn't know what else to do. I couldn't have you wandering around the city by yourself, lost and confused and falling down. I wanted to keep you safe, and then that nonsense with the disc. You had me going for a minute there. You almost had me convinced that it was real, that you'd made the find of the century, but it was just another fantasy as crazy as your magic ship. I checked, and there was nothing in your safe. The whole thing was in your head."

He checked and there was nothing there? If he didn't take it, who the Hell did?

"I'm so sorry, Papa. When Dr. Mansour called, I had to tell her it was all a terrible mistake, that you were suffering from dementia."

I turn my head to glare at him, but I don't see the blustering bully I expect. I see a little boy who's lost his father.

"Papa, it broke my heart, but I didn't want your reputation sullied. I wanted them to remember you as the great scholar, the esteemed Dr. Jacob Kanter. Do you understand? It was for your sake. Can you forgive me?"

I can't speak, but I try to nod. He acted without malice out of love. My index finger stirs, and I press it against his hand. It says, I forgive you. It says, I still love you, son.

Michael sits beside me holding my hand until long after dark. My eyes are closed but I'm awake listening to the ticking of the wall clock, and to my son's heavy, irregular breath. I. feel the weight of shadows shifting across my bed as the fan stirs the curtains and I wish Bess was here beside me. I think about the disc and how I almost had the chance to explore its mysteries, to decipher an unknown language, to reach across millennia to commune with a vanished culture. That would have been something, but it seems I've run out of time.

I hear the door open then the nurse's gentle voice. "Go home now. You need some rest. We'll call if there's a change. I promise, we'll take good care of him."

Michael raises his great bulk from the small chair where he's been sitting, kisses me on the forehead, and leaves the room. I hear the door close and the sound of footsteps as he makes his way toward the elevator. *Good-bye Michael,* I whisper in my head.

"Well, that was quite the confession. I'm glad your son got that off his chest."

How did the nurse know about our conversation? Had she been eavesdropping? Had she been standing at the door the entire time?

I force my eyes open and turn in her direction. She's taller than I remember. Her uniform glows in the light streaming through the window. Her straight white hair, always neatly combed and pinned beneath her cap, stands away from her head electrified and wild.

"I came to let you know, your ship is back in port. I told you, you have options."

"The *Aqua Meridian*?" I'm amazed by the strength and clarity of my voice.

"Yes, and I'm authorized to offer you a first-class ticket, but you'll have to hurry. She won't be docked here long."

"Impossible, I'm much too weak. Can't you see the state I'm in?"

"You can do it. I'll help you dress. We'll have to slip out the service entrance."

I feel her strong arms beneath my shoulders and a moment later I'm sitting up and she's pulling an *Aqua Meridian* T-shirt over my head. Once I'm dressed, she lifts me to my feet. "Come on now, let's get you to my car."

"But I can't walk. We'll need a wheelchair."

"Lean on me. I'll support you until you get your sea-legs back."

I do lean on her and my legs move as she propels me forward. To my surprise, no one gives us a second glance as she guides me to the elevator then out the back door onto Shuter Street. It's a beautiful evening in July and Toronto is vibrant even at this late hour. I turn to her and shake my head, mystified to find myself alive. I inhale the scent of a city night: gasoline, French fries, hot asphalt, and a hint of the lake a few blocks to the south.

"Thank you," I whisper, overcome with gratitude for this beautiful night.

In response, she reaches into her pocket and takes out a small package wrapped in gauze. "Here you go, take this with you. Those closet safes aren't worth a damn, and I was concerned about your visitors." She drops the disc into my hands. "Enjoy solving the puzzle. I understand it holds some surprising secrets."

I put the disc into my pocket overcome with joy. "You were the nurse who told Arcus's father to keep this disc, weren't you?"

She looks indignant. "Just how old do you think I am?"

I shrug apologetically. I have no idea. But I know Dawson will be astounded when he sees this. We can work together on the project. We don't need the university, fame, or recognition, just the joy of trying to solve the puzzle, the pleasure of resurrecting a bit of a long-lost past. What luck that I met Dawson. He's just the man for the job.

"Thank you," I say again as we climb into her old gray Chevy. I pat the disc inside my pocket as we head off toward the lake. "You know, there was a woman on the ship who looked exactly like my wife. It's odd but I think she knew my name."

The nurse smiles but doesn't say another word until she pulls up alongside the dock where the *Aqua Meridian* is moored. "Out you go. Enjoy the trip."

I open the door, tentatively place my right foot on the pavement, and stand up. To my relief, my legs hold. I take a deep breath and turn to see a small group of people waving from the lower deck.

"Go on now. They're waiting for you," the nurse says.

"Thank you." I give her my best nautical salute and make my way up the gangway as she drives off.

The little group waiting to meet me is dressed to the nines. Joanie's got herself dolled up in a long blue gown with flouncy sleeves that shimmer beguilingly in the moonlight. Her dark curls are parted to the side then done up in little ringlets and waves. Even more astounding is the sight of Dawson in a tuxedo and Sam in his best dress whites. Clearly, I'm undressed for the occasion.

Joanie greets me with a hug. "You're back. We were worried about you. Did you know they've moved you to first class?"

"Yes, my nurse told me. Wonderful news."

Sam puts his arm around Joanie. "We're celebrating with supper in the first-class dining room tonight. You'll love it. The chef is amazing."

I turn an admiring eye to Joanie. "You look lovely. What's the occasion?"

"We're celebrating the Golden Age of Hollywood tonight. Everyone's dressing for dinner and then they're showing old Marx Brothers movies. You'll find an appropriate outfit in your new stateroom."

"You know," I tell her. "I met another beautiful woman while I was in the hospital. She and her daughter both looked exactly like you, except, of course, she was older." I'm about to tell her about the coincidence with the matching necklaces when Dawson pats me on the shoulder.

"Good to have you back. We've missed you," he says.

"Good to see you too. In fact, I've brought you a little present"—I pat my jacket pocket—"a second Phaistos Disc."

His look of astonishment is gratifying. "No! Impossible. Can I see it?"

His excitement is palpable, but he'll have to wait since Joanie is pulling me inside where a big band is playing a schmaltzy rendition of that old chestnut, "Cheek to Cheek." The conductor, wearing a curly blonde wig, comically oversized evening coat, and battered top hat is doing an impressive imitation of Harpo Marx.

Elegantly dressed couples are dancing in the large lobby that's been decked out as a speakeasy from the thirties. Champagne is flowing and everyone seems to be having a wonderful time. I'm no dancer, but I feel myself swaying to the music when I notice a familiar figure. The woman who looks like Bess is standing with her back to me chatting with another woman and for once, she's not racing away.

"Excuse me," I say to my friends as I make my way in her direction.

"Excuse me," I call out louder, hoping to get her attention. "Excuse me." She's wearing a beautiful green dress that shows off a figure that brings back memories of Bess in her prime. "Excuse me, Miss. May I have a minute?"

She turns, but I still can't see her face because she's wearing Groucho glasses with a bulbous nose, a small moustache, and bushy eyebrows she wiggles lasciviously in my direction. Above the music and the chatter of the crowd I can hear Joanie laughing.

Amy
July 1993

NICK WAS COMING home. He'd attend his rally, do his bit to save the world, and then we'd head to cottage country for a month. I folded shorts and T-shirts, underwear, sunscreen, and insect repellent into my suitcase, but my mind was on Dr. Kanter. I kept seeing the panic in his face before he went stiff and fell backward on the bed.

Poor Dr. Kanter, that stupid disc had meant so much to him, but why? It was probably just an archaic shopping list or an ancient recipe for cheese dip. How had I let myself get caught up in the old guy's delusions when I knew he had dementia? He'd most likely hidden it himself and then forgotten where. There was a reason he was moving to a memory ward.

I took my old swimsuit from the bottom drawer. It was a navy one-piece decorated with small white fish that swam across the fabric in neat horizontal rows. I smiled apologetically at the fish. In all the years I'd owned the suit, they'd never gotten wet. I occasionally wore the suit for sunbathing far from the beach, but never for swimming. The moment I thought of stepping into a lake or river alarms would go off in my head and I'd hear my sister's screams for help. No point ruining a good vacation by reliving that nightmare. I refolded the suit and put it back in the drawer.

Cady was my main concern. We had to tell her about Arcas, but I couldn't find the words. I kept rehearsing one scenario after another, but none of them felt right. I tried, *Guess who stopped by yesterday evening?* But that was too casual. *It seems your dad isn't quite as dead as we thought.* No, too glib. Maybe, *You'd better sit down, we have some shocking news.* That might work if it didn't scare her to death. I'd just have to play it by ear.

A pan of lasagna sat steaming on the dinner table. Tom and Cady tucked in with their usual enthusiasm, but I didn't have much appetite.

"What's Nick going to do at the cottage? He can't go swimming with that cast." Cady took a sip of wine and turned to me for an answer.

"I guess he'll just keep me company and work on his tan," I answered. "He could go fishing. We have a couple of fishing poles around somewhere."

Tom couldn't imagine anyone being bored at the lake. "He can go out on the boat, he can play board games, he can read, he can go bird watching. Don't worry about Nick. We'll make sure he has a good time."

"Absolutely, Nick's loves bird watching." Cady was being sarcastic, but she was right. Nick wasn't made for sedentary activities, but he'd have to learn. We were picking him up from the hospital first thing in the morning. Thinking of the hospital brought back the memory of my visit with Dr. Kanter.

"Did I tell you what happened this afternoon? I was visiting Dr. Kanter and he seemed perfectly fine, sitting up and talking normally. He wanted to look at the disc, but when I opened his safe if wasn't there. It was shocking, I mean I was shocked, but he was absolutely stricken. He fell back on his pillow, his eyes turned glassy, and he couldn't talk. It was terrifying. I don't think he knew what hit him. The nurse threw us out of his room, so I don't know what happened after that."

"Poor guy, sounds like he had a stroke." Tom tore off a hunk of garlic bread from a knotted loaf and stuffed it in his mouth.

Cady stopped eating and turned to me with a stunned expression. "That's awful, I hope he's okay. He was my absolute favorite patient. Does Nick know? Nick really liked him too."

"No, I just went home afterward."

"Then we'll have to tell him. He talked to Nick about politics and the Second World War. He was teaching me about Greek medicine before Hippocrates." She took another sip of wine and went back to her lasagna. "Did you know they had a medical school in 700 B.C.? And he told me the US Army Medical Corps uses an insignia with two snakes but that's the Greek symbol for trade, liars, and alchemy. The real symbol for medicine only has one snake. Someone just thought two snakes looked better." Her face brightened as she spoke. "It's amazing how much that man knows. Could you drop off some flowers for him when you pick up Nick tomorrow?"

"Absolutely, assuming he's well enough for visitors. He was in bad shape when we left."

"We? Who else was there? It wasn't Nick. You said he doesn't know what happened." Cady looked puzzled.

I bit my tongue, but it was too late. Well, I needed to tell her about Arcas and this was as good a time as any. I hated to cause her more pain, but there was no way to sugar coat the news. "No, Nick wasn't with me. It was someone else, someone I never expected to see again."

She cocked her head, waiting to hear what I'd say next. She looked curious, but certainly not alarmed. She must have thought I'd run into an old school chum or a neighbor from my childhood back in Rochester.

"It was your father." She turned to look at Tom. I took a breath. "No, not Dad, it was Arcas. He just showed up on our doorstep last night."

Cady's eyes widened. "But he's dead. You always said he died before I was born. You showed me the letter."

I took her hand across the table. "The letter was a hoax. He's been alive and living in Greece all this time. Apparently, he was married and sent me that letter himself so that I wouldn't know. He wanted me to remember him as a hero and not—"

"A two-timing, adulterous liar?" Cady finished for me.

"Yeah, that's about it," I agreed.

"My God, so my bio-Dad has been alive all this time and never even sent us a post card."

"In fairness, he never knew you existed. He'd already left for Greece by the time I found out I was pregnant, and then I didn't tell him because I thought he was dead." I stroked Cady's hair, trying to soothe her. "Nancy ran into him in Athens and told him he had a daughter. He flew to Canada the minute he heard about you."

"Well, isn't that touching? What's he expect me to do, jump in his lap and call him Daddy?"

Tom nodded in agreement. "That guy has no right butting into our family. You don't have to see him if you don't want to."

"Good, I don't want to." Cady crossed her arms and sat back in her chair. Her lips were pressed together, but tears glistened in her eyes.

When the phone rang later that evening, I knew it was Arcas and I almost didn't answer. There was enough drama in my life without having to deal with this relic from my past, but we'd parted so abruptly that I'd never even thanked him for meeting the professor. I reluctantly picked up the receiver.

"Hello, this is Arcas."

I stiffened my spine and tried to strike a cordial, but business-like tone. "Good evening, I thought you might call. I'm so sorry for the way things turned out this afternoon."

"I was wondering if you'd heard anything more about Dr. Kanter. Do you know if he's going to be OK?"

"I don't know, but I'm planning to see him tomorrow when I pick up Nick. I'll let you know how he's doing. Also, I'm sorry about your disc. Dr. Kanter has memory problems and I'm guessing he misplaced it. I'll ask the nurse if she knows anything about it when I see her."

"Don't worry, it was just an old souvenir. To tell the truth, I'd forgotten all about it."

"Still, I'm sorry for the way things turned out. I'll let you know if it turns up." I was ready to say good-bye and go back to Tom and the current episode of *Seinfeld*.

"Amy, I'm not done. We need to talk. I've been thinking about what you told me and the more I think about it, the less I like it. You and Tom weren't sleeping together while I was in Toronto. He was in love with Nancy and you weren't the type to sneak around."

"What are you saying?"

"I'm saying you're lying to me. I'm saying that Cady *is* my daughter."

"And I'm saying that I don't want to go through all this again. I need get up early to pick Nick up from the hospital and then I have to get ready for a family vacation. I don't have time for this. I'm sorry."

"No, if she's my daughter then you have to . . ."

I hung up on him. It was a coward's response, but I didn't know what else to do. Maybe he'd fly back to Greece and this would all just go away.

NICK WAS DRESSED and sitting on the edge of his bed when I arrived the next morning. It was the first time I'd seen him in his own clothes in two weeks. He looked paler than he had before the accident, but he was his usual impatient self.

"All my stuff is in that bag." He indicated a plastic bag full of books, toiletries, and his snack stash. "We just have to sign some papers and they'll spring me. I'm a free man."

"Letting you out on good behavior, are they?"

"You bet. Are those flowers for me?" He reached for the bouquet of daylilies I'd bought on my way over.

"Sorry, they're for Dr. Kanter." I pulled the flowers out of his reach. "He had a stroke or seizure yesterday and I wanted him to know we're thinking of him."

"Is he going to be OK?"

"I don't know. I hope so, but I was there when it happened and frankly, it looked bad. Why don't you wait here for the discharge nurse while I take these to his room."

It was only a short walk from Nick's room to Dr. Kanter's. As I got closer, I could see that his door was wide open. Was that a good sign or a bad one? The moment I looked inside I knew. The room was empty, stripped bare of any sign of an occupant. There were no books, no empty dishes, no eyeglasses, or potted plants. A bare mattress and two pillows without pillowcases sat on a metal bed frame as though no one had ever occupied the room.

I remembered the spring I'd found a clutch of robin's eggs just outside my bedroom window. I'd watched them emerge as naked hatchling with wide yellow mouths that never seemed to close. I'd cheered them on, delighted when their loud, persistent chirps for food were answered with a tasty bug tucked down their throats. I checked on them numerous times a day, watching their baby down turn to speckled fledgling feathers until one day they were gone. Just like that. No note, no fond farewell, nothing, just an empty nest and a few stray wisps of down. They never even said good-bye.

"Excuse me, are you looking for Dr. Kanter?" I turned to find the nurse standing at the door.

"Yes, I wanted to give him these." I held up the flowers. "What happened to him?"

"I'm sorry, I'm afraid he's gone. He left us late last night." Her expression was so sweet that it softened the sad news. I remember thinking that she must have a lot of experience comforting the bereaved.

"I see, that's too bad. He was a brilliant man and very kind. I'm glad I got to know him."

"He was glad to know you too. He enjoyed your visits very much."

"Excuse me, but there is something else. Do you remember that clay disc he had in his safe, it seems to have disappeared. Do you know where it is?"

"Oh, it probably just sailed off somewhere. We'll keep our eyes open, but hospitals are notorious for losing things."

I nodded. What was there to say?

She came closer and put her hand on my shoulder. "Can I get you anything, a glass of water?"

"No, no I'm fine, but would you take these flowers? Put them at the nurses' station or give them to another patient. I don't want to take them home."

"Of course." She took the flowers and inhaled their sweet scent. "They're just lovely, I'm sure someone will enjoy them."

Her hand was still on my shoulder, making me feel awkward. I wasn't the bereaved. "Well, I'd better get going. It's a big day. We're taking Nick home and then we'll be leaving for a month at the lake."

"I hope you have a wonderful time. We're going to miss Nick. He's a fine young man. Take good care of him and don't let him get that cast wet."

"I promise. I never go near the water. I have a little, what do they call it, aquaphobia?" I laughed, although it wasn't a joke. "He'll stay high and dry with me this summer."

The place where her hand touched my shoulder became warm and that warmth flowed through my entire being. My heart slowed and I felt as though I was floating in a dense fog. She pulled me toward her and whispered in my ear, "This year you'll go swimming, and you'll find her well. There's healing in the water."

"What?" I pulled back and she stepped away.

"Well," she replied, "I won't keep you. Enjoy your holiday and thank you for the flowers."

"Yes, I mean you're welcome. What did you just say?"

"I said, thank you for the flowers." She smiled again and bustled off to find a vase while I stayed behind, staring at Dr. Kanter's empty bed. Her words, the words I thought I'd heard, kept repeating inside my head. *This year you'll go swimming, and you'll find her well. There's healing in the water.*"

I don't know how long I stood there before I remembered Nick and realized I'd better collect him before he started to worry. As I retraced my steps down the hall, I heard a familiar Greek accented voice coming from his room. The unmitigated gall of the man, had he no shame, no boundaries, no decency? Hadn't I made myself clear? Didn't he understand that we didn't want anything more to do with him?

I burst into the room and caught him *in flagrante delicto* chatting companionably with my son who greeted me with the happy news that an old friend from Greece had noticed our name on the door and stopped in to say hello. "He says he knew you before you married Dad, back when Papandreou was in Toronto."

Arcas looked at me with no sign of embarrassment. "Hello, Amy, nice to see you again. I've just had the pleasure of meeting your son."

"So, I see. How nice of you to stop by. Unfortunately, I need to get Nick discharged now. I'm afraid I don't have time to visit." I stepped back and pointed toward the door, hoping that he'd leave.

"That's too bad. Nick was just telling me about your lovely family. He says you have two children, him and his older half-sister, Cady. How sad that her father died before she was even born. I bet she would have meant the world to him."

Wow, that man was an operator. How had he gotten all that out of Nick in the few minutes I was gone? "Arcas, would you step outside a minute? I'd like a few words with you in private."

"Certainly." He turned an ingratiating smile in the direction of my son. "Will you excuse us for a moment? Your mother and I have some catching up to do."

Once we were safely out of earshot, I turned to him and hissed, "She's not your daughter. Tom was there to hold me when I was sick with morning sickness and sick with grief because you'd died. He was the one who got up at night to feed her and to change her diapers. He was there for her first step and her first word and her first day of school. He's Cady's father and don't you dare say otherwise."

He listened intently, nodding, but in the end it didn't matter. He wanted Cady.

"Yes," he agreed. "Tom has been an excellent father, but she is still my daughter. Let me meet her. She deserves to know who her who her real people are."

"We told her about you yesterday. She doesn't want to meet you."

"One hour, that's all I'm asking. Tell her I only want an hour." He looked desperate and I could tell he wasn't backing down. "You and Tom can come too, all of you can come. Tell her tonight at seven. We'll have dinner at my hotel. Will you, do it? Will she come?"

"Arcas, I don't know. Listen, our son is being discharged from the hospital and . . ."

He looked away and drew a long, ragged breath. "Your son, it must be nice to have a son."

"Yes," I agreed. "It is."

"So, will you come, all of you, including your son? I beg you. It isn't only Cady. I've missed you and Tom as well. I left so much of myself here, more than I knew, and I want a second chance."

"I can't promise anything, but I'll talk to her and let you know."

TRUFFLES WAS THE classiest restaurant in a city famous for upscale dining. We tried not to gawk as the maître d led us past Roman columns and through cream-colored arches to a table set with crystal goblets and gleaming silver cutlery. Arcas was already seated, but he rose as we walked in. He was wearing an immaculately tailored suit and a shirt whiter than the cloths that dressed the tables. He gave the impression of a man in his milieu. How improbable that a socialist goat herder from a small Greek village had morphed into a man utterly at ease in this opulent setting. Cady was wearing her Audrey Hepburn dress, a sleeveless black sheath accessorized with the pearls we'd given her at her high school graduation. She looked lovely and she knew it, but she was wearing her beauty as armor not as a magnet.

"Thank you so much for accepting my invitation. I've come a long way to meet you." He held out his hand.

Cady stiffened but surprised me by offering her hand in return. She was playing this by the book, proper etiquette without a scintilla of warmth. "How do you do?"

He pretended not to notice and smiled graciously, the charming host, as we were seated. "I hope you don't mind, but I've ordered a special wine for the occasion. You do drink wine, don't you?" He looked at Cady.

"I'm twenty-one years old."

"Of course, you are a grown up young lady."

Cady glared at him.

"I wanted to order something Greek," Arcas babbled on, "but they don't have a single bottle from our country. Can you believe that? They hand me a wine list with hundreds of bottles and not even one Argyros VinSanto. But don't worry. I think you will enjoy this vintage. It's an old Barbaresco from the Piedmont region in Italy. I've had it before. It's very good."

I felt bad for Arcas. He was trying so hard and failing completely. He was never going to impress Cady with expensive grape juice.

The sommelier arrived and made a great show of uncorking the bottle and offering a taste to Arcas for his approval before filling a glass for everyone but Nick. We all sat rigidly still as he performed this ritual, awkward and ill at ease. As soon as he left, Cady pushed her wine over to her brother. "Here, you drink this. You're the one who has something to celebrate."

"Of course, we must toast Nick who is home from the hospital today." Arcas raised his glass. "And also, I toast this lovely young woman who I hope to know better over time."

Tom and I dutifully raised our glasses while Cady stared at her plate and Nick took a big gulp from the glass she'd offered him.

Arcas continued, undaunted. "I am sorry that I didn't meet you sooner. I would have liked very much to have known you as a baby and as a little girl, but I am so glad to meet you now. Do you know, you look a bit like my mother? Here, let me show you photos of your family."

He took out his wallet and for the first time Cady looked at him with interest.

"This is my mother." He handed Cady a photo. "She's old in that picture, but she looked like you when she was young. My father would never have gotten such a good-looking bride, but my grandfathers arranged the marriage and he got lucky. She's about sixty in this photo."

Nick studied the photo over Cady's shoulder. "I don't see it. Cady looks like Mom, but she does have bushy eyebrows. She might have gotten her eyebrows from your side of the family."

"I do not have bushy eyebrows," Cady objected.

"You do when you don't pluck them." Nick took a sip of wine and grinned. He was the only one at the table who seemed to be having a good time.

"Did she really raise sheep? Mom said you were shepherds. I pictured you like Peter in the Heidi story, only Greek. Now you don't seem like that at all."

"Yes, we absolutely raised sheep when I was a boy. We raised sheep and goats and made cheese. It was just a little family business back in those days."

"So, what happened?" Tom leaned forward, curious about the transformation of his old comrade in arms.

"It was a combination of things. First, I make exceptionally good cheese and second my wife's family had money and they helped me buy the commercial equipment you need to make product at scale. Then we had political connections that helped me get my first big contracts and well, as they say, the rest is history."

Tom shook his head in disbelief. "Boy, did I have you wrong. I never figured you'd have a head for business."

Arcas looked genuinely surprised. "Why? We were studying economics."

"I thought we were learning how to remake a corrupt capitalist system into something more fair and just, not how to profit off the machine."

"My business is fair and just. I create jobs and my employees are well paid. Believe me, Canadian workers don't get half the benefits they'd get in Greece. Papandreou's government is doing good things for the people. In fact, he's squeezing us capitalists hard. It's difficult to make a profit these days."

"You seem to be doing okay." Tom gestured around the room where a well-heeled clientele conversed in hushed tones over plates of expensive food with fancy French names.

"Yes, I have done very well in some respects. Arkadiko Tyri exports cheese all over the EU and even to a few of the old Soviet countries. In other ways my life is not a success. My parents are gone, I'm getting divorced, and I have no children." He turned to Cady and looked at her with eyes full of hope and longing. "That's why I've come. You don't know me, but I know you. My family's blood flows through your veins, and I see my mother in your eyes. So, I've come to you with a proposition."

Cady froze. She'd reluctantly accepted Arcas's invitation at my urging, and now he was going to press her into a corner. I leaned forward, ready to jump to her defense. Tom looked ready to grab Cady and bolt.

"As I said, Arkadiko Tyri is a large company and very profitable. I am still relatively young and plan to run the company for many years, but eventually I will want to retire and leave the company to someone I can trust, someone who will continue the business and my family's legacy. Your mother tells me that you're thinking of a career in medicine, but maybe I can change your mind. Medicine isn't the only way to help people. A well-run business provides jobs and good jobs allow people to live full, healthy lives."

"Sorry, not a chance." Cady leaned back in her chair and cast an evil eye at Arcus with a proficiency she must have inherited from her Greek grandmother. "I'm going to be a doctor. We may have a genetic connection, but that's it. You're not my father. You're not even the man Mom told me about."

Arcas listened intently, nodding as she spoke. I could see the negotiator in him trying to close a deal. "I understand. This has hit you out of the sky, out of nowhere, but you don't have to decide today or tomorrow, not even this year. Just think about it. It's a wonderful opportunity. Most young people would jump at a chance like this."

"I don't need to think about it. I'm not giving up a career in medicine to move to Greece to make cheese. Who would do a thing like that?"

"I would," Nick said and all eyes turned toward him. "I could study business in college then work for you when I graduate. I love cheese."

Arcas started to laugh, but when he saw Nick's earnest expression he stopped and only grinned instead. "Do you speak Greek?"

"A little, I'm not fluent but I'll study it at university."

"I see." The two stared at one another in silence for several long moments. They seemed to come to an agreement without words. "And you could practice when you work for me in the summer between classes."

"Yes, that would be great. I could do that. I'm a good worker and a fast learner."

"And a good salesman." Arcas tipped his glass in Nick's direction. "To my future sales associate, Nick Savas." He turned back to Cady, but the emotional temperature had dropped. Something had shifted in the dynamic around the table. He laughed, an open relaxed belly laugh. "The offer's still open if you change your mind. Your brother will always find a place for you in the company."

We drank expensive wine and ate truffled spaghettini, noisettes d'agneau, and coquilles en sauce pernod while Arcas told us stories about his childhood in Arcadia, the sheep he'd known by name, the social problems still plaguing Greece, and the prospects for Papandreou's government. Tom gradually allowed himself to be drawn into the conversation and soon the two were reminiscing about the bad old days of the colonels and the junta. They applauded Nick's plan to stand with the ARA against the neo-Nazis and offered their support, Tom by accompanying his disabled son to the rally, and Arcas by donating a substantial sum.

By the time we'd wiped the last crumbs of cream filled mille-feuille from our lips with heavy linen napkins and sipped the last drop of coffee from gold rimmed cups we'd reached a détente. Maybe we'd even taken a first step toward renewed friendship. Cady had agreed to visit the family farm the next time we were in Greece, while Nick was clearly dreaming of becoming an executive at Arkadiko Tyri.

I arrived home exhausted, sated, and at peace. Arcas would be returning to Greece in two days, and we'd be leaving for the lake. My kids were doing well, my marriage was strong, and my business was thriving. A pang of guilt hit me deep in the gut, the same pain I always felt whenever things went too well. "What about Joanie? How could I be happy when she missed all of this?"

There was a knock on the door and Cady poked her head into the room. "Mom, do you have a minute? Can we talk?"

"Sure, come on in. What's up?"

"I just feel all weirded out. Arcas isn't who I thought he was at all." She threw herself on the bed, scattering my neatly folded underwear. She'd taken off her *Breakfast at Tiffany's* outfit and put on a floral nightgown that was more *Rebecca of Sunnybrook Farm*, all innocence and vulnerability.

I brushed a tangle of dark curls from her forehead. "He's not the man I thought he was either. You don't have to see him again if you don't want to."

She sat up and looked at me, as though I had the answer to a question she hadn't yet asked. "I don't know what I want. He seems nice, but can we trust him? Maybe he's still lying. Maybe nothing he says is true."

I picked up the stack of underwear, refolded each piece, and put them into the suitcase. "I talked to Nancy, and she says his story pans out, at least the part about Arkadiko Tyri. He really is a cheese magnate."

"Figures, perfect job for a rat."

I laughed, but felt a spasm of regret. For better or worse, Arcas was Cady's biological father, and I didn't want her hating him. "I can't argue with you. What he did was despicable, but in the end, he's the one who lost out. He had a loveless marriage while I have you and Nick and your father."

"Exactly, *my* father. My father is Dad not Arcas."

"And nothing will ever change that. Like I said, you don't have to let him into your life if you don't want to, but I kind of feel sorry for the guy. You must have seen how he was falling all over himself trying to impress you tonight."

"Yeah, it was kind of pathetic."

"I think he really regrets what he did, not that he can undo it with a fancy dinner."

Cady picked up a framed snapshot of our family from my bedside table. It was the same photo I used as a screensaver on my computer. She stared at it for several long seconds as I watched. "He didn't get me with the dinner, it was the photographs. It's odd seeing pictures of relatives you never knew existed. I might have his mother's eyebrows. Isn't that creepy?"

"Not at all. You share his DNA and that's not a bad thing. He's a very clever and capable man. I'm not condoning what he did, but I suspect he'd still be tending sheep if he'd followed all the rules."

"Do you think Nick will really go to work for him?"

"Who knows? Nick's still young. His life could go in a million different directions, but it's possible. He sure perked up at the prospect."

"And you'd let him, after everything that man did to you?"

"I don't see how I'd stop him, besides . . ." I turned and looked out the open window where wind was blowing through the branches of the maple tree. Its leaves made a sound like rushing water and I paused, remembering. "Besides, that was a long time ago. We were stupid and selfish, but we never meant . . ." Joanie was dead and Cady had grown up not knowing her real father. I lowered my voice as though I was speaking to myself. "And yet we caused so much pain." I turned and looked at my daughter, not sure if she had heard me.

She stared back at me with deep, solemn eyes. "Will you ever be able to forgive him?"

"Yes, I think so. I think I've forgiven him already."

She got off the bed, gave me a quick kiss, and left the room.

I closed the window and sat beside my packed suitcase, wondering if I'd ever be able to forgive myself, when the nurse's words came back to me, replacing the litany of shame that played inside my head. *This year you'll go swimming, and you'll find her well. There's healing in the water.* I wasn't sure what she meant. I wasn't even sure I'd heard her correctly, but I stood up and took my swimsuit from the bureau and packed it for our trip.

THE LAKE WAS always glorious in August. We'd rented the same cottage outside Picton since the kids were small. It wasn't on a fashionable stretch of lake, and it wasn't the pristine turquoise of the Mediterranean, but it had its own exquisite palette of greens and blues, grays and browns. The kids had gone swimming, biked, hiked, and eaten ice cream there while Tom and I had enjoyed winery tours and dinners at little lakeside restaurants. Cady and Nick were grown up now. They'd soon be too busy with their own lives to join us at the cottage, but this year they were still mine. I watched Cady and Tom tossing a beachball in the water from my usual perch on a chaise lounge set well back from the shore. Nick was sitting on his own chair with his cast propped up on a stool. He was trying to capture the gentle waves, the wispy clouds, and the silhouette of a ship far off on the horizon with a set of colored pencils. We'd been at the cottage three days and I still hadn't found the nerve to venture into the water.

Tom waved and Cady gestured for me to join them, although I knew they expected me to stay riveted to my chair. I shook my head no from habit, but then I remembered. "*This year you'll go swimming, and you'll find her well. There's healing in the water.*"

I put down my book, stood up, and picked my way across the beach as Tom and Cady watched, incredulous. The water was colder than I'd expected this late in the season. I felt pebbles and wet sand beneath my feet as I moved slowly forward. Waves lapped my ankles, my calves, and then my stomach. I gazed out at the ship that hung suspended at the edge of my vision. I took another few steps and the lake floor fell away. The water rose above my head, and I remembered how to swim. I dived below the surface where strands of algae brushed my face, sunlight danced above me, and from somewhere in the distance I could hear my sister laughing.

Patricia Averbach began her writing career at sixteen as literary assistant to Anzia Yeszierska, the Jewish-American author of the immigrant experience. A native Clevelander, she's a former director of The Chautauqua Writers Center. Her third novel, *Dreams of Drowning* (Bedazzled Ink, 2024), was a finalist for the Tucson Festival of Books and Chanticleer's Somerset Award for Literary Fiction. Previous novels include *Painting Bridges* (Bottom Dog Press, 2013) and *Resurrecting Rain* (Golden Antelope Press, 2020) which was nominated for a Pushcart Prize. Her poetry chapbook, *Missing Persons*, (Ward Wood Publishing, 2013) won the London based Lumen/Camden prize and was cited by *Times of London Literary Supplement* (November 2014) as one of the best small collections of the year. Her work appears in the anthology *101 Jewish Poems for the Third Millenium*. She lives with her husband in Beachwood, Ohio when she's not visiting her daughters in Toronto, Maui and Peru.

To learn more visit her website at www.patriciaaverbach.com